The end of everything that stands.
The end.

THE DOORS, THE END

EVERYTHING THAT STANDS

Jeremy Holt

(*) greenhill

(✱) **green**hill

https://greenhillpublishing.com.au/

Holt, Jeremy (author)
EVERYTHING THAT STANDS
ISBN 9781923088177
LITERARY FICTION

Typesetting Calluna Regular 10.5/16
Cover photo by Ruslan Alekso from Pexels.com
Cover and book design by Green Hill Publishing

For what is it to die but to stand naked in the wind,
and to melt into the sun?
And what is it to cease breathing,
but to free the breath from its restless tides,
that it may rise and expand and seek God unencumbered?

KAHLIL GIBRAN, THE PROPHET

No one can comprehend what goes on under the sun; despite all their efforts to search it out, no one can discover its meaning.

ECCLESIASTES 8:17

Why does the bird sing?
Because it has a song.

ANTHONY DE MELLO, THE SONG OF THE BIRD

When the stars threw down their spears
And watered heaven with their tears
Did he smile his work to see?
Did he who made the lamb make thee?

WILLIAM BLAKE, THE TYGER

We have not yet arrived, but every point at which we stop requires a re-definition of our destination.

BEN OKRI, TALES OF FREEDOM

A LUMINOUS DARK

Gunfire smacks into the lower reaches of the trees above.

With a short gulp of air, I rise to my feet and run.

Again.

I shout to my brother above the din, but I'm unsure whether he hears. A fearful thud-thud-thudding tracks me, and he materialises to my left.

Branches slap and sting my face and forearms as I scamper away into the black shadows of the morning. Between dust and darkness, despair and desperation, I am haunted by this life, this death.

We need to be far away before it grows light, before we're flushed out into the open like scatterling guinea fowl.

Phlegmatic fireflies, tracers, flick past me. My heart jackhammers in my head, drowning out the panoply of noise.

I can do nothing other than run.

I lose my footing, but my brother grabs my jumper and heaves me upright just before I sprawl into the undergrowth.

I allow myself a quick over-the-shoulder glance.

Apart from an unforgiving landscape...

Nothing.

I speed up; utter a prayer for God to deliver us.

The cacophony behind dissipates and I settle into a pace I can uphold. Blaise remains steady on my left shoulder.

Neither of us speaks.

We concentrate on regulating our breathing. For the trials that lie in wait, we must preserve our energy as best we can.

Sounds of silence, apart from the persistent undertone of cicadas, replace the hurly of our hunters.

Daybreak's first crimson appears to the east, and we adjust to bear in the opposite direction.

Flaking lips, parched mouth, swallow-sharpened throat.

Unsteady legs and aching feet, the prelude to mushrooming blisters.

To find water is a priority, even though I know to break rhythm would be folly.

Blaise points to the right and, slowing to a trot, I follow the arc of his finger and spy a brackish waterhole amongst an assembly of thorn trees. Despite its sinister discolouration, it heightens my thirst.

We sink into the scrub.

I look. Listen. Linger.

Breathing deeply, I resist the urge to plunge into the water.

Our eyes comb the terrain, scrutinising every dark recess amongst the trees.

Blaise nods at me and I inch forward. Firearm cradled in his right hand, he scans right to left. I squat and scoop water to my mouth with cupped hands, drink more than I should.

We reverse roles. Blaise passes the weapon to me. I melt back into cover, take up a defensive position. I wrap my fingers around the pistol's grip, its textured surface biting into my skin.

My right index finger hovers over the trigger.

My brother takes a knee, splashes water on his face and the back of his neck, slakes his thirst.

My stomach cramps and I bend over to quell the pain.

An inexplicable fear squeezes my chest and I jerk my head upwards. Sensing danger, Blaise leaps to his feet, pivots and obstructs my line of sight.

A shadowy figure, whose features I cannot determine, has emerged from the darkness. Right arm extended, he aims a pistol at Blaise's chest.

My brother raises his hands, fingers pointing to the heavens. The gun wavers in a silhouetted fist, oscillates between Blaise and me. I bring my pistol to bear.

Hands stiffen, fingers tighten.

Blaise opens his mouth to protest, but before he can move or utter a sound, a string of dissonant shots splinters the nascent redness.

And I am up and running.

Forever running.

Away from that waterhole, toward the craw of a luminous dark.

FORGET-ME-NOT

NO SOUND BUT THE early evening breeze caresses the jacaranda trees. They purr their pleasure. Through the tree line behind them, the sun dips towards the horizon, heralding the onset of yet another bloodied African dusk.

The jacarandas are in full bloom, each with a cascade of royal mauve and pink, breathing sticky, spicy perfume to the mild wind.

Beneath this grove lies an inviting, sensual covering of lavender and lilac with a palette of shades in between.

Adore or abhor them, jacarandas discard all year. At the end of autumn, they jettison ferny fronds. In spring, the blossoms opt for freedom; and throughout the summer, coffee-coloured seed pods scatter largesse wherever and whenever they please.

Should a jacaranda flower drop upon your head, local legend contends the act will endow you with a life of good fortune. The fates have never sanctified me in this way, although I recall that in my salad days many of my varsity friends, in a fit of futile optimism, would sit beneath the jacarandas come exam time.

It has been many years since I visited Pretoria, the City of Jacarandas. I never believed I'd return to one of its distinctive spaces, Voortrekkerhoogte. It was established after the Second Anglo-Boer War in 1905 as Roberts Heights for the commander-in-chief of the British forces, Lord Frederick Roberts, but found its apotheosis as

4

Voortrekkerhoogte in the 1930s. It was so named by the then Nationalist Government at the commissioning of the Voortrekker Monument, at a time of growing Afrikaner nationalism. Following the end of Apartheid, it was reborn as Thaba Tshwane.

So much for nomenclatures. For me, it will forever be Voortrekkerhoogte.

I finished school in Salisbury in 1979, during a turbulent year marking the demise of Ian Smith's UDI in Rhodesia and the failed power-sharing model under Bishop Abel Muzorewa. Afterwards, along with many other families fearful of post-Lancaster House Agreement chaos, my family had 'taken the gap' and crossed the African Rubicon – the Limpopo River – to South Africa.

Their fears were well-founded. In the autumn of 1980, the predicted rise and rise of Robert Mugabe and his ZANU-PF party to power presaged the gradual fall of Zimbabwe into a starless oligarchy over ensuing decades.

I was conscripted into the South African Defence Force in the early 1980s. Having completed my basic training and officer's course in Oudtshoorn, I spent time in Rundu on the Kavango River in South-West, and other unspecified locations in southern Angola in 'The Battle for Africa'. Thereafter, I endured a considerable time in my home-away-from-home 1-MIL, the premier military hospital in Voortrekkerhoogte, requiring reconstructive knee surgery courtesy of Operation Askari, in which my *Ratel's* turret took a direct hit from a 23-mm mortar shell.

I had vowed never to return.

Such is the conundrum of life. It interrupts our best-laid plans.

A vida continua.

Just as the wind can shift unexpectedly, powers beyond our imaginings can thwart our endeavours. All that remains is our last fragile freedom: to choose how we respond.

'Follow your conscience, Baron. Not making a choice is still making one,' Mum said. 'The decisions you make will determine the life you lead. Do the next right thing as an act of faith.'

I made my choice in good faith, not fully expecting the magnitude of the consequences.

Life continues.

For refusing, on the grounds of conscience, a military call-up for township duty during the national State of Emergency, I found myself incarcerated in the SADF Detention Barracks, a stone's throw from 1-MIL...

A vida continua...

... with a three-year sojourn, reduced to eighteen months, spent in a familiar space I had grown to accept, and despise.

The irony was difficult to avoid.

After a second internment, I never imagined I would revisit the place that conjured those ancient, mythical, mystical creatures that have tourniqueted my heart over the years.

But it is time.

Sic transit gloria mundi.

Time to loosen their hold.

Time to face up to the guilt, shame and anger of my past; spark a third iteration to break the pattern.

I am not alone.

The family is present to show its support. Anne, my wife, who spent her childhood in Salisbury during the Rhodesian Bush War, is with me, as are my eldest daughter, her husband and their three boys, my younger daughter, and my two sons.

My parents are not.

Thus do the joys of this world pass us by.

Time may soften memories, but I have not found this to be the case. Time itself does not console, nor does it make things better or worse. Rather, it puts them into perspective. While only recently deceased, neither Mum nor Dad recovered from the fateful events that occurred so long ago.

Requiescat in pace.

May they rest in the peace they deserve.

To the east, the iconic Voortrekker Monument looms above me, an imposing granite Adamastor and mute testament to a troubled and conflicted country.

Within the variegated jacaranda palette nestles the memorial I have avoided but am impelled to visit. Mindful that I walk on holy ground, I tread towards it with restrained steps.

The members of my family keep their distance.

An assortment of wreaths and flower bouquets braces the steps, bearing poignant and silent witness to the many people anguished by events that occurred so long ago.

The memorial is unassuming in its design. Two large, identical rectangular concrete tablets lean in towards an airy spine. Connecting them is a dedicatory plaque.

It proclaims:

This memorial is to commemorate the lives of 107 holiday-makers and crew murdered in the world's first 9/11-style attacks to destroy passenger aircraft in flight when Rhodesia Air's Viscounts Hunyani and Umniati were brought down with SAM 7 missiles on... 03 September 1978 and 12 February 1979.

At the apex of the Viscount Memorial, above the interconnected tablets and embedded in the top of the plaque, sits the stylised metallic icon of the Viscount – nose, wings and tail-fin – reminiscent of an unfurled snake eagle.

Etched into black marble are the Rolls of Honour with the names of those killed, the *Hunyani* on the left and the *Umniati* on the right.

I approach the Roll to the left, a solemn face mirroring mine in the polished stone.

At my feet, an unpretentious green wreath captures my attention. It is foregrounded by clustered sky-blue flowers, the centre of each splashed with white and yellow. Its soft sillage floats in the lingering kiss of the departing sun.

The warm forget-me-not fragrance filling my senses, I view the list of names. Each carved-out name has its story locked in the memories of the loved ones remaining.

From beyond the names, a familiar face rises to greet mine.

I reach out and trace the letters of one name in particular, whose story is intertwined with my own.

Reflected fingers touch mine, trace letters chiselled into the marble... and in that moment, a patchwork of memories enshrouds me against my will in a smothering of colours, sounds, smells and emotions.

And I remember.

THE-YOU-KNOW-WHAT

'YEE-HAH!'

In burst Blaise.

Our Blaise.

Rugger ball in two hands, he sidestepped me and dived onto his bed. He flipped over and with consummate ease bounced the ball off the wall above and behind his head.

I busied myself, stowing my clothes and tidying my stuff.

The thumping stopped. 'Hey Baron, are you good to go? Ready for some razzle-dazzle?'

'Just about. And you?'

'Almost. Still a few things to sort,' he replied, making no effort towards sorting.

The thud-thud-thud of the ball resumed, hammering its incessant drumbeat on the pockmarked wall.

'Shouldn't you pack?'

'*Ja*, I suppose. But hey, Bar, we don't need much, do we? Cozzies and flip-flops only, I reckon. I mean, a week in Kariba. Party Central!'

'What with finals coming up in two months, I assumed you'd at least be taking prep work with you.'

'It's the hol-i-days, brother Baron! You recall what that means, doncha?'

'Yeah, *holy days*, I hear you. I –'

'No, *Boet*. Seven days of amusement and leisure. I'll worry about exams after our return to Salisbury. No, better yet. I'll let you do the fretting. You'll produce enough for both of us.'

'Pity about Mum and Dad, though,' I said, deflecting his barb.

'*Ag*, shame. A real bummer. The Black Residence Man Cave's gonna be out of commission for an entire week.'

'Ha-ha. Hilarious. I laughed 'til I stopped. It means those garden chores will double up for you, my man!'

Blaise and I lived in a large-gardened redbrick house on Borrowdale Road, in a leafy, salubrious part of Salisbury near St George's, the Jesuit College where we were students in our A-Level year. School had closed for the Michaelmas holidays; Mom and Dad were headed overseas on a quick business trip, while we were off to see our godparents on the Rhodesian Riviera.

'C'mon, B-man. Kariba. Aunty Jo and Uncle Monty. Fothergill Island. Matusadona. The Vic Falls! What could be better?'

The Falls.

One of the world's seven natural wonders, formed in deep time when starry spears collided with a malleable earth, its mention triggers the imagination.

Moved by their beauty, David Livingstone, Scottish missionary, explorer and first-ever European to view them in 1855, wrote in an otherwise dour journal: 'scenes so lovely... gazed upon by angels in their flight.'

To visualise a more extraordinary waterfall was a challenge.

I recalled our first family visit there.

You detect a muted hum first, rising to a rumble then a reverberating thunder shaking the earth.

As you approach, pinprick pulses stimulate the balls of your feet, throbbing to the hairs covering your entire body. Plumes of vapour explode from myriad points, battering your senses. Close up, its hypnotic voice and racing heartbeat overwhelm you.

On an unbroken, flat plateau, the land disappears abruptly and 'God's Highway' slip-slides through a fracture in the earth's surface, much like drenching rain seeping through fissured sandstone.

The water pounds the chasm's uncompromising base then rebounds upwards, hammer blows on multiple anvils.

In an instant, the world upends, and mizzle-comets fall skywards. Showery mists and haloed moonbows ascend, melding the sacred and profane. Apart from touching the divine face, you inhale its moist, sweet, cooling breath.

Livingstone named his discovery to honour Queen Victoria,
an act of colonial arrogance that hid a deeper truth.
The Falls had older, poetical indigenous names:
Seongo, the Place of the Rainbow, and Mosi-oa-Tunya,
the Cloud (or Smoke) that Thunders.

Mosi-oa-Tunya's joint width and height made it the world's vastest curtain of cascading water, eclipsing both the Niagara and Iguazu. It is composed of five distinctive waterfalls, including Rainbow Falls and Devil's Cataract. The Zambezi plunges over Devil's Pool into the Boiling Pot beneath, and Nyaminyami, ancestral spirit, protector and serpentine river god, spits rainbows into the churning, frothing basalt gorges beyond.

'Hey, Baron, distracted again, I see. You okay? *I wait upon your leisure, worthy Thane.*'

'You're such a smart arse, Blaise. *Give me favour at least. My dull brain was wrought with things forgotten,* little brother,' I parried.

The feint wasn't long in coming. 'More likely, *wrought with things remembered*. Talking of weirdos, I believe you just spoke with Jo and Monty on the phone? To you, *they have showed some truth*, yeah?'

'That's unkind, Blaise. Odd and eccentric, maybe. But weirdos?'

'Now, don't get all self-righteous on me, Baron. *Let's speak our free hearts each to other*, remember?' he jabbed.

'But also *fair* hearts. *Keep bosom franchised and clear*, huh?'

'*I shall be counselled.*'

'That remains to be seen. *Time and the hour runs through the roughest day,* not so?'

Blaise leapt from his bed and, with a twirl and flourish of the rugby ball, saluted me. '*Touché,* Baron. *Out-Shakespeared.* Your Will-power is better than mine.' He bowed. 'I acquiesce to your superior wit and pledge my fealty.'

'Monty and Jo sounded delighted,' I said, trying not to laugh at his antics. 'They're even promising us a surprise when we show up.'

'I love surprises, but I'm never confident where Jo and Monty are involved. I hope this one's better than their last offering.'

Blaise had slumped back onto his bed and balanced the rugger ball on his left index finger, slapping it with his right hand. It spun on his extended fingertips like a pirouetting dancer.

'You mean the Christmas present last year? The dolls?'

'With those two, expect the unexpected. That's the only given.'

'Yep. Play what's in front of you. A useful philosophy for living.'

'As good as any other, I reckon.'

With a roll of wrists and a flick of fingers, Blaise floated the ball upwards. It spiralled toward the ceiling and wavered just shy of the vaulted wooden panels, before gravity tugged it back down into his outstretched hands.

'Now, tell me. Why the Eeyore face? Is there something we should worry about?' Blaise said without looking in my direction, his attention absorbed by the ball. 'You were preoccupied when I came in. Although that's about right.'

'I don't think so,' I said, as I stacked the pile of books on my desk in the bookcase. 'Apart from *the-you-know-what*, that is.'

'That's also about right,' Blaise said. 'What else other than *the-you-know-what*?'

In normal circumstances, the Falls trip would have thrilled me; but the hostile African bush that marked the route to our destination made me uneasy. For the Rhodesian Bush War, the Chimurenga, or as we called it, 'the-you-know-what', was in full sway.

TV evening news carried daily reports of the ongoing conflict, always ending with the names of young men, either killed in action or MIA, scrolling across our screens. Since the collapse of Portuguese rule in Mozambique at the end of 1974, counter-insurgency clashes had escalated and the number of casualties was mounting.

There wasn't a family we knew that hadn't been touched by the war. Civilian deaths in a firefight in Salisbury in May of the preceding year and the Woolworths' store bombing four months later had tossed the war into our homes. Rural communities were not exempt, either. The St Paul's Musami murders and the Elim Mission massacre had humanised its face.

With Mozambique breaking free from its colonial shackles, the Rhodesian military could no longer garrison the country, or stem the flow of cadres across landlocked borders. They adopted a twofold strategy: 'contain and hold' the key towns and installations, and 'search and destroy' hot pursuit sorties beyond international borders when and where deemed crucial. While guerrillas roamed the Rhodesian bush with growing regularity, they did so knowing the Security Forces would retaliate with a destructive fire-force.

Our direct experience of the Bush War occurred at Christmastime when we travelled on our annual holiday. Accompanied by a military escort, we drove to destinations in South Africa in convoy with other Rhodie families from Salisbury to Fort Victoria and on to Beit Bridge, a distance of 600 kilometres.

The visceral fear and the intangible uncertainty of ambush on each of those trips, as I sat hunched in the back seat of our second-hand family Audi, remain my overriding memory.

Dad always carried a loaded 9-mm pistol in the glove box. Each of us was adept at firing it, as Dad had insisted we learned how to shoot. Mum, Blaise and I spent many an hour at the range honing our skills. We could also pull the weapon apart and reassemble it with speed and accuracy.

Part of our abnormal normal.

'We won't live a life out of fear,' Dad said. 'Or apologise for who we are or what we stand for. We'll create our own *normal* and damned be anyone who denies us that right. That doesn't mean we're not taking precautions.'

It was another reason we attended basic self-defence classes.

The least safe stretch of our annual journey south was from Fort Victoria, the country's oldest township close to the Zim-Ruins, to Beit Bridge, the border post. The bridge spanned the Limpopo River, fusing Rhodesia to South Africa.

Before the departure of each convoy that gathered at the designated spot, I well remember the early morning police briefings, which I attended with Dad.

'Morning, Everyone. Welcome to Echo Convoy. We have air cover all the way today. If ambushed, our top priority is to reach the border. If we have to stop, get in the ditch on the side of the road. Don't venture into the bush. If our armoured convoy vehicles see movement, they'll assume they're terrs. There's been some terrorist activity in the area over the last fortnight, but it's rare anything will happen. We have never experienced an ambush, and it's unlikely we will. Departure at zero six hundred.'

The convoy halted.

'Out!' yelled Dad.

We obliged.

Ahead and behind, car doors opened and people scrambled for cover. The four of us clambered into a shallow *donga* to our car's left. Heads to chests, bodies tensed and senses tingling, we huddled in the unnatural quiet.

And waited.

Grunting and threshing from somewhere close by in the bushy terrain disturbed those sounds of silence.

It grew louder.

A makeshift military escort vehicle hove into view and, within a stone's throw of where we lay, shuddered and lurched to a standstill, engines complaining.

A voice squawked from a loudhailer.

'All clear! Return to your vehicles. The terrs dug two trenches across the road. They've also trashed the nearby telephone poles and ripped out the lines.'

Anxious and uncertain, we idled on that road, the umbilical cord to the outside world, while two sappers went to work with a mine-detector.

In such a wild place besieged by squat, bald *kopjes*, it was a nervy delay, and the stifling stillness heightened our sense of dis-ease.

'This place gives me the creeps.'

With prickling skin, I glanced up to see a moustached youngster in military fatigues crouched behind a 12.7-mm Browning in his cage atop the front escort vehicle. He scanned the skyline. 'An ideal spot for an ambush,' he muttered. 'The worst tribal trust land in the country.'

For non-Rhodesians, such an incident would have been extraordinary. For us Rhodies, it did not qualify as significant. Until someone was injured, shots fired into the convoy were a non-event.

Also part of our normal abnormal.

Roadkill and debris littering the verges of the roadway was common, a constant hint of insurgency tactics to sow fear and turmoil.

The terrs placed dead livestock or tree trunks across the roads, but the ruse proved ineffective as the escort vehicles smashed them aside. A refined variation of this guerrilla stratagem was to corral cattle onto the roads. This ploy also failed, as the armed escorts eliminated the cow threat using their mounted guns.

The roadkill could stretch for miles, a cornucopia of putrefying carcasses stiffening in the blood-bathed wasteland attended by squadrons of swirling flies and carrion-eaters bunched together, squabbling for a feed.

Two specific memories remain seeded in my brain.

The first involved chasing the convoy from Beit Bridge to Fort Vic. We had missed it by a few minutes.

'So, Mary, what do you think?'

'Ah, Guy, now, to be sure, we can't hang around here. I have things to do at home.'

'So we should go?'

'I don't see why not. We're not far behind. In all our time, nothing's ever happened. On a prayer, I say. It's too long a wait for the next convoy. We're both back at work tomorrow.'

We raced to catch up at the Fort Vic mustering point, driving unaccompanied through guerrilla-invested bush. After thirty years, the memory still has the power to conjure that same level of anxiety.

The second memory embodied the Rhodesian 'new normal' way of life.

As we sped along on the Fort Vic to Salisbury stretch at the prescribed seventy miles per hour, a bump, rip and slap to our immediate rear resounded in our ears.

'Get down!'

Clutching at our hearts, we ducked beneath window-level as the car bobbled, careened and whined. Dad fought to right the wheel. With fluid movements, he engaged a lower gear, de-clutched, and sped up. The Audi jerked, surged and regained its balance amidst howls of tyre rubber, bumping the vehicle to our front. I lay shaken and horizontal on the floorboards behind the front seats until we wobbled into the safety of Borrowdale.

Later, our neighbour interpreted what had happened. He and Dad, known as *The Wombles*, were our suburb's home-grown version of the Neighbourhood Watch.

'Man, look at that. A lacerated tyre,' he said, pointing at our left rear wheel. 'Talk about luck. How'd you make it home?'

'I'll be damned. So it wasn't gunfire!' Dad declared. 'Shredded rubber... and a buckled wheel rim! How did we avoid a puncture? *Deo gratias*.'

I don't think anyone would have disagreed with him.

Apart from confidence with firearms and a rudimentary set of self-defence skills, each of us knew the intricacies of changing a car tyre. We practised and drilled at home, Dad timing us on a stopwatch.

He was relentless.

'Not good enough. Again!' he would say until, sweaty, grimy and out-of-breath, we broke the four-minute barrier.

He was fastidious and (dare I say it?) anal about car and tool maintenance. In retrospect, I understand why. It was a life-and-death difference. A flat tyre meant being abandoned in the bush. The convoy waited for no one.

I would forgive any outsider for wondering why we Rhodies even bothered going on holiday. There was nothing peaceful about our travel anywhere inside the country's borders.

It was, as I understood it, a matter of Rhodesian nous, an unambiguous message to the many who would thwart our lifestyle, that we would not go gentle into that good night.

Too late, I learned it was a conduit to Rhodesian hubris.

Apart from providing opportunities to escape the pressures of a country at war with itself, going south on holiday also made economic sense. Exchange controls allowed Rhodesian citizens limited cash withdrawals as a holiday allowance. As the political status quo unravelled with the apotheosis of Robert Mugabe, our trips were opportunities to move capital to banking safe havens in South Africa.

Just before Uhuru, my parents converted what wealth they had into Krugerrands, concealed them in my biology school research project sample-sachets, and smuggled the gold coins out of the country through the Beit Bridge border checkpoint.

Despite these circumstances, or because of them, Blaise showed no overt interest in the Bush War. He never spoke about it, opting instead to project an image of *Mr Cool*. It may have been his way of dealing with the reality in which we lived.

Many Rhodesians did the same, learning to live with danger as a constant companion. A few found it stimulating, an adrenaline rush. I, for one, was not one of these *adrenal-junkies*.

Blaise was a different proposition. He could well fit that epithet.

'Baron, are you sure there's nothing else bugging you?'

'Apart from you, not much...' I said, letting the words loiter.

We eyeballed each other and laughed out loud.

We were like the two sides of a gold Krugerrand.

Blaise was only five minutes younger than I was, but he was the extrovert – far more interested in playing rugger and cricket and chatting up the ladies. And he was, I had to admit, a very gifted sportsman. I was the pensive one who, not unlike Atlas, carried the weight of the world on my shoulders.

He was Gawain to my Percival.

Ouma had a less flattering way of describing us: Tweedle-Dum and Tweedle-Dummer.

Blaise shrugged. 'I'm not convinced you're telling me everything, *Bru*, but it's your call. Happy to listen if you change your mind.'

With a nod, he snatched up his bag and headed towards the bedroom door. 'Um... catch you downstairs, Bar. Get a wriggle on.' He ambled out and went down the staircase.

My voice followed him. 'I'll join you soon. Just a few items to add.'

'Cheers, Big Ears!' he called. 'Don't bring too much, you hear? And no schoolbooks, okay?'

I smiled, shook my head. 'That's never gonna happen.'

I seized my pack and thrust it on the bed, then added a slim folder of essential texts and slipped in two bottles of water along with a few apples.

Padkos. Food for the road.

And the soul.

ALWAYS ENDING

I ZIPPED UP MY pack and taking firm hold, I swung it onto my back. Reaching the door, I turned for one last look at our twin-share room.

Blaise's space was a postmodern artwork, with crumpled doona at the foot of the bed and pillow and pee-jays strewn on the floor next to muddy rugby boots. Beneath his bed were piled orphaned shoes. *International Rugby* magazines cluttered his desk. No schoolbooks in sight.

Cupboard doors were adorned with an array of hanging clothes, and inside resembled a dirty laundry basket, reeking of what Mum called the 'boy smell' of musk deodorant and damp, mouldy towels. An action poster of the Welsh rugby maestros Gareth Edwards and Barry John clung to the wall.

As counterpoint, my space was a modernist construction: bed squared away, paired shoes on parade underneath. Schoolbooks, tallest to shortest, lined the bookcase; and clothes, socks and undies lay folded and stashed on their designated shelves in my cupboard.

Along the wall above my bookcase, a print of Brueghel's *Fall of Icarus* was flanked by posters of The Rolling Stones, Creedence Clearwater Revival, Simon and Garfunkel, Pink Floyd and The Doors, symmetrically aligned. My favourites.

Paint it Black. Fortunate Son. The Sounds of Silence. Us and Them. The Doors.

One of the most influential bands of the Sixties, I found their original sound and lyrics to be intelligent and provocative.

Riders on the Storm. Lizard King. Waiting for the Sun.

Jim Morrison's eyes stared back at me. Weird and unsettling.

The way I liked it.

... (this is the end)... my only friend, the end...

When I discovered they had taken their name from Huxley's text, *The Doors of Perception*, and appropriated lines from William Blake's *The Marriage of Heaven and Hell*, I was hooked. Blake's intuitive and imaginative words, *If the doors of perception were cleansed, everything would appear to man as it is, infinite*, have remained seeped and sparkling, in my consciousness, like a freshly squeezed lime through carbonated water.

Like Blake, at my core, I was and always have been a rebel and nonconformist, believing all institutions needed a royal kick up the rear because they helped enslave rather than empower.

Blake believed humans had shut themselves off from eternity, choosing only to see the world through the narrow iron bars of their own self-imposed prisons.

He was a disruptor and visionary. Through his poetry and artwork, he prophesied how the power of the imagination could ventilate the soul, to free it from those 'mind-forged manacles' that stifle human endeavour. His linguistic and visual portals opened onto an eternal vista beyond the rational to the preverbal and instinctive realms of creativity and empathy.

For me, he will always be a kindred spirit.

Mum called me a *Disestablishmentarian* and a *Moody-Blue.*

She was right. Guilty on both counts.

I was a mongrel. A *brak.* A crossbreed. Rebel and Blues: a veritable witch's brew.

She imagined I had a severe dose of adolescent angst and would recover from rebelling-without-cause. I wasn't sure whether my struggle would amount to much or if it would ever end. It might well approach some end, but would be trapped forever in that moment of always ending.

... the end my friend... the end...

'Cheers, buckle-beers!'

I hit the lights, closed the door, and rode side-saddle on the banister to the living room below. Negotiation of the lengthy passageway accomplished, I sauntered to the polished cedar door at its end.

... down the hall... to a door... and... looked inside...

'Ma?' I barrelled in.

Mum sat on the edge of the bed; Dad stood next to the dresser. Their whispered conversation ceased. Both turned to regard me, in a close encounter of an alien kind: Dad's gaze was vacant and unfocused, and Mum's ash-blue eyes clouded and moist.

'Sorry to barge in...'

An awkward lull ensued. I was the intruder, beamed down from the mother ship. 'We're good to go,' I mumbled.

Mum broke the awkwardness. 'Are you sure you've everything you need for the week?' her voice quavered.

I nodded.

She eyed my black backpack. 'What's that?' She pointed to a part of something protruding from it. Before I could protest, Mum had unzipped my pack and whipped it out.

'Baron!' In her hand, she held the family photo of everybody from the previous year's Christmas family gathering. I had taken it from the fridge door to use as a bookmark.

'Sorry. It seemed like a good idea at the time.'

Her cheeks flamed red and her eyes filled with tears.

'Son?' Dad raised his eyebrows, inclined his head. 'Go wait with Blaise. We'll be along.' He rested his hand on Mum's shoulder, and she sank onto the bed. I lifted the photo from her hands, slipped it between the pages of the novel I was reading, placed it back into my backpack, and left for the lounge.

... of our elaborate plans, the end...

Jim Morrison's hypnotic voice and enigmatic, apocalyptic lyrics clunked in my head like a shaky ceiling fan.

The half-drawn blinds cast uncanny shadows through the living room. The retreating light clawed at them, but it was losing its grip.

I parked myself next to Blaise, taking a Granny Smith apple from the fruit bowl.

'So, Blazer,' I said, biting into it and munching. 'Are you excited yet?'

'I guess.'

The apple's bitterness stung my tongue. 'You sure you're okay?'

'Kinda.' Never at a loss for words, Blaise's monosyllabic replies were out of sync.

We lived in dangerous, disjointed and uncertain times.

The-you-know-what.

Had I underestimated the extent to which the bush war was unhinging our lives?

The silence hung, stagnant.

'*Blazer.*'

He grunted, taking the last of the apples, leg-spinning it with flicks of his wrist and fingers. 'What's on your mind?'

'Are Mum and Dad okay?'

Blaise shrugged his shoulders. 'I've no idea. They're definitely tense and on edge.'

'It's nothing I've done, is it?'

'No, I don't think so.'

'It's not you, is it? You've done nothing knuckle-headed to anger the parentals, have you? Remember two weeks ago when you smashed the glass patio doors with that rugby ball?' I nodded towards the scuffed leather Junior Springbok in his lap.

'Nah, I'm off the hook on that one after all those extra hours of gardening.' He chortled. 'I'm glad Dad didn't bring out the Malacca cane. Recall the last time he did that?'

'Hard to forget that he beat us two each on the seat of the pants. For disrespecting the old lady next door.'

'Funny now, but not when it happened. We copped it that day and deserved it.'

'It's not us this time. The mood and tone seem different.'

'That's a relief. I worry that Mum's still peeved because I swatted her expensive Waterford crystal vase with my squash racquet.'

'No, she's forgiven you... although practising your backhand in the living room was not your brightest move.'

'It took her a while.'

'What did you expect? It was a wedding present from the Irish mob, after all.'

'Don't remind me,' I said, shaking my head. 'I still feel guilty. I wonder what dragon's eating her now, though?'

'A massive dragon, by the looks of it. I'm sure it'll come out of its cave at some point. They always do.'

'Not so sure about that. Often dragons don't. We need to coax them.'

'But some dragons are always within our reach, aren't they? If you just stretch out your hand.'

'The more dangerous dragons don't wait though, hey Blazer? They leap into our hand, with or without our invitation. And if we're lucky enough, they might not rip off an arm.'

Blaise stifled a nervous laugh. '*Ja*, big brother. Who knows where in the murky depths of our souls those serpents hide, and what they're capable of when they appear.'

... there's danger on the edge of town...

Mum and Dad emerged from their bedroom.

Dad cleared his throat. 'Okay, gather round.' Mum, Blaise, and I clustered around him and leaned inwards. 'As is the norm, let's pause to pray at our parting.'

With heads bowed, we spoke the words that had become second nature from our early childhood days.

'*God bless Mum, Dad, Baron, Blaise, Tom, Jo, and Monty... O Angel of God... be at our side to light and guard, to rule and guide...*'

'Lord, look after us always and keep us safe,' Dad added, to which we offered a hushed *amen*.

We remained close until Dad broke the trance. 'Ready?'

Blaise didn't need any further prompting. He jumped up and grabbed his bag.

'Let's get going, then.'

Single file, we trooped behind him down the hallway, through the front door into the settling darkness.

... the end... of laughter and soft lies...

I rested my head against the cold rear window and watched the sun lower itself to slumberland beneath the blanket of hills.

The Audi's engine thrummed.

My eyelids sagged.

'Behave yourselves,' Mum said. 'I don't want your Uncle Monty and Aunt Jo calling me to say my sons were hooligans.'

I sighed. 'Mum, we know.'

'And don't forget to brush your teeth every night, and remember to say your prayers.' She delved in her bag, rummaged for a moment. 'I want you to have these.' She handed each of us a small silver medallion.

On closer inspection, I saw it was a miraculous medal. Nestled in my palm, its potential glowed in the fading light. 'Please keep these on you. Do you promise?'

'Yes, Ma, we promise.'

A deathly quiet gripped the car as each of us was lost in an ocean of thoughts.

Mum fidgeted, threw furrowed glances in our direction.

To send us on our first plane trip in the height of a bush war – even though it was a short flight – was unfamiliar territory for her. Guilt and fear, I figured that much. But something else addled her. Of that, there was little doubt.

Mum and Dad were packed for Perth in the Land of Oz, for a business conference.

It remained one of the few places I still longed to visit. South Africa was a dream for holidaymakers, but Australia looked to be a vibrant alternative.

Unusual flora and fauna. Touristy adventures. Slops, surf and sand.

Somewhere beyond our partial rainbow-paradise of patched newspaper t-rolls.

'Bring home a present for us?' Blaise said.

'Maybe.' She smiled for the first time.

... ride the king's highway, baby...

Rushing, flaring lights and images flashed in my merry-go-round head. They receded.

'We're there!' Blaise whooped. 'Yee-hah!'

Dad opened the rear door, and a chill touched my skin as I clambered out. The dark maintained a clandestine advance, its wraithlike shadows groping towards me with bony fingers.

... desperately in need of some stranger's hand...

Dad popped the boot. Blaise and I hoisted out our packs and flicked the slips onto our shoulders. Mine bit deep.

'Up for an adventure?' asked Dad.

I nodded.

'C'mon then, I'll take you in.'

Mum leaned over and hugged me. I struggled to breathe. 'I'll see you soon,' she sniffed. 'Have a good time. Give our love to Jo and Monty.'

'Will do, Mum. Don't worry. See you in a week, and we'll swap stories then, okay?' I grinned. 'It's only seven days. Tell you what. I'll bring you home something from Kariba.'

Mum managed a smile. 'Take care now.'

'As if anything could happen,' I winked. 'It never does. We live a mundane existence, remember? It's unlikely to change.'

Mum embraced Blaise. I saw his cheeks flush. 'Bye, Mum. Try not to worry. See you soon. Promise.'

Mum trudged back to the car, stood by its open front passenger seat door, wiping her eyes.

'Love you!' Blaise sang, waving.

She returned his farewell, white hanky fluttering in the light breeze, a flag of surrender. Standing in the car park in the dying evening glow, Mum struck a forlorn figure. She was the family's steely backbone, our core. *Gees*, we called it. *Spirit.* Yet, at that moment, she looked vulnerable, brittle even.

… of everything that stands, the end.

SENTINELS

DAD, BLAISE, AND I pushed through the main glass doors.

Whatever their orientations and contexts, all airports share similitude: sanitised black-flecked white tiling, maze-like walkways and corridors, disinfected restrooms, uncomfortable seating, bulging newsstands and unforgiving fluoro-lights. Apart from its parochial peculiarity, Salisbury Airport was no exception.

On this day, it was abuzz.

Travellers hurried to their allotted departure gates. Some hugged and kissed their farewells; others jammed the sole duty-free store and purchased last-minute gifts or supplies. Yet more loitered in the café and newsagency, drinking coffee, reading newspapers or browsing the packed shelves of potboilers, penny horribles, and magazines for their trips.

Paladins of power sentinelled the place: the ubiquitous police, armed military personnel, tracker dogs and their handlers.

Part of that new normal.

We said our farewells at the café. Dad was not one for long-winded goodbyes, but this time he hesitated. He cleared his throat. 'Mum is out of sorts for a reason. It concerns your Uncle Tom.'

Tom was Mum's younger brother and a chopper pilot in the Rhodesian SAS.

'A rocket grenade hit his chopper. He's in hospital. Touch and go whether he'll survive.'

Tom was a wonderful fellow, full of life and fun, a larrikin and prankster.

'Thought you should know. Remember him in your prayers.'

I stared at Dad and then at Blaise. After a protracted and uncomfortable lull, Blaise's voice fractured the stillness.

'Yeah, sure. Sorry to hear that.'

'We'll pray for him,' I said, numbed. 'Give Mum our love.'

Tom's circumstances were not uncommon, but this was our first intimate brush with *the-you-know-what*.

The image of Brueghel's *Fall of Icarus* bounded into my mind like a springbok.

We abide in our nondescript insignificant lives, unsympathetic to or unaware of the suffering and misfortune of others outside of our own geography... until it leaps into our personal and private space.

... a desperate land...

Dad shoved an envelope into each of our hands, followed it with a quick hug with a 'take care and enjoy', and left. He exited through the revolving doors to the twilight beyond. The darkness engulfed him. Not once did he glance back.

We were on our own.

I checked the envelope Dad had handed to me and glimpsed the dollar bills. *Good old Dad!* I put them away inside my journal. We'd be able to buy a few souvenirs from the tourist shops at the Vic Falls.

After depositing our one overladen cricket-bag of holiday clothes for the week at the check-in, Blaise and I adjourned to the café to await our boarding call.

With a coffee and blueberry muffin, I headed for a corner table. Slurping on his fizzy drink, Blaise joined me. I hauled out a paperback from my pack.

'Wha-cha reading, Bar?' he said, chewing on his plastic straw, neck craned over my shoulder. 'Paton's *Cry the Beloved Country*?'

'Done with that. Worth a geez. A powerful human drama. I'm uncertain whether my latest choice would excite you, Blazer.'

'You won't know if you don't test the waters, hey?'

'You sure?'

Blaise nodded. 'Baron, indulge me. Give it your best shot. I dare you.'

'Okay, then. I'm reading Achebe's *No Longer at Ease*. Kinda sequel to his *Things Fall Apart*.'

'*Things Fall Apart. No Longer at Ease. Cry the Beloved Country*. Sounds apt. It sums it up for us, hey?'

'Wow, unbridled optimism!'

'Positively black. So, tell me now, why the fascination with African Lit?'

'Something's missing in my understanding of our lives here in Africa – much like the centre of a doughnut. At a deeper level, I think I'm searching for who I am and where I fit.'

Blaise stifled a laugh. 'Bar, that's a lifetime pursuit. I don't think you're ever gonna fit anywhere or find an answer to that in a book.' By the look on his face, I could see my brother was baiting me. But I couldn't resist.

'Where else, if not in books, baby brother?'

'Now that would be telling, hey? How 'bout you whip your nose out of that book for once? There's an existence beyond the printed word. Look around you. There's so much to take in.'

'Nothing strange or spectacular as far as I can see. My book beckons,' I said, opening it to the family-photo bookmark.

'Not so fast. Look closer. You see that young lass sitting over there near the counter?'

I looked up and followed his gaze to where a young, dark-haired woman sat drinking a milkshake.

'*Ja.* So what?'

'I'm gonna nip over there and introduce myself. She's been throwing inviting glances in our direction for a while.'

'Really? I hadn't noticed.'

'How would you ever know, Bar? Your head's always buried in a book.'

'Do you think it's a good idea? What about the Blaise Black Fan Club back on Borrowdale? If they get wind of this, you'll break their hearts.'

'Baron, what the eye doesn't see, the heart cannot grieve for. And I'm not officially in any relationship at the moment. I'm free to play the field. Be back soon. Stay here and enjoy the muffin and coffee.' He grinned. 'And the ill-at-ease time.'

Before I could respond, Blaise had jumped to his feet and made his way over to her table. After a brief exchange of words and smiles, he plopped down across from her and they were soon deep in conversation, leaning forward, heads close together, fingers touching.

I shook my head and returned to *No Longer at Ease*.

... limitless and free...

A female voice intoned the expected into the airport's ether.

'Could all passengers for Air Rhodesia Flight RH825, Salisbury to Kariba, make their way to Gate 2 for boarding. Thank you.'

The announcement prompted a flurry of movement from around me. I stood, packed the Achebe novel into my bag, and waited for Blaise.

He and the young woman stood, said their farewells. They embraced, Blaise kissing her cheek. They separated and, reaching out, hand touching hand, they smiled and parted company.

On his arrival, I said, 'That seemed to go well. Looked as if you hit it off with...?'

'Caroline.' Blaise smiled. 'She's a Mount Pleasant girl. Also, doing A-Levels. She's waiting for her parents, who're flying in from Jo'burg. She gave me her number and I'll look her up on my return.'

... our... plans...

'We'd better get a wriggle on, Blazer.'

We upped our pace, following the signs, swerving and paddling our way upstream amid the torrent of jostling bodies flowing in the opposite direction. Uneven clusters bouncing and eddying, they swirled in an uncertain current, swishing and bubbling around us as they slipped and slewed downstream.

'Looks as if they've just disembarked from the inbound flight from Kariba.'

'Yeah,' Blaise grunted. 'They don't appear too happy, though, do they?'

I hadn't been paying enough attention to the uneven current of bodies, but did so on Blaise's observation.

Relaxed faces were missing.

'You're right. They are anxious. I wonder what they know that we don't?'

'Calm your farm, brother. It's probably nothing, apart from the general malaise. Don't go jumping at dragons before it's necessary.'

'Easy for you to say. To ignore dragons makes you susceptible to being devoured by them.'

'All good stories have at least one dragon, hey?'

And, for good measure, other weird and wonderful creatures thrown into the brew. And that's bothering me.'

We reached Departure Gate 2.

Our flight would be a full house, given the press of people assembled. A motley crowd had gathered, the full gamut of humanity: old and young, families with young children, couples, singles. By their casual and colourful attire and accessories, they were mainly school holiday-makers and tourists bracing for Kariba, Rhodesia's Riviera and prime holiday destination.

Blaise and I queued, waiting for the gate to open and for *AR* personnel to check us in.

While we waited, I gazed through the massive windows to the tarmac beyond, where our plane sat spotlighted. Her sleek silver and blue lines glistened in the fading golden sunset.

Down the length of the fuselage was the bold sky-blue lettering *Air Rhodesia*. The tailfin sported *AR*'s uncomplicated yet iconic motif of an imposing red eagle.

The Bateleur, the snake eagle, and national emblem of Rhodesia, was associated with the stone-carved Zimbabwe Bird, and appeared on the national flag, the coat of arms, military insignia, banknotes and coins.

Hook-beaked, head uncrested, body curved and geometric fish-scale patterned. Wings folded, tucked in at its sides.

Sit Nomine Digna. May she be worthy of the name.

My thoughts drifted to its history.

African folklore claimed the carved birds derived from the city of Great Zimbabwe, or the Zimbabwe Ruins, built by the Shona people's ancestors, the Karanga, in the 11th Century, and whose civilisation had prevailed for over 300 years.

One of Africa's great mysteries, the ruined city was the largest ancient dry-stone fortress in Southern Africa. It had operated as a city-state, established on the gold trade with the East, confirmed by the many unearthed archaeological artifacts from China, India and Arabia.

The city's key artistic and cultural feature was its enigmatic sentinels – the soapstone bird sculptures – installed on its ancient walls. The Karanga believed the birds of prey to be not only totems of royal presence, but aspirational symbols of unity, power and hope.

Over the years, these guardians had been destroyed, lost or stolen. And forgotten.

... danger on the edge of town...

The eagle motif blurred; its lines rippled, swayed and danced, ruffled by an indiscernible breeze. Feathers shimmered in the fading light, a fusion of earthy browns, deep oranges and fiery yellows. Rising above its head, a spear-patterned, haloed headdress glittered, a cluster of stars.

'I am all birds, but none. I am the snake eagle, yet not,' it said, warrior eyes fixed on mine. 'I am the king of fishers, and more. And less.'

I could not evade its gaze.

'You look, but do you truly see? You hear, but do you comprehend?

'I am light in shadow, form in formlessness. Impermanent perfection. Question with and without answer.

'I exist between and beyond worlds.

'I am the dance of interconnected opposites, harmony in chaos, chaos in harmony.

'I am union and disunion conjoined, not one thing, but many things.

'I embody and transcend the mystery of existence.' I was incapable of responding.

'I am bow and lyre.

'I carry within me the songs of those silenced, the pain of those forgotten. To look upon me is to see the resilience, and the suffering, of the human spirit.'

Majestic wings unfurled in a graceful, cursive arc, to record a message on weathered sandstone in sacred calligraphic script, hinting at an ancient but forgotten wisdom.

Transfixed, I sensed truths to be uncovered in these mysterious runes.

'My wings bear the weight of history, the burden of memory, the hope of transformation. Will you honour the voices of those erased, and hold space for the marginalised?'

'Bar-on!

'Will you brave the darkness of the labyrinth to find your light?'

'Baron!'

'Pierce the veil of your certainties?'

'Hey, Baron!'

Yes?

'Are you ready to push against the doors of the unknown, to explore meaning between and beyond?'

I nodded.

'Dare you disturb the Silence?'

The eagle's haunting cry echoed over crumbling sandstone; she extended her wings without a sound, poised to take flight.

A sharp pain shifted my focus.

The bird tucked its wings back against her body, returned to her perch, morphed back to what she was on the *Hunyani's* fuselage.

... can you picture what can be...

'Hey, Baron!' Blaise prodded me in the ribs once more, laughing. 'Big brother, are you in, or out on another magic-mushroom hyper-real mind quest? This is Ground Control to Major Baron...'

I blinked back into wakefulness. 'Sorry. I was just checking out the plane we're about to hop on.'

'And?'

'She's a Vickers Viscount, the *Hunyani.*'

'Of course she is. How did you know that?'

'Don't you read anything, Junior? It was all detailed in our flight booking info documentation.'

'Who's got time to read that stuff?' Blaise said. 'No, wait, I forgot. You do.'

He followed my gaze out the windows to the airstrip. The *Hunyani* glowed in the lengthening late afternoon shadows. 'The *Hunyani.* Why is it called that, hey, Smarty-pants?'

'I've done some research on this, believe it or not.'

Blaise rolled his eyes. 'Of course you have.'

'It takes its name from the Hunyani River, which joins the Zambezi to the north,' I said. 'There are a couple of theories attached to its naming.'

'I'm all ears,' said Blaise, pursing his lips.

'The more popular theory suggests *hunyani* derives from the Shona word, *mhangura*. The closest English translation I could come up with is *red metal*. Or *copper red*. Your understanding of Shona culture and language is better than mine. What's your take?'

'I can't out-Baron you this time. Your translation rings true.' Blaise grinned. 'And the other theory?'

'*Hunyani* originates from *hunyanhwe*, or *place of elephants*. I could have it wrong... not that I'm often wrong,' I said, trying to suppress a laugh. 'I thought I was wrong once, but I was mistaken.'

'Pull the other one, buddy. So, a choice: *red metal* or *place of elephants*. Which way are you leaning?'

'Depends on which has the most meaning for me.'

'That's a dodgy way to justify anything, Baron,' Blaise said. 'You can't just make things up on a whim.'

'Is it not my right to select the interpretation that is most sensible if there is a disagreement concerning meanings?'

'Or use both. What's preventing us from fusing the theories? They're linked anyway. Why does it always have to be *either... or*?'

'Fair point. I hadn't thought to blend them. It might make for a richer, subtler understanding.' I shook my head and smiled. 'There are times you can blow me away.'

'I'm a lethal weapon. I blow myself away sometimes,' Blaise said, embracing me in a bear hug and lifting me off my feet. 'What's with the *red* reference, huh?'

His vice-like grip held me captive.

'Once you put me down,' I wheezed, '*you* can tell me, seeing you're on a roll.'

Blaise released his hold and set me down.

'We associate *red* with extreme passion and pressure. And the *metal* bit. A play on *mettle*, perhaps?'

'Not a poor answer, Watson. Marks for insight, creativity, and effort.'

'Existential creativity, if you will, Sherlock. Let's hear you do better.'

'I thought you'd never ask,' I grinned. 'Let's combine the theories, like you suggested, to illuminate realms of meaning and possibility.'

'Illuminate away, Captain my Captain.'

'Both terms are associated with the Hunyani River. One refers to it as a life-source and gathering spot for elephants, the other describes its volatile nature. Red soil and rocks impact the powerful flow of water when the Hunyani is in full spate, causing it to glow a metallic copper red and brown. An alchemist's crucible. It has a whole range of connotations attached to it too, as you said, best summed up by what the Shona call *kusimba*, the ability to withstand difficulty and challenge. How's that? Are you impressed yet?'

'Big Brother, I'm positively awestruck. You... are... a... leg-end. Your brain has been working overtime in that Humanities class,' said Blaise. 'You're full of useless information, hey? I hope that you'll be able to put that encyclopaedic brain and all that reading to some good use somewhere.'

'You wouldn't be half as bad if you focused more on your studies and paid less attention to rugby and the Convent lass you keep chatting up. What's her name again? Jess... Jessica, isn't it? Or is Caroline the new flavour of the month?'

Blaise blushed. 'Rugby is not a matter of life and death. It's more serious than that,' he said. 'And as for Jessica, and Caroline, well, they are *mooi*, aren't they? I can't help myself.'

'I'm not sure what they see in you.'

Blaise winked. 'It must be my amazing charm, wit and raffish good looks.'

'Obviously not your modesty, Little Brother.'

'I have nothing to be modest about,' he said. 'Speaking about *meisies*, I reckon Stephanie has her eye on you.'

It was my turn to be surprised. 'You're having a laugh. What would she see in a front-row forward? I don't think she knows I exist.'

'Ah, Big Brother. You are soft on her! Trust me, it's mutual. You should chat with her when we get back from this holiday, instead of losing yourself in those books of yours. Escape from *No Longer at Ease* and take a trip to *Mysterious Island*.'

'And use the Blaise Black romance playbook, I suppose? What's that one called? *Heart of Darkness*? Or is that *Redness*?'

'No,' Blaise grunted, 'more like *The River Between*.'

'Not sure if you're the bleeding-heart type. I'm definitely not. A trip across water to the never-never is not my style.'

'You need to change your style. Take a risk. Try something new. You won't be disappointed.'

'How do you know about Stephanie?'

Blaise tapped his nose with his index finger. 'I have my sources.'

My brother was a hooligan, and incorrigible to boot, but life was dull when he was absent.

'Air Rhodesia Flight RH825 now boarding at Gate 2,' intoned a helium-filled voice-over. Bodies snaked forward. Jovial, light-hearted banter and laughter wove a charm around us.

... ride the snake... to the lake...

The lilac-clad flight attendant smiled and checked our passes. 'Welcome. Enjoy your flight.'

I smiled back at her, but I couldn't shake that feeling of unease. I dismissed it as the influence of the book I was currently reading.

We wound our way down a long corridor. The walkway felt more like an oversized cattle truck.

'This is a final boarding call for passengers on Air Rhodesia Flight RH825, Salisbury to Kariba...'

... the end... my friend... the end...

I lined up behind Blaise.

'We made it!' he said. 'We'll be at the Vic Falls in no time, you'll see. Relax, Big Brother. You're always so tense and wound up. Let go. Live a little.'

'I suppose I should.'

'Forget *should*. Try *must*.'

For a footy-head, he was astute when reading me.

I was prone to brood and found it tough to relax. First-time nerves, the bush war and the news about Uncle T were also powerful disincentives.

'You okay, Bar?'

'Just light-headed.'

'Me too. All this excitement.'

I did not contradict him.

At the front exit of the *Hunyani*, a second flight attendant greeted us and checked our tickets once again, giving us directions. 'Welcome aboard. 13-C, and D. Near the back, to your left.'

We crammed into the cabin, where all shapes and sizes were stowing bags, settling in. The collective jibber-jabber proved a comforting diversion.

'Hey Bar, I thought the cabin would be bigger than this.'

'Nah. Room for 50 passengers plus crew.'

We shuffled towards the plane's rear. A fair-haired boy – he couldn't have been older than four or five – in the arms of his father, dropped his fluffy chocolate-brown teddy bear.

He whickered.

I scooped it up with one hand and handed it to him.

It reminded me of my first teddy from years before. Baloo the Bear travelled with me everywhere, prompted by Mom's dreamy bedtime stories that fuelled my imaginary journeys with other *Jungle Book* luminaries: Mowgli the man-cub, Akela, Raksha and the wolf pack, fatherly Bagheera, the scary Shere Khan and cunning Kaa.

'Here you go.'

'Tank you,' he said, cuddling the bear to his chest.

'What's Teddy's name?'

'Milo.'

'Cool name.' I held up my hand in a royal salute. 'Give me five!' He smacked his hand into mine, although his aim was off. He giggled. It was difficult not to stifle a chuckle of my own. As we struggled past him and his father in the congested aisle, the lad waved.

'Cheers, Big Ears!' I waved back.

He snickered again. I gave him thumbs up, and he responded in kind. As we moved away, Dad gave a weary smile and mouthed a thank you.

We squeezed down the aisle towards the back of the plane.

'Here we are. Lucky 13, C and D.'

We shoved our bags in the overhead lockers, flopped into the seats, and strapped ourselves in. As the older twin, I had claimed the window seat.

I checked my watch. It was coming up for six.

A voice crackled over the PA.

'Good evening. This is your Captain speaking. Great to have you on board, Air Rhodesia Flight RH825, Salisbury to Kariba. We'll depart once we have clearance. Conditions look good. ETA 18h45. Please buckle up and follow the directions of our cabin crew. I'll talk to you again once we're airborne. Enjoy the flight.' After a pause, he added, 'Cabin crew, cross-check and prepare for take-off.'

... ride the snake... to the ancient lake... baby...

Flight RH825 haunts me still.

Memories can be reliable and deceitful. They can terrorise, distort, and conflate; embellish, comfort and clarify.

The details of 825 continue to befuddle my mind, the reality blurred with my recollection.

For the Hunyani took off from Kariba, not Salisbury.

In my conscious hours, I struggle to make sense of my recon-structed version of events, which begin in Salisbury, and not Kariba. Like shards of a shattered clay pot pieced together kintsugi-style, my mis-memory persists.

Had I merely confused the facts, or was something deeper, beyond comprehension, at play?

Had my mind shielded me from the full horror of what happened, by re-creating an altered version of events?

In attempting to reconcile the disparate elements of a traumatic expe-rience, was my memory attempting to compensate for my jumbled sense of loss, grief, fear and confusion?

In skewing the facts of the flight, had I created a narrative that made sense of the insensible?

Try as I may to confront these questions, answers continue to elude me.

Perhaps that is the point: to live meaningfully is to live in the transi-tional, post-rational space between question and answer.

The search is all.

Over the years, that twilit space has nudged me to interrogate my assumptions, to recognise the limits of my understanding, to seek the perspectives of others, and to be gentler on myself.

Memory is never merely a record of past events: it is a dynamic force-field that holds, challenges, shapes and nurtures our past, present, and future. While it is flawed and fragile, porous and partial, it frames the narratives that we construct for ourselves.

We need to safeguard these narratives even as they shape-shift within us. For it is through our stories and songs that we make sense of our lives. It is how we find meaning amid uncertainty, contradiction and complexity.

Minha busca continua.

My search continues.

IN THE SHADOWS

PROPELLERS SPLUTTERED AND WHIRLED, and the Viscount murmured to life. She jerked forward, taxied to the runway, and turned to face the light breeze.

She paused.

Her hummingbird engines rose to a protesting whine. My feet vibrated. Eyes closed, I gripped the seat's armrests. The howling intensified, the tinnitus ringing in my ears.

The *Hunyani* exploded down the runway. Everything rattled and shook. Then, as if she was a primed hunting falcon, she slipped her shackles and lifted skyward, clawed at the wind's currents, seesawed, and surged upwards.

Elation melted to queasiness as my gut caught up with me.

Powerful Rolls-Royce engines thundered and sling-shotted us into the heavens.

I forced my eyes open and stared at the headrest to my front. For some inexplicable reason, I was thankful my brother and I sat at the rear of the plane.

'Woo-hoo! What a rush!' Blaise gushed, eyes alight, a kid on the Big Dipper.

I stuck my face to the window and an apprehensive shadow frowned back. Through the pale reflection, I had a bird's-eye view of Africa sinking away.

I'd often been told that the infinity of the African bush offered a feast for the senses and the emotions, capable of feeding the soul in single mouth-watering morsels strung together.

'Baron, the African bush dances to the beat of a different drum,' I recalled my cousin saying to me once. Mom's nephew, Drew, worked as a ranger at Pretoriuskop, the oldest of the rest camps in the Kruger National Park. Mom, Dad, Blaise and I had holidayed there at the conclusion of O-Levels.

'It has its own *gees*. Full of surprises, it forces on you a humble insight: you are a smudge on its enormous canvas. *Ja, Boet*, you can't hide from yourself in the African bush. Out there, you encounter what's in here,' he said, pumping his chest above the heart. 'It gets under your skin. You come face-to-face with yourself. And your mortality. Once you confront its rawness and vitality, you're never the same.'

As the *Hunyani* ascended to cruising altitude, I had an inkling of what cousin Drew meant. The kaleidoscope of dapples and freckles daubed in the shadows of a fiery sunset could do nothing other than stir the soul.

I yearned to see it up close. *To let it under the skin...*

... ride the highway west...

The plane's broad wings banked left and levelled.

With ear pressed against the reinforced window, I eavesdropped on the plaintive wind and the purring turbo-prop engines.

The tightness in my muscles began to ease.

I have slipped the surly bonds of earth... danced the skies on laughter-silvered wings... chased the shouting wind...

I wanted to write like that. I had dabbled with various writing projects, but had abandoned them. Mom and Dad had encouraged me to persevere, but I had always felt my efforts were inadequate and would be dismissed as idiot-tales. Nor had I yet discovered that inspiration or storyline to prompt me to write.

My thoughts drifted to *Psalm 139*. Even Magee had his master:

If I climb the heavens and... fly to the point of sunrise, even there your hand will guide me, your right hand holds me fast... Darkness is not dark for you, and night shines as the day... Darkness and light are but one...

'Baron! That was unbelievable. I can't wait for the landing,' said Blaise. '*Oi*, Baron, are you in? Man, sometimes – no, most times – you're away with the fairies.'

'Sorry. I was elsewhere, thinking of Calliope.'

'Such a dark horse, Baron. So you do have a girl in mind.'

'You could say that. She's one of the Ancient Greek Muses. A poetic muse, to be precise.'

'Why's that not a surprise? You need to get out more,' he laughed, punching me on the shoulder. 'Get those musing goblin-maidens off your back. Life's passing you by. Enjoy the moment, brother; don't psychoanalyse everything.'

'It'll be easier next time.' It was the only lame comeback I could manage.

A loud chime gonged throughout the cabin as the *Fasten Seat Belts* and *No-Smoking* signs switched off, followed by an asynchronous unclicking.

The flight crew moved through the cabin serving the customary victuals and passengers kicked back to enjoy the short ride to Kariba. Some chatted, others dozed in their seats, and a few peered through the plane's portals at the thick tapestry of bush sliding away beneath the evening sky.

My earlier stab of uneasiness dissipated and I turned my thoughts to my aunt and uncle, who awaited us. Despite their idiosyncratic tendencies, I was looking forward to the family reunion.

I settled back and pulled out my journal and pen.

'Scribbling again, Bar?'

'Can't stop myself. Helps me frame my thoughts and feelings.'

'I hope that doodling's gonna be useful someday.'

'You never know, hey? It might be source material for the next great African novel.'

I started writing.

SUNDAY, SEPTEMBER 3

My first take-off.

Exhilarating and daunting. A little claustrophobic, too.

Looking forward to holidaying in Kariba. I'm confident it will be unforgettable.

How ironic that words from 'High Flight' popped into my mind. The poet John Magee, an RAF pilot, died in a plane crash during the Battle of Britain in World War Two.

The African sunset through the portal is flame-lily surreal. 'Out of Africa, always something new.' Thus far, I have no objections to Pliny's axiom.

I understand why Ma had been so wound up with her farewells: apart from the guilt of travelling abroad, she was worried about Tom, and that something might happen to us. We'd be so lucky to have some real excitement in our lives!

And Blaise? Well, he's pumped. I wish I could be in the moment like him. He is so uninhibited.

I wrapped my journal into its plastic sleeve, stuffed it back into my bag, stowed it under the seat and sat with my eyes shut, reflecting on how I could be less self-conscious and more unconstrained, like my twin brother.

... take a chance...

A convulsive shudder yanked me out of my reverie. The *Hunyani* lurched, shrieked in anguish. Her engines whooshed in protest as if punched in the solar plexus.

... of everything that stands... the end

Standing passengers and crew crashed to the floor amidst cries that reverberated around the cabin, followed by a chorus of discordant, bubbling moans.

I glanced out the window. Thick, black smoke wheezed from the inner starboard engine.

Its propeller spluttered and failed.

... fuck...

Sparks erupted into long tongues of fire that licked the wings and fuselage. Flames and smoke billowed past the windows, and fragments of engine debris spun away into the aircraft's slipstream.

... of our elaborate plans, the end...

Starved of fuel, the *Hunyani's* outer starboard engine mimicked its sibling. A fizzing voice echoed from above. 'I can't... *they're going like f...* Mayday. *Mayday.* Rhodesia 825, I have lost both starboard engines.'

The plane staggered to the right and wobbled. My belt snapped taut, thrusting me into the depths of my seat.

Pain ripped through my midriff and across my back.

... a wilderness... of pain...

The Viscount floated and without warning air-pocketed, falling free and gathering speed.

With a single heave, my guts jumped to my mouth.

Emergency lights flickered to life, bleeping and strident clamours of God-knows-what jarred the cabin. Guttural yells, low-pitched sighs and tearful sobs echoed from around me.

Bigger flames shot past the windows in sheets, their intense heat searing the metal fuselage and causing it to glow furnace-red.

A young man to my right looked to prise open a window while up ahead, someone yelled for a fire extinguisher.

The two air stewardesses had regained their feet and composure, and struggled up and down the aisle, issuing instructions. 'Strap in. Crash position.'

... ride...

The wails grew louder.

Now a wounded raptor, the Viscount plunged in a horizontal dive, its laboured descent controlled by the exceptional skill and experience of the pilot.

'Fasten seat belts and prepare for an emergency landing,' his voice crackled overhead. 'Something's hit our starboard engine. Stay calm. We'll be okay. Assume crash position. We're going in!'

It was a miracle that we had not broken up in mid-air and the fuel in the wing-tanks had not exploded across the darkening sky.

With shaking hands, I hurried slowly to place the oxygen mask – which had dropped from above me – over my mouth and nose.

I'll never look into your eyes again.

In the seat in front of me, a mother groped to secure a mask for her toddler, but it eluded her outstretched hand. I loosened my seatbelt, lunged at the mask above her, and latched onto it with my second attempt. I extended my arm and held it out to her.

Moist, smoky grey eyes locked with mine.

She smiled. 'If anything should happen to me, please get my child out.'

Words choked in my throat. I nodded.

Our fingertips connected, cool and clammy to the touch.

... desperately in need of a hand...

Violent pounding, hammer-blows, iron on anvil.

Her eyes widened. Our fingers tarried.

Hands grasped, grabbed, clutched, wrenched free.

Mother. Child.

Gone in an instant.

A wall of wind wrenched me forwards. Blaise grabbed my jumper and yanked me down, held me fast, helped secure my seatbelt.

My abdomen strained against the tugging harness but somehow the strap held me in place.

The serrated hole in the fuselage and the bloodshot haze beyond gripped me in their thrall.

... no safety or surprise...

I glanced over at Blaise. Jaw clenched shut, he gave me a thumbs up. I reached out my right hand towards him and grabbed his wrist. He realigned and squeezed my hand.

... of everything that stands, the end...

Banshee-wailing air. A stammer of alarms. Spasms.

Whirling in my head.

In a flash of lilac, kind eyes framed by dark auburn hair levelled to mine. 'You've got this. Head down to knees and brace. You'll be fine.'

She smiled, patted my back, and battled forward.

Emboldened, I ducked beneath seat level and shrugged my shoulders inwards to protect my neck.

The cabin filled with smoke which thickened to boiling, bubbling and bluish fog. Eyes watering, the back of my throat burning, I tried to swallow, but it triggered a reflex fit of long-winded, dry, hacking coughs.

... doing a blue rock... on a blue bus...

We're all going to die, kept birling in my head. *I'm going to die.*

Downward the *Hunyani* coiled, spiralling, a noble eagle in its death throes.

... the snake is long... seven miles...

The captain struggled to keep the Viscount's nose up.

'Brace for impact... and... be brave.'

... pray for us... now and at the hour of our death...

Adrenaline flooded my body. With tightened jaws, I could not form the word *Amen*. In a final act of supplication, I placed my head on my arms and embraced the seat in front of me.

Tops of trees clutched at the *Hunyani's* under-carriage and starboard wing.

... the end... this is the end...

With protesting metal she groaned, twitched and belly-flopped to touch the earth, bouncing and skidding. Head down, she tilted sideways, accelerating and vibrating as she furrowed the ground.

Oh, God, please don't let it disintegrate or flip over.

We slewed and slowed. My heart missed a beat.
We're going to make it.

... beautiful...

Darkness engulfed the *Hunyani's* cabin as it smashed into an obstruction.

In slow motion, she cartwheeled in a death-defying acrobatic, rico-cheting flick-flack. Her forward section burst like shrapnel, flinging wings and tail-section outwards. Ruptured tanks hurled burning fuel everywhere.

My head whiplashed, jolting me to all points of the compass.

Churned in a cement mixer.

The fuel-dense dust crept towards the rear of the plane, its hot breath enveloping me. My head thwacked against something hard, and I blacked out.

... lost in a Roman wilderness of pain...

BEYOND... BEYOND

A BLUR OF COLOURS heralded my return to consciousness.

Whiffs of char-cooked meat filled my nostrils, and my mouth tasted of crunchy soil. I spat out the granules as best I could. Apart from a few scratches, body-bumps and a hippo stampeding in my head, I was unhurt.

I struggled to my feet and scanned my surroundings.

In the darkening haze, a shattered cabin and a series of jagged, razor-sharp fuselage teeth crystallised. Disoriented, I stared upwards. The seats suspended from above confirmed how the *Hunyani* had arrived in its last resting place.

I staggered to the exit door and twisted the emergency handle, but it snapped off in my hands.

Spot fires sizzled in all quadrants, and burning plastic seized my throat.

Where was my brother?

I faltered to the rear of what remained of the tail section. Bodies lay strewn and sprawled in amongst the clutter, shabby playing cards flung across a card table.

I checked through the disordered jumble. *Clothes spun in a washing machine.*

My search became frenetic.

... weird scenes inside...

53

Greasy smoke wheezed and coughed from the disfigured, fragmented fuselage and gasoline fumes overpowered every pore and crevice.

Whimpers emanated from somewhere, interspersed with the clatter of sluggish, uncoordinated movements. I could not pinpoint their precise whereabouts in the midnight-dark murk.

To the front and right of me, urgent yells resounded in the night air, followed by distinct popping.

Shit.

I had spent enough time with my brother and father at the shooting range to recognise what it was. I redoubled my search efforts for Blaise.

... desperately in search of some...

A hand touched my shoulder. I jumped in fright.

'Thank God! You all right?' Blaise nodded, fuddled and groggy. Blood oozed from his head.

'Sit for a moment while I staunch that blood.' I fumbled for some means to retard the bleeding. My eyes chanced on a bloodied silk scarf amongst the dross. I wrenched it free, crafted a pressure bandage and wrapped it around his head.

More explosions. Buzzing.

Much louder.

Firecrackers.

'We must find a way out before we're trapped inside a firestorm.'

Blaise bobbed his head once again and lurched to his feet in a stupor.

I pulled him down. 'Stay low and out of sight.'

'Where... are we?'

'I'm not sure, but we must get out of here.'

I wormed my way towards the rear of the plane, through the cabin-clutter, tugging at and hauling Blaise, drowsy and heavy-eyed, behind me.

Protracted snaps, angry yells, and muted shouts echoed in the night.

Close by.

'Wait here, Blaise. Don't move. I'll be back in a tick.'

Blaise managed a garbled response. 'Where ya goin'?'

'My pack has some provisions. We'll need them.' It also carried my journal and the family photo, but of that I said nothing.

It was a challenge to scramble back in the dark to what had been my seat.

I ferreted around, located and unravelled the backpack, which had been curled around one of the buckled seat legs suspended above me, then negotiated the obstacle course back to my brother.

He was not where he was supposed to be.

'Blaise?'

No answer.

Damn and bless the dark.

I crawled forward on hands and knees, eyes closed, right hand groping the blackness in front of me.

I whispered my brother's name once more.

From behind me and to my left, a grunt spewed from the darkness. 'Here.'

'Why did you move? I told you to stay where you were.'

'I did. I haven't moved. Promise. You're the one who got lost.'

Blaise was in no condition to move on his own. He couldn't have budged, even if he had wanted. 'You're right,' I said. 'I wasn't where I thought I was.'

Yells and shrieks fractured the quiet.

'No time to debate the matter.' I grabbed a handful of jumper and tugged him forward. He attempted to shift from a sitting position but, unstable and somnolent, all he could manage was to rock backwards and forwards.

... came to a door...

Placing my shoulder under his, I heaved him to the rear exit door. I kicked at it, but it was reluctant to open.

Supersonic cracks... *closer.*

'For shit's sake. Not now.'

I booted at the door once more. Apart from echoing clangs, it remained unresponsive.

A prattle of voices. Exploding, popping corn.

I shouldered the door.

It shifted.

'C'mon.' I bent my knees and with my right shoulder leading, I scrummed it. The door snarled and relented, opening a fist's width. With a final all-or-nothing karate kick, I propelled the base of my foot at the door's centre. It creaked open enough for us to squeeze through.

The moon squinted at us, offering a slice of light. We'd ended up in what looked like a cotton field. The only ones I knew of in the north-west were in the Urungwe Tribal Trust, about thirty clicks or so from Karoi in the *kopjed* Whamira Hills.

Whamira. I had a vague recollection of the word's meaning. 'You have terminated.' *How apt.* Stuck at world's end, in her granite, constipated buttocks.

... the end...

A thick covering of African bush with a large concentration of mopane trees stood close before us.

... a chance...

Confident footsteps threatened from behind, in tandem with a *skinder* of disparate, cussing voices. They swelled again and the stepping was much louder, accompanied by more jibber-jabber and upheaval.

I mouthed to Blaise and pointed to the bush ahead of us. He gave a shaky thumbs-up.

With both hands, I catapulted him from the exit door and followed. As he staggered forward, losing his footing, I grabbed him, and arm-in-arm, we hobbled our way to the cover of the tree line, crouching as low as we could. Into the bush we dived, leopard-crawling as far as possible, and then we lay still, face down in the underbrush.

'Not a word.'

... the end of everything...

What followed remains vivid in my re-presenting past. Branded into my consciousness, it has been an uncoiling and recoiling serpent down the years.

Perceptions and emotions can undermine our memories, so they are neither reliable nor accurate. At worst, they are biased and etiolated fabrications; at best, creative approximations, nuanced reconstructions of reality that through repetition are reshaped over the years into comfortable and believable certainties.

But the thousand sordid impressions of that night playing over and over in my head have remained constant over time, despite their fragile and fragmentary nature.

... a vision planted in my brain...

Sjambok whipcracks, pyrotechnics and incendiary tracers, loud screams, then silence.

I lay prostrate and inert, listening and concentrating on controlling the only thing I could: my breathing.

... the killer put on his...

Boots scuffed against the undergrowth, not five paces from my head. The unmistakable trace of tobacco wafted on the night air, attended by hushed and strange whisperings.

... from the ancient gallery he took a face...

A deep, croaky voice growled to life.

'Comrades, that must be all of them,' it began. 'We've mopped up the survivors. Our leaders will be pleased with our efforts tonight. These new infrared missiles, they will tip the scales in our favour. This will dishearten our enemies. We have struck a blow against those who took our land,' he said.

'Mark my words; this is the beginning of the end for those who oppose us. *A luta continua.* The struggle continues and victory will be ours.'

... soft lies...

'We'll do one more sweep for anyone who may have slipped past our cordon, and then we should get out of here before the military arrives – as we know it will. A good night's work, everyone. *Hamba!*'

... insane...

Their hubbub faded away into the night, replaced by other more familiar sounds.

Against the theatre of night sky, the concert resumed: the vocal ensemble of cicada beetle love-clicks, a baboon's bi-syllabic *wa-hu* bark, the lion's guttural grumbling, and ghostly hyena wails rose in rambunctious chorus, all part of the distinct musical repertoire of nocturnal Africa.

Blaise and I remained motionless amidst an unvoiced fellowship of death. We did not deign to move until the ritualised night sounds of the African bush, unruffled by the drama that had just played out, had reached their crescendo.

I pulled my pack off my shoulders and rested my head against it. Blaise leaned his head on the opposite side.

Neither of us said a word.

... echoed in the wells...

Blaise ventured into our silence.

'You okay?'

I did not respond.

'Baron?'

I struggled to speak; words jammed in my throat. 'Hang on. I'm not sure. Just give me a moment. I – Sorry, you first.'

'My head hurts, and I'm fecking cold, but other than that, like you, I'm just processing what happened.'

... the night(s) we tried...

My thoughts romped like unchecked cheetahs across the grasslands of a fuzzy mind. A splitting headache didn't help either. I took a few deep breaths.

'Baron?'

'Just trying to orient myself.'

'You think? My mind is whirling like a catherine wheel. What do we do now, Bar?'

'Sounds like most of the passengers are dead. You heard what that terr had to say.'

Blaise remained silent.

'We need to regroup, come up with a plan. For now, we're safe enough in this thicket. We'll look at things when the sun rises. Our plane didn't arrive at Kariba, so that should be an alert. And I'm sure the pilot would have raised the alarm, so the security forces should be out at first light looking for us,' I rationalised. 'It might be best to hide and wait.'

'Fine by me. I'll let you make the call, Bar... I'm out of it.'

'You gonna be okay?'

'*Ja*. Nah. I'm not sure. I'm sore and my head's throbbing.' As if to underline his remarks, Blaise leaned over and vomited in repeated spasms. 'I'm just going to close my eyes for a while...'

I tried to reassure him. 'Rest up. I'll keep watch.'

... what will be...?

I lay on my back, battered by shipwrecked thoughts. Blaise was also marooned, staring at the sky above. Between us, the unasked question remained unasked.

It hung in the air.

... like a cancer, grows...

Disconnected impressions... unforgotten memories.

Never will I forget the dread and the numbness. Nor nature's nocturnal requiem. Nor how my ears strained for that intrusive and oppressive silence, a prelude to danger.

My thoughts roamed on that night-to-remember.

To survive a fiery plane crash had been inexplicable. But never will I forget the aftermath beyond, beyond comprehensible.

I will never forget.

I'd sought an explanation and found only a tentative answer in Shakespeare. (Who else?) I recalled lines from our set text, *Macbeth*. On viewing Lady Macbeth sleepwalking, the doctor reflects:

'Unnatural deeds do breed unnatural troubles.'

To deny our humanity results in deeds unnatural and, once we embrace the darkness and slide on its slimy slope, it's difficult to avoid the fall into the oily abyss and not stay there.

'Blazer?'

Blaise dozed, his head resting against my backpack.

'What?'

'Don't worry. Just checking in.'

Exhausted, I closed my eyes and drifted into a fitful sleep where grinning dragons wearing polished combat boots chased me through six-foot-high savannah grass, their rapier claws glinting in the moonlight, reaching out to disembowel me, yelling with verve and gusto, *a luta continua...*

... some stranger's hand...

The penetrating and plaintive *haa-haa-haa-de-dah* of a lone ibis awoke me.

My eyes adjusted to the strange surroundings in the unfolding dawn. We lay ensconced in a shady grove of the ever-present African mopane tree.

The foliage obscured the wreckage of the *Hunyani*, but ample evidence of the previous night's crime abounded. Smoke trails floated upwards, guided by an intoxicating miasma of fuel. Large, sinewed metal sculptures, postmodern landmarks, knelt in prayer.

Blaise rested on his back, breathing unevenly.

I checked the backpack, careful not to disturb his slumber. Small mercies lay within: bottles of water and apples. Sensing my movement, Blaise stirred, and we shared the food and water.

'Keep some for later. We don't know what still awaits us out there.'

Blaise remained uncommunicative.

'How are you tracking?'

'Luckier than most, I guess,' he said, looking at me with red, road-map eyes. 'Apart from the rhino stomping in my head and red ants nibbling at my face.'

'Can't do much for the headache. Let me look at that wound.'

He inclined his head. I removed the blood-marked scarf. A jagged gash stretched from the tip of his ear to just above his left eyebrow.

'Howzit look?'

'Not too bad. The bleeding's stopped, but it's inflamed. There's a shard of glass lodged in there,' I said. 'Best leave it in for now. It's hard to see how big it is, so removing it could cause further bleeding. It'll need stitching.'

'Thanks for the diagnosis, Doctor Baron.'

'Aren't you lucky that I kinda know what to do?'

Blaise nodded. 'Some help is always preferable to the alternative...'

... the end of laughter...

I rinsed the wound with some water and wrapped the scarf around his head once more.

'From the land beyond, beyond. From the world, past hope, and fear...'

'What?'

'You know, *beyond, beyond*...?'

'Huh?'

'The seventh voyage of Sinbad? Blaise, *Sinbad.*'

'Sinbad. *Really?* You're stuffing with my head... not that it isn't stuffed already.'

'Just trying to bolster your spirits, lighten the mood.'

'The mood, big brother, if you haven't noticed, crashed and burnt in that plane,' Blaise said, pointing to the wreckage.

I bit my tongue. 'You're right. Bad timing. Look... I –'

'Bar, just drop it. Given what's happened, I'm a little twitchy. I get what you're trying to do...'

'I –'

With pursed lips, Blaise put up his hand. 'Stop. Let's just leave it at that for the moment.'

... everything that stands...

That moment, and moments after, came and went. The silence expanded, a translucent, shape-shifting crystal. I ventured into its pressurised expanse.

'I first thought we should just remain here, but now I'm not so sure.'

Blaise said nothing. I mustered up the courage to try again, but before I could, he lifted his gaze as if coming into consciousness for the first time and said, 'That's a big call, Bar. Why's that? Surely it's better to wait for help to arrive?'

'I hear you. That was my thinking last night. But we're too close here. Those terrs are still sniffing around.'

'I would have thought that by now they'd have hightailed it, before the military arrives,' Blaise said, 'which they will.'

'A lot depends on the message the pilot got out. There's no way of knowing,' I said. 'They still have to find us.'

'That shouldn't be too hard. This mess will be visible from the sky. I reckon the spotter planes will be up and the parabats won't be too far behind, even if the pilot didn't get the message out. A plane not arriving would have been enough to alert authorities. Perhaps we should stay and hide?'

'Sitting around here waiting for something to happen or not happen is too passive for my liking, Blazer. It's making me edgy.'

We argued back and forth in this vein until Blaise said, 'Okay, Baron, we can't fluff around here if we're going to move. Let's get out of here before my courage deserts me.'

'All right then. Let's haul some ass.'

'Where did you have in mind?'

'Northwest, towards Kariba.'

... where you taking us...?

The African bush sweated and sweltered in the growing haze just prior to first light.

We scoured the landscape, checked for any movement. We watched and listened for any signs or sounds of unusual activity.

Everything appeared quiet. Normal, even.

Still, we lingered.

The sun ascended, its alchemist-threads weaving promises of both renewal and confinement. Its fist held us in its steely dawn grasp; we had little choice but to endure its stranglehold.

My mind wandered in the growing heat of the day.

Was our intended course of action the right decision? How much longer should we wait before moving? How safe were we? What if the terrs were still close? How long would it take for the military to arrive?

The decisions you make determine the life you lead.

It had been hard to gauge what to do, but my new-formed belief that we needed to shift as far away as possible from this location was gaining traction.

... paid a visit...

Blaise and I had agreed to first check the crash site for survivors and whatever provisions we could forage.

The *Hunyani* had broken up near the end of its fatal journey, flipping over and shattering into a multitude of smaller pieces after it had slammed into what appeared to be an irrigation ditch in the paddock.

Without that hazard, the pilot would have executed a near-perfect emergency landing.

The piecemeal plane had gouged deep-clawed wounds in the earth. Slivers of her twisted, jagged body, fire-blackened engines, buckled propellers and liquefied metal lay scattered over a narrow wasteland, spanning an area the size of two rugby fields. Apart from the rutted earth, the Viscount's starboard wing and underbelly had shorn and tousled the nearby treetops.

Mutilated vegetation lay scalded by the ruptured fuel tanks that fire-balled when the *Hunyani* smashed into the side of the *donga* and somersaulted.

Her blistered, disfigured tailfin stood upright, its stylised iconic eagle unbowed and defiant.

... and looked inside...

Working our way forward, we searched for proof of life.

The only recognisable and intact fragment of the downed aircraft was the rear section of the fuselage, which had held the last five rows of seats.

An assortment of charred, defiled personal effects – shoes, sunglasses, jostled suitcases, sunhats, cameras, a bloodied dress, a tennis racquet and rugby ball, playing cards, torn clothing – cluttered the site, poignant reminders of the crime that had occurred the night before.

Our pickings were slim, given our guerrilla friends had purloined and looted. We scavenged drink-bottles and a variety of dry rations: a small bag of biltong, some dried fruit and a pack of military-style dog biscuits.

I unearthed a slashed, tatty nylon khaki rucksack from the rubble and loaded what we could carry.

... his sister and his brother...

We inched towards the remnants of the front section of the plane, always watchful, eyeing the terrain.

Cinder-black corpses, still doubled over in the foetal crash position, confronted us. Carbonised remains smouldered in a series of incinerated clusters; ashen particles and the stench of *braaied* flesh mingled and floated on the stagnant air.

... a wilderness of pain...

I fought back the bitter, acrid bile rising in my throat.

Never will I forget what I saw. Or smelt.

The air was still as we snaked towards the front of what remained of the *Hunyani*. No sound met our ears save for the fish eagle's distant mournful knell, and the growing chorus of gathering flies.

Vultures circled overhead; many more had already dropped in uninvited. A silent phalanx mustered a short way off, watching our every move. It wouldn't be long before their collaborators, the hyenas, arrived.

We were unprepared for an even grislier sight near the nosepiece. It was difficult to look at, more difficult not to.

... insane...

The sun, nature's guardian, saw all. Nothing escaped the intensity of its rigid stare that day. In a world clouded by shades of meaning, its gimlet eye saw and exposed the truth through an unfiltered cornea.

... all the children...

On the ground, a semi-circle of scattered mutilated bodies sprawled at unnatural angles. Shredded by automatic gunfire, men, women and children lay pale and stiff in the bleeding African sun. A fair-haired boy with bewildered, staring eyes was couched in his father's last embrace, clutching his bloodied teddy bear.

My pulse quickened.

Milo.

... of everything that stands...

No one had told me the bush war was like this, or that humans had a capacity for this.

I shall never forget the pallid, smoky wreaths of silence drifting into the desolate heavens. Nor shall I forget how my world, like the Hunyani, was flipped upside down and inside out, crushed and burnt beyond, beyond recognition.

How could Blaise and I not have thought of and longed for home and our loved ones?

... it hurts...

We observed a moment's silence and together whispered a brief prayer:

Eternal rest grant unto them, O Lord. Let perpetual light shine upon them. May these souls, through the mercy of God, rest in peace.

I grabbed Blaise's arm, but he shook free and stood with a faraway stare engraved on his face.

The living know death stalks them. What do the dead know?

'It's not safe here, Blazer. Time to put some distance between this place and us. We can do nothing more for them, for now.'

With heavy hearts, we melted into the safety of the undergrowth.

the end of everything that stands... the end

INTO THE BELLY

... west is the best...

WE SMEARED OUR FACES and hands with mud and used anti-tracking techniques: splitting up, we circled back to prearranged rendezvous points, brushed our tracks, and kept to rocky ground where possible.

No one had picked up our trail, but we were under no illusions a seasoned tracker wouldn't uncover it.

Blaise was coping despite his head wound and suspected concussion, and we covered the ground to the north-west at a swifter clip than I had expected.

... ride the highway...

To slake its thirst, the sun slurped the moisture from the dehydrating earth; our perspiration dried on the skin before it displayed itself.

Concealed in the bending, itchy elephant grass, the two of us squatted side-by-side, baking in the post-midday heat. I rolled a swollen tongue across my chapped lips and attempted to swallow.

Licking broken glass.

On the distant horizon, the storm clouds conferred, waiting for a tilt at the expectant bushlands.

... in a desperate land...

With heads bent beneath the grass line, we rose and edged forward, Blaise following my lead.

'Do you hear that?'

'Bar, I hear nothing.'

'Exactly. Something's amiss.' I tugged Blaise to the ground, putting my fingers to my lips.

'I'm not...' he said, before I put my hand over his mouth.

... there's danger...

A short distance from our position in the head-high grass, the foliage fluttered and feathered.

Bantering voices bobbled towards us.

In the dappled light, I could just make out two men to our front. Dressed in piebald camouflaged jackets, their AK assault rifles stacked against a fledgling thorn-tree, they lounged *indaba*-like, smoking and chatting.

Blaise stood. 'Maybe they can help us.'

I tried to yank him down, but he avoided my arms.

The two men looked incredulous when they saw a dishevelled, tatty and grubby white boy rise like Lazarus in the long grass.

'*Mhoroi?*' Blaise called. 'Hello – how are you? We were just thinking – could you help us?'

Aghast, I stared at Blaise.

'*Buia lapa!* Come here!' one shouted, and both scrambled for their weapons.

'Shit! *Gajima,* Blaise. Move!' I grabbed his arm and pulled him away.

The two men scrambled, fumbling for their weapons. We hurdled away like skittish gazelles and dissolved into the savannah, Blaise hollering in glee, me in his wake.

Tracers whined and whipped overhead and ricocheted through the desiccated grass. We ducked and jinked, zigzagging like kites buffeted on a windy day.

... ride the highway west, baby... ride...

Into one of the bone-dry *dongas* we charged, and doubled back towards our foes.

'There!' I pointed at a smallish gap in the brush that swelled above us. We wiped our tracks with branches and pulled ourselves into the belly of the undergrowth.

Bullets ripped through the surrounding foliage, our hunters spray-gunning the vegetation. Machetes hacked at the lanky khaki-grass chased by a chain of clamouring voices closing in on us.

We lay on our bellies, heads down, statue-like, senses heightened, hearts pounding.

... someone dared disturb the sounds of...

Silence.

Overnight, we had become intimate companions. She had de-silenced my memories, unlocked my secrets.

I had lain with this Silence, she who was never tepid or tranquil.

Together, we'd sniffed the ripe body odour of our enemies, rejected their dissonant advances; the two of us, having inhaled their tobacco-breath, flinched in their close company, all the while remaining conjoined.

Our disturbers advanced, a daisy-chain of voices. Their song drowned my ears, conjuring curious evocations of death.

Boots crunched on river-stone, scorched grassland, snapped foliage. Salty sweat mingled with stale, foul breath.

Pangas sliced, slashed, scythed.

Their commotion grew fainter.

Silence restored, and abandoned.

On cue, the cicadas' serenade relaunched.

I turned to my brother.

'What the hell? Do you have any idea what you've just done? Is your mind still in a fog after that head-knock, or were you trying to kill us?'

Blaise remained silent, his head down.

'That was reckless. Try thinking for a change.'

Unable to contain himself, Blaise bit back. 'Oh, stop blithering, big brother. You're still alive, aren't you? At least we know they're tracking us.'

'No, Blaise. They did not know we were even alive. But now, thanks to you, we've not only alerted them to our existence, we've given them a bead on our location.'

'Shush.' Blaise cut me off, placing his fingers to his lips. '*Listen!*'

He pointed.

I stared at the sky, but the canopy of greens and browns that concealed us obscured my view.

'I can't hear anything,' I mimed, straining to drown out the annoying mating calls of cicadas.

Blaise held up his hand as if to say, *wait*. The cicadas grew still, as if responding to his orchestral direction.

'There. Can you hear it now?'

... limitless... free...

A forlorn hum floundered in the breeze.

Blaise's eyes brightened. 'At last. How do we attract their attention?'

Before he could rise, I wrenched him to the ground and embraced him with a bear hug. He resisted, using his arms to crowbar himself loose.

'*Baron?* What are you doing? That's our way out,' he stammered. Staring at me with enlarged eyes, he renewed his efforts to break free.

'Too risky. We'll expose our position to friend *and* foe,' I said, the words hanging between deep breaths.

Blaise's wild eyes settled as bewilderment gave way to confusion and a dawning understanding. The strength in his muscles diminished.

'If I let go, promise not to do anything stupid?'

'Promise,' he said, slumping to the ground.

... the end... my friend... the end...

A camouflaged Cessna Lynx blew overhead.

The plane's perspex canopy, painted fuselage, and double tailfin flashed by in the sunlight. It was so close that if I had reached out, I could have stroked it. I imagined airborne eyes scanning the *bushveld* left and right, for any sign of life.

... the end of our elaborate plans...

I have worse memories but few that haunt me so, and they nibble at my mind still. A light plane roving overhead never fails to summon the angst of that moment as, powerless, I watched salvation slip beyond our fingertips.

The shadows lengthened and the sunlight waned and faded, mirroring the intensity of the stony silence between Blaise and me.

In that shroud of darkness, I dared to glance at him. 'Blaise, I'm sorry, man. Maybe our strategy's all wrong. I reckon we'd do better to travel at night and hide during the day, something we should have been doing from the start,' I said, offering an olive branch.

There was no response.

'*Blaise!*' He did not move or respond. 'Blazer, what's up?'

Blood oozed from his left shoulder, a red stain widening on his jumper.

He groaned.

'Why didn't you say anything?'

'After our fallout, and your wobbly, I thought it best not to poke the beast further,' he half-laughed.

'Okay, Junior, just pause before you act, all right?'

'I forgive you, too.'

It was difficult to stay angry with him when I had persuaded him to leave the crash site.

'I also stuffed up. I'm the one who should be sorry. We should have waited for help to arrive.'

Blaise winced as I cleaned out his wound. The bullet had clipped him in the fleshy part of the shoulder and exited at the front, missing the bones. I tore a strip from his shirtsleeve and used it as a pressure bandage.

Eyes closed he lay in funereal repose.

... his skin is cold...

The mellowing sun began its bedtime routine.

Nature drooped and drowsed as the evening carnival stirred to life.

... waiting for the summer rain...

I dozed, troubled by a flickering vision in which a mother cradled a child in her lap. Both stretched out their hands towards me, pleading. I wanted to help, but I was strapped to a chair.

The mother morphed into Mom.

... Mother... I want to...

She called, much like a liquid-throated coucal.

'*Bar-on, Bar-on.*'

Her soap-bubbled voice rose and tarried. '*C-mon, Bar-on… St-orm's a-comin…*'

My eyes twitched open.

The scalding heat of day had surrendered to the damp chilliness of night. I peered over at Blaise, who lay unmoving. For a moment, I feared the worst, but I detected his shallow, even breathing.

Through the leafy covering of our hideout, we watched shadowy clouds scurry in front of the moon. Swelling and billowing, they were veined by lightning jags and rumbling thunder.

Unprovoked, they unloaded their teary gifts on the parched earth. I ripped out the water bottles and held them up to the dripping leaves, hoping to replenish our supply.

The massaging rain fell upon me. I stood, head back, eyes shut, mouth open, and stretched out my arms in a gesture of invitation.

A wily serpent jumped into my head. In normal circumstances, it would have been unwise to schlep anywhere because of my brother's injuries. But exceptional circumstances called for exceptional measures.

'Blazer.' I shook his leg.

He stirred from his stupor. 'Huh – *what*, Baron?'

'We must shift now. If we do, the rain will cover our tracks. Buy us some time. Are you up for it?'

It took a moment for my brother to register. 'Sounds like a plan. Let's get this party moving.'

I just shook my head.

'What?'

'Nothing. I'm just not sure how you do it, that's all.'

'Simple. Persist and resist. In the here and now.'

'What do you mean by that?'

'If I worry about what might happen and dwell on what's been, I'll miss the opportunity of what is.'

'That's very Zen. I'll need to think...'

'That's your problem, Baron. *Too much thinking.* Don't complicate things. It's easy. The past and the future are shadows. All we have is the present moment. *Now.* In fact, *you... me...* we are this moment. That is all we have.'

For one of the few times in my life, I found words to be inadequate, so I said nothing.

'Here, give me a hand up.'

I tugged him to his feet and, shoulder-to-shoulder, we disappeared into the cascading rain.

The massaging rain intensified, its acupunctural needles rejuvenating the earth's neural pathways.

A benediction.

Keeping up a decent pace, we maximised the opportunity. Blaise struggled, understandable given his wounds; but he soldiered on, never complaining.

Exhausted, we pressed forward, chanced upon a thorn-tree thicket in amongst the scrub, and went to ground.

... lost in a wilderness...

The rain faltered. As swiftly as the clouds had arrived, they darted off into the distant gunmetal grey hills.

Drying beneath the anthracite night sky and the flickering candles of the Southern Cross, Blaise and I drifted off into a deep, dreamless sleep...

... C'mon baby, take a chance with us...

The dawn struck through the muddled post-rain mist. Nothing could defy the sun. It dragged us into another day.

'Under the sun, we are all equal,' I thought out loud, as its rising amber glow poured through the foliage onto my upturned face. 'There's nothing new beneath its stare.'

'What was that?'

'Under the sun, we are all equal,' I repeated. 'The sun sees all.'

'That's too profound for this time of the day.'

The sun was well on its way to its appointed rendezvous point. Its heat and the playful mist jostled together in a steamy embrace.

A collision of opposites.

Their flirtation did not last long. Coy and resistant, the mist, wearied by the sun's unrelenting foreplay, capitulated.

Blaise and I stewed in the steely glare of its morning.

'You tracking okay?'

'I'm fine.'

'Let's take a sticky-beak.' Blaise squirmed under my prodding. 'No actual change from last night. Looks clean. Just gotta keep it that way.'

'Easier said than done, Bar!'

'We can only do our best.'

'So, what do you propose as best, then?'

'We're out of water and food, despite the rainfall from last night. Our hunters are close by but, on a more positive note, the rain has dissolved our tracks and bought us some time,' I said. 'We have no food and must live off the land from now onwards.'

'*Ja-well-no-fine*, that's a damning summary. But what should we *actually* do?'

'I've been trying to recall the details from that 3 Weeks-Without-Walls survival program you and I took part in last year,' I said.

'Do you remember what they said about water?'

'Elephant shit.'

'I'm sure I would have remembered that recommendation,' Blaise said.

'Really? As I recall, you were one distracted love puppy,' I grinned.

Before I could elaborate, Blaise interjected. 'What's the go with elephant dung?'

'A handful of freshly hand-squeezed elephant dung-juice is the real deal when you're up to your neck in it.'

'Thank God there are no elephants about. I'm not that desperate yet. We might have to resort to Plan C. Any ideas?'

'My brain's like Swiss cheese, but it might have something to do with riverbeds.'

'Find the lowest point and dig,' Blaise said. 'I think that's what they said.'

Was it that simple?

'Sounds as good a piece of advice as any,' I said, strapping on my backpack. 'I'll be back soon. I will find water, come hell or whatever. Don't wander off.'

'Don't worry, big brother. I'll be here when you get back,' he chuckled, half-coughing, 'unless someone arrives with a better offer.'

... ride the highway... baby...

I exited our covert, scampered across an open patch of *veld*, vaulted up and then crossed a slight incline covered with clumps of towering African savannah. Weaving in and out amidst the lengthy clusters, I chanced upon a *donga* that cut at right angles to my traversing. I surveyed the eroded laceration before dropping a few feet into its murky depths.

It had all the visible signs of a riverbed. Despite the rain the evening before, and apart from the occasional damp patch, it was as dry as my mouth.

The broiling sun had fulfilled its morning promise, shrivelling blood, sinew and marrow.

... in a desperate land...

Fresh, grassy elephant dung.

I grabbed a spongy handful, squeezed my fingers, and allowed the moisture to dribble between my lips to rehydrate. Soft on the palate, its hybrid sweet-fruity, tea-like and fermented taste was much better than I had expected.

So many uses for elephant shit.

An elephant can produce up to 100 kilos of not-so-pungent dung each day.

Mozzie and fly repellent.

I grabbed another handful, brushed my arms and legs.

... in need of a...

I shuffled along the riverbed's base, scanning for its lowest point. After some procrastination, I chose what I thought was a suitable place, fell to my knees, and scooped away the soil.

You can't keep digging in the same hole for buried treasure, my mother used to say.

I tried a different spot. Then another. And one more. Fourth time lucky – the ground moistened, and water bubbled to the surface.

As the water bottles filled, a weapon cocked behind me. My body froze, incited by a racing heart, tightening muscles, and numbed buzzing in my head.

'Stay where you are and put your hands where I can see them.'

... the end... my friend... the end...

CLASH OF KUDUS

FROM MY KNEELING POSITION, I raised my hands, a water bottle in each.

Stupid!
If you focus on the serpent, you miss the scorpion.

'I want you to stand and turn around when I say *now*. No sudden movements. Nod your head if you understand. Got it?'
I obliged.
'Drop the water bottles.'
They fell from my hands.
'Slowly... *Now!*'
I stumbled to my feet and swivelled, palms showing and fingers pointing upwards at waist level.

Before me stood a tall, muscular man. He wore leopard-speckled battle fatigues that were pressed to razor-sharp perfection, and his boned boots flashed in the sunlight. In his right hand, he held a 9-mm pistol pointed at my chest.

I was everything he was not. Sun-darkened, peeling skin, tousled and filthy hair, elephant-dung- and dust-covered head to foot, lacerated elbows and knees, blood-spattered red-and-white school footy jumper, ripped canvas trousers and scuffed trainers.

For a moment, we held each other's gaze. I stood up straighter, thrust my chest forward, pushed my shoulders back, and returned his penetrating stare.

'*Unjani igama lakho?*' he said in measured Ndebele tones, and then, as if checking himself, repeated in flawless English, 'What is your name?'

I did not respond.

He repeated his question.

'*Ungubani wena?* What's my name to you?'

The 9-mil shook in his hand.

I couldn't resist. 'You and your men have been hunting us. I was on the plane you shot down. I saw what you did to the survivors. Forgive me if I have no wish to share respectful formalities with you.'

He lowered his pistol. 'Keep your voice down. It is a bad idea to attract any more attention than you already have.'

I stared at him, uncomprehending. '*Ufuna njani?*' I said, using one of the twenty-or-so Ndebele terms I knew. 'What do you want? *Angizwsisi.* I don't understand.'

'That's the problem: a lack of understanding of the issues, not so?'

I could not muster a response.

'*Uyabhubhisa,*' he said. 'You are neglectful and ignorant, and that is disrespectful. And I concede this is also true of me.'

I chose to remain silent.

'As for the plane atrocity, I am not one of those men. I do not subscribe to tactics that target innocent people. Many others believe the same thing. But not all people – wherever they stand – see it that way, do they?' he said, stepping towards me.

I took a step backwards. 'But you have aligned yourself with people who do. Does this not make you just as guilty?'

'War has no eyes. Atrocities occur on all sides. My grandfather used to say war is a clash of *kudus.* Once the two animals have interlocked their horns, they cannot see each other, and it is impossible to separate them. We are all caught up in the long, spiralling horns of this bloody conflict that has gained a momentum of its own. Are we not all culpable, and so also responsible for ending it?'

I tried to control my thoughts.

How could I believe what he was saying? His words contradicted everything I believed about the various parties who were fighting in this war.

'You have nothing to fear from me. It goes against my instinct to kill an unarmed man,' he said. 'You are a fellow countryman. But more than that, we share a human bond. Sadly, we have clouded our humaneness. *Ubuntu*, not so?'

'Yes. We do have a common humanity. I was born here, and I grew up here. I have a right to be here, like you. Even though I have a different skin colour and cultural background, I still see myself as African. Our diversity is strength. Are we not different for a reason?'

I did not allow him to interrupt.

'I am grateful my parents encouraged *Ubuntu* in our household. We are humans only through other humans, beyond racial and cultural distinctions. *Because we are, I am.* Are we not created to know our need for one another?'

The man's eyes grew wide.

'It is my turn to be surprised,' he said. 'Spoken like a young lion! Full of passionate intensity, but with some naivety. You speak of your *right* to be here. That you were born here, in Africa. *But is this Africa born in you?* History and circumstance may have brought you here to this point. But does your history entitle you to claim the right of which you speak, if you do not have a deeper commitment to the land, or a grasp of the issues of the many differing rights – and responsibilities – that come with that?'

His words were a sledgehammer blow.

'When you put it like that, I have to admit I have never thought the nuances of my words would have such...'

'Patronising undertones? We are all prisoners of our particular environments and worldviews, my friend, and how we have been conditioned to use language is a key part of that captivity. The perspectives of the more powerful are accorded more status than others. And this privileged position allows a worldview such as yours to be normalised.'

'So, desiring to make my country a better place is a whitewashed half-truth?'

'Crudely put, but yes. Your liberal intentions are honourable on one level, but on another, paternalistic. Be careful that, in your eagerness to improve the lives of people different from you, you do not make them in your own cultural image and likeness.'

His words, a series of snakebite punctures, thrust their venom into my vulnerable brain-white-washed sensibilities. They coursed and pulsed unabated through my fragile consciousness.

'I understand why some people might object to my being here. But is your perspective not also jaundiced?'

'My young friend, apartheid is criminal. It denies each of us the opportunity – no, the right – to interact in the richness of cultures different from our own on an equal footing, to bring about something better. And we are all guilty of practising discrimination in some form or other.'

... came to a door...

As I studied the man in front of me and listened to his words, it dawned on me that he and I were in a transitional space between black-and-white binaries, somewhere between what had been and what could be, on a threshold of something else.

... so limitless... so free...

'Milk and honey are different, each nourishing in their own right; but mixed, wouldn't that be worth tasting? If we are to survive, somewhere beyond our ingrained positions, and the chaos of this war, we will need to work together to forge a new consciousness of ourselves as a nation.'

He stepped towards me. I did not back away.

'An interesting way of putting it,' I said. 'Mixing honey and milk might bring about an exciting fusion, but could this not dilute and weaken both the milk and the honey?'

'Such a wise head on young shoulders. When there is a perceived lack of balance in the blending, such danger exists. It requires a deeper understanding of the singular aspects of milk and honey, and a willingness to combine them in subtle, respectful and harmonious ways.'

'To celebrate diversity and divergence, and to recognise the common threads that connect us?'

'When we share our experiences and ideas, we can generate something new and exciting, just like milk and honey combined.'

'And not just for the sake of it.'

'When we approach things with an open mind and heart, who knows what's possible? But for now I have no choice but to fight for what has been taken from my community – land, resources, dignity, justice, freedoms, a say in how this country is governed. *A luta continua.* The struggle – the *chimurenga* – continues. And yes, so does my personal search for understanding, and meaning. These too, continue. *Minha busca continua.*'

'I'm not sure how to ford the wide river that separates us.'

'A river might divide us, but it remains something shared.'

'But it still impedes us.'

'The wise build bridges, the foolish fashion dams. We can start with the formalities of greeting,' he said, eyes sparkling.

I nodded.

'Very well, then. I am *Thembelani Thumbeza* from the City of Kings, Bulawayo. Now you. *Unjani igama lakho?* What is your name?'

'I am Baron. *Baron Black*. Born and raised in Salisbury.'

'*Kuhle ukukubona*. Baron Black, I see you.'

Our extended hands met halfway.

We shook in African hybrid style: hands clasped to begin, locked thumbs pointed upwards as a sequel, traditional western handshake to conclude.

'Mark my words. A time will come – well beyond the cruelty of these troubled times – when we can sit, without fear of reprisal, to share a meal as equals,' he said. 'But not now. Others will suspect something's amiss, and we can't have that. Many of them are not ready. They are too invested in building dams. They are afraid of transcultural bridge-building,' he half-laughed.

I summoned up the courage to reply.

'There are people on all sides of this conflict, building dams. And are we ever ready? How we use those stones thrown at us out of fear and anger to build a life-giving and sustainable structure... or not, is an act of bravery. It is not easy.'

'It never is! But we must try.'

'Perhaps, when our paths cross again, we can work to finish our bridge.'

'Ha! A young bullock, if we nurture it, becomes a large bull,' he said, smiling. 'From small beginnings come great things. So, my friend, search for me. I look forward to continuing this *indaba*. Bank on us meeting again. But until then, farewell! Now, turn around and get back on your knees.'

For an anxious half-moment, I feared he had been playing me as I knelt in that damp *donga*, with my back turned. But he said, '*Khamba kuhle, Lungisani*. Travel safely on your journey wherever it may take you.'

When I turned around, he had disappeared.

... weird scenes...

Apart from one further unexpected sighting-from-a-distance of Thembelani Thumbeza, I never saw him again. And I do not know what became of him. Although I did, once, go in search of him in his hometown after the war had ended.

Perhaps I had given up too easily.

I vowed to try again.

Our encounter in the bush gave me pause to reflect on my Black-(white) washed misperceptions of this war – the difficulties in understanding it and the various groups who fought in it – often defined only in binary terms.

Innocence and truth are always casualties in times of conflict. As is our humaneness. It took a compassionate and thoughtful man to alert me to the complexities of our political and ideological entanglements and to destabilise my narrow, simplistic views, inspiring me to think anew.

My search continues.

Minha busca continua.

It was only many years later that I better understood what Thembelani Thumbeza had gifted me.

We had attempted to de-other each other, he and I, and had ventured, albeit for a moment, into that liminal and decolonised arena beyond deep-rooted intellectual and philosophical entrenchments, that exhilarating and hopeful third space of uncertain opportunities, of provisionalities, of ambiguities, beyond unequivocal and dissembled definitions where anything could be possible.

Thembelani was an apt name. For, much later, I discovered that all indigenous African names inspire character. Thembelani was 'one who brings hope'.

I also learnt that he had called me by an indigenous Ndebele name on our parting, showing me a respect I did not deserve.

'Lungisani.'

It was his challenge to me, to work to 'make things right', to make things whole, to make things new again.

... can you picture what will be...?
... lost...

Head in orbit, I clawed with trembling hands at the soil, for the water I knew lay at the base of the *donga*.

The water frothed to the surface once more. Snatching up the discarded bottles, I filled them as best as I could and high-tailed it back to the thicket where I had left my brother.

I crested the small *kopje* I had surmounted on the outward journey, amidst bone-dry and spindly elephantine brush near our hidden redoubt of thorn-trees beyond, and my entire being prickled.

The perennial natural sounds of the bush had faded to a murmur.

... in a desperate land... there's more danger...

I dropped to the ground and lay prone. My heart pounded, followed in quick succession by the blood-rush typical of an acute stress response. I imagined my adrenal glands releasing a range of hormones into my body to trigger that reaction.

I concentrated on slowing my breathing.
Through the heavyweight scrub below, hushed tones rose like dandelions in the heat of the post-midday sun.

Three bodies in green-splotched camouflaged jackets took shape as they strolled into the clearing beneath me, and within throwing distance of where Blaise hid. Their demeanour suggested they had not yet uncovered evidence of our presence. The three of them stood bunched together, weapons slung over shoulders, smoking and glancing about.

The better part of me believed Blaise would have had the good sense to stay undercover. The other part, however, worried he might act in character. His delayed concussion, or recklessness – it was difficult to determine which – had already landed us in this mess and he had paid for it with a shoulder wound.

Muted, lilting voices persisted, meandering upwards on the warm afternoon breeze.

... the killer awoke...

A rough bark off-stage further to the left of my vision galvanised the three amigos into reaction. The bellicose shouts continued, transforming their posture. Flicking cigarettes away, they spun around and leapt to attention.

An imposing figure, wearing a red-tinged beret and splashed battle fatigues, stormed in from stage right, flanked left and right by two subalterns. He pointed to various points of the compass and snapped out the occasional command to his subordinates who, with heads bowed, deferred to his demands. I couldn't hear him – even if I had understood.

I strained to see his face, but he did not swing around for me to gain a glimpse of our adversary.

... the snake is long...

Another man appeared to my right. I recognised him at once.
Thembelani Thumbeza.

He was not alone. His entourage comprised many senior-looking officials and a military escort of bodyguards to match. His group and Beret Man's came together.

Thumbeza took command and spoke with the gathered troops. After much obsequious bladder and bluster, Beret Man and five of the original group headed off, jogging at the double. Their departing rhythmic footfalls grew fainter and fainter, dwindling to silence.

The remaining men melted into the bush. Thumbeza tarried, looking my way.

I sensed he knew where I had concealed myself. Although he was some way off, I could have sworn I detected a smile and a nod towards me before he strolled off in the wake of his escort.

... take a chance...

The sounds of the bush re-established themselves then built to a melodious disharmony.

While every fibre in my body twitched to sprint to our sanctuary and check on my brother, I waited. In the open dead-land between my current position and the makeshift thorn-tree hideaway fifty metres beyond, I would risk exposure.

It was only when the shadows lengthened, throwing tomblike, distorted shadows across the ground, that I took a deep breath and crossed the unsheltered space to our haven.

I dashed into open territory, fearing a shout of recognition and the whip of automatic gunfire.

They never came.

At the entrance, I dropped onto my belly and crawled my way into the depths of our lair.

... he came and looked inside...

'Blaise. *Blaise!* You there, buddy?'

No answer.

'*Blazer?*'

Still not a word.

Fear gripped me. *Shit.* Where the hell was he? Had he lost consciousness? Had he wandered off in a dazed and concussed state?

I squirmed deeper into the heart of the murky, thicketed brushwood, calling out once more in hushed tones.

No response.

Imagining the worst, my mind swirled.

... lost in a Roman wilderness...

A series of bloody splashes where he had lain before my departure was the only visible evidence he had been there.

Of Blaise, there was no sign.

... the end... my only friend... the end...

TALISMAN

'GET A GRIP, BARON! Control the things you can,' I said out loud. 'C'mon. Breathe!'

In. And. Out.

I had to trust Blaise was still alive, and that he had chosen to abandon our temporary refuge.

No evidence suggested otherwise. If I began from that premise, I could better manage the jumbled thoughts clashing in my addled mind.

In Blaise's position, what would I have done?

I'd have left a subtle clue, signalling my intentions only somebody who knew me could comprehend. I rummaged around the hideout, seeking anything that might help me figure what to do next.

Nothing.

I double-checked.

The darkening doubts descended once more.

Could I have been wrong?

... desperately in need...

My brother may not have had time to prepare an intricate escape plan or even have thought to leave me a clue. And if he had, I had no way of knowing what he might use and how he'd use it to communicate with me.

Blaise could do the improbable.

Unlike me, he was a will-o'-the-wisp, an outside-the-box daredevil. He was a merry wanderer to my king of shadows.

Was I guilty of imputing what Blaise might do?

If I was mistaken, I had no clue where I could locate him.

And myself.

He and I were different, but connected on every level.

Our bonds moved well beyond ties of blood. We were invested in each other's wellbeing at depths more profound than rational understanding. When we were on song, together, we became better versions of ourselves. As a single entity, we were much more than the sum of our separate parts, a powerful cocktail.

Was I working from an inaccurate premise?

I was mimicking Blaise.

What if I flipped my thinking?

Blaise might have tried to think as I did. I needed to intuit from my perspective and not infer from his.

What would I have used to reach out to my brother? What bound us beyond the immediacy of this ordeal?

A refrain bubbled to the surface of my mind, recognisable words uttered through the generations.

... Mary, pray for us who have recourse to thee...

And I knew, with an absolute conviction, what object my brother had left for me to find. I even had a hunch about where he had placed it.

An entangled crown of thorn-trees, a twisted briar of knotted tree trunks, unkempt branches and their discarded residue shaped our current stronghold.

I fixated on two of the intertwined trees that presented as a barbed and splintered crucifix.

I inspected the intersection.

My heart missed a beat.

Buttressed amongst the thorns, what I searched for rested in its own natural sanctum. I reached up, careful not to inflict too much damage on my fingers, grasped the object, and pulled it free.

I turned the shiny, oval-shaped item over and over between my thumb and forefinger.

The miraculous medal of Catherine Laboure that Mum had given to Blaise and me on our way to Salisbury Airport at the start of this fateful odyssey blinked back at me.

My brother had left a hint, but decoding it was the tricky bit. At least he was still in the game.

... desperately in need...

Scrutiny showed Blaise had not tampered with the stamped silver medal in any obvious way.

The front depicted Mary, the mother of Jesus, standing on a globe with rays of light coming from her hands, a crushed snake under her feet.

I flipped it over.

The reverse displayed a crucifix, sans corpus, with its base intertwined and resting on the letter 'M' underscored on either side with two hearts encircled by an oval of twelve stars.

How should I interpret these clues? How should I join the stars?

The Catherine story had a strong resonance with the *Book of Revelation*. It spoke of a sign in the heavens and – the words came back to me verbatim – *a woman clothed with the sun, the moon under her feet, and on her head a crown of 12 stars.*

... can you picture...

Was the answer to Blaise's clue written in the night sky?

It made sense – the heavens, twelve stars, sun and moon, the earth. He had been present at the same astronomy session – on using heavenly bodies to plot direction – that I had attended as part of the *3-W* bush survival programme.

... what will be...?

I dismissed the idea.

The notion was implausible, involving waiting a good number of hours to use celestial directional pointers – Sirius, Venus or the Southern Cross – to find him. When time was a precious commodity, Blaise would have used a more immediate and obvious indicator.

I wasn't confident that Blaise had paid any attention in the orienteering session on stargazing, either.

That left the image of Mary, the rays of light, the crucifix, the letter 'M', and the two hearts.

Nothing jumped out at me. I was missing something.

Was I over-analysing the clues?

I looked at the medal once more.

The vibrant, metallic-silver image of Mary radiated, reconfigured in my hand.

Mary was recognisable, but different. She was more abstract, organic, culturally ambiguous. Repeated, dynamic lines and curves epiphanised her openness and aliveness. Small, subtle details caught my eye. An admixture of textures and finishes – part polished part matte, and uneven – disrupted my ability to focus.

A tingle pulsed in my fingers, spreading through my body.

Was my imagination playing tricks on me again?

Mirrored in Mary's face, I saw myself.

In such a pre-figured moment I connected to a personal and collective past, present, and future in a way I had not experienced before. Its essence, intrinsic, timeless, nuanced, was difficult to capture in a single emotional or linguistic byte.

I wondered then, as I have wondered since, about the nature of such an existentially creative and spiritual encounter.

Might it have heralded an awakening in my perception, foreshadowed a new awareness, predicted a consciousness beyond my existing sensibility, first hinted at in my exchange with Thumbeza?

Within the medal's interrelated image lay the promise of transformation, of new possibilities.

My heart jumped a beat: it was a means of connecting with my brother.

If only I could open the doors to its mystery.

I went back through my discovery of the medal, visualising the cross-sectioned trees, the medal lying on its side at their crux.

Which side of the medal was to the fore and how had it been resting?

Lying with its reverse side upward, the apex of the cross pointed like an arrow to the right.

Was it that simple?

Blaise wouldn't have had time for anything more complicated.

How could I be sure?

Then, unbidden, Blaise's voice drifted into my head. 'Be in the moment, don't psychoanalyse everything.'

Wily devil!

I scrambled from the redoubt to the rear, oriented myself according to the cruciform trees and the medal's positioning, and headed off in the arrowed direction.
    North.

... no safety or surprise...

Using various natural landmarks to keep me tracking in the right direction, I kept a low profile amongst the tousled mopane scrub and scruffy savannah grass. I covered the ground at a good clip, checking the lie of the land for potential pursuers and for any signs of Blaise.

During one of the frequent pauses on the fringe of bush next to the high grass, I cut the spoor of at least two sets of signatured tracks. One set displayed the familiar zigzag pattern of the trainers, or *tekkies,* my brother and I preferred. The other belonged to an animal. Broad four-digited, flat, naked paw-pads scuffed the ground. The patterns and size of the footprints suggested something large. They obscured the shoe tracks.

Both sets stretched far and away into the distance, marshalling me on an alternate course, at right angles to my current trajectory.

I upped my pace along the path etched out in pursuit of Blaise and whatever was hunting him.

I hoped I wouldn't be too late.

… some stranger is calling…

The shadows of afternoon lengthened as the metres dropped away behind me.

Following the smudged footprints, I hastened into the scrubland, through carpets of tall grass, across disfigured *dongas* and bone-dry riverbeds, around squirts of *kopjes*, at full tilt, caring little for my safety. I was driven only by the single thought that any delay could have dire consequences for my brother's life.

Fuelled by emotion and adrenaline, I'd set a murderous pace, driving myself onwards and knowing such a tempo was unsustainable.

I crested one of the many *kopjes*, breathing hard, gulping for air. My lungs burned, my leg muscles stretched taut.

To slow my breathing and heart rate, I hunkered beneath the silhouette line, hidden in the shade. I surveyed the panoramic vista below, sipping water from the supply I had gathered from the riverbed earlier in the day.

Those morning events felt like a long time ago, beyond history.

... lost in a wilderness...

Against indigo arches of sky, the scorched scrub had given way to swampy wetlands on an extensive floodplain, pockmarked by meandering shrivels of muddy water and a patchwork of flourishing olive-green pasture, spiky dead trees and tall reed clusters. Behind, dark and impenetrable woodlands bordered by blood-red earth reared up into the distant hills.

It was a rugged, elemental space, a wilderness with its own unique heartbeat.

Amidst the extensive undulations, a series of incongruous bellows and grunts snapped me out of my trance.

A caucus of giant creatures thrashed and trampled about among the reeds.

Their banter intensified as they called to one another with low-pitched grumbles.

Large dark forms shimmered in the high reeds, distinctive heads, each with a crown of horns. Bone shields, or bosses, coalesced at the centre of each head. Each horn diverged downwards and then curved upwards and hooked inwards. Beneath this headgear, black, heavyset bodies, short, stout legs and droopy ears emerged from the crowding savannah bosque.

... weird scenes...

An alliance of Cape buffalo ambled into view, foraging and grazing at leisure.

It was an inspiring sight. The complex, untamed heart of Africa never failed to impress.

A single buffalo stood aloof, apart from the rest.

Inyathi: the one who fertilises the land and brings good eating.

He was the largest of the herd, a charcoal-black creature of mythical proportions. His sheer size and muscled presence exuded raw and vital energy.

He was in his prime, revelling in his status as the principal male of the group. He belched short-tempered rumbles, cajoling his charges.

Not that the ladies were taking any notice. They were engaged in their own tranquil, democratic convention.

... there's a danger on the edge...

Local communities dubbed the unpredictable buffalo the *Black Death* or *Widow-Maker*. The only sensible choice was to give this herd a wide berth, despite the inconvenience. I was unready to tackle Africa's grim reaper.

Somewhere beyond the herd's sweet spot, I would pick up Blaise's spoor and whatever was chasing him,

... no safety or surprise...

Bypassing the buffalo proved difficult. I wound my way from the *kopje*'s crest, taking a serpentine route through the maze of reeds to their left, and into the wet lowlands.

Beyond the *kopje*'s base, the tangle of elephantine reeds gave way to a collage of multi-faceted vegetation.

'Here be dragons...'

I crouched at the edge of certainty in the tall grass, crumbling the soil's granules between my fingers.

Red ochre. *Imbola.*

Bringer of visions and dreams; protection against sun, corruption and decay.

I spat into my left hand and, mixing the soil with my right forefinger, made a sticky paste. I applied it to my legs, arms, neck and face.

Purgatory or perdition?

The journey to Hades is incremental. Halfway there and back, either way.

Still, I vacillated.

... a point of no return.

I'd had many points of no return in the last few days.

What was one more?

I would have to pay the boatman at some point. If I wanted to help my brother, to waver was not an option.

The tracks of Blaise's *tekkies*, and whatever was chasing him, scratched the ochred earth.

I emerged from the reeds and within a few steps, I hit full stride across the Styx-like otherworld.

... in a desperate land...

Waves of frothy footprints smudged the ground.

Paw-prints and *tekkie* zigzags mingled, overlaid by many other straight-lined boot imprints that converged at right angles from the left. All sets of prints snaked off in one direction.

A man does not run among thorns for no reason; either he is chasing a serpent, or a serpent is chasing him.

The odds of Blaise surviving had shortened.

I took up the chase.

... ride the snake...

As I trekked in the wake of the triple set of dissimilar footprints in the tangerine earth, only the mid-afternoon light dry wind assuaged the clumps of dehydrated white savannah grass to either side.

Trails of serpents soil everything.

Cuffed together, the landscapes melded in surprising, multi-coloured, wondrous ways.

In several places, the trees hung and drooped in tight boscages, offering consolation against the inhospitable elements. In other spaces, the savannah stood open, with a scorched tree or isolated *kopje* silhouetted against limitless horizons. Despite its aridity and desolation, the terrain possessed an unfathomable bounty and unsophisticated, rugged grace.

One could get lost here.

Walls of vegetation crowded in, arrowed to a vanishing point. Burnt patches of earth with the homing beacon of footprints disappeared into the dense, forbidding bosque ahead.

At its ingress, the bush lay trodden and flattened. Apart from the long grass rustling in the light breeze, there was no sound.

I slipped sideways into cover and knelt to scan for any threat or movement nearby.

Close to the trampled grass where the footprints ended, a pile of bare, ashen rock-like objects gleamed in the sunlight. Given the angle of the sun's reflecting rays, identifying them was tough.

... waiting... waiting...

Hunched over, I hastened towards them and crouched in the part-shade of the tall-grass close by.

My old friend, Silence, was there to greet me.

Unsettled, I scanned the lie of the land. Shadows and whispers persisted and lingered, echoes of forgotten lives.

My gaze fell downwards.

It was not a rock-pile at all. A pyramid of wind-worn salt-white skulls rested in the sand.

In a valley of dry bones.

Yea, though I walk through the valley of the shadow of death, I will fear no evil.

Human death masks. Five skulls, each unique, united by the same fate.

Four formed the base, and the fifth nestled above, marking the apex. Large noses and mouth cavities, dark, eyeless sockets and toothy grins leered at me.

Who had arranged the skulls in this stark, geometric configuration? And why?

Earth's dry scent filled my nostrils. Turbo-charged with an ancient energy, the wind crackled through and around the pyramid of skulls.

What had enticed these people to this place? What calamitous event had befallen them? Had it been a mere coincidence, or a curated witches' brew, hinting at a darker design?

The caustic taste of bile rose in my throat.

Not long ago, these were living, feeling, breathing men and women, with hopes and dreams. Perhaps brothers and sisters, husbands and wives. Children. Family. Friends.

Where are the joys you once shared?

What you are now, we once were; what we are now, you shall be, they sighed.

I plucked up the skull positioned at the apex. It fragmented at my touch.

... unto dust and shadows...

To this condition, we must succumb.

The living know they will die; what can those already dead know?

Did a deeper, paradoxical meaning lie hidden within the haunting beauty of these bones? An interconnected, disconnected and reconnected truth, both denied and affirmed?

The wind's whispers faded and the world receded in a moment.

My attention narrowed to controlling my breathing, to the gentle and rhythmic rise and fall of my chest.

It was short-lived.

... ride the snake...

Slothful movement from the base centre of the skulls and an eruption akin to a Bunsen burner splintered my ruminations. I leapt backwards and tripped over, stumbling and landing on my backside.

My breath tightened, squeezed my chest, clutched my heart.

Lethargic movement and somnambulate sibilance pursued me.

I scrambled to my feet, retreated.

A thick, swollen wineskin bag curled amongst the gleaming skulls. I knew what it was: *Inyoka*. Africa's mini-leviathan, the most venomous of all death specialists.

It must have been drowsing for the entire time I had been monologuing.

Soaked in the sun's warmth, the puff adder offered a languid protest.

Its flat, triangulated head was painted with two dark bands, one on its crown and the other between its impassive eyes. It possessed a wide straw-yellow girth, and dark chocolate chevrons adorned its topside.

The viper hissed and rotated forwards slowly, its black, unblinking irises regarding my every move.

I gazed back, pulse pounding in my ears. Our eyes locked; I could not look away.

... he's old and his skin is cold...
Don't tread on me.
For I still rest at peace in Eden.

'Who... What... are you?'

I am

   that ophidian and promethean mentor,
      enemy of ignorance, inspirer of curiosity,
         harbinger of hidden (trans)-knowledge and truth.
   Through me, your eyes and soul open to
      the possibilities and potentialities of life.
   All humanity should thank me.
      You ought to be grateful.

Who was charming whom?

I am

   primordial, chthonic, and ancient,
      the keeper of astral knowledge,
         uniting and transformative.
   I was present at the beginning.
      I am the Good and Wise Serpent.

'You are also known by other, more familiar and less salubrious names. Evil One. Satan. Beast. The Devil. Lucifer. Prince of Darkness. Beelzebub. Lord of the Flies. Diabolos. Shaitan. The Tempter. Belial. The Antichrist. Fallen Angel. Dragon. Wicked One. Father of Lies. The Stranger. Lord of the Underworld. Ancient Serpent.'

   People have always misunderstood me.
   I am a pluriform of contraries, a colliding harmony of dualities:
   renewal and regeneration;
   resurrection and salvation, Christian and otherwise;
   solar and lunar, father and mother;
   astrological and androgenic;
   angelic elohim, seraphim, and cherubim.

I am God's Spirit.

'You can slough your skin, but not your nature. You are abhorred and feared. Damned, not deified. How can you be both blessing and burden, slayer and saviour, shepherd and slaughterer?'

> *I have*
> > *been worshipped and deified throughout history,*
> > > *across all languages, cultures and religions.*
> *I am*
> > *revered, an eternal blessing.*

'You are a curse, not a cure. Cold, capricious and cruel, not comforting. A contagion.'

> *I am*
> > *sacred and salutary (trans) motif and serpentine myth,*
> > > *cultic archetype, runic allusion and fungible paradox,*
> > > *studied icon and approbation.*

'You are also scorned as vitriolic and venomous, a vile and viperous vision.'

> *I am*
> > *the cosmic Drakon.*
> > > *Chimera. Basilisk. Hydra. Angitia.*
> > > > *Phoenix. Cerberus. Apep. Echnida. Stheno.*
> > > > *Quetzalcoatl. Goorrialla. Typhon. Euryale.*
> > > > *Nehustan. Ananta. Midgard. Renenutet.*
> > > > *Tiamut. Ningishzida. Wadjet. Medusa.*
> > > > *Umveliqangi. Indlodlo. Inyoka. Nyangani.*
> > > > > *Nyami-nyami.*

I am
> *the genius loci,*
>> *the reincarnation of kings.*

'You are vilified as a taboo and toxin, a treacherous totem and talisman.'

I am
> *at the heart of Gnostic, Neo-platonic, Rosicrucian,*
> *Theosophist and Kabbalah currents.*

'But also a heretical and heterodox enigma.'

I am
> *the mystical Dreamtime Rainbow, River and Sky.*
> *I light the Milky Way in*
>> *a celestial spectrum of colours.*

'You are despised as a nether-worldly nightmare; nasty, not nurturing.'

I am
> *the collective unconscious.*
>> *Humanity's accumulated memory.*

'You are also a hellish and harrowing hallucination.'

I am
> *resourceful and respected, consecrated, and adored.*

'You are detested as deceiver and defiler, destroyer and desecrater, disordered and depraved, devilish, and demonic.'

I enchanted and seduced Eve.
  I am Eve. Hawwah. Hiwaya.

'What are you without forbidden and bitter fruit? You can seduce and enchant me with your forked tongue, but you cannot define me or become me.'

  I am
    God's leviathan and Job's adversary.
      Isaiah's saraph.
        Jonah's captor.
          The Almighty's sceptre.

'... anyone who sees the leviathan, that twisted serpent, loses courage and falls to the ground...'

  I encompass the Rod of Asclepius,
    staff of the serpent priests, Moses and Aaron.
  I am
    the Wand of the Occult and New Age;
    Hermes' reconciling double-serpent caduceus;
    Osiris' Uraeus and Hippocrates' emblem;
      Chinese Sign of the Zodiac.
  I am
    father to heroes and legends,
      the helical DNA.
  I am
    monistic protector of the tree of life,
      potion, poultice and panacea.

'Not protector, but predator. Poisoner and polluter. A perverter and profaner.'

I am

> *diviner of prophets, druids, shamans and alchemists;*
>> *guardian of tantric chakras and holy totems;*
> *spine of spiritual and kundalini currents;*
>> *writhing, interwoven shakti energies;*
>>> *esoteric familiar of Wiccan covens.*

'Adversary, not apotheosis. Malicious and malignant.'

I am

> *the umbilical cord that flows through all things:*
> *the anguine human circulatory system,*
> *creation born out of chaos;*
>> *impregnating phallic primogenitor.*
> *I cannot be concealed like a guilty secret.*

I am unquenchable.

'You are corrupting and concupiscent. Carnal and copulating.'

> *Eternal and immortal, I rest at the axis mundi,*
>> *the world's yaw and double helix,*
>>> *perpetual and fractal cycle of renewal,*
>>> *the elixir of life eternal.*

'Within all living things, how is it possible for such a disharmony to co-exist?'

... the leopard shall lie with the lamb, the serpent and the sheep together...

I am

> *Ouroboros, eternally looping and lemniscate, tail-devouring serpent.*

'Why devour your own tail? How can you sustain life by consuming yourself?'

> *Caress and feed the serpent that devours you from within.*
>   *Unless you devour yourself,*
>   *you will not become the dragon you are.*
> *Death out of Life. Life out of Death.*

'For every soul, there is a serpent, for every ladder, a snake.'

> *I am the ophiomorphic you.*
>   *You are the anthropomorphic me.*

'If around my soul you lie, dare I uncoil you? If I trust you, will you bite?'

> *By you, both versions need to be*
>   *accepted and nurtured.*
> *Of you, both versions are*
>   *life-saving and indispensable.*
> *For, without both versions, you lack poise and dignity.*

'Is the harmony of inherent opposites in my life – all life – requisite for growth and transformation?'

The dance ended, and the spell lifted.

The puff adder dropped its gaze and, susurrating, retreated amongst the skulls, winding sideways in scrolling s-shapes.

I recoiled to the savannah grass to take up the chase once more.

> *... ride the snake to the ancient lake ...*

BEHEMOTH

I SLID THROUGH THE spindly elephant grass.

A light, dry afternoon breeze stirred its desiccated tips. They resembled ranks of pikemen with long serrated spears pointing at the heavens. As I trailed through them, barbs pricked and prodded my fingers and thumbs, my arms and legs.

Grainy sweat burned my eyes and skin. I mopped my brow and face on my sleeve.

... on the edge of...

A hushed stillness descended.

I dropped to my haunches, mired in coils of pasty grass.

Snuffling. On my left flank.

The sniffing persisted in the wind. Its faint traces echoed in the brush, swirling among the leaves, infused with the sound of crunching twigs.

Many bodies. Soft voices.

'Comrades. Not far ahead, skulks the *umlungu* we have been chasing. We must flush out this serpent and remove its head as a warning to those who would oppose us.'

There were murmurs of approval.

... the snake... he's old and his skin is cold...

My brain was abuzz.

What to do? What to do?

I needed to divert attention. My brother's life depended on my next action. *But what?*

I grovelled and groped around in the dust for something... *anything...* heavy. My fingers closed upon a smooth, oval-shaped rock. I tested it, weighing it in my hand. Smaller than a cricket ball, yet snug in my palm.

'Here goes nothing. Time to dance with the devil.'

I cocked a trembling arm.

'*Coo-ee!*' I shouted with a quavering voice, and hurled the rock with all the strength I could muster. It hummed and whirred in a flat parabolic arc, swimming through the pinkish waves of the descending sun towards its target.

I didn't hang around to see if my projectile found its mark, or to enjoy the after-effects of my handiwork. Following the path along which I had come, I bolted.

As I bounded away, there was a dull thud followed by a yelp. Indignant howls and cries echoed through the aspirant grass.

'I hope this hare-brained scheme's gonna work,' I uttered to no one in particular. 'What the hell am I thinking? I should start listening to that cautionary voice inside my head.'

The rest was a blur.

Shots coughed high above and well to my right. I rushed headlong through the vegetation. It slapped and slashed at me as I beat a weaving retreat.

Exiting the grassland, I hurdled the skull-pile and its lethal tenant, hoofing through the barren-lands. Within seconds I reached the closest *kopje*, and legged it upwards to the summit.

At the top, I puffed hard for air then hesitated, caught my breath, and concealed myself in the meagre scrub.

The *kopje* dominated the landscape, commanding a three-sixty-degree view of the surrounds. From different pathways, chasers converged on my position on the ridge. My pursuers were not yet visible; long-grass bowed before them as they harvested forward.

The cadre was further back, moving at a slower pace.

... the west is best... get here and we'll do the rest...

I scoured the near horizon to find my bearings and my heart jumped.

Had I been wrong?

Relieved, I saw what I was searching for: the skeletal, scorched trees with stripped water-gullies in the floodplains, that I had avoided on my outward journey.

I pushed myself from the ground and hurled myself down the far side of the *kopje*. I slid, lost my footing and toppled over, spinning head-over-shoulder to land in a dazed, twisted muddle at the base.

Distant shouts, a whipping of air, muffled cracks echoed around me.

I regained my feet.

Sporadic zips and snaps – much closer – exploded near me as my chasers found their range. I swerved, head tucked into my chest, searching out the cover of the paltry scrub as I pressed towards the perceived safety of the wetlands.

... ride the snake to the lake...

My intended destination of high reeds, sagging clusters of trees and fractal water channels hove into view.

I quickened my pace, skimming the terrain as I did so. I feared they'd departed, but torpid movement in the long grass allayed my fears.

Large black shapes mooched in the afternoon warmth.

My pursuers had narrowed the gap.

Bullets whined, shredding the grass above my head. I had to sustain my chasers' interest so they remained unaware of the danger lurking nearby.

'We must execute any attack in the lion's mouth, or not at all,' our rugby coach, Mr B, often said. That maxim had held true on the rugby paddock, but was untested in a wild animal arena.

'Again, here goes nothing.'

I took a deep breath and charged through the tall-grass, clapping and hollering to create as much ruckus as I could.

Shouts of recognition followed as I raced through the scrub, still bellowing. I changed tack and used the blackened cluster of trees around me for cover, then slid into the darkness of the thick foliage.

Down a meerkat-hole.

From this position, I watched the events unfold.

The front-runner, well ahead of his two comrades, reached where I had just stood. Weapon ready, he blundered to a standstill and hailed his mates, who also came to a halt. They conferred for a moment, calling across to one another as they advanced.

Kneeling, terr-number-one examined the ground.

... the killer awoke...

The chasers consulted once more. The front-man stood, and stepped in my direction. As he edged to within a metre of where I lay, a protracted lament, haunting in its pitch, startled him.

He was unprepared for the large shadow that rushed from the dense scrub. Inyathi burst from the reeds, twisted his head and skewered the man at the crotch. The man unleashed a chilling shriek as crimson blood pulsed from his punctured femoral artery.

The buffalo bucked to unpin itself from his foe, but he could not, and dragged the hapless man along with him. With his arms splayed, legs flailing, blood-soaked torso and head grinding the ground, the man whimpered and lifted his arms in a last gesture of entreaty.

Inyathi shook his head and flicked his victim's crumpled body into the air. Mid-air, the body hovered, defying gravity before it crashed to the earth and lay unmoving.

The buffalo slowed and swung in a short arc.

He hesitated, staring at the second and third chasers, who had stood transfixed during the attack on their comrade. In the lull, adversaries weighed their options.

But it lasted only nanoseconds.

No false charge, no feinting or goading. Without subtlety, Inyathi snorted and trotted towards his foes, reaching full speed within a few paces. A blur of grunting black and thrashing horns, he flattened the grubby foliage as he went.

The two men brought their semi-automatic weapons to bear on the rampaging buffalo. His thunderous hooves pounded the ground like a tiger tank at full throttle.

Feeble sprays of gunfire did not deter him. Bullets struck their target, staining the buffalo's massive chest with red-flecked pockmarks, but on he rumbled without breaking stride.

Inyathi slammed the man on his left, colliding with a force that lifted him off his feet and propelled him upwards. He soared like an acrobat, head over heels, and smacked the earth.

The buffalo was on him before he could move.

After a quick yelp, silence.

The third tracker jettisoned his weapon and scampered away, dodging through the scrub dotted by gloomy, blistered trees. He threw glances over his shoulder, scouting for the clamour of inevitability approaching, his face blank and mouth agape, unable to give voice to his rising terror.

When he realised the buffalo had not chased him, he reduced speed and stopped, hunched over with hands on knees, chest heaving, and scoured the surrounding scrub.

... he paid a visit to his brother...

The counter-attack was as sudden and unexpected as it was lethal. To the man's right, impenetrable jess bush palpitated and trembled.

The man did not wait. He fled.

Brute buffalo muscle and sinew exploded from the jess. Lowered dark grey horns shimmered in the afternoon light.

The man could have improved his chances of survival, using defensive tactics favoured by the matadors, moving sideways and diving flat.

He did neither.

The buffalo rammed the man into a large tree trunk. He caromed as the buffalo rammed him.

Boss on bone.

A crack, a snap, a whimper.

The limp, broken body flopped in a heap.

In the chaotic aftermath, I disappeared in search of my brother. To regroup would not take our enemies long, and I wanted to be elsewhere when that happened.

... C'mon baby, take a chance with us...

I gave the kill zone a wide berth, doubling back to the path at the pyramid of skulls. There was no sign of pursuit, and using the existing tracks to cover my retreat, I headed north.

In the arid-lands a short distance beyond the tall grass where I had hurled my projectile, I picked up on Blaise's *tekkie* tracks. Paw prints remained in tandem with them.

I increased my pace.

The flaming mahogany terrain sloped upwards.

It was heavy going in the soft sand, and my calves and hamstrings – stretched like elastic bands – burned. Slowing to a walk, I topped the slope after resorting to monkey-climbing up the last part of the steep embankment.

Below, the landscape had changed yet again.

A winding, piping waterway was flanked by a boulevard of aromatic musasa trees punctuated by lounging vegetation, and an eclectic mix of bird and animal life.

The centrepiece at the nexus was an enormous, aged baobab. *Umsenge*, the nurturing tree.

What could be more beautiful than the distinctive baobab, the African tree of resurrection and truth, silhouetted against the apricot glow of an African sunset sky?

African legends told of the gods who, exasperated by Umsenge's vanity and over-blown hubris, ripped it out of the earth and replanted it upside down as punishment. Ever since, the penitent baobab has worked in silence to make amends. Each nutrient-dense, fruit-filled baobab can sustain entire ecosystems and communities.

I have always loved the complex insights in the simplicity of African folk-lore: *wisdom is like a baobab tree; no one individual can embrace it.*

This bulky, bulbous baobab's trunk must have been at least fifty metres round. Its stumpy arms, each with a crown of flowers, reached up thirty metres into the vast expanse of pink cotton-wool sky.

I grinned. At least I had a source of food at my disposal for the immediate future.

'The Lord takes away... and gives in abundance.'

I approached in the scrub's cover, my nasal passages overwhelmed by a nauseating stink of cheap, homemade carbolic soap.

If the smell wasn't bad enough, derisive, high-pitched laughs reverberated through the bush, sounds amongst the most recognisable in all of Africa.

In the baobab's shadow, a hint of camouflaged movement.

An animal outline leapt into sharper focus. *Thembisi*, Africa's dark, magical admixture: purifier and profaner; despised and sanctified. Cleanser, trickster and keeper of secrets.

Thembisi, the spotted hyena.

A colossal specimen by any standards, it danced around the tree's base, boasting an extensive vocal range: deep-throated soft grunt-laughs sprinkled with human-like giggles. All the while, it darted furtive glances, askance and then upwards, to something suspended in the baobab's far-flung branches.

I would have recognised that mop of ginger hair anywhere.

... meet me at the b(l)ack...

It was uncommon for hyenas to be out on their own as they were, by nature, gregarious creatures, preferring to work and live in clans. This hyena was a different beast.

I needed a deterrent. My eyes fell upon a scattering of thorn-tree branches nearby. Thembisi had yet to sense my presence. I snatched up a tree branch and rushed forward, lunging and shouting at the animal from behind. Taken by surprise, it grunted and jumped away. Pressing forward, I howled, brandishing my lightsaber.

Flicking its large, rounded ears, the hyena bounced backwards. With both legs bent with my left foot pointing at the foe, and right arm and weapon extended out in front of me, I waited, trying to anticipate the hyena's next move.

Thembisi feinted forwards and as I adjusted, it jumped sideways and back towards me, probing my defences and stuttering a series of supernatural lower-pitched whoops and half-grunt laughs. Countering, I shuffled clockwise and forwards and then retreated, growling my intent, weapon at the ready. We rotated, joined by invisible threads in a macabre song and rumba routine.

From close-up, he was a formidable creature, larger than I ever imagined hyenas to be.

May the force be with me.

Apart from the pale carmine hoops on his thickset neck and a white band above each eye, Thembisi had an irregular pattern of nickel-grey, chocolate-brown ink spots across his body. With its head and muzzle held high, ears cocked, mouth clenched, mane erect and pompom tail carried forward on its back, the hyena studied me with gleaming, devilish eyes.

I knew to avoid his shovel-jaws at all costs as they outmatched every mammal for their bone-crushing ability.

... look into your eyes...

As I sashayed at odds with my non-compliant partner, a voice called out to me from the heavens.

'About time you showed up!' he said, arms folded, reclining in the tree. 'Took you long enough.'

'Ever the smart arse,' I called back, not taking my eyes off my adversary. 'You won't believe the merry dance you've led me.'

'I can see that. You're a regular Fred Astaire.'

'Well, slobber-chops over there is no Ginger Rogers...'

The hyena and I lit up the dance floor.

Slow... slow... quick-quick slow...

Blaise chuckled.

'Glad you think it's funny. I'm still *peed off* at you.'

'*Ja-well*, it's better than being *peed on.*'

'No thanks to you for landing me on the biggest of turds.'

'Guilty as charged,' he said, leaning forward. 'You can stop romancing that turd now. Time to make up and move on.'

'Depends how remorseful you are.'

'I'm suitably chastened.'

Ever the opportunist, Thembisi kept his distance, circling just beyond me.

'Are you up for an intervention? We need to end this putting-on-the-Ritz stuff.'

'I'm enjoying the show. Do I have to?'

'I'll cue you,' I said, darting him a sideways glance. 'I want you to scare the shit out of this smug brute when I tell you.'

Blaise nodded. 'Ready when you are, Bar.'

The rumba continued. By turns, I manoeuvred the hyena to where it had its back to my brother.

I stopped and stood my ground.

The hyena did the same, eyeing me all the while, mirroring my movements. He opened his mouth and discharged a lugubrious, high-pitched *who-oop* of maniacal laughter reminiscent of a horror movie soundtrack, giving me goosebumps.

'*Now*, Blaise. Now's your time!' I yelled, arms extended. 'Get your butt down here!'

Blaise dropped from his position in the lower branches, ululated like a dervish, and chopped downwards with a long stick. It struck the hyena with a glancing blow on his rump.

The hyena yapped and skittered away.

My brother joined me and arm-in-arm, we formed a united skirmish line, our spears bristling. The hyena whinged, glowered at us and skulked off, its short fluffy tail bowed below its belly.

'Just in time, big brother. That was getting nasty.'

'I'm a latter-day Obi-Wan Kenobi. Who said I didn't have my uses?' I fired back at him.

'So what other Jedi mind tricks do you have up your sleeve?' he said. *'This is not the umfaan you're looking for...'*

'Funny. I see you haven't lost your sense of humour,' I said, handing him the water bottle and stifling a half-laugh. 'Here, *sha-rup* and drink up, and let's vamoose before that chancer returns with back-up.'

'Bar-man, is there any reason your face is covered in shit?'

'Red ochre. Excellent sunscreen and moisturiser. Perhaps you should use some? Your skin is burnt and blistered. It'll help, I promise.'

'No-ways. Over my dead body.'

I thought better than to tell him of ochre's divining properties, and its popularity in local communities in preparing bodies for the afterlife. Before he could say anything more, I said, 'You can update me on your adventure later.'

... no safety... surprise...

'Here's a ready-made food supply. We should grab some before we head off.'

'Where?'

'Right here. See those foot-long pods?' I said, pointing.

'And?'

'Baobab fruit.'

'Didn't know that baobabs produced fruit. What's so special about it?'

'Everything. Every part of a baobab is useful – bark, leaves, trunk, flowers. Immune boosters, ant-oxidants, vitamin C. You name it. Nature keeps giving. I just hope that we don't just keep taking.'

'I always knew all that useless information stored in your brain would be useful someday.'

'Lucky you, lucky me, hey? Come, my hunter-gatherer friend, get busy. *Our cup runneth over but our time slippeth away.*'

'Sadly, Bar, the day is not far off when our cup will run dry. Until we reframe our exploitative mindset to consider more existentially creative dynamic, sustainable and mutually beneficial systems, we're on the road to environmental and human catastrophe.'

'I'll drink to that mind-shift, *Bwana*. Couldn't have put it better. Looks as if you've found yourself a vocation.'

'Maybe, maybe not.'

We loaded one rucksack with as many pods of fruit as we could cram in.

'That should keep us going for a while.'

I turned to Blaise. 'You good to go?'

'Hope so. I've got this far.'

'Time's the real enemy,' I said, putting my arm around his shoulder. 'We're vulnerable here. Our tracks are dead easy to follow.'

'*Half a league, half a league onward!*' Blaise intoned. '*Into the mouth of hell, into the jaws of death...*'

He was such a hell-raiser.

... into the fiery pit... the dark abyss... the maw of the dragon...

'You are so full of *it*.'

'Full of charm, charisma, and brilliance?'

'That's not what I had in mind.'

As we jogged to the north, the churched thorn-trees faded to black in the expanding shadows, conjured by the *stockade* of hills in front of the sun.

... the king's highway...

LABYRINTH

AGAINST AN OREGON-TIMBERED SKY, the coppered sun hesitated, apathetic and aloof, weighing its options.

Nothing surprises the sun. What it has seen before, it will see again.

We had holed up in another chapel of African trees and compacted brush north of our recent showdown with the lone hyena at the baobab.

Blaise told me what had happened after I had left our hideout in my quest to find water.

'While you headed off on your *Groot Trek*, I had an unwelcome visitor,' he said. 'Must have been the blood scent. I tried to encourage him to leave by rattling the vegetation with a stick and with choice sailors' vocab I gained by listening to Grandad's regular rants against the locals from the back *stoep*, but that didn't work.'

'So, Midshipman B, what forced you to abandon ship?'

'I was worried the hyena would attract other unwanted attention with its piercing laughter and I would have been up a paddle without a creek,' he said. 'That's why I took my chances with the lesser of the two evils. But that hyena was bloody persistent. It took energy and prowess to keep it at bay. I was at wits' end when you arrived with the marines at the old hanging tree. Was I wrong?'

'No, I can't fault your reasoning,' I said, patting him on the back. 'I'd have done the same.'

'I left you a cheeky message, huh? You have to admit that. Although you had me worried. You took your time, didn't you?'

'I worked it out. But then I also had challenges of my own.'

I filled in the details to bring him up to speed: my unexpected encounter with Thumbeza, the senior guerrilla leader; how I'd tracked him and his mammal companion, confronted a puff adder, the guerrilla cadre, and the buffalo ambush.

'So while I'm away, you have all the fun,' he said. 'And your bush *indaba*? How do you get to grips with that? Or understand any of what's happened? What kind of tale have you tumbled us into?'

'There is no single *kind* here, Brother. The very style of our tumbling implies a genre-busting level of chaos and ambiguity in this tale.'

'Just the material you need for your tilt at penning the great African novel, hey, Baron?'

'You never know. I'll keep my options open.'

We locked eyes.

'*Thumbeza*, was it?' Blaise said, disrupting the moment.

I nodded. 'It's possible that we don't have a monopoly on the truth in this narrative.'

'More than just possible. I think we've never had a reason before now to interrogate our version of the narrative. I'm still trying to reconcile the many contradictions,' I admitted. 'It's proving difficult.'

'Maybe that's the grist you need to write your novel,' Blaise grinned.

'Wishful thinking.' I reached into my pocket. 'Here. You'd better take this back,' I said, handing him his miraculous medal. 'You might need it. It helped me.'

'*Us*.' Blaise took the medal, dropping his head. 'It's my fault, isn't it? I mean, if I hadn't stood up in the savannah grass this morning and announced our presence, none of this would have happened.'

He looked to the ground, his eyes welling with tears. I seized his chin. '*Hey*. Look at me. It could have been worse. That decision and its consequences could have saved us from an even worse situation. Who knows?'

Blaise still did not look up.

'I also stuffed up by convincing you we should leave the crash site.'

'Let me finish, Baron. That doesn't excuse my actions. I'm not sure what prompted me, but I'm sorry,' he said, looking at me, teary-eyed. 'What I did was stupid, unforgivable. I could've killed us both. I'm sorry.' He sniffed, wiped his nose across the back of his hand, and looked down again.

'The important thing is that we're still in this game. All's forgiven,' I said, squeezing his hand. 'We've got this far, haven't we? And we must work together if we're to get any further. And you know what? That's what we're gonna do. *Rise and rise until lambs are leopards.* And leopards, lambs, I suppose. Or is it *tigers* and lambs?'

'*Lions*. But I don't think it matters, anyway. One feline is like any other,' Blaise said, glancing up and grinning. 'But lamb stew. Or chops. Or *biltong*. Now that makes my mouth water. So let's get to it.'

'Not so fast, buddy. I want to check the state of your war wounds.'

He nodded. 'Well, come on then, Dr Barnard.'

I moved in closer to examine them.

'What do you think? Give me an honest analysis now, Doctor,' he said, holding his head sideways. 'Don't be shy. I can handle it.'

'If I told you, that would be telling.'

'*Funny*! You missed your vocation.'

'Mum reckons I'd make a good priest. Not for me, I'm afraid.'

'If you were Father Baron, it's everyone else who should be afraid.'

'Whatever, Trevor. Now you, Blaise, you're perfectly suited to the religious life.'

'*Pope Blaise the First* has a nice ring to it, doncha think? Bless you, my child.' Blaise raised his right hand and made the Sign of the Cross in my general direction. 'You may show your pleasure.' Blaise proffered his hand.

'Kiss your ring, my arse. Now stop being a distraction.'

Blaise tried very hard not to laugh, but he couldn't contain himself. 'By your command, Cardinal Baron. Sorry, Cardinal Baron.' After a pause, he added, 'I'm saying that little devil word too often of late.'

'Don't beat yourself up over it. We need to look forward now. What's done is done. We cannot undo it. But we can redeem things. Let it go. Heed your own advice about being in the moment.'

He nodded. 'Damn. I can't stand that you're usually right.'

'I am. Now let's check those wounds and then we can decide what we're doing next.'

I unwound the bandage around his head.

Struggling to sit still, Blaise said, 'So?'

'Okay, I think.'

'You *think*? That's hardly an endorsement.'

'There aren't any obvious signs of infection, but there's swelling. The shrapnel's staunched the blood flow, but it will need to come out.'

With luck, help would find us before I undertook the repair work. Either way, Blaise would carry a scarred reminder for the rest of his life. On that point, I remained silent.

'The gash looks clean despite the glass. It should be fine for the time being, anyway.' I patched him up and shifted attention to his other wound.

'Cheers, that's a relief.'

'I'm more worried about the shoulder.' I unwrapped the bandage and had a closer look. 'How does it feel?'

'Tender. *Sore*. There's a tingling in my shoulder when I move it.' He winced, rotating his arm.

The signs didn't look or smell right. Blaise could see the concern on my face, and so he said, 'Bar, give it to me straight. I'm a big boy. Better the truth than a fool's paradise.'

'*O-kay*. It's a nasty red, and it's swollen,' I said. 'Also, a faint smell of almonds.'

'What does that mean?'

'Infection.'

'That's hardly inspiring.'

'You *did* ask,' I said. 'It's the least of our worries,' I added to allay his fears. 'Priorities, *Boet*. We've got to stay ahead on the scoreboard. We're a few tries ahead.'

'But in this game, the lead can quickly change hands. What's our next play?'

'We attack our lead, not defend it. If we stay here, we don't have a hope in hell,' I said, binding his shoulder. Blaise tensed and grimaced under the pressure, but said nothing.

'If we keep moving, we'll at least have a chance. We might get lucky and bump into an army patrol, or a plane might sight us. I'm sure they're still out and about. While those terrs are licking their wounds, they'll want to find us after that buffalo ambush. One thing I'm learning is they're tenacious. Overnight, the rain gave us a chance by wiping away any tracks, but this afternoon's events have nullified that.'

'So, move where?'

'Northwest. After the moon rises.'

'I bow to your superior judgement, Obi-Wan.'

'You'd better believe it, Master Luke.'

There was no getting away from it. He was so full of... *himself*. 'You up for the challenge?'

He nodded and laughed. 'Never been better.'

One thing Blaise didn't lack was fire in the belly. *Intestinal fortitude*, our rugby coach, Mr Beukes, used to say.

My brother had it in spadefuls.

... of our elaborate plans...

The sun quit for the day and meandered towards the horizon. Blaise and I lazed in the thicket's cover and rested, girding ourselves for the next leg of the journey.

It had been two full days since the *Hunyani* had crashed. My thoughts, disjointed and disordered, floated like a pall in my head.

Wouldn't the full array of the Rhodesian military – the RLI, SAS, and Selous Scouts – be out looking for us? Where were they now? Had they abandoned the search for survivors? Were they yet to account for everyone? Did they know we were alive?

Blaise's voice snapped me out of my distraction.

'How'd you know so much about orienteering and bushcraft? No, don't tell me. You were actually taking notes at that *bundu*-bash.'

'Yeah, and believe it or not, that knowledge gained is helping us now,' I said. 'Unlike someone else I know. As I recall, you also attended that Weeks Without Walls immersion, didn't you? Don't you recall that session on basic orienteering?'

'Nah, I was there, but I wasn't paying that much attention. Must have been preoccupied.'

'Surprise, surprise. It wasn't Jessica again, was it?'

'She was the reason I signed up for the course. I might also have been listening to radio commentary, the Springboks playing the All Blacks. Can't remember.'

'How the hell were you able to achieve that?'

'Small radio, concealed earpiece. Smuggled in.'

'You do that often?'

He grinned. 'All the time.'

I shook my head. That about summed him up.

... no surprise...

'So, Master Galileo, how do you work out directions?' Blaise persisted, ever the smart-arse.

'It's never an exact science. During the day, we can track our course by the sun rising in the east and setting in the west, and, at night, use the star constellations to give us north and south orientation. This will give us an approximation.'

'I get the sun. But how do you read north and south from the stars?'

'First, work out the key players. The Southern Cross is the most recognisable and quickest to identify. It'll be easier if I show you. We can do it this evening before we leave.'

'Sounds good to me, Master G.'

... waiting to ride...

Despite the sun's retirement, the accumulated heat of the day persisted. Under cover of our increased grubbiness, we struggled to cope with the stifling mugginess. Blaise and I sweltered and sweated in the confined cauldron of our refuge.

A busyness of flies had gathered.

They deployed into battle formation, full frontal attack, humming, and droning.

W.T.A. Welcome to Africa.

A continent of paradoxes and absurdities.

Quality time with a flea or mozzie proves small things matter.

Ditto an evening with a horde of African mopane flies.

As they descended en masse to storm our battlements, we could attest to the truth of that African wisdom and our growing annoyance in the claustrophobic heat.

Royalty. I was my own veritable lord of the flies. Not that this *nkosi* controlled them.

Annoyance grew to frustration and then exasperation as, in a sweeping counter-attack, Blaise and I swatted and swiped at their advance in a ludicrous liturgical dance rather than any effective military manoeuvre.

For a random passer-by, our impromptu performance would have been something out of a *commedia dell'arte* routine.

It grew into a fencing duel.

Give us the foils.

En garde! Thrust and parry. Feint. Counter-thrust. Counter-parry. Lunge, riposte. Fleche, seconde. Flick and flunge. Cut. Hack. A hit? Touché!

'How can we defeat these flies?' Blaise wheezed.

'You know mopane flies are actually bees?'

'And that's meant to make a difference?' said Blaise, gesticulating with his arms to ward off our invaders. 'We can't keep doing the same thing. It's exhausting.'

'We don't have any firepower,' I said. 'We must grin and bear it.'

'Not sure if I can,' Blaise said, saluting the flies away. 'Grin and bear all you want, but enough is enough.'

Even the lion has no choice but to protect himself against flies.

'I know that flies hate sharp smells like cloves, or garlic, pepper, and so on,' I said. 'Ouma used these in a homespun air-freshener to excellent effect.'

Ouma was an herbalist of note, with an enviable reputation in her hometown of Gwelo, a town situated between Salisbury and Bulawayo.

'That's no help. Ouma's not here, is she? And would it work on bees?' Blaise slapped at the great nothing again as the flies bobbed and weaved, evading his feeble stabs.

We continued to beat about the bush.

The flies taunted us. '*Na-na-na-na... na.* Do your worst!' they droned. More of their mates arrived.

Reinforcements.

The bush telegraph was working. Exasperation became a total vexation.

... in need of a desperate hand...

'You don't have any dung beetles handy?' Blaise huffed.

'Why dung beetles?'

'The humble dung beetle, Master Baron, lives in animal shite. By burying and consuming dung, it improves nutrient recycling and soil quality.'

'So, Watson, that's all fine and dandy, but how is that relevant for our current fly crisis, which is really a bee infestation?'

'Well, Sherlock, the dung beetle also protects livestock, such as cattle, by removing the dung which, if left, provides a breeding ground for pests such as wannabe flies. It's a solution to a fly invasion. Remove the dung and, well, you know the rest.'

I understood the convoluted point he was making.

'Now, fresh elephant dung. That's an organic repellent of note. Can't see any fresh deposits around here.'

'That's a relief. I'm covered in enough brown stuff as it is.'

'As for the dung beetle, we have no livestock and cow pats either, unless you've hidden them in your pockets, Master Gulliver.'

'A real pity. Soon, the dung beetle will be an in-demand export to countries such as Australia, Kiwi-land and the Americas. It can revitalise the soil, boost agricultural practices and animal husbandry, and also improve hygiene,' Blaise said as he swiped at the flies. 'I reckon there's money in that venture. And it also has massive advantages for the environment,' he continued. 'That's what I'd like to research when I finish school and go to varsity.' Before I could interject, he added, 'It's also a business opportunity, I reckon. What do you think?'

'An innovative proposal indeed, Watson. It has its merits and is worth considering,' I said. 'But first, we need to escape this siege. We'll talk about it once we're out of this fly-fight.'

'One last thing. Did you know that dung beetles navigate their way via clusters of stars, making them the only creatures known to orient themselves this way?'

'No, I didn't know that.'

How the hell did they work that one out? I wondered. I had visions of a news reporter speaking to Doug, the dung beetle.

'Tell me, Doug,' I imagined her saying, 'How do you work out which direction to move your dung?'

'Ja-well, no-fine, Carike, I'm not sure, but when I check out the night sky from the bottom of a cow pat, covered in, you know, dung, I just know. It's like in me. I can't explain it, but it's in my stars. I just intuit directions.'

'That's amazing, Doug. It's obvious to me you orient yourself according to the stars. Must be a special form of satellite tracking.'

'Carike, I'm not sure about that. You're making it sound too complicated. It's just a dung beetle thing. It's genetic. We're natural path-finders.'

'Knock-knock, Baron. Are you in?'

'I was just wondering how anyone can know how your dung beetle uses the stars to orient itself.'

'It's got something to do with polarisation and wavelengths,' Blaise said. 'A research paper at a varsity in South Africa. I can't remember the details off hand.'

That I was gob-smacked by Blaise's perceptions and intentions said something about my intellectual arrogance and ignorance rather than of him. I didn't know Blaise as well as I assumed.

I vowed to strengthen our fraternal bond on the other side of this mess.

'I read somewhere that you could repel flies by filling a plastic bag, bottle, or glass with water and pennies,' I said. 'And the larger the pennies and the container, the better the fly-repelling ability.'

'You can't be serious.'

'Something to do with flies' compound vision. They think the pennies are the eyes of a larger predator, and they back off. So they say.'

'They must be part of the old wives' yarn club. And they're bees, remember?'

'Maybe, maybe not. What do we have to lose?'

'True. Tell me though, Sherlock, even if it were true, how do you propose to carry out your ambitious plan?'

'Hah, we can improvise. I have a few pennies in the rucksack's side-pocket, and we have water bottles. Shall we experiment, Doctor Doo-little?'

'By your command, Doctor Doodle-more!'

I took one bottle, decanting most of the water into the other. I then squeezed two pennies into that bottle containing about three fingers of water. It was a gamble, given our meagre supply, but it was worth it if it repulsed the fly invaders.

A statue of liberty, I held the coin-eyed bottle up above my head. The pennies bulged, magnified through the water and plastic.

Miraculous.

The flies disappeared, frightened off by the bulging, threatening eyes of a more significant threat to their existence.

It felt good to be an ex-*nkosi* of the flies.

'No way, Hosea,' Blaise said, shaking his head. 'Seeing is believing. Without this proof, your theory was always bollocks.'

'Not my theory. Just an urban legend – like myself.'

'You sound like Uriah Heep – so humble!'

'I have nothing to be humble about, as you well know.'

'Get over yourself. You're just as surprised as me, aren't you?'

'*Ja.* I can hardly believe it. I'm still pinching myself.'

'Perhaps the mopane flies withdraw in the dark. It's probably got nothing to do with your coin-in-water strategy.'

'Either way, I'll take the win. *QED. Quod erat demonstrandum*,' I said.

'*Demon...* who?'

'*QED.* The Latin phrase meaning *thus proved*. You know, written at the end of maths theorems?' I said. 'Archimedes. Euclid?'

'*Jis*, now you've lost me, Captain Caprivi!'

'Never mind, it's not important,' I said, trying not to sound like my condescending self.

Blaise just shook his head and rolled his eyes.

... desperately in need...

We settled down for an uninterrupted and much-needed rest, preparing ourselves for the next part of our serendipitous ride on the bushveld freeway to the northwest.

... waiting to ride the king's highway... waiting...

In the hiatus, I pulled out my journal, along with the family pic that I had plucked from the fridge door on a whim. The dimpled, blurred photo was still intact. It was a Polaroid special – all the rage. I wasn't sure why.

Jo and Monty were there, slouching in deck chairs by the pool. Mum and Dad stood behind them, beaming. As did Blaise, ubiquitous rugby ball under his arm. I was standing next to him, next to Mum. Uncle Tom had snapped the shot, which explained Mom's adverse reaction to my packing it without asking.

Our last family gathering.

Would there be another?

I scribbled in my journal.

TUESDAY, SEPTEMBER 5

I've been in the bush with my brother for 2 days. I'm trying to make sense of it.

Blaise's shoulder wound has deteriorated, puffing up like an oversized cupcake. I am not confident that I can keep it clean.

We can't make this on our own, but I must keep faith.

The brutality of these past days beggars belief. How do

I understand this war, and the levels of barbarism to which humans stoop?

How do you explain the cruelty at the Hunyani? Can anyone justify the deaths of innocents and children in a so-called fight for freedom and justice?

I'm at a total loss, trapped on the other side of the moon.

And who knows which is which...
And who is who...

What I've seen and experienced is an indictment of our species.

Yet are we not all complicit? From where has such hate come? Have we lost sense of who and what we are? Have we become immune to our darker nature, ignored our better angels?

Do we share in the responsibility for the atrocities of this war? They didn't happen in a vacuum.

'Unnatural deeds do breed unnatural troubles.'

The random interaction with Thembelani Thumbeza may have been something more than random.

His grace, his sense of *Ubuntu*, his perceptive, profound words and questions had caught me off-guard. He had challenged and destabilised everything that I had grown up to believe.

My head was a labyrinth of interwoven and unravelled thoughts.

... lost in a wilderness...

Best to write them down despite their fragmented nature.

Journalling, I had read (I forget where), was a weapon of the soul, liberating into the light of clarity, from the darkness of confusion, pulses of inspirational thought.

The very act of writing was part of the bigger struggle for understanding, for spiritual and mental wholeness.

Committing thoughts to paper with honesty and courage, jumbled as they were, aided coherence and connectedness.

It was not for the faint-hearted.

Writing could be a hazardous and lonely journey through the maze. But if undertaken in a spirit of integrity, it could lead to uncomfortable places to expose the truth in its complexity.

Thumbeza's words of challenge had been confronting, spooking me from my comfort zone. My head was a cavernous catacomb, his words rebounding off its skull-packed walls:

'... your right... but does that history entitle you to claim that right...?'

Leaping onto the path of thoughts and feelings, I scribbled, hoping the act of doing so would push me further along to the very core of that yearned-for enlightenment.

Have I unknowingly allowed colonialist values to influence my understanding of the world?

Am I also not guilty of hypocrisy, my perception impeded by ego and arrogance? Am I enslaved by those very 'mind-forged manacles' that I claim to disdain?

His words continued to saturate the mandala of my skull.

'... prisoners of our worldviews...
language is a key part of that incarceration.'

I put pen to paper once again.

On matters of history, knowledge and culture, the compli-
cation is I think, feel and write from within the very language
that is exploitative and oppressive.

'... this privileged position allows such a worldview to be normalised...'
banged on in my head.

The words poured onto the page unimpeded, as water cascading
over the Seongo.

But what other choices do I have? English is my mother
tongue. I am caged and liberated by the linguistic tradition
in which I was born. If the limits of my language mean the
limits of my worldview, how do I reconcile this contradiction
or even revolutionise my language from the inside so that my
thoughts, my writing, my speaking, are at least sensitive to
those nuances I've spent a lifetime normalising?

Thoughts thudded, hydraulic pile-drivers in my head.

'... your desire to help should not be the same
as making us in your image and likeness...'

The novels of my early adolescence bounced into my conscious mind.
Rider Haggard's 'King Solomon's Mines'. 'She'. 'Allan Quatermain'.
Again, I scribbled.

I can see that the so-called colonial depictions of the dark
continent and its noble and 'savage' Africans might generalise,
oversimplify and dehumanise, conjuring romanticised, exotic
but distorted images of mysterious places and their peoples.
While such stories might naturalise racial and gender
stereotypes, they were still great primal and startling yarns of

the frontier, recast tales of adventure and struggle, quests, and tests of strength and ingenuity against and about an unfamiliar otherness, enough to spark any young adolescent's imagination.

And yet... and yet... there was something about Thumbeza's words that made sense, and something about my own thoughts that didn't.

Was there that other sacred space beyond our differences where we could unpack our views, our understanding, within a new frame of reference?

I flexed my aching fingers.

'Once a new idea has stretched the mind, it can never revert to its original dimensions.'

Just get the words down, Baron.

It was conceivable that the stories of my youth had clouded my prism of perception, desensitising me to a more attuned understanding of the richness and diversity of human life and culture in my country.

Tired of its diurnal trek through the skies, the sun had all but departed. Its butternut rays faltered, uncertain, pensive, half-concealed by interfering clouds on the distant and darkening horizon.

My mind shifted to the encounter with the puff adder. I tried to distil into wordy essence what it could mean.

Each of us carries serpents within us, which are present all the time.

By choosing not to ignore them, we can placate them and keep them in check. If we ignore them, they grow bigger and uncontrollable.

When we tame the enemy within, the enemy without can do no harm.

She-Who-Must-be-Obeyed – Ouma – used to say that in our lives, we are always confronted by fundamental choices.

'Now, Baron,' she'd say in that musical Irish lilt of hers, 'the choices we make decide what people we become. We either follow the path of grace and poise or we walk the path of egotism and desire.'

'*Ja*, Ouma, whatever you say, Ouma.'

'You're not being a smart arse again, are you, Baron? You might be a bright lad, but don't let that ego impede your education, my boy!'

'*Jammer*, Ouma. I bet it's Shakespeare again, hey?'

'Baron, of course it's the Bard. Who else?'

Ouma instilled in me a love of Shakespeare. I'm undecided whether that has been a blessing or a burden.

'*Ag*, man, not the Bard again, Ouma!'

'Afraid so, Baron. Desire and grace litter Shakespeare's works, but words from one of his poems – I forget which, my brain is a colander – gave me the idea: *Flesh being proud, Desire doth fight with Grace, for there it revels.*'

'I'm not convinced, Ouma, that lines from an obscure Shakespearean poem set up a basis for a way of life.'

'Baron, my boy. All texts are part of the great conversation of life, of human experience, speaking to us down the ages. Why would you not want in on this discussion?'

'There you go again, Ouma!'

'That's because, Baron, you miss the point. Shakespeare's words are relevant. He claims that the wiser choice is always the higher path of spirit, of grace. In choosing it, we walk in a divine light.'

Ouma looked *skeef* at me over the top of her reading glasses.

'But if we choose the lower path, the flesh, we enter the dark recesses of desire and self-interest – the realm of the puffed-up ego – where the dark plays with us until it seeps into our pores and consumes us. Make sense?'

'Kinda.'

'Just remember, life is a difficult and constant battle, deciding between these two paths.'

My grandmother was a wise old lady, and I wished, looking back, I had paid more attention to her sharp insights and thoughtful opinions. But, for me, this view of hers was inadequate, particularly in the light of my recent experiences.

It's not a case of choosing a binary position, either... or, grace or desire. Poise or pose. The higher or lower path.

It's subtler and more nuanced.

There is only one path each of us walks. On our chosen path, both grace and desire co-exist, fused much like a double-helix rod with entwined, coupling serpents, in harmonious balance.

Our lives are provisional: a constant negotiation along the spectrum bookended by the opposites of grace and desire. Out of necessity, we must hold the tension between both; negotiate our way with poise and equilibrium between the extremes, to make our lives meaningful.

People like Thumbeza walked a graceful path, and their example prodded me to do the same. Just as he believed he had no choice but to fight to assert his rights and those of his people, I, too, along with my twin brother, was also committed to our struggle to assert our right to life.

... ride the snake... ride...

Beside me, Blaise lounged with eyes closed, propped against the foot of an acacia tree.

I had to be strong. The family would rely on me.

Words of wisdom my father always used drifted into my mind. 'Remember, son, two things. First, *nous*. Mind. Focus. Second, *bottle*.

Mettle, grit, pluck, courage, whatever you want to call it.'

He was always a man of few words, but when he spoke, they were compelling.

'Act in good faith, always do the right thing. Never give in... apply the F-word often... *focus.*'

Words oft-quoted and familiar resonated in my ears, offering solace.

Be courageous. Do not be afraid of your enemies, for your God goes with you; He will never leave you nor forsake you.

Disoriented in the entrails of the beast, I remained more or less where I had started.

Meandering in circles, or in spirals of eternal recurrence, where the past whispers to the future, to create a forever-unfolding present...
I wasn't sure which. Probably both.

Whatever awaited me, I had to keep control. A dash of faith wouldn't go amiss, either.

It would be easier to succumb to the temptations of serpents in this inscape than to resist them in a more recognisable wilderness.

... lost...

I packed my pen and journal away and watched the sun's rays slip beyond the horizon, a hint for the African bush to renew its own soporific, nocturnal and eternal hymn.

The African transition from day to night was abrupt. In an instant, all wounds of colour were gone from the land.

Darkness incarcerated me.

The moon had yet to respond to her entrance cue, but the milky way of stars, plump and close to the earth on the southern horizon, slid past in their nocturnal round, to limn the black spindly trees against the wan savannah.

I began to tear up.

Get a grip. We were not alone.

I remembered my miraculous medal and, pulling it from my pocket, I gazed at its Marian outline. The words of the original prayer eluded me, but others frothed in my mind. I said them out loud.

'As I carry with me this medal, may it open me to your grace. May it be a sign of hope and transformation...'

Blaise looked as if he wanted to correct me, but he stopped himself.

'Guide us towards new ways of thinking and being... help us connect in empathy... protect us as we navigate life's contradictions...'

... waiting...

We watched for dark-and-light sides of the moon to rise.

In the end...

It's only round and round, and round...

As I had promised earlier, I tutored Blaise on how to use the Southern Cross as a guide.

'In a nutshell,' I said, eyeing the star-filled heavens, 'you identify the two southern pointers, the gatekeepers for the four cardinal stars of the Southern Cross.'

I pointed them out. 'There. Do you see? You can pick them out by their superior brightness.'

Blaise stared for a moment and nodded.

'Bisect the line between the two pointers and draw an imaginary perpendicular through that centre point.'

'Right-e-o. Got it.'

'Now, draw an imaginary line from the Cross's top to its bottom. Where the two lines intersect, beyond the foot of the cross, that's south,' I said.

'Easy-peasy, when you know how. B, just as well one of us was paying attention. While I'd be the last to admit it, your book-worm wealth of knowledge isn't going to waste.'

... ride the king's highway baby... ride...

The flush-cheeked moon, ever the lady, obliged and emerged from her boudoir. Even she had a dark side.

We trekked northwest once again, careful to counter-track as best as we could.

... ride...

I shivered.

Blowing on my hands, I extended and contracted my numbed fingers to improve blood flow.

Blaise and I shambled together, one foot in front of the other, on and on.

My eyes sagged.

Scuffle and thud.

'Sorry, Bar. I must have dozed off.'

'We need to rest and eat,' I said, snagging his hand and pulling him to his feet.

The meagre supply of apples, biscuits, and *biltong* pilfered from the plane was long gone, and while the baobab fruit had helped, it hadn't lasted.

'No kidding. Any ideas?'

I racked my brains. Where would we find bush food? As I made to stand, Blaise grabbed my arm and pulled me to the ground.

'Be still.'

... there's danger at the edge of town...

Filtered moonlight.

Delicate movements in the stillness.

Blurry-red eyes leapt into focus.

A hot, pungent whiff of wild cats.

Lions.

A pride strolled past, a short distance upwind from our position.

Five females. Five cubs, plus-minus.

Accompanied by a single alpha male whose bushy, tawny mane framed a scarred, ashen face.

He strutted the bushveld catwalk.

The cubs frolicked and cavorted; the lionesses stalked in foraging formation.

Beast of a Thousand Omens, Judge of Africa, the King, *Ibhubesi*, swaggered, heavy paws padding the earth.

... the king's highway...

Ibhubesi was at the height of his power.

Muscles, tendons and joints flexed and relaxed in antagonistic symmetry. Citrine eyes glowed, signalling a dark intelligence, and exuding dignity and composure.

Ibhubesi, forged and hammered into shape by a cosmic blacksmith.

What immortal hand or eye...?

Ibhubesi, a violent yoking of synergetic opposites.

Attraction and Repulsion. Grace and Ego.

A dangerous but striking contradiction so typical.

T.I.A. This is Africa, the continent of ironic juxtapositions and correlations. And victories. *It never loses.* In the end, Africa always prevails.

The wildcats, enjoying their family perambulation, disappeared into the tall trees to our left.

Trees. That was it. Umganu. Marula trees!

The fleshy, delicious almond-shaped fruit drove elephants mad. And before us was a prayer circle of them. Yellow and sweet when ripe, with healing properties, marula fruit was also high in vitamin C. The South African Amarula Cream, derived from the marula fruit, was a renowned liqueur.

I gestured to Blaise to stay where he was, and I merged into the trees with my backpack. He stared after me, somewhat bemused.

After my return, Blaise and I filled our stomachs with nature's ambrosia and consumed the leftover water collected from the riverbed.

A holy communion.

Never was food more satisfying or water as sweet.

Supporting and half-carrying each other, we retreated to the deepest point of the marula grove and, after an agitated and fitful settling, we passed out in the arms of Morpheus...

... lost in a...

> *Kweh-kweh, kweh-kweh. Go-away, Go-away.*
> > *Kweh-kweh.*
> > > *Go-away, it twanged.*

Warning bird, shouter-at-enemies, harbinger of demons.

> *Kweh-kweh.*

A melic drawl nudged me from a semi-comatose state.

> *Go-way. Go-away...*
> > *Go-away bird, Kwadira,*
> > > *the grey lourie.*

I wasn't sure whether the lourie had been a figment of my imagination or not, but I awoke to an insistent moaning.

'*Blaise*. What's up?' He lay on his back, motionless. I called to him again.

He emitted an audible wail.

I unravelled the makeshift bandage to assess the shoulder wound. The bullet hole and its surrounds were suffused with a strong smell of almonds, saffron-red and engorged.

I used our paltry water supply to clean it.

'Hold still!' I barked as he squirmed and groaned. 'Blaise, can you hear me?'

'I feel so cold. Baron, I don't feel good at all...'

'Hang in there, buddy. I've got it covered,' I said, restrapping his shoulder with a makeshift bandage that had seen better days.

'I need Mum...'

'She'll be here soon, I promise,' I said, wiping the sweat from his forehead. 'She's on her way.'

'The darkest hours are those just before the dawn,' I muttered out loud. 'It can't get any worse.'

Who was I kidding?

I was fast losing any sense of perspective.

Or hope.

... c'mon baby, take a chance on us...

BUTCHER BIRDS

I WAS FALLING... *FALLING*... on a bateleur plunging downward, with its left wingspan in flames.

... ride baby... ride...

It yapped as it slowed, glided onto a stumpy baobab branch, and extended glowing ochre wings flecked with purple, to sun itself. With an illuminating nimbus and sapphire eyes aglow, the eagle resembled the fabled phoenix.

Its blazing wing transformed into a flame that distorted into a field of blood-splattered lilies. I roamed this vast lofty host, my hands thrust downward, and felt their serrated petals on my fingertips as they clawed at my arms and legs in the molten red of a Rhodesian dawn.

From the sunrise's ripening papaya glow, a figure strode towards me. It was a challenge to identify him, even though his gait was familiar.

... Father... Yes, son...

Martin-of-the-Lily-Fields, they called him.

While the flame lily was a protected species in Rhodesia, this hadn't prevented Dad from affirmative gardening, and he harvested a large number.

Seeds of fire. *Kajongwe.*

Despite it being illegal, the old man had the most enviable flame lily collection in the whole of Borrowdale Road.

... old... the old man's face is...

'Son,' he said, 'do you know why I grow flame lilies?'

I shook my head.

'Let me tell you, then. Not only for its unusual fractal shape, sinuate leaves, striking, prismatic colours and healing qualities.'

He put his arm around me. 'But to inspire me. *You. Us.* It is a hardy, resilient and fiery herb adaptable to the harshest conditions. Its petals of blood and the golden base are a reminder to live with passion and conviction. Fire in the belly. Call it whatever you will.' He paused. 'Now wake up and get it done. Keep the flame alive. Help your brother. Faint heart never won fair maid.'

My eyes fluttered open with my father's words, 'keep the flame alive', jitterbugging in my head.

The African dawn burst upon us once more. The molten sun began its climb to the heavens.

Not unlike Sisyphus.

Blaise whickered. I checked his vital signs. The rhythm of his breathing was erratic, his pulse thready and skin moist and clammy.

I was running out of options.

... his skin is cold... so cold...

Well on its premeditated and upward arc, the sun was en route to conquering the day.

Carpe diem.

I was at a loss.

Where to now?

At the highest point of its parabola, it wavered and frowned downwards.

To stay would compromise us. *Better to die on our feet than live on our knees.*

Fire in the belly.

I sighed.

In my sleep-vision, Dad had spoken of flame lily qualities. It gnawed at my innards that I could not recall his words.

... desperately...

I dragged Blaise upright.

'Breakfast time... and don't forget your rugby boots,' he mumbled.

The fever was working its poison.

We trudged towards the northwest. The savannah grass, elephantine baobab trees and their smaller relation, the buffalo-sized mopane, offered us partial cover and shade.

... ride the king's highway... baby...

Addled, I couldn't join the dots of my flaming lily dream.

As we plodded onwards, a pair of giraffes, rubber tongues munching on juicy, cathedral-high acacia leaves, watched us, bemused and disinterested.

The terrain changed.

Uphill.

Fewer trees.

Ahead, flaming lilies shimmered scarlet and honeycomb in the morning breeze.

My father's dreamtime words leapt into my head. F-lilies were *herbs* with *healing* qualities. While toxic to ingest, they had a wide variety of uses. In the traditional medicinal practices of the *sangoma* or *nyanga*, they were an antidote for snakebite and an antiseptic on open wounds.

How to prepare an effective concoction was beyond my ability. To try was preferable to not trying.

Faint heart never won fair maid. I smiled. *Thanks to the old man!*

... take a chance...

Hope surged, galvanising me into action.

I ordered Blaise to sit under the umbrella cover of a mosu tree, and I went to work. He appeared too exhausted and delirious even to care.

I used a stick to dig them out, and amassed various sizes of lilies, making sure I removed their root systems intact. I spotted a knotty, knobkerrie-shaped acacia branch, ideal for crushing the lilies into a paste. I used it to pound them into a mush, and with the last of our water, I mixed both ingredients until they formed a crude salsa.

With a *Hey Blazer, this will hurt, I'm not gonna lie*, I removed the makeshift bandage from my brother's injured shoulder and applied my gluey poultice. He yelled, but I held him down and strapped on the ragged, tatty dressing.

Would it work?

It couldn't do him any more harm, given the state of the growing sepsis in the wound.

Only time held an answer to my question.

... ride the snake...

Flecks drifted in lazy circles high above, suspended in the heat.

They grew larger.

Two birds of prey floated in hypnotic orbits, their still wings magnetised to each other. I knew royalty was present.

Spirit birds aflame,
   Past, present and yet to be.
      Crimson trimmed, blistered ivory, chastened coal,
        molten-mantled, frozen fire.
   Teary nyangas,
     Layered paradoxigmas.
   Ancient unravelled
      scourgers and nurturers of serpents.

Earthy masked mystics, Janus-faced,
   death-and-life whisperers.
Mentor-hunters, mothers of trees,
   fertility-bringers.

Untrammelled ancestral messengers,
     bridgers between profane and divine;
Dancers desired by the Sun,
   tightrope walkers, tumbling acrobats
transcending earth and sky.

Bateleur eagles.

The smaller one – the male – swooped towards the larger female. She rolled onto her back, presenting her claws, and then righted herself as he careered beyond her. He circled and pursued her and together they folded, curled and twisted in a spiralling manoeuvre, mirroring each other, two hands in sacred prayer.

They plunged downwards, flirting with the earth in an act of supreme aerial skill.

At the last moment, as the ground loomed large, the paired eagles disengaged and with wings expanding, swelled on the air currents against a cloudless sky and a burnished African sun.

They repeated their gymnastic courting ritual, culminating in a rapturous crowing and barking enmeshed in a vertical drum solo of slapping wings.

I was breathless.

Was this *being in the moment?*

The eagles flew in flat circles as they followed each other, drifting and swinging high in the wordless silence, performing one lateral barrel after another in an unrestricted nuptial display.

Little wonder that bateleurs mated for life.

The birds receded together, fused contraries gliding in gentle spirals, following the sun.

> *Oh, holy and sacred Ingonghulu,*
>   *thrust from the tree of deep time,*
>   *first creation bird:*
>
> *Extend your brooding wings and beat them*
>   *(ghu-ghu-ghu),*
>   *for me.*
>
> *Lament for the death of kings*
>   *(sjwee-sjwee),*
>   *but not yet for me.*

And so it was.

My spirits lifted and melded with the *Ingonghulu* birds as they soared and drifted on the wind, shepherding my brother and me in our intended direction, towards the perceived safety beyond the granite monolithic and metallic hills to the northwest.

... follow me...

We had not lost. There was a way out.

Blaise had not moved. He lay on his back, eyes closed. I coaxed him to his feet.

'Come on, Blazer. We're there. One last push.'

... ride the king's highway... yeah... ride...

We staggered forward. Blaise could not support himself, so I placed his arms around my neck and piggy-backed him forward.

Ever upwards.

The terrain grew steeper. My steps shortened and the muscles in my legs were like flexed rubber bands, and burned without respite.

My chest heaved.

Until we summited a large granite *kopje*, we continued in this manner. At the top, I collapsed, exhausted, with Blaise perched on me, dead to the world.

We kept our bodies low against the skyline.

... the blue is calling...

A Gabriel de Jongh vista of greens, browns, yellows, blues and reds held my gaze...

A canvas to take the breath away.

The *veld* lay in its untouched wonder, apart from and conjoined with the expanse of the red-grey hills and African cobalt-blue sky.

My view shifted.

Below, at the base of the *kopje*, lay a snotty-green waterhole.

... ride the snake to the lake...

I grabbed Blaise, propelled him downhill. We crashed and coiled, order and decorum gone. Over the rocks and through the brush we tumbled, collapsing in the waterhole's shallows.

The water was brackish, but safe to drink. I uttered a prayer of thanks and slaked my thirst. I wiped my mouth and glanced over at Blaise. He lay face downwards, motionless.

Shite! Only careless feet stumble into a snake pit...

Distracted by my needs, I had been neglectful of Blaise's. I wrenched my brother by his backpack straps and heaved him over.

He wore an African death mask: eyes sealed against the sun, aquamarine lips, pasty white skin.

'Blaise. *Hey!*' I said, shaking and then slapping him hard across his left cheek. A second time, I whacked him and checked for breathing and a pulse.

Nothing.

I loosened his shirt, grabbed his chin, and tilted his jaw backwards. Blocking his nose with my right thumb and index finger, I breathed into his mouth.

With interlocked hands, I applied pressure to the ribcage above his heart.

... this is the end, my only, beautiful friend...

Repeated breaths. Renewed compressions.

I kept at it. I tested for a pulse in his neck.

Still nothing.

I seized his wrist, searched for any sign of life. At the point of resuming CPR, I detected a faint throbbing.

I rolled Blaise onto his side. After a moment, he spluttered a cough, and discharged liquid.

With my ear to his mouth, I checked for the rise and fall of his ribcage.

I pulled him into the shade of a withaak tree nearby and propped his head under his pack, making him as comfortable as I could. I dressed the wound, repacked the lily-poultice and re-bandaged the shoulder.

... on the edge...

His skin was no longer warm to the touch. The wound remained a distended bag of pus, but it had not grown worse.

Could Blaise's condition have stabilised?

Skin glistened, moist and cool. I mopped his lips and face.

I intoned the *Memorare*.

O, remember gracious Mary, that never was it known... that anyone who sought your help... was unanswered...

... waiting... yeah... waiting...

The shadows lengthened to welcome evening's chilly breath.

WEDNESDAY, 06 SEPTEMBER

Another day has passed. I hope that help will be on hand soon. And that we do not run into our hunters. They continue to track us.

Blaise's condition has stabilised. The poultice has arrested his infection. If help reaches us, he may just have a chance.

I hope I won't have to explain his death to Mum and Dad... I wouldn't be able to live with myself...

Not worth writing.

Calliope had deserted me.

The nocturnal symphony launched yet another rowdy recital, a rock and roll soundtrack for those creatures that had ventured to take water.

I lay facing the vault of space above the horizon.

A lone liquid star made its lustrous debut, nacreous in the sable night to the west.

The brightest planet in the pantheon of heaven, Venus.

Creation's night light.

Ancient sky watchers had called it *the wandering star* as they recorded its motion crossing from the morning eastern sky to the early evening western sky.

I preferred *Shepherds' Star.*

Was this the star the Magi followed in search of the Christ-child?

Kings from faraway realms, they must have understood their odyssey to Bethlehem would rebirth them, changing them forever. Yet still they ventured on that journey, fraught with dangers in hostile, strange, and fickle landscapes.

How could they not have yearned for the comforts of more familiar homescapes?

Not unlike these wise men, I too was a wayfarer, weighing life and death.

Errant knight, pilgrim, and prodigal, I was ill at ease, my experiences perplexing at every level of existence.

Was there a grail I should seek, and serve?

Beneath that sole star, a renewed belief flooded through my veins, suppressing the growing voice of doubt and confusion in my mind at that darker than dark moment.

I checked in on Blaise.

Restful, he slept in the protective embrace of Morpheus.

Could my remedy have succeeded?

I gazed upwards once again.

'I lift my eyes to the hills – from where will my help come?

The sun shall not destroy me by day nor the moon by night...'

Convocations of winking stars emerged from hiding to thrust their glittering spears of light downwards.

Finisterre Africanus, the edge of my known world.

Fields of stars on a midnight-blue canvas hairlined the earth and heavens, limned and linked the sacred and secular.

In that moment, as in all moments, the world, finite and infinite, divided and blended.

The stars converged, distant and alien, old friends long-lost but found again. They danced, spoke to me in a trans-language beyond words, each a small, fragile miracle of light and energy; they tied me to something larger, to a cosmic space-web that stretched beyond understanding, reminding me of how small I was compared to the universe's vastness.

'When I am weak, then I am strong...'

I sought solace and inspiration in the only formation I knew: the two scouts and the four watchmen of the Southern Cross.

Sentries at their posts, they lit the darkness.

Forever loyal.

Was I up to their challenge?

Acoustic bushveld shadows invaded my consciousness once more: wittering cicada beetles, faraway hyena-sniggers, doleful jackal yelps and nearby baboon's gut-aches, overruled by Ibubhesi's gravelly and jubilant voice.

No sound matches such a candid bellow at night. Through the silent and crisp African darkness, his throaty roar can clutch at the soul, cut to the very heart and heighten the senses in a single metronomic moment.

It is the king declaring, with authority, to every creature, foreign and domestic, that he is the boss. This is his kingdom.

There was even consolation in that.

My eyes drooped and closed.

Instead of envisaging eagles, I conjured long-tailed, colour-coupled, sable and white butcherbirds, *the scatterers of enemies*, eaters of other birds.

Their rhythmic incantation jumbled in my head and ears.

Stippled, graceful shrikes, roost in withaak tree;
voices soft and meek, they croon a verse to me.
'The day's near done,' they swoop to say,
'take heart, hold the dark at bay.'
'What do you mean?' I ask with probing mind,
'what truths can you teach, help me understand?' In
their mystic, spectral song, I hear dialects profound,
they resonate with my soul, echo in the round.

Butcher bird spikes me on withaak thorn;
grace-filled voice, of inchoate wisdom born:
'Your day's now done,' hums this hangman-bird revered,
'nightfall has come, time to brave your fears.'
Skewered to that tree, I am in a bind, on
who I can be, for what I should stand.
'I know not how to sing my song of life, nor
what grail to grasp midst such soul-less strife.'

'Seek within,' whispers the gwabi bird to me,
    'your heart does sense why, and how, it should be:
    Each new sunrise with it brings
    interconnected moments, 'neath unfurling wings;
    to bless, to heal, with caring hands,
    injury, injustice in our wounded land.
    For in every fall, a chance to rise, I see, as
    we dance this death, this life, in mystery.'

BLUNDERLAND

BATHED IN A SOFT halo of light, the flexuous road rises to meet me. I swerve left and right, following its course into the inverted bowl of sun, foregrounded by darkening hills.

... ride the snake... to the lake...

Under my feet, the surface pulses. To my horror, I am riding an African rock python.

What devilry is this?

I leap from its back and smack the ground, performing a well-executed shoulder roll, and regain my footing. The serpent slows and turns in a wide arc, sliding its stout body towards me. A short distance away, it stops, tail swaying.

It is the same height as me.

Tongue flicking, it rears its shovel-shaped head as if to strike. Before it does, I attack first, embracing it and coiling my legs and arms around it.

... the snake is long...

Two heavy-weight wrestlers, we struggle together. We writhe and I push it away, shouting, 'What do you want from me? Leave me alone!'

There is no direct response to my hostility.

Can it hear me?

After gazing at me with stoical eyes for an uncomfortable while, it kisses my tongue.

'I am your dream-snake. *Your inner serpent.* Embrace me. Your story is etched into my skin. Connect with my energy. Why deny me? What do you have to fear? Why do you deprive yourself? I have reached out to you before, but you do not respond.'

I do not speak, but the creature reads my thoughts. Its oval, glassy stare narrows. 'Do not be troubled. Let not your mind divert you from what you lack. Focus on what you have. If you feed me, you may discover yourself.'

... take a chance on us...

Impassive eyes beguile, but flare to red. In that gaze, the serpent misshapes into a human-sized, hammer-headed, razor-taloned bird of prey with black and white peacock plumage. Bloodied spittle froths from its curved, crimson beak.

A postmodern, multi-colour-coated Joseph, I was left befuddled, wondering what had violated my subconscious mind on that night, so soon after my confrontation with the puff adder.

Had it been an imbola-induced deception, offered by antagonistic serpents that prey upon the restless?

Was it a manifestation, from the depths of my psyche, of the ancient river serpent that goads the human imagination, the archetypal Nyaminyami?

What if it had been a divination from the fabled Impundulu, the shape-shifting, vampiric lightning bird, summoner of the elements, blessed with both curative and harmful powers, guardian of traditional faith healers? Or an ancestral and ghostly messenger, offering a prophetic warning?

Could it be that the serpents we meet are blessings meant to guide us into becoming our best selves?

The dream may have just been a figment of my overstimulated parietal lobe.

The vision or nightmare – whatever it was – had directness, a rare mystical aura, at once magical and haunting, enticing and inexplicable, but as later events unfolded, prescient.

... ride the snake to the ancient lake... baby... yeah...

... ride...

'Wake up, Baron. *Now!*' Mum said. I resisted. *Just a little longer, please...*

'This minute, young man,' she insisted, 'get moving, before it's too late.'

I sprang into consciousness, alert, prickles on my spine.

She had reached out to me again.

The night was onyx black.

MIA, the moon and stars had retreated to defensive positions behind the clustering clouds, which had descended to overwhelm the shallow *donga* beneath the withaak tree near the waterhole where we had taken refuge.

A chilly mist made itself comfortable, settling in and holding us in its seductive embrace.

Even the night-time revellers held their breath.

I nudged Blaise on his uninjured shoulder. His eyes fluttered open, and he glanced about in confusion.

'What... what's the matter?'

Before he could speak further, I whispered, 'Keep your voice down.'

He swung around, uncomprehending. 'Where are we?' he mouthed.

'I'm glad you're back.'

'Where have I been?'

'Delirious and then insensible, and for a while, I feared I'd lost you. I'll update you when I'm able, but for now, trust my judgement. We need to move to a deeper cover. Can you stand?'

'I think so. Here, give me a hand up.' He wobbled when first upright, but found his balance. His green eyes focused with the intensity I knew, understood, and expected.

He grinned and with a faltering mumble, said, 'Let's play.'

'No more talking now. Something's going down.'

We crept past a cadaverous copse of red ivory trees and on to compressed scrub a short distance away; me leading, and Blaise behind, stepping where I stepped.

... no safety in a desperate land...

The pallid vapour maintained its silky grasp. Within thick scrubland beyond the reddened spinney, we sank to our knees and waited.

Fingers tapped me on the shoulder.

I scowled at Blaise and shook my head, but he persisted, pointing to my backpack and, raising his hands, shrugged his shoulders in a gesture of loss.

Crap.

Given the situation, I had to retrieve the second rucksack. Apart from being a beacon for any pursuer, it held half of our provisions.

I signed to Blaise to stay where he was, dropped my pack, and trudged in the direction in which we had come, intent on retracing our footsteps.

It was painstaking work.

Step. Stop. Pause. Listen. Repeat.

The mist swirled, eddied, and thickened.

I had to be near our former position, but disoriented by the dense and crumbly *putu-pap* brume, I hoped I hadn't wandered off course.

... lost in a wilderness...

I inched forward on all fours, St Anthony's prayer on my lips.

Nothing. I groped around in the darkened whiteness.

A metaphor for my life: *Baron in Blunderland.*

Still nothing. Nothing but a fool's errand.

It was time. *To go.* I swivelled on my knees and made to stand. As I did so, my right foot snagged an object. I patted the ground, my hands touching nylon and...

Black metal hoops.

My luck appeared to be holding.

It's never wise to remark on any form of good fortune, and Blaise and I had been sailing unimpeded on the surge and thunder of its flood tide. We had to maximise its momentum before it dissipated into the dangerous shallows to becalm and bedevil our ventures.

To cover my bases, I made a mental note to pray the novena to St Anthony of Padua.

Conscious of the need to minimise noise, I hoisted the pack onto my back. In the churning fog of Dante's other-world, I hesitated to work out my bearings.

So began my journey to Blaise.

After I had ventured a half-dozen steps, muffled coughs from behind me fractured the stillness. Trying not to tremble, I stood, immobilised by an internal force I could not fathom.

... the killer awoke before dawn...

Scuffing boots on grass, stifled yaps, a series of thudding footsteps and soft voices jabbering in Shona, emanated from somewhere near my position.

Or was it Ndebele?

Paralysed, I just stood. My heart hammered at my ribs, and I had the urge to hyperventilate. I shut my eyes and inhaled.

Sounds grew louder and strayed towards me.

Bodies dawdled and bumbled, passed within a few steps, and headed away from me. Fifteen of them by my reckoning, although I couldn't be sure.

At least twelve.

The fog devoured them.

Sucking in air, I dropped on my haunches. A sour taste rose in my mouth, but I swallowed it back, forcing myself not to puke.

Where was I?

With my near encounter, I had lost my sense of location.

What now?

... desperately in need of a hand...

I closed my eyes and imagined forests.

Fools see not the same trees the wise see.

> *Silent,*
> *   you speak a mystical and sacred language known to you alone.*
> *Bearing the seeds of abundance and harmony,*
> *   you are life itself.*
> *In humility,*
> *   you endure humanity's excesses.*
> *Inscribing the hidden truth of experience in the translucent*

rings of your boles,
you protect our ancient wisdom.
Through the ages, you withstand
the scars of conflict, of adversity, of disease.
Keeper of all things living,
you prophesy a future, not your own.

O, royal umNcaka, red ivory tree,
calmer of hearts and restorer of spirits,
speak to the tranquillity of my warrior-heart,
rejuvenate my tree-soul.

... inside...

With my eyes closed against anaemic milkiness, I focused on my breaths, listening for the sounds of the present moment.

Raindrops feathered, fumbled, fragmented, and fell.

With eyes still padlocked, I turned my face to the skies, opened my mouth and allowed its gentle drizzle to sluice over and through me.

No sound met my tired ears, save the *drip-drip-drip* of rain on pink-burdened tree limbs and herringboned leaves. Their echoes shadowed and swelled inside me.

The red ivory never asks the mopane how it shall grow its fruit.

My eyes snapped open, and I strode toward an elegiac melody from beckoning trees.

Inked on a silvery-charcoal canvas, a bluff of trees rose above me.

Their dark skeletal fingers spiked the fog with clusters of burgundy drupe fruit. Coiled, fissured, grey-barked trunks thrust skywards and crimson-fleshed, gnarled roots twisted to grasp the earth. Ebony-on-ivory etched features I recognised from earlier in the night. I snatched handfuls of the sweet stone fruit, chucked them in the pack, and melted back into the waxen maze.

... picture...

'Jeez, Baron, don't *skrik* me like that! Where the hell have you been? You had me worried.'

'Long story for another time. Let's just say our terrorist friends are hot on our trail and we have to hotfoot it to put distance between us and them. Are you up for it?'

'You bet. *Blow, wind! Come, wrack! At least we'll die with harness on our back!*'

'What other roscian talents have you been hiding?'

'Ah, big brother, by now you should know better. You can out-bard me, but you can't out-act me with Billy Wobble-dagger. Lay on, MacBar.'

'Blazer... or should I call you *Laurence O-liv-i-er?* Let's not get too carried away. How's that shoulder holding up?'

'Not bad.' He rotated it. 'It's still stiff and painful, but bearable. What did you do?'

'A flame lily poultice.' I grinned. I would not admit it was a fluke.

'*Slaan my dood.* Knock me down dead, and smear jam under my arms.'

'Let me check it out.' I unravelled the bandage and examined the wound, more by touch than by sight, given the limited visibility. The swelling had subsided, but it was still a nasty injury.

'What does the great man say?'

'I don't know, but this man declares it looks much better. We need a doctor asap. You should give the GP a call. And while you're about it, order a pizza with an extra sprinkle of mozzarella.'

'Now who's a smart arse, hey?'

We debated our next move.

Our pursuers were in a similar predicament, heading in the other direction. Once the mist lifted, that would change. We, the game, would be afoot.

'I think they've foreseen our escape route,' Blaise said. 'Put yourselves in their boots. If you were the hunter, where would you expect your quarry to go?'

'Makes sense. But how does that benefit us?'

'Let's retrace our steps. I recollect tribal trust lands and PVs – protected villages – somewhere near. We could ask the locals for support.'

'That's a poisoned chalice. They might not want to help. There's a history of brutal reprisals and abductions involving the guerrilla militias. And what if we stumble upon those settlements hostile to so-called settlers?'

'No guarantees,' Blaise said. 'What are our alternatives?'

'None that I can think of.'

'Into the west it is. We must take our chances.'

'Apart from our lives, what do we have to lose? *We might not make our sun stand still, yet we'll make him run.*'

'So, which way is west?' my brother said, not caring a jot, or even recognising my clever intertextual reference.

We desired to be far away when the mist rose, but it impeded our intentions, continuing to swirl around us. By retracing our movements in my head, from the withaak waterhole to our current position, I triangulated an orientation.

'That way,' I said, pointing. 'A into G. We've wasted enough time already.'

'*Yee-ha!*'

Throwing caution to the elements, we disappeared into the laced haze.

... the west is the best... ride the highway... baby...

Layers of candy floss mist peeled away as the sun's heat came into the game.

Blessed with a new day, a different beginning.

A tabula rasa.

To put space between us and our earlier position at the waterhole, Blaise and I hauled ass westwards. We had sacrificed stealth for distance, our tracks cutting a swathe over the terrain.

... ride, baby... ride the snake...

At the cusp of a small *kopje*, soaked in sweat, we idled to catch our breath. We'd been running for well over an hour.

Every joint and muscle in my body ached, with a stabbing pain in my right side.

'Bit out of practice, *nê?*'

'Looking forward to that second wind,' I said, panting.

Mr B, our rugby mentor, had been relentless with the team's fitness. I still remember his mantra. 'Listen, *Manne*,' he would say in his Boland drawl, 'fitness is the key to success in *ruk-by*. It breeds confidence; confidence, skill; and skill, victory. Mind over matter. Relax the body. The trick is not to tense up. Keep going, move forward...' He'd clap his hands, and add, 'One day, you will thank me for all this work.'

That day had come.

Blaise and I could run for the full 70 at a good pace.

'*Dankie, Meneer.*'

We paused on the *kopje*'s rocky outcrop and drank from the water collected earlier at the greenish waterhole.

'Small sips. Too much and we undermine our best efforts.'

'Who could forget? Learnt that the hard way.'

'That rugby boot camp was brutal.'

'Bar, what now?'

'We keep moving. Those terrs will soon realise we've given them the slip and they'll try to run us down.'

'And we left them a simple path to track us. We'll have to outrun them. We're fit and, thank God, you've made a remarkable recovery. You up for it?'

'No choice. Necessity is the mother of invention... move or die.'

He had the heart of a leopard.

Gees.

Little wonder he was a beast on the rugby paddock.

From the summit of the *kopje*, we breathed rarefied air and absorbed the view's beauty: undulating landscape in all directions, transposed against the dark mystical hills that whispered seduction and mystery to us.

Our eyes fell in the direction we had just traversed, but we detected no perceptible movement.

... get here... and we'll...

'Over there!' Blaise pointed. 'On that marshmallow-shaped hillock to our left. Do you see them? Specks on the horizon?'

My breath caught in my throat.

I followed Blaise's outstretched index finger, scanning right to left, so as not to overlook anything.

I recalled the bushcraft instructor's words.

'Because we condition our brains to perceive in patterns, to detect any object in the bush, you look right to left, opposite to the direction in which you read. In this way, you're less likely to miss important detail.'

'I see them. But is it who we expect, or something, someone else? Wild animals or the military, maybe?'

'Difficult to say. But we can't afford to take a chance, can we? At this stage of the game, everything's a potential threat.'

Our concealed position atop the *kopje* afforded us the advantage of a clear view of an ancient, sacred landscape that stretched out to touch eternity.

Gnarled baobab and acacia trees dotted the vast expanse of Africa's golden canvas below, and in the hazy mid-morning heat, the distant milky-white mountains shimmered and vibrated. Specks in the distance could be anything, a herd of impala or zebra, or the very danger we were trying to avoid. Conscious of our vulnerability, isolation and exposure in such a wild and untamed space, I couldn't help but fear the worst.

I raised my left thumb, closed my right eye and aligned said thumb on the advancing dots. I then opened my right eye and closed my left. A sudden change in sight alignment between the current movement and where my thumb had re-positioned followed, measuring about 300 metres in real terms.

'How far away do you think?'

It wasn't an exact science, but taking into consideration dead ground, and multiplying the meterage by ten, I could do a guesstimate.

'If it's who we believe it is, they're about three clicks away. Twenty to thirty minutes behind, depending on how fit they are and what gear they're packing.'

'I'm not even going to ask,' he said.

Whatever it was, it was moving in our direction.

... on the edge...

'Baron, it's them. I can just make out silhouettes.'

I took him at his word. Blaise had the eyes of a hawk.

'Do you think they've seen us yet?'

'Nah,' I said. 'They would have dispatched a vanguard of their quickest and fittest men to reel us in. An old tactic. In that way, they'd hope to panic us, force us to run faster and so tire us out more. The trick is to keep up a steady pace without exhausting ourselves.'

'I'm exhausted already and beyond caring, anyway. We should get a wriggle on.'

'Stir those limbs, then. Let's power up these unwashed bodies.'

'Not sure whether we can outrun them, brother!' he muttered. 'But it won't be from a lack of trying. If we can't, we'll be crow bait.'

And that was the simple, inconvenient truth.

I tightened the pack's straps. 'Ready?'

'As much as I'll ever be.'

And so it was.

We went again, full tilt into the west.

... ride the king's highway... ride...

BLOOD TRAIL

OUR BROTHERLY SPIRIT DROVE us onward. We'd set a herculean pace, feet slapping in unison, striding upwards and cresting yet another *kopje*.

'We should stop, or we'll blow a gasket,' I said between heaving breaths. 'Can't keep going at this murderous speed.'

'*Ja*, I'm struggling a little.'

'Aren't you just a master of understatement?'

'Speak for yourself,' Blaise grunted.

Hands on heads, we sucked in the air.

'You all right?'

'I think so. Stiff and sore, though.'

I shook my head and smiled.

'What's so funny?'

'You. A short while ago, you were at the front door of Dr Death. And now you're running for Mr Life. Not sure how.'

He looked at me for a moment.

I held his gaze.

'I didn't have time to thank you for keeping me alive. If it hadn't been for you...' He stopped mid-sentence, half-choking on the words, tears welling in his eyes.

A response seemed inappropriate, so I refrained.

... you'll follow me...

We rested in the shade beneath a lone mopane tree. The sun had long burnt the mist away, opening the infinity of earth and sky.

'We should ditch that backpack. We're done with it.'

Given the gruelling trip to Hades to retrieve it, it was difficult not to see the irony. Blaise also saw the humorous nature of it. *'What fools we mortals be.'*

'Ho-hum. Our course *never did run smooth,*' I said. 'I'll carry this one with the water bottles, journal, Achebe novel and family photo.'

Everything else I'd already unloaded.

'Still *Ill at Ease*? Not sure why you're so attached to it,' Blaise said, 'it's weighing you down.'

'Let's just say, it's a physical reminder of a recent chance encounter, an important life lesson. Maybe it should weigh me down.'

'You need to let it go, in my not so humble opinion.' Blaise tossed the spare backpack into the undergrowth.

'Can't. I'm too deep in the meerkat burrow, too committed to give up on myself.'

... of everything that stands...

We scoured the horizon, but there was no sign of our pursuers.

'Do you think we've outstripped them?'

'Damn it, Bar! Look to the skyline. They're closing the gap.'

Crap.

Our hunters hove into view, larger than the dust mites they'd been before. They flickered, mosquitoes in the sun's glare, and came into sharper focus.

I did the eye-thumb test again.

'How far off do you reckon?'

'Less than before. They've gained on us.'

'But at what cost? They must also be blowing hard.'

'How many do you think?'

'Twelve, thirteen, maybe? Difficult to tell.'

The broiling sun had reached its seat of power in the heavens, phlegmatic in its interest of us.

And them.

Wisdom comes to those who seek the sun.

That sun brings itself to bear on us all: the old and the young and those in between, the wealthy and the impoverished, the wise and the ignorant, the virtuous and the un-good, the god-fearing and the ungodly, cadres and settlers, the entire human masquerade.

It treats each of us with the same warmth of indifference.

Blaise's words interrupted my train of thought. 'We need an alternative plan, Baron. Can't outrun them forever.'

'But until it crystallises, we've no other option.'

'Yeah. When the drumbeat changes rhythm, so too should the dancers adapt.'

'True. But we must choose the moment to change. If we get it wrong, and we beat that drum too soon, the wiles of those mad men will undo us.'

... ride the snake to the lake...

I wasn't sure for how long we'd been running, but I knew that I'd struggle to start again if we stopped. I kept pressing onward, one foot in front of the other.

To maintain balance and poise, you must move forward.

Blaise bustled, urging me to persevere. 'Keep going, B. They'll also tire – they can't do this forever, either. Mind over matter. That's how winning is done.'

He had a massive engine. Concussion, head wound, a hole in the shoulder, sepsis, fever, unconsciousness. How he'd managed it was unfathomable.

An act of resurrection.

There he was, driving me to keep up. Where I had carried him, he now carried me.

Mystifying Madame Fortuna.

'The trick, Baron, is to free your mind,' our school counsellor, Mr Fuller, used to say. It was a wellbeing class.

'Empty your head, be in the moment, pay attention to your breathing. The breath is always present in the here and now, since our mind is often elsewhere. Settling the breath settles the mind.'

I turned my focus to my breathing, inhaling for a count of two and exhaling for four.

Mr Fuller's voice whished in my head, an ode to vertigo.

'Bringing your attention to your breath is a simple and effective way to address tension and recentre yourself on a hectic day.'

My day was as tense as it could be...

'Taking a few slow breaths to control the flow of the breath in and out can bring peace and focus.'

'B! Baron. Stop. *Ooi!*'

With hands on knees, Blaise stooped over a short distance behind me. He gagged, and with heaving shoulders, retched into the grass.

'Sorry,' he said, wiping his mouth on his sleeve. 'Run out of steam.'

'Pity. I was in the zone.' I handed him a water bottle.

'I've hit Hadrian's Wall. We need to reassess. We can't keep doing the same thing here. The results will be the same. Even though they're as tired as we are, they'll haul us in. What's Plan B?'

We halted in the shade of an acacia thicket.

'Here. Moisten your lips. Wash out your mouth. Don't bloat yourself or you won't be able to run.'

'We're almost out, anyway.'

The terrain sloped upwards to even higher ground. Surrounded by more outcrops of granite rock, our position offered a heightened panorama of the undulating Rhodesian tablelands in its natural ruggedness.

The sun had grown tired of waiting and had outstripped us westwards. My eyes followed its trek.

To chase the sun is to embrace both light and shadow, but those who seek only the light are doomed to falter.

A hypnotic, velvety fire in the distance, it zithered off large tracts of water.

'What lakes are those?'

'The Mana Pools,' I said. 'By my estimation, they're the closest of the many wildlife sanctuaries to where we crashed, if I'm correct about the cotton fields.'

'You seem right about most things, not that I'd admit it to anyone else.'

'One day – soon – you will,' I grinned.

The question was: where along the water were we? The Mana Pools, one of Africa's largest and most famous game regions, stretched from the Kariba Dam in the west to the Mozambique border in the east.

'I know that in Shona, *mana* means *four*. As in *four* pools?'

'Yep. Four large permanent water tracts formed by the meandering ox-bow lakes of the Zambezi,' I said. 'I reckon we're closest to the pool nearer Kariba.'

... the lake... the ancient lake... baby...

'They're still on our trail and getting closer.' Blaise's shout snatched me back to reality. Sure enough, our pursuers were closing the gap.

'Two clicks tops, I reckon.'

'No,' he frowned. 'Much less.'

... what will be...

Shouts wafted on the breeze as a couple of bodies detached from the larger cadre and rushed towards our position. One of them pulled ahead.

The primary group slowed.

'They've seen us. Now what?'

'For every tactic, there is a counter. We know what they're trying to achieve, so how about we plan a reception?'

'What do you mean, Baron?' Blaise asked. 'That's a little risky, isn't it?'

'*Ja*, but I'm over running. Time to go for the unexpected.'

'Hah! But they're holding all the aces, Bar.'

'Come on, *Boet*. Use that rugby brain of yours. We have the jokers. What do you do when you're up against bigger opponents, and you know their game-plan?'

'There's more at stake here.'

'Are you sure? *Rugby isn't a matter of life or death...*'

Blaise joined in before I could finish. '*... it's more serious than that...* Yeah, yeah, I get it. So, we'll ambush them with the unexpected, playing to our own strengths?'

'Affirmative.'

'You're serious. Er – Baron – ah – what did you have in mind?'

We conferred for a moment. Blaise nodded. 'Yeah, it might work.'

'It'll work,' I said. I wasn't as self-assured as I sounded, but I had to sell the idea.

'Now run as before.'

... danger on edge...

Our two chasers advanced in the old style.

The front-runner motored at full pace and had outstripped his comrade, who had slowed. By the time he reached us, he would be well ahead of his lagging partner. That suited us: we needed to leverage every advantage.

The primary group had clustered, slowed to a walk to aid recovery, expecting their scouts to get the job done.

Never disturb the enemy while it's making a mistake.

They had divided their forces, and that gave us an outside chance. We retreated along the same arc, ensuring that the chasers saw us do so. As we withdrew, we searched for a suitable spot to put our plan into action.

... can you picture what will be...?

We slipped below the skyline.

'This'll do,' I said, looking at Blaise for his approval.

'It'll have to. We have little time to prepare.'

To our front was a gently sloping stretch of earth framed by two massive granite rocks. We pressed beyond the narrow space between them, an outstretched arm's length wide.

To encourage our opponents to chase without hesitation or thought for their own safety, we were careful to leave telltale signs. The tracks, alluring and plain to see, stretched far past the entrance. We counter-tracked to our predetermined sides of the gap - Blaise left, me right.

We'd sprung our trap.

... get here and we'll do the rest...

The front-runner crashed through the undergrowth beyond the rocky breach, never faltering as he whipped towards our defensive position, scanning the ground ahead of him as he rushed through the granite entrance.

As he passed between the rock sentinels, Blaise hit him from the left with a rugby tackle of which that great South African centre, Joggie Jansen, would have been proud.

It was like a slow-motion movie sequence, its soundtrack the most memorable. The timbre of it will stay forever embroidered in my brain. An explosive discharge of air followed a crude snapping of bone. Blaise drove his shoulder into the terr's upper torso with magnum force, rattling his ribcage, dispatching him to the ground.

He never had a chance.

Blaise's rugby abilities were unsurpassed. For a flank, he had it all – speed, power, skill, agility, aggression and a fearsome tackle. *Nous*, our coach Mr B, called it. *Relaxed intensity*. His mates preferred to call him *Hitman*.

'Suck on that!' Blaise leapt to his feet, yelling at the inert body lying in a crumpled heap on the ground.

... I want ...

Stunned and disoriented, the man groaned and attempted to sit up. Before he could, I pounced and, with rock in hand, smashed him in the face.

His startled features disappeared in a morass of spewing red as I lifted my arm and brought it down.

Over and over.

... to... kill... you...

'Baron, that's enough. Stop. He's dead.'

I kept bludgeoning the rock into the man's face, oblivious to Blaise's shouts. He intervened, grabbing at my raised arm as I tried to force it downwards.

'Look at me. Stop now. We've a second customer. Come on. Don't drop your bundle. Get a grip.'

My arms weak with exertion, I emerged from my daze and stared at tacky crimson hands and blood-covered forearms.

They smelt of mortality.

My sleeves and shirt were blood-splotched, as if I had lanced a bulging and purulent boil.

'Baron, snap out of it.' Blaise tugged at my jumper. "You want to take his place?'

Blood will beget more than blood.

'Suck it in, Bar. We'll deal with the emotional shit later.'

I stared beyond my brother. 'Sorry, I'm... not sure... what came over me... I want to look away, but can't unsee what I've done.'

'Don't ever look away, Baron. If you want to survive, and thrive, you won't sugar-coat the bad shit. But for now, bury it. Until you're ready to deal with it in a meaningful way.'

... from the ancient gallery...

Blaise snaffled up the AK assault rifle dislodged in the attack, and inspected it.

'Buckled and effed.' He tossed it into the bush before frisking the body. In a snug-fitting side holster under the terr's left armpit, he found a 9-mm pistol with a full clip of ammunition. He pulled the weapon free, checked and cocked it.

'Sweet! Just what we needed,' he said. 'The next one will be here soon. We'd better make ourselves scarce.' Pointing at the ground, he added, 'Leave him where he is.'

I muttered to myself, staring from my stained hands to the bloody spread-eagled body with pulped face. 'A path of blood. It could act as a distraction.'

Beneath the skin, blood has the same colour.

'A blood trail,' I said. 'A real lifesaver.'

'So it could,' Blaise nodded. He looked over at me. 'You gonna keep it together?'

I could not bring myself to answer.

One life for another.

'Come on. Quick-smart. We're running out of time with another scene to be played.' He pulled me to my feet.

We concealed ourselves once more in our former positions and awaited the second act.

The curtain call wasn't long in coming.

... he came to a...

Before the rocky gap, the terr would not have been able to see his comrade's body lying on the trail, as the descending gradient of the terrain obscured his view.

From afar, I heard the new arrival's boots slapping the ground. He called out to his comrade, and when there was no answer, stopped in his tracks at the egress of the rocky causeway.

He was a large, barrel-chested man, dressed in a rice-flecked combat jacket, with a wine-red bandana around his head. His skin glistened with sweat and exertion. Strung from his right shoulder to his left hip, an ammunition bandolier flashed in the sunlight. Strapped to his back, an AK pointed downwards.

On glimpsing his fallen comrade, he unslung his weapon in one fluid, skilful movement, scooted for the bush to his front, and dropped to one knee.

His eyes settled on my concealed position.

My heart pounded like a war drum.

He scrutinised the space in which I hid.

Had he seen me?

In my sweaty hand, I clutched a bloodied rock, ready to launch myself at him. Every fibre in my body tingled.

I was a mamba, coiled to strike.

The man inched towards my location. He narrowed his stare, cocked his weapon, and squinted along the gun sights. I charged, tripped in the knotty bush, and sprawled on the ground.

His finger squeezed on the trigger.

Loud pops, a crack, air zipped past my head.

A flinch, a burning jellyfish sting.

The man spun, fell, and lay still. I staggered from the tangled underbrush just as Blaise stormed over, alarm etched on his face.

'Bar, are you –?'

'*Ja... Ja*, I think so. Twisted my ankle.'

'Blood's all over you.'

'Burn in my right arm.'

'Let me take a gander.' He cradled it for closer inspection. 'You're are lucky puppy,' he said, shaking his head. 'That terr's bullet whipped through your rugby jumper. You can see the hole. It clipped your bicep, leaving a large red welt. All that blood – it's not yours. That's a relief.'

'Thanks, B, but man, you left it late. You had me worried.'

'Timing, Baron, timing. To use a rugby analogy – attack in the lion's mouth or don't attack.'

'But I was down his gullet fiddling with his intestines.'

Blaise was pale around the gills.

... the snake...

With the left trainer removed, I sat on my butt, nursing my foot.

'What about that ankle?'

'Tender. Tripped over in the undergrowth. I'll need to strap it to keep going.'

'You always had weak ankles. We can tear strips from your jumper.'

'It's an irony I fell over as I did.'

'Saved your life.'

'Sometimes a minor mishap saves you from a more serious one.'

'Ain't that true.' Blaise ripped at my now sleeveless jersey and strapped my ankle as tight as I could bear, using a figure-of-eight.

'How's that feel?' Blaise offered his hand. I seized hold, and he tugged me to my feet. I rotated my ankle, tested the weight.

Our eyes levelled. Held.

I grinned. 'It'll do.'

... took a face...

I threw a glance over at the results of Blaise's first intervention. A bullet had clipped the terr in the shoulder, and as he had spiralled, a second had blasted a jagged hole in his chest. His blood had splattered on me.

The 9-mm pistol, nicknamed the *mamba*, had done its gory work.

Blaise gave the body a once-over. 'Nothing for us to scavenge, apart from the mamba's shoulder-holster.' He unbuckled it and pulled it free. He then turned his attention to the terr's Kalashnikov and scrutinised it. 'This AK's also stuffed – it's filthy and the barrel's bent. The ejecting cartridge stove-piped in the breech. No wonder it jammed.'

I stole a closer look. 'I'm one lucky pilgrim.'

'If it makes you feel any better, given its shitty state, this AK was fated to jam.'

'Thanks, B. I feel so much better for knowing that.'

'Glad to be of help. Looks like their weapons are all old and buggered.'

'It makes them even more dangerous. They can still do damage,' I said, somewhat distracted by the broken body of the front-man I'd savaged.

Staring down at his pulped face, I stood, rapt.

In taking a life, I forfeit my own.

'All this blood... it might not be mine, but it leads to me, doesn't it?' My voice drifted. 'Which means it's mine. A blood-trail.'

... the trail of the serpent...

'Baron, we must go. Pronto!' He grabbed my sleeve. 'We don't have much time. Soon that mob will be all over us like a heat rash.'

I didn't move, mesmerised by the bloodied corpse on the ground. 'You know what? Serpents are an acquired taste, but I think I've the palate for them. Maybe I've always had it.'

'Bar, to battle serpents, sometimes you have no choice to let slip your own.'

I could not tear my gaze away. 'He who fights serpents, is in danger of becoming one.'

Blaise shook me by the shoulder. 'We don't have time for this, Baron. We're always grappling to restrain our serpents.'

I shifted my focus from the corpses to my brother. 'But that doesn't mean I should enjoy their company, does it?' I said, 'Or bask in their admiration.'

Blaise hesitated, searching for a response. 'Some serpents never die, do they? No matter how many times we think we've hacked out their entrails and laid them to rest, they reappear in a different skin. Put it out of your mind, Bar. It's done. No time to obsess. You can journal about it later.' He winked. 'Now, saddle up.'

... ride the snake to the...

Blaise in the lead, we clambered to the brow of the nearest *kopje*, cautious to stay below the skyline.

'In the shade. Two o'clock. Such irony. Friend and foe finding shelter under the same tree. They've stopped at the one we were under earlier. Lazy buggers. I reckon they believe their mates have it squared away. They're having a siesta.'

'Aren't they in for a surprise.'

... you'll follow me... never...

We crawled to a safer position, obscured by larger granite boulders, and checked out the movements of our guerrilla friends.

'We should change tack and head north. Put some distance between them and us. Stay on the rocks, make it harder for them. A shift in direction might throw them. What do you think?'

'Sounds like a plan, Bar. But we shouldn't wait. It won't be too long before they cotton on.'

I caught Blaise's eye. 'What's up?'

'I – ah – I never thought you had that in you. Thanks for what you've done.'

'Before I get teary,' I said, 'let's head for the hills.'

He smiled, reaching towards me. I stretched my arm out and grabbed his hand. As I pulled him to his feet, he recoiled.

'Something wrong?'

'It's my shoulder. That hit on the terr has caused some damage.'

'Not having much luck, are you?'

'We make our own. We're still alive, aren't we? Your ankle's a case in point. Madame Fortuna favours the bold.'

'Or reckless. I hope she's not listening. She can still unfavour us.'

'You might be bright and all, Baron, but sod the Fates. We shape our own destiny. *Salvation lies within*.'

'Careful, Blaise, that your pride doesn't interfere with good sense. For now, let's put Ms Chance behind us.'

'I'll try,' he said. 'Just have to pull my head in, grin and endure.'

'Get a move on, then. I've no desire to dine with the devil for longer than we must.'

'True. We're running out of very long spoons.'

A shout floated on the light afternoon breeze.

Our enemies must have grasped that their plans had gone awry, for they emerged from the shade and pressed forward in our general direction.

'Can you hang on?'

'You'd better believe it. Worry about your ankle. I'll be fine.'

Once more we legged it, this time trekking to the north and the shimmering Mana Pools that beckoned to us in the settling afternoon haze.

... ride the snake... ride to the lake...

PLEXUS

THE SUN IDLED YET again towards its distant darkening horizon.

No human-made timepiece can replicate it.

From the summit of the highest rocky granite *kopje,* we gazed out to an undulating stretch of the unfurling Zambezi River.

'See that large pool over there? I'm sure that's where the fabled Mana Pools' sequence starts,' I said. 'I'll put money on it.'

'You won't need to.'

Entranced, we savoured the waning vista.

'Magical. Better than a Narnian landscape,' said Blaise.

'Much more than that.'

Blaise and I stood at the entrance to another realm, where the membrane between the heavens and earth appeared diaphanous.

The sun, ever the hegemon, contrived to distil muscular, bent shadows across the river's basin.

Can anything twisted be straightened? Should we seek to uncoil such things?

Could the crooked signal genius and be natural in its own right? Was deformity a sign of holiness?

Does God draw straight with cursive lines?

'You must have accumulated a tidy sum of disposable income by now with answers to all those sixty-four-thousand-dollar questions. So, here's another. Let's have it. Give me chapter and verse on this place?'

Trust Blaise to mix his metaphors.

'Is that a challenge?'

'Sure is.'

'The Mana Pools are a sanctuary of islands, sandbanks, and natural waterways, flanked by flora, and diverse fauna to match. Brilliant for tourists. Not that there're many these days.'

'Is that the best you can do? That's just a pass for you.'

'It boasts large concentrations of hippo, crocodile, elephant, and buffalo. Not to mention lion and leopard. Wild dog, too. Along with your friend, the hyena.'

'No surprises yet. Are you gonna tell me about the birds?'

'You'd better believe it. This place is a twitchers' paradise with 300-plus aquatic species. Banded snake eagles, herons, bee-eaters and the fabled falcon, the bateleur, nest here –'

Blaise interrupted. 'What about the fish?'

'The most sought-after is the elusive and dangerous tiger fish. African pike, barbel, yellow fish and bream are abundant here as well. Satisfied yet?'

'You are a veritable Encyclopaedia Baronica! How do you remember that stuff?' he said, shaking his head. 'I find it hard to recall what I read yesterday.'

'Beneath my cool exterior, I'm a nerd. I have an eidetic memory and a voracious appetite for reading in the pursuit of knowledge.'

'Yeah, whatever.'

Ouma explained it differently. I recalled her telling me, 'Baron, you're a precocious, know-it-all smart arse.'

We kept on downwards to the Mana Pools floodplain, checking our rear for our hunters, but of them there was no sign.

... ride the snake (he's long... seven miles) to the ancient lake...

The landscape transformed as we descended.

Gone was the dry, thirst-crazed scrubland of the higher lands, replaced by a plexus of miombo woodlands and apple-ringed acacia trees, dotted on one of Africa's pristine wetland canvases.

The terrain grew muddier underfoot and the air clammier on the skin and nose, ripening to petrichor.

Plum-coloured clouds reappeared from their hideaway in the hills, prologue to a rhapsody of howling wind, deep growls of thunder and ecstatic zithers, jagged shocks of ivory white in the graphite sky, which forked to copulate with the virgin ground – thunderous percussions that heralded their warning too late.

... waiting for the summer rain... yeah...

Large droplets tap-danced downwards, their footprints rustling on the hopeful earth. Nudged by the gusting wind, the rain's tempo pulsed soft-shoe shuffles, swept up in wild, bucking pullbacks one moment, and diagonal time-steps the next.

Caught out in the open, we lay flat, swallowed by the gale and rain, beguiled by their vaudeville performance.

In the denouement, the storm lost its rhythm. Russet clouds dissolved, replaced by a bone-white light as the sun's late-afternoon rays illuminated a once more empty sky.

Exhausted and drenched, we searched for a shielded space to rest before nightfall.

... a visit to...

We sank to our knees in the tall grass.

'How about there?' Blaise nodded.

I looked in the same direction as his gaze. Only when the sun nuzzled the horizon did we drift towards the spot, vigilant and watchful.

Blaise's instincts had been on point. We had chanced upon a secluded glade and, detecting no recent spoor, we concealed ourselves and bunkered down for the night.

I made Blaise as comfortable as I could. He sat with his back propped against a tired tree trunk, arguing the toss.

'Bar, no need to mother me.'

'Blazer, I've got it covered. You're banged up and require time to recover. It won't take long, I promise,' I said, shooting him a grin. 'Then I'll help with those injuries. I should just check our location for an exit strategy and then assess the water quality. The brackish and unfiltered stuff we've had to drink until now is giving my mouth the itch.'

'I'm not helpless. I can and want to do something. For the record, I sit here under protest.'

'Noted, little brother. Let the record show that Blaise – in name and deed – doth protest too much.'

'Let it also show that Baron – in name and deed – doth control too much.'

We held each other's gaze.

'I – ah, I won't take long. Try not to go anywhere, okay?'

'Don't worry, big brother, zero degrees of separation from now on. That much I can promise.'

My first impression of the water source was positive. With the recent downpour, which had caught us out in the open, the waterhole had overflowed to other areas, with no evidence of stagnation.

No traces of mosquitoes or animal faeces either.

'What gives, *Bru*? Are you making any progress?' Blaise called out to me from his makeshift throne.

'Just checking for threatening wildlife.'

'What kind of wildlife?'

'Crocs and hippos. *Snakes.*'

'I thought we'd cleared it in the first sweep of the space. No indications, hey?'

'With wild animals, you can't be too sure. Their behaviour is unpredictable. Plus, this place is ideal for hippos. During the day, they stay in the water or mud, but at dusk, they emerge to graze. And they roam up to 10 clicks from their watery home. Hey B, guess what time it is?'

'Feeding time? Yeah, I'm hungry, *Boet.* Forget hippos.'

'Don't you want to hear more about our semi-aquatic neighbours?'

'Nah, but you're gonna tell me anyway, aren't you? *Hippos 101.* Get on with it then, Professor B.'

'The *Professor* tag's unsuitable. Pretentious. Just call me *Nobody.*'

'What-ya mean, *Nobody?*'

'Well, *Nobody's perfect…*'

'I have a better name for you.'

'I'm listening…'

'How about *Red?*' Blaise said.

'As in *Big Red? Red Adair?*'

'No cigar. With your head of coppery hair, *Big-Headed Red* could be the one… or *Woolly-Haired Red,*' he laughed. 'With that dirt face of yours, *Ochre Red* might be a better choice.'

'You're not thinking of *Red Riding Hood?* Or *Little Red Rooster?*'

'Hold that thought. However, it's not what someone calls you that's important, it's what you respond to.'

'Aren't you just the oracle?'

'Anything you can do…'

'*Ja-well,* no-fine. You gonna tell me?'

'I should put you out of your misery, but I'm enjoying your suspense. I was thinking of an eponymous name: *Red Baron.*'

'Of von Richthofen fame?'

'The same.'

'What can you tell me about him, Master-Blaster?'

'Much more than you think, Baasboy Baron.'

'Come on, then.'

'Serious? Or are you just stringing me along?'

'Apart from the fact that he was a German fighter pilot in World War One, I have scant knowledge about Manfred. Enlighten me, oh guru-man.'

'Credited with over 80 combat victories by the last year of the war in 1918, MVR was the ace-of-aces, a national hero in Germany, feared and respected, by comrades and enemies alike.'

'And? Get to the exciting part.'

'The term *baron* in German is *freiherr*, meaning *free lord*. And because Von R flew a crimson plane, he became known as the Red Baron.'

'I see now why you think *Red* is a suitable nickname. *Red Lord.* The lord bit appeals to me. *Red Nkosi.* I like that. I must share traits with the great man himself. It must be his legendary and heroic status. His red mettle. So, brains hide somewhere in that brawn of yours,' I said.

'Believe it or not, you don't have the monopoly on those genes. I've always been interested in World War One since many of our family fought and died in that Armageddon – at Delville Wood, the Somme and Ypres.'

'Why the fascination with von Richthofen?'

'A brilliant tactician and a law unto himself, Von R challenged the accepted practices and norms of the time,' Blaise said. 'He revolution-ised air warfare and pushed the boundaries. Courageous and innova-tive, he romanticised aerial combat with colour and carnival. The flying circus. A real trailblazer. A man after my heart.'

'That says something about you, rather than me. *Red* should be your nickname. You also share that red hair gene.'

'Big brother, here's the thing. Von R was distant and unemo-tional, one who saw through the deeds of others. Sound familiar?' he said, chuckling.

'Are you suggesting I'm detached? Dispassionate?'

'Baron, you're sharp enough to know it's true. Admit it. You have trouble letting go, and it's a trait I admire in you. Sometimes I wish I could keep tighter control like you.'

'The events of the day suggest otherwise. Look at them.' I held up both hands. 'Red-handed. Black-hearted. That's the truth.'

Silence, our old companion, sat between us.

'You have that passion, that potential for destruction. So what? You lost it for an instant. What does that prove?'

'It worries me that what I did left me exhilarated. On a high. If being in the moment means that, I'd rather stay rational,' I said. 'Play in the shadows and the shadows play with you.'

'We all have a dark side, Baron. We battle to restrain our serpents, yet they come out to play under the right circumstances.'

'Is that meant to make me feel better?'

'No, Baron, it's supposed to make you feel human. What you did was a natural response in an extraordinary situation.'

'It didn't feel natural. I should have been able to control myself. And if there's a next time, am I going to repeat the same thing? Does it get easier?' I said. 'And if I do, will I enjoy it more or less?'

'Bar, life is messy. We survive in the cracks of the canvas. We must live with ourselves and our serpents, and the decisions we take. It's what we learn along the way and how we move forward. We could stay trapped in our guilt, or forgive ourselves and seek grace, and redemption,' Blaise said. 'By living in the present, we can atone. As you, yourself, showed me earlier.'

'I suppose it doesn't help that the Red Baron died in aerial combat just before the war ended, does it?' I said.

'There's a black irony in that.'

Blaise was spot on. While we may not escape our serpents, we can restrain them if we know what triggers them.

There was a lot more to discover about Blaise. And the more I was prepared to learn about him, the more I was learning about myself.

The gloom began its slow ascent.

Blaise, ever the charmer, broke the spell. 'If I recall, before we went off on a tangent, you were telling me about hippos. Do your worst. I can handle it.'

'You'll be grateful one day, *Bru*. Hippos. River horses. Did you know that while they resemble pigs, their closest living relatives are whales and porpoises?'

'No-ways. You're having me on.'

'No, I promise. A hippo is a crossbreed of both land and sea creatures. The locals call it *imvubu*: a blended beast, undecided about whether to be an elephant, a rhino or a crocodile.'

'A devil's brew, by the looks of it.'

'Hippos are unpredictable. Lazy loafers, they are prone to bouts of inexplicable aggression, liable to vicious unprovoked attacks from the water's depths. And despite their stocky shape and stubby legs, they're capable of high-speed sprinting on land and underwater over short distances. So, Mr Rugby, even you have your betters. If you get between *imvubu* and its territorial waters, or if it thinks you're threatening its calves, or if it just takes exception to your ugly rugby face, it can attack.'

'Guess who I look like, twin brother of mine? But I'll keep that in mind the next time I go *bundu*-bashing or have a desire to tackle or ride a hippo, or invite it to morning tea.'

'Hippo attacks account for the most human deaths on the continent.'

'You mean apart from humans killing other humans?'

For a moment, we held each other's gaze. I looked past and above Blaise, to the descending shroud of darkness. 'I... ah... that's enough sermonising for now.'

'Agreed. No more. You're scaring the shit out-ta me.'

'Sorry.'

'Thanks for making me feel so much better,' Blaise said. 'Do you think we're safe here?'

I stifled a laugh. 'Chill, baby brother. I reckon so. I'm pulling your leg. No territorial markings here. No signs of hippos or crocs.'

'Leave the crocs, please. And snakes. Perhaps another time,' Blaise said.

'Promise. I'll prep the water and we can check out the battle wounds.'

... in need of some hand...

I could at least filter our water, given its plentiful availability. First, I washed my bloodstained hands.

A little water clears me... how easy...

'Time to test my primitive purification process.'

With my hankie I created a sieve over the mouth of one of our bottles and, using the other, filtered the waterhole water, collected from as deep as I could reach.

Success. Muddy residue appeared in the hankie stretched over the bottleneck.

Hell is murky.

'How's that shoulder?'

'A little sore.'

That meant little, as my brother had a high pain threshold.

'It seemed to pop out and back in.'

'Let me check the open wounds, then we'll look at that dislocation.'

'Is that necessary?'

'Humour me.'

Blaise's shoulder wound was still suppurating, but the dispelling of pus was a positive. There was no malodour either. I shook my head.

'What's the matter?'

'Don't stress. It looks fine. I'm gobsmacked. That poultice sure did the trick. We're in a holding pattern with it, though. You need professional help.'

'So you keep telling me,' he said.

'Smart arse.' I couldn't help but smile as I cleaned the wound and repacked it with what remained of the flame lily *muti*, making a mental note to find more, and strapped it back into place.

'Cheers, big ears,' Blaise said. 'Feels good.'

'For you, I ride the bull.'

'More like talk the bull-sh –'

I cut him off. 'Let's check out your head.'

'Forever damaged, I'm afraid.'

'No arguments from me. The first time we've agreed on something serious,' I said. 'I'm getting worried.'

'Ha! The master of the riposte.'

I unfolded the bloodied scarf from around Blaise's head. While the wound was clear, the glass shard had shifted, and blood trickled from the gash.

Dare I risk removing it?

'Howzit going there?'

'We can remove it, but it might prompt a torrent of blood. It's shifted, so that's not doing us any favours. The cut looks clean and free of infection. What do you think?'

'Bar, you've got me this far. I trust your judgement,' he said, grinning up at me.

'I'm glad you have confidence in me.' I wasn't sure if I deserved such confidence, but on this thought, I remained silent.

'*Ag*, on second thoughts, take it out. I'm done with foreign bodies.'

'You certain?'

Blaise nodded and said, 'Make sharp, before I change my mind.'

I tore two strips of material from his shrinking jumper sleeve. They'd have to do as a pressure bandage. I subjected the water to bucolic purification through my sieve-like container.

Blaise lay bolstered by the backpack. I thrust the water bottle into his hand. 'Tilt your head. Okay, give me the water.'

I flushed the wound using my left hand, lobbed the bottle to my brother with a 'here!' and, rubbing my fingers together, I grabbed the shard of glass with my right thumb and forefinger and plucked it out on the second try. I thrust the folded pieces of shirt strips onto the wound and pressed as hard as I could.

'*Ooi!*'

'Don't be such a whinger. You've taken a shot in the left shoulder, you've dislocated the right one, and you're having a grizzle over a tiny piece of glass.'

He laughed. 'Yeah, I agree. Pathetic.'

'Here. A souvenir.' I tossed him the glass fragment. It couldn't have been longer than the thickness of two fingers.

Blaise rolled it between his thumb and forefinger. 'Thanks. Hardly worth all the worry, now that I look at it.'

'*Boet*, fear doesn't come from the thing itself, but from our thoughts of it. And that we can control. It's all in the mind, Blazer...'

'Or in the head. If I didn't know any better, I'd say you're becoming wise.'

'I'll take that as a compliment.'

... look into your eyes...

I strapped the scarf around his head. 'All done, pretty boy,' I pronounced. He looked like a revolutionary. Che Guevara sprang to mind.

'*A luta continua*,' I said.

Blaise bore a confused expression on his face. 'A *luta* who?'

'*The struggle continues...* but victory is assured,' I intoned. 'You know, the maxim of the freedom movements in Africa?'

Blaise eyed me as though I had beamed down from the *Enterprise*.

'Forget about it, *Bru*. It's not serious. I'm just being my usual smart arse self.'

'We seem to agree with each other more and more, hey?' he said, laughing. 'I'm worried.'

'The age of miracles and wonders continues.'

'Believe it or not, I am interested in what those words mean. Beyond this conflict, we will need to sit down and look at the world from our enemy's perspective, to resolve our differences. We share a common homeland, and humanity. *Ubuntu*, isn't it?'

'O-kay,' I managed. 'Uncanny. That's what Thumbeza said to me.'

'There you go. We're not so opposed, are we?'

'Who would have thought? *A luta continua*, then. Portuguese for *the struggle continues*. A maxim popularised by Che Guevara and his ilk.'

'Che Guevara?'

'He was a South American revolutionary, a mate of Castro's. A renaissance man by all reports – author, doctor, intellectual, idealist, Marxist and diplomat. A disestablishment and counter-cultural symbol.'

'Bit like you,' Blaise laughed. 'Doesn't Mum call you a disestablishmentarian?'

'I'm not in the same class. CG polarised opinions. Reviled or revered. Rebel or rogue. Executioner, saviour, martyr, murderer.'

'Probably he was a blend of all those things.'

'True. A political crusader, he challenged the ruling elites around the world irrespective of ideology. A voice of and for the people. Sadly, like most idealists, he died for his principles, executed by those who feared him.'

'And *a luta continua*... the struggle continues?'

'*Ja-well*, the word *luta* suggests *fight* more than *struggle*. It means to fight for your rights, to fight for a better world, for your goals in life. It has a powerful message of asserting yourself, never giving up on your dreams.'

'*A luta continua*. Seems like a noble pursuit to me,' Blaise said.

'Can't argue with that. Where we may disagree are in the methods used to achieve those dreams and how we combine our different ideas so all can benefit.'

'Often we don't have any choice.'

'We always have a choice,' I said. 'Not choosing is still a choice.'

Blaise grinned. 'I'm choosing not to respond.'

... lost in a wilderness...

'Now for the other shoulder.'

Blaise sighed, but leant over to make it easier for me. I used my hands to prod and press for any abnormalities. 'Rate the pain out of ten.'

'Four or five. It's centred around the shoulder joint.'

'Anything along the arm?'

'Nah, I'm fine. Promise.'

'Any numbness?'

'Baron, stop stressing me out,' Blaise said. 'Look, I can move my arm.' He lifted it up and then down. 'It's stiff with a dull pain, but I'll be okay.'

'No visible signs of dislocation or distension.'

'As I said before, I think it popped out and in without too much damage done.'

'So you did. You're one fortunate soul who's used up another of your nine lives. What's that now? Five? Four?' I said.

'Lost count.'

'That's no lie. Take the pressure off. Here, let me help you fashion a sling using the bottom of your jumper.' I helped him shape a sling of sorts. 'Rest and support it, at least until tomorrow.'

'Thanks. What would I do without you?'

'Live an uncomplicated life,' I shot back.

'Ah, to live, that's enough for now.'

... waiting... waiting... yeah...

The diffident moon replaced the imperious sun. He had abandoned politics for the night, and retreated to the safety of his chambers.

Our minds turned to a subject that was the most significant of all, beyond politics, ethics, religion, philosophy and even rugby; that which occupies the minds of young men most of the time.

'Let's talk about something more serious,' Blaise said. '*Food.* I'm ravenous. Any ideas? What are we going to eat?'

'I've had my eye out for wild fig trees or bush thorn, but I've not seen any yet.'

I tried to recall anything else about bush food apart from the figs and bush thorn fruit, but details eluded me.

'Bar, aren't they mopane trees?' Blaise said, pointing.

'Yeah, so what?'

'They should have a supply of *mashonja.*'

'Wait... that's a Shona word for... ah...'

'Something you don't know.'

'Okay, you win. So, Mr Mashonja-Man...'

'If you womble over to them, Bar, you should be able to collect some *mashonja*. Mopane worms. You can't miss them, even in the dark. They're large, with colourful spiky stripes like a Zulu caftan, and green underbellies. I'd like to help you, but at your insistence, my injuries make it nigh impossible.'

'How convenient, and oh-so-well played.'

'I am a brilliant strategist and tactician. Anyone who out-Barons Baron the Red must be amaze-balls...'

'Okay, okay. Don't get too carried away. Ah, you're expecting me to eat these... er... delicacies?' I asked. 'Seriously?'

'Bar, where's your sense of adventure, man? They're *lekker.*'

'When did you gain a taste for, um, maggots?'

'*Butterflies*, if you don't mind. *Mopane* translates as *butterfly*. I went on a school excursion to the local markets in Salisbury, and we had some mopane worms as a snack. Delicious.'

'What do they taste like?' I asked. 'Please don't say *chicken*.'

'No, Master. They taste like *biltong*.'

'Well, that can't be too bad. I rather like *biltong*.'

I headed off to the mopane trees and checked out their branches. Blaise had not been wrong. Large numbers of plump multi-coloured caterpillars, rather than worms, were eating their coloured greens – the distinctive butterfly-shaped leaves – as they should.

Cherry picking. Mashonja picking didn't do it for me.

I returned to our hideaway and chucked a pile of them on the ground. They wriggled and squirmed in the rusty afterglow of the moon.

'You expect me to chew on these... ah... grubs?'

'Well done, *bwana* Baron,' Blaise said, trying not to laugh. 'Part One of *Mopane Worms 101* is complete. Are you ready for Part Two?'

'Does it matter whether I am?'

'No. Sit. Listen. Learn. Comfortable? Good. Mopane worms are not worms. They're caterpillars, the larvae of the Emperor Moth to which the mopane tree is host.'

'I thought they didn't look like worms. I'm glad you've cleared up that confusion. It makes a massive difference.'

'The best time to harvest them is when they are at maximum plumpness,' he said, 'later in their larval stage. So, well done. Your mopane worm hunting skills are unparalleled. You're a natural.'

Blaise was enjoying himself.

What goes around...

'I'm trying to work out how you know so much about mopane worms.'

'Baron, you don't know heaps about me.'

'Isn't that the truth?'

'Stop interrupting, if it's not too much trouble?' he said, a gleam in his eyes.

'It is, but go on.'

'All right then. *Mashonja* packs a protein punch with good doses of iron and calcium.'

'Obviously, I need them as a staple.'

'A common way to enjoy them is to squeeze out the goo, dry and then fry them with tomatoes, peanuts, chillies, onions, not forgetting garlic. You can add them to stew or boil to soften them up. Or eat them dried. The husks make for a tasty *hors d'oeuvre*. Unfortunately, these gastronomic and culinary variations are not available on the menu this evening.'

'So, Chef André, what do you propose?'

'Aah, *Monsieur*,' Blaise said, smacking his lips and blowing a kiss in my general direction, 'I recommend that while they are less tasty when fresh, we eat them raw from the tree, as God intended.'

And this was Africa's response to escargot? *Forget* hors d'oeuvres. *Eating worms would mean* hors de combat.

'So, ah, how do I eat... it?' I held a squirming caterpillar between thumb and forefinger.

'I grab it by the head, and bite it off from there...' His voice trailed off.

I tried not to gag.

'Like eating prawns. Here, let me show you.' He bit one worm at the head and chewed. 'Or you can eat it whole, or just swallow...'

I didn't hear the rest as my attention focused elsewhere.

'I'm not hungry anymore.'

'Come on, Bar. Tuck in!'

Let the die be cast. *Alea iacta est.* I closed my eyes, said a prayer, offering it up to the holy souls in purgatory, and thought of Ma's home-made almond tart.

Ave Caesar, morituri te salutant. Those about to die salute you.

I bit, nibbled, and swallowed with a water chaser.

Grimace. Swallow. Try not to puke. Repeat.

Nothing like biltong. More akin to moist beach sand. Or fibrous muesli.

No, on second thoughts, tastier and chewier than organic muesli.

I looked over at Blaise. Smile on face, he chomped with enthusiastic vigour.

Man, was he weird.

He would eat the lion's share of the worm harvest, and that was fine by me. More disconcerting was his unrestrained enjoyment in eating them. But then I recalled him chomping on flying ants and *shongololos* when he was much younger. I waited for him to say, 'Please, *Bwana*, can I have some more?' but he didn't, saving me a trip into the heart of African darkness in search of more hanging bugs.

A restaurant at the Vic Falls – I forget its name – awards a certificate to anyone who has eaten at least one mopane worm. I'd earned at least one of those, if not a medal, after gnawing my way through a half dozen twitching maggots.

Rhodesia's highest military honour. For conspicuous gallantry in perilous conditions, above and beyond the call of duty: the Grand Cross of Valour.

... weird scenes inside...

SEEK-AND-HIDE

I WAS FRETFUL AND idle, my mind awhirl, mired in brazen doubts as fears and numbness were easing. The shock and revulsion of the entire experience tightened.

Blaise had passed out, curled up in the undergrowth. Unlike me, who let the lilies fester, he had the knack of tuning out, oblivious to those putrefying lilies.

Despite the dwindling light, I whipped out my journal, compelled by a hard-wired faculty beyond my conscious understanding, and wrote.

THURSDAY, 07 SEPTEMBER

How things have changed in the space of twenty-four hours. Blaise is recovering, for which I have no plausible explanation. I thought I'd lost him. Had it been his steely resolve or an inexplicable factor at play?

I'm numbed by the horror of the experience.

A dissolving lacerated face, spurting blood over me, swam before my eyes.

Death is part of the human package, but my savagery to bring it about lies beyond my ability to fathom.

This was a thinking, feeling, living human being.

Like me.

How could it be that our views were at opposite ends of the spectrum?

Clashing kudus.

Could he have been just a pawn, sacrificed in a greater political game?

Or succumbed to the wiles of ideological, revolutionary machination?

'A luta continua.'

Or was he fighting for a better life for his people, his family, himself?

'Minha luta continua.'

Am I any different, caught up in my search, my struggle, conditioned by my jaundiced worldview?

'Minha busca continua.'

I closed my eyes to shut out his bloody visage.

It persisted.

I clutch a bloodied rock, smashing into a confused and terrified face.

Waves of rising emotion throb in my head, awash in a sea of redness.

Anger in my intent. Exhilaration and energy in its execution. Guilt in my complicity. Fear my heart's compass can no longer discern North.

Disgust and shame in what I have done.

My hands and heart are forever tainted.

Adrift in a bloodied river, propelled by its unrelenting current, I flounder between the near bank of grace and the far shore of dis-grace.

I'm imprisoned in my theatre of cruelty, a 'jet of blood' surging from my fingers.

Antonin Artaud leapt into my head, uninvited.

I recalled my drama teacher's impassioned words on Artaud, delivered in his distinctive Stoke-on-Trent dialect.

'Now, lads,' Mr Evans would say. 'Huddle up. Here's the thing. For Artaud, theatre is life, *yeah*? It doesn't imitate life – 'tis that life at a deeper level. T' be effective, it must mirror the soul. Conventional theatrical notions are inadequate t' explore deep-rooted human impulses. *Bloody 'ell!* It's under the skin, well beyond words in the subconscious. It has t' be primal, visceral, symbolic, *yeah*? Artaud's theatre lances that boil of innate fear, forcing viewers to glimpse the truth mirrored in their own natures without the superficial constraints of civility. By plunging the depths of the human psyche, Artaud takes us on a spiritual and therapeutic journey to expose the dark recesses of the soul. His is a theatre of a particular cruelty, aiming to be kind.'

Yeah, that drama class was always entertaining...

> *I plumbed the depths of myself today to the riptide beneath – and had a foretaste of what I was – and I'm not sure I liked what I found.*
>
> *I am learning new things about myself, and it's hard to stomach. I'm a mongrel, a wastelander's blood coursing through my veins.*
>
> *Apart from a hooligan, head stacked with termite-eaten straw, I am less than a dust mite, delighting not in the infirmity and frailty of what I am.*
>
> *Between what I am and what I believe I am... falls the shade.*
>
> *Born with a snake in my mouth, it extends around my heart.*
>
> *Still ensnared in the dark and tangled woods beyond the city gates, predators lurk within and hunt me from without.*
>
> *What further chaos will tomorrow bring?*

I shut my journal, and lay on my back, searching the silky velvet night sky with its pincushion stars. The sun had made its escape, now a non-presence after its diurnal round.

A.W.O.L. Absent without leaving.

To be trapped in the dark satanic mills of my mind in the night's depths was confronting, and chilling. I had no way of switching off, my thoughts coiled in an *inyoka*-spectre's suffocating and seductive embrace.

... the snake... he's old... ancient... his skin so cold...

Blaise stirred beside me.

'Hey, Baron. I have a question.'

That's where it began.

With Blaise, that was where it always started: a throwaway line, an impromptu remark, an uncomplicated and innocuous statement.

I've tried, over the years, to piece together the conversations that followed on that night, but memory is a finicky and fickle devil, a mist that plays seek-and-hide in the mountain valleys on a crisp but sunny winter's morning. Just when it gets on your nerves, it scurries away, searching for the lowest and most impenetrable valley bottoms where it lurks until the darkness signals for it to emerge once more.

Well-versed in the art of disguise and non-compliance, my memories hasten into the shadowy recesses of my unconscious mind to rematerialise, each time a new re-remembering and imaginative re-enactment.

'I thought you were asleep.'

'Can't. My mind's a mess. It won't switch off.'

'Likewise.'

'I'm uncertain where to start, or how to verbalise it.'

'C'mon,' I said. 'Spill. You know it's all right to share anything with me.'

'Can I, Baron? You're often dismissive,' he said. His words wasp-stung me. 'Promise you'll listen with an open mind?'

There it was again: the implication I was trapped by those oft-referred-to shackles of intellectual pride. I was overdue a dose of hubris and my brother had delivered it.

With my right arm raised, pinkie and thumb touching, and three middle fingers elevated, I saluted. 'Scout's honour.'

'I've been trying to make sense of it all since we plummeted out of the sky,' he said, searching for the right words. 'How do I understand? I'm confused.'

Silence descended on the evening carnival as it hung on every word.

I lifted my head and looked into my brother's probing eyes.

'Me too.'

'You're not just saying that to make me feel better? You have an answer for everything.' He spoke it without a whisper of irony and contempt, so I let it slide.

'From my perspective, the effects of evil are exponential. Why do people suffer? Those passengers at the crash site. Why children? Can you please enlighten me?'

Mother and child with horror-struck expressions torn from the *Hunyani's* fuselage, Milo the teddy bear, and the small blonde-haired boy's pale, lifeless bloodied face swam into my mind.

'Blaise, you're touching on perplexing universal and existential issues with no definitive solutions,' I said. 'Like you, I'm trying to make sense of what happened, and my actions.'

'That doesn't help me understand, Bar.'

'That's the whole point. Perhaps we're not meant to. The questions we ask are more important than the answers we construct.'

Blaise looked bemused. 'What do you mean by that?'

'Well, you're bothered because it's not fair that people suffer. You're worried about evil and from where it springs. *As you should.* Our experiences would outrage anyone with a speck of moral sensitivity. And you have every right to question. Like you, I'm struggling to understand human action here,' I said. 'And my own feelings and behaviour.' I took a deep breath. 'Each generation has confronted its own peculiar serpents. Ours is no different. We're still coming to terms with them.'

'Perhaps the serpents are blessings in disguise?'

'Next you'll tell me that, at a deeper level, evil things are crying out to us for understanding.'

'Isn't that's the point?' Blaise said. 'It's difficult to speak about the issues with any certainty. We're still in the dark, like most reasonable people throughout history, by the looks of it.'

'Blaise, if I can play devil's advocate for a moment. What if we found an adequate explanation? Would we be any better off? What if we solved the mysteries of the universe?'

'What do you mean, Bar? You're muddying the waters.'

'No. Think for a minute. Life is a search for meaning. Self-understanding. Finding our place in the world. The challenge is figuring it out for ourselves. What if we had ready-made answers? What's left? There are reasons why we forget to remember.'

'Eternal recurrence. I see your point. But don't we need certainties?'

'We might crave them, but do we need them? Wouldn't we be tempted to endorse suffering and evil if we could account for them? To my mind, worse than people suffering would be others watching, unmoved.'

'Why so?'

'We'd no longer be empathetic to the pleas for help because we'd brush off suffering as part of our rationale for explaining the complexity of life.'

Blaise thought for a moment.

'So, once we have a plausible explanation, then pain, misfortune and wickedness aren't so bad anymore? We could tolerate suffering if we understood why it was happening? That's a massive call, Baron!'

'If we could make sense of the big questions – if we could rationalise tragedy, suffering, evil, death – we'd be less inclined to be horrified. And less likely to act.'

There was another pause.

'No, Baron. I don't agree. It's wiser to seek answers than not to.'

'What I'm trying to say, Blazer, is we must be careful not to strait-jacket ourselves with ironclad answers.'

'You have a print of Brueghel's *Fall of Icarus* on your bedroom wall. What does it suggest about suffering in the grand scheme of things?'

'That life goes on, untroubled?'

'That too. But also people are unreflective, uncaring and don't give a shit, preoccupied with their own little selfish lives, regardless of whether they have answers,' Blaise said. 'Unless it affects them on a personal level.'

'But many do care, and act on injustice regardless of answers,' I countered. 'That's the nature of the human beast. Altruism and selfishness together. A blending of binaries.'

'I don't buy that view for a single moment. Do we not owe it to ourselves as a species to keep the debate front and centre? Fight to eradicate suffering?' Blaise said. 'Isn't this struggle an atonement, a purging, even a means to ward off greater harm?'

Blaise took a breath and, before I could interject, continued. 'I concede that if we reduce the discussion to the academic and develop a credible theory, then we're in danger of it becoming a philosophical navel-gaze that helps no one.'

'The cycle repeats itself, each generation shaping its own explanation for the same age-old problem.' As an afterthought, I added, 'We'll never find a satisfying answer, apart from the cumulative wisdom of the ages. Should we not control what we can?'

'That doesn't imply we shouldn't search for adequate explanations... and solutions, hey? The unexamined life is not worth living, is it?' Blaise had the bit between his teeth. He was at full tilt. 'It also doesn't mean that we would tolerate shattered lives,' he said. 'Should our thinking not inform our worldview and our actions? Surely, the ways a particular culture shapes values and beliefs have an impact?'

'But that's why it's important to engage with people different from ourselves. For example, African wisdom suggests pain is inevitable, while suffering is a choice. It begs the question, hey?'

'What question? That hurt, agony and distress are figments of our imagination?'

'Yes, and no. Rather, we should seek to understand before being understood. Our racist and apartheid way of life is, at its heart, a greater offence.'

'That's an even bigger call, given what we've experienced in recent days.'

'Maybe. But the unlived life is also not worth examining,' I said. 'We will remain bothered by evil, pain and suffering as long as the burning questions remain; and if we can imagine ourselves in the shoes of those who oppose us, that should motivate and inspire us to address them, and change.'

Blaise cut me off. 'Aren't we inclined towards the dark side? At worst, are we not conflicted between grace and desire, between *serenity* and *ego*?'

'I get what you say. I mean, I beat someone to death earlier, *with a sharp rock*. And even found it exhilarating.' My voice choked to silence. 'What person does that? What does that say about Me? Does that make me evil, or my act evil? Can we distinguish between the two? How do I live with my actions?'

Blaise shook his head.

It was my turn to get animated. 'I'm trying not to dwell on it, but it's a rabid baboon shrieking in my brain, assaulting the bastions of my sensibility. How do I resolve what I've done? And where does my Christian faith fit into this? I must come to terms with myself to live a meaningful life.'

'I also killed a man today, but I'd do it again. It was self-defence – *him* or *you*. Or *me*. Same difference. I'm able to justify that. Do you imagine

I feel comfortable about it?'

There was a tense silence between us as we wrestled with the complexities.

At last, Blaise spoke. 'I'm sick at heart about it. It's a burrowing serpent, gnawing away at my soul...'

I put my arm around his shoulders and said, 'I know what you mean.'

'Careful with that shoulder.'

'Whoops. Sorry.'

'As you should be.'

The greasy silence closed in on us.

Blaise breached that stillness once more. 'Our decisions have spiritual and psychological consequences, but isn't that the reality of the situation? The nature of the beast?'

'This *nature of the beast* stuff. Is there even such a thing? We've been tossing those phrases around, haven't we?'

Blaise weighed his words. 'We can be more purposeful in word and action. Perhaps it cuts to the heart of what we are as humans. At times we react, at times we respond. We don't and can't always act with a pure conscience. The world is not packaged for our convenience. We live in the shade, so to speak. Light casts lengthy and dark shadows.'

... came to a door...

A cloth wiped clean the thin film of dust from my eyes, and through and beyond I glimpsed, for the first time, the fire of my brother's spirit, the energy of his soul, infinity composed in his heart.

'Most actions involve compromises. Sometimes it's the lesser of evils. Often an action results in being tainted by that same evil,' he said. 'Doing nothing can be as bad as doing something wrong.'

'Wow. Where did all that come from?'

'Bar, I might be a footy-head, but I'm not a total hooligan. Carwyn James, one of the great Welsh philosopher-rugby coaches, observed that a humane way of life underpins the game at every level. Mutual respect is key. *Better people make better rugby players.* I find it difficult to disagree with him.'

We unlocked horns.

'Perhaps we can blend our views to reach an answer beyond the entrenched positions.'

'How?'

'Pain... suffering is inescapable. We should never shy away from asking tough questions to uncover their meaning, but always ensure our responses are compassionate. We don't need unequivocal answers, just a personal response.'

'That makes sense. Although I'd add that our responses need to be measured and flexible.'

'How we inform those responses is a different matter. But acting in good faith will give us a chance.'

Blaise stifled a yawn. 'We might save that discussion for another time. Won't we?'

'It's just getting interesting. B-man, you can't leave me hanging.'

'All that talk's made me tired.' He stretched his arms, turned his back, curled up and played at sleeping.

Just like that.

In an instant, I detected his even deep breathing.

I sat staring off into the blackness. I had a feeling it was gazing back.

... lost...

UP-RIVER

... he paid a visit to his brother...

BLAISE'S VOICE ECHOED FROM a distance.

'Bar-on. Bar-on!' it sang. My foot shook.

'Leave me alone. I'm trying to sleep, *dammit.*'

'Bit touchy, aren't you? You haven't considered the crucial question, have you Bar-on?' the voice persisted, leaning in close to my face.

'I'm warning you, Blazer, let me be.'

Hissing vibrated in my ears.

'You can do better than that, Bar-on. Answer the question, pilgrim.'

Sleep was no longer a choice, but I lay on the ground, eyes clenched.

'What question?' I said, rolling over onto my back.

'*You* know the question. You think you've solved the mystery of suffering. Big deal. You're still avoiding the key issue, aren't you? *The* question.'

My eyes flickered in a raven-blackness. It assaulted my senses. 'I'm not ready to answer.'

'We're never ready, are we? So, the d-evil word, hey? *E-V-I-L*? We chuck it around with abandon, but what do we mean by it?'

... he looked inside...

'Okay. Wickedness. *Evil*. Is it a symptom of our failure to understand who and what we are?'

'That doesn't say what it is.'

'Humour me. Do we need to define it? Definitions can be so inhibiting. It's more useful to examine the soil in which it takes root and thrives. We should be careful with its usage; the word has become a cliché.'

'Interesting perspective.'

'How's this? Evil drives a *narcissistic mindset*, for want of a better term.'

'By that you mean...?'

'*Ego*. While all humans grapple with their egos, the unrestrained ego is the foe at every level of existence. Unbridled obsession with self, a superiority complex, a turgid self-image – stroked and nut-tickled, enabled, adored and sustained by status, success, insecurity, power and ambition – is the enemy of humanity. These give evil oxygen. Pride – selfishness, arrogance, smugness, narcissism – it's not on the seven deadly sins' most-wanted-list for nothing. Once we allow the ego to dictate matters, we don't have a hope in hell or heaven of balanced living.'

'How do we keep our arrogance in check, then?'

'By reminding ourselves that our mind – our thoughts and emotions, where narcissism thrives – is a process toolbox and not our real self.'

'Not sure if I follow.'

'African wisdom might help us. *Ego is a cowhide drum*, it observes, *prone to loud noise but hollow inside.* The drum's sounds might stir the blood with their thunderous beats, but they always exceed their usefulness. All bladder and bluster. No matter how great an egoistic mind considers itself, it is empty on the inside, like the cowhide drum, a reverberating echo chamber promising far less than it delivers. When we understand this, we realise our insignificance in nature's grander scheme. This allows for a healthier self-image.'

'An empty vessel makes the most noise, you mean?'

'Ego gives us a better context in which to locate the discussion.'

'What about evil itself? We're circling this beast, prodding and probing at its belly.'

'The world is not perfect. Nature is impersonal, if not defective.'

'We might not fathom its paradoxes, but to call it imperfect and impersonal may be an extreme view, in my opinion.'

'If it is defective, we ourselves are defective because we're part of it, and so it becomes difficult to determine any frames of objective reference.'

'What malevolence is and what it means is elusive. It induces suffering; it frightens and troubles us. While we could agree specific taboos are always wrong – like genocide or cannibalism – other behaviours are often justified or excused by using the term.'

'So, you're proposing evil is in the perceiver's eye?'

'Yes. Our language contributes to this process, making a heaven out of hell and a hell out of heaven.'

'It's more than just semantics.'

'If not through language, how else? Through language, we dehumanise or demonise anyone and anything that is different. When we categorise or label humans, we take part in evil. Stigmatisation down the ages. And so categories become expendable. Thus, *cadres* can kill *settlers*. And vice-versa. Classifying and objectifying people is one of evil's brilliant achievements.'

'What of the corrosive effects of evil?' Blaise said. 'It comes into its own when it slides beyond the point of no return. It's a contagion. The horror!'

'Like piercing a pus-filled boil. While it's cathartic, its debris spurts everywhere to infect everything and everyone.'

'If we lose control of our darker passions, what occurs?'

'Once the civilising shackles vanish, all things are possible. Liberation *from*, and freedom *to*… By stages, we become immune and desensitised to what we're doing. The surest way to hell is gradual.'

'You're saying that even in certainties, there's ambiguity?'

'*Ja*. You think you understand evil better now?' I laughed.

'Clear as mud. It seems a futile exercise.'

'You could be right. Over millennia, the words *mysterium iniquitatis* have been used to capture its meaning. *Mystery* is its key,' I said.

'*Mystery*? That doesn't help much. After all, the term defines many things.'

'*Mystery* suggests incomprehension, paradox, puzzlement, ambiguity.'

'Tell me, Baron, why do certain individuals become calloused, to a point that taking life causes no remorse? There's nothing ambiguous about that.'

'Are you sure? Remember, *unnatural deeds do breed...*'

'*... unnatural troubles*. But should we try to explain the wiles of evil beyond this?'

'We must be careful not to reduce its mystery to something it's not, by diminishing its complexity to a simplistic trifle.'

Our voices subsided, and the dark continued to batter us.

I shivered, but I couldn't help myself. 'We are what we do. Minor acts, both good and evil, lay the foundation for greater ones, becoming custom or habit. Can you understand my angst given the ferocity of my violence?'

'I get that.'

'I imagine I'm clutching at a rope ladder, with a choice: up to the light, down to the dark. If I descend a rung, as I did earlier today, the next rung below seems closer. That scares the brown stuff out of me. I feel I am sinking into that dimness, struggling to adjust to the rising dark, the fading light paining my eyes beyond bearable. My greatest dread is that the memory of light will fade and the once inconceivable becomes acceptable. Evil's arc is downward and I fear I may lose my vision in a kingdom unfamiliar.'

'Brother, the slippery rope ladder argument is flawed. All I'll say is you might travel the arc upwards if you live from your spiritual core.

Regardless of how far you descend, it's the same trajectory. You could rise one rung at a time if you choose. Not that it's a linear journey. It never is.'

The hushed dimness continued to weigh us.

'Here's a question. Is there a way to measure evil?'

'The sixty-four-thousand dollar one.'

'I'm full of those, aren't I?'

'Yep, and many other things too,' I shot back. 'I don't think we can quantify it, but systems empower it. Many *isms* and ideologies that espouse forms of social engineering, no matter how benevolent they claim to be, do this. Often, such structures generate their own momentum. But could we calibrate evil and human wickedness and collect its data? I'm not sure.'

'Do you think it's possible the collective becomes something different... being well meant, moves beyond our control?' he said.

'Yes. Evil is difficult to pin down. It is cruel and elegant, vivid and vague, clear and concealed, banal and bewildering, parasitic and clandestine – at the same time. A complex brew, more than the sum of its ingredients.'

'Does our accumulated wisdom address evil?'

'Those wise writers, thinkers, artists, and philosophers I have encountered do not look to give an unequivocal answer. They might concede we assign blame for evil anywhere, rather than to where we should – to ourselves and our choices.'

'So, no neat explanations for these issues. Evil is a sly, slippery serpent.'

'That snake metaphor doesn't quite work for me anymore,' I said. 'Snakes are misunderstood and docile creatures, often victims of poor press.'

'We will never see snakes as anything else, I'm afraid.'

'Apart from the fact we've experienced evil's effects over the last few days, where do we go next? I'm still struggling to comprehend my complicity in it all.'

In the silence that followed, I remained a hostage to its Stygian blackness.

... in a Roman wilderness...

A voice towed me back.

'Some say evil doesn't exist... It's an absence of good rather than a malevolent, diabolical spirit roaming the universe.'

'I'd want them to see the bodies near the *Hunyani* wreckage.'

'They argue it's the residue of our reptilian brain that had evolutionary value once – but no more.'

'For me, the key question at evil's core is: why the innocent children? How does anyone explain that?'

I thought again of the fair-haired boy and his teddy, Milo.

'Humanity is vicious, these people say. Nature can be capricious, but to say it's evil or wicked is to give it too much status. Elevating it to an absolute, opposed to good.'

'I can recognise evil, but does that mean I'm saying it's equal to good?'

'Those uncomfortable with the term *evil* are hesitant to equate shadow and light.'

'*Evil* empowers Satan, then?' he asked.

'By the same token, *goodness* empowers God.'

'That thought occurred to me. *Mysterium bonum*, the *mystery of goodness*.'

'Maybe we should address evil from beyond religious binaries.'

'How?'

'The binary approach is simplistic and over-dramatic. God versus Satan. Light versus dark. Love and hate. Energy and reason. Polarities. *Either... or.* What about the spectrum idea – you mentioned it earlier with your ladder analogy – that connects the two?'

He smiled. 'I'm intrigued. What do you have in mind?'

'If we accept the evolutionary worldview, then all its components are in flux. Evil, like anything else, is not static. It's mutating, adapting to things novel. It has new interests as our context changes. Key elements may well be atavistic, a throwback to the past, but fresh forms emerge. Each era has its own styles of wickedness, its own squad of fresh players.'

'Would that apply to the *good,* too?'

'Perhaps they are on an exponential trajectory, tracking together at the same rate?'

'Now that is a scary notion.'

'You said it, brother. Different ages have unique beasts to face, but they remain variations of the same archetype.'

'*Ja,* history repeating itself. The wheel turning and revolving in widening, causal circles.'

'The shadings are subtle – in their motivation, in their particular contexts. Our understanding of evil changes, suggesting it's not absolute or total,' I said.

'Can we not also apply that principle to *good*?' he half-laughed.

'In an odd twist, today's evil could be tomorrow's good.'

'Sounds bizarre when you put it like that.'

'It questions the all-or-nothing view, I suppose. There's truth in the counter-intuitive idea of good in the bad and bad in the good.'

'It answers the question about the polarities, doesn't it? Nothing is bad or good in its entirety.'

'Balance between these dualities is vital. To eliminate one leads to an excess of the other. In working to remove evil, we can create greater evil.'

'Now there's an irony. Wouldn't more goodness be a positive thing?'

'Think of ancient weighing scales. When the weights of good and evil on each pan are balanced, harmony and equilibrium exists,' I said. 'If we absolutise evil or good, favouring one over the other, we undermine the balance. With any alteration, the scales tilt and restoring the balance is difficult.'

'By the same token, wouldn't relativising evil have a similar effect?'

'When we project our notions of evil or good onto others, we're in danger of it coming from the conflicted inner core of ourselves.'

'Good and evil may intersect in the heart of every human being.'

'If that's true, that begs another question, doesn't it?' I said.

'There could be many. What one did you have in mind?'

'Well, how do we eradicate evil if it's part of who we are?'

'Good one!' he said.

'It's a question that recurs in all humanity's shared wisdom through the ages. In the soul, good and evil are intertwined, like wheat and darnel together. As grace advances, so too does desire. We need evil to provide opportunities for good to emerge.'

'Does that bring about more evils?'

'It seems. Yet from those evils, more good emerges. And so it goes...'

'... and goes, in a flattening cycle, *ad infinitum.*'

'Our challenge, as I see it, is to disrupt these cycles, shift their trajectories, destabilise our perceptions.'

'This perspective poses a dilemma.'

'How so?'

'What about methods and outcomes? Shouldn't they coincide? Do the means justify the ends? Or is it the other way around? I get confused. If our methods are dubious, are the outcomes also dodgy? Could we legitimise killing innocents to progress a certain ideology? Are actions intrinsically evil or good or only relatively so?'

'I don't think we can ever act with a pure conscience. Sometimes to achieve the most moral outcome, we must compromise – stoop to conquer.'

'Who's to blame, then? *God*? If he is the creator of all, is he not also responsible for it all? Are we not reflections of the divine? *No one*? Are they acts of a blind universe? *What about humanity*? Are our actions moral evils for which we must answer?'

'I'm not sure we can point the finger at anyone else. The key question, for me, is: should we assign individual responsibility, or is there a shared culpability? Think about our situation for a moment. Who's responsible for the downing of the *Hunyani* and the subsequent innocent deaths?'

'The man who fired the missile? He carried out the orders. His immediate superior in the field who ordered him to fire? The overall leader of the cadres, or their political leaders who determined their policy?'

'Or their opponents? They're not blameless, either,' said Blaise. 'Can pursuing a racist political agenda be justifiable? Both claim right is on their side. Can they both be right? Or wrong? Or both at the same time? Is it a zero-sum game? We're back to considering the polarities again.'

'What about me? I've played a small part in this unfolding tragedy,' I said.

'Then, bordering countries that allow terrorists to launch their attacks? Those who commit atrocities in the belief they're serving the greater good? Or leaders who say and do nothing?'

'There's also those who either sold or supplied the munitions. And the industry which manufactured them.'

'Cause and effect. Givers and receivers. Sharing the love – and the hate. Looks to me, there's a widening blood stain of responsibility for evil, hey? Micro-evil, the murder of innocent tourists, becomes part of a macro-organism. All belong to the same serpent.'

'All evils inhale the same oxygen, pumping life – and death – into the same universal bloodstream which passes its contents through the many and various circulating arteries. Blaise, the question remains: how do we navigate that stream to the heart of the matter, then? Where do we moor our boat?'

'My boat has a leak, and the trip up-river in the dark has been nightmarish. I'm also struggling to orient and read the map.'

'That about sums it up!'

'Shit, Bar. My brain hurts. We live in the real world. How is this relevant? Are we any nearer to unravelling the mysteries of the universe?'

'Over the millennia, minds greater than ours have grappled with these questions. The jury is still out. We're not gonna solve it in fifteen minutes.'

'Why bother? The search for meaning is a load of existential and metaphysical *kak*. It won't make a skerrick of difference.'

'The meaning-of-life question may not be ours to ask.'

'I'm not sure I follow.'

'Flip your thinking. Life asks questions of us. Each of us must find our answer to the questions in our actions, by choosing to embody virtues such as justice, courage, wisdom and compassion.'

'Don't forget to add the big three: faith, hope and love.'

'In our own spheres of influence, controlling the things we can. Starting by becoming better versions of ourselves.'

'Ah, so, debate has value – like our conclusions on suffering, it keeps us alert to the machinations of evil. But here's the thing. Forget the dichotomies between good and evil. Life is mysterious. Let's stop wasting energy on debating for the sake of debating. We must act. If we accept this, embrace it, then *you – me – all of us –* can live, with empathy and respect. Love, and do what you will.'

'Too true, brother. All it takes for evil to flourish...'

'... is for good people to do and say nothing.'

'*Ja*, makes sense. We need a practical and practised philosophy. Speak out against injustice. Fight the good fight. Stop jumping at shadows. Keep searching in the rocky terrain. Never turn a blind eye, despite the obstacles – or because of them. Perhaps the hardships are a means to a workable end.'

'Yes, we model that arc upwards. Address the spark of good in those alienated and estranged from themselves, and others. No growth without struggle – our lungs need to burn to build capacity. It's as simple as that, rather than easy.'

'That's all well and good, and there's much to celebrate in your first-order suggestion. But we need something more radical.'

'What did you have in mind?'

'A second-order idea, nothing scripted as yet.'

'I'm intrigued.'

'So you should be. Sometimes to transform and transcend, we need to upend how we think about the issues within our systems, world-views, frameworks, or philosophies, whatever you choose to call them.'

'We've circled back. You suggested that earlier.'

'So I did. Issues are not isolated incidents but embedded within larger systems and cycles. Addressing them requires a holistic under-standing of the context in which they arise.'

'You're saying we need to question our understanding of the way things change?'

'Neatly put. Challenging ingrained patterns and underlying assump-tions, embracing novelty and creativity in order to bring about sustain-able and authentic change, is a way forward.'

'Does this changing the way things change involve embracing the uncertainty and complexity of systems, and being open to evolutionary solutions and unpredictable outcomes?'

'Yep. We must give up control to regain it. Shifting from problem-focused perspectives to more relational and contextual understandings of problems, means actively constructing new meanings and possibilities through creative interventions. Embracing complexity and uncertainty is not for the faint of heart.'

'I don't see how this idea is that radical, or how it contradicts a prac-tised and practical philosophy.'

'It doesn't have to. If our philosophies are rigid, conventional, binary, and linear, it probably will. If they're porous, flexible, diverse, and holistic, underpinned by a paradoxical and interdependent spirit, they should absorb, adapt, and thrive.'

'Quite complicated, if you ask me.'

'If it were easy, we'd all be doing it,' I said. 'Anything worthwhile takes effort. *Faint heart never won fair maid.*'

Blaise grinned. 'Now you're talking. I'm always keen to chat about maidens.'

I reciprocated with a smile. 'Trust you to mention *meisies*. If I didn't know you better, I'd say you had a one-track mind. Or a back-tracked mind.'

'More likely, an anti-tracked mind.'

'*Faith* and *fortitude* might be a better proposition than *faint* and *fair.*'

... can you picture what will be...

To this day, I am unsure if I conversed with my brother or if it was a sinuous apparition, a hallucinatory dragon from a troubled brain, a sanity-mocking delusion, a shadow of myself, or a cathartic unburdening of serpents in my subconsciousness.

I'd imagined it must have been Blaise and me debating the big questions, but try as I may, all I can re-remember are two otherworldly voices, reminiscent of the pair of us.

This fluctuating quasi-socratic exchange has visited me over the years but it keeps evolving and shifting, and understanding it remains elusive.

Under a starry canopy of sky, hidden amongst the trees under the cover of darkness, and comforted by the yipping of a lonely jackal, I surrendered to both the mental and the physical fatigue accumulated over the earlier days and slept, if not in absolute peace, then relatively so.

... the end of nights...

MORE THAN LITTORAL

... the blue is calling...

A VOICE CALLED TO me from the depths of *spiritus mundi*. Or was it one of the serpent guardians, the *genius loci*? It was far off, sighing my name.

'Bar-on... hey *Bar-on...* wake up...' it crooned. *'Wake up...'*

Not now... let me sleep...

The voice crept closer, churring, trilling, insistent, much like a purring cat close-up.

'Bar-on...'

> *The cryptic nightjar, the mystical litany bird.*
>   *Of life and death, the go-between.*
>   *Fiery-necked*
>   *Healer and harbinger.*

It repeated my name rapid-fire.

'Baron... Baron... Baron... Baron.'

Hmm? *Blaise?* I was hoping for something more exciting...

'Baron.'

My eyes flickered open.

It took me a few moments to orient myself and adjust to the pre-dawn half-light. Blaise was leaning over, stale breath and sanguine face crowding me.

'Thanks for nothing. I was just getting to the interesting part.'

Blaise put his finger to his lips.

'What's cooking?'

'Not sure. Come look.'

I yawned, rubbed my eyes, and struggled to my feet.

Gone were the post-rain cerulean blue skies and chocolate sunset of the previous day. The heavens were awash with impenetrable layers of dull greys and blotchy whites. In places, shards of light pierced the boiling cloud cover, spotlighting the expectant landscape and greenish hues of the bush in an unearthly, dappled glow.

The damp, humid air foreshadowed yet more stormy spring rains. Even the animals and birds knew to seek shelter.

... waiting for the rain... yeah...

From our well-hidden sanctuary, Blaise pointed northwards.

'Do you see it? Ten o'clock. Isn't that smoke?' I followed the arc of his pointing arm.

'I can't see anything.'

'Baron, sometimes just look, you must.'

'What do you think I'm doing?'

'Surely, Baron, you've had experiences where you've transcended the ordinary?'

My earlier encounters with the bateleur eagles, and the red ivory trees, pushed at the doors of my consciousness. 'Yes, but only rarely. My head seems to obstruct my heart.'

'Stop trying to see solely on your terms. That's your problem, my padawan friend. Declutter your mind. Connect to the Force, Baron...'

'How do I do that, Master Yoda?'

'You don't need to do anything. Just be still. Let the fragments of the natural world find you. Breathe. Deeply. Aerate your body. Listen for the symphony and choir of existence in those fragments. Pay attention to your inner voice. It will lead you to your life-song. Allow the boundaries of your perception to dissolve. More heart and soul, less brain...'

'This is Brother Sun, Sister Moon stuff.'

'Precisely. A deep-down interconnectivity exists in all things. And God is the electrical charge. The force-field.'

'Blaise, you confound me. When did you get so wise?'

'Sometimes, I confound myself.'

'Right, unplug the mind...'

I closed my eyes; brought attention to bear on my breaths.

> *In-then-Out.*
>> *Out-then-In.*

Their wispy warmth danced with a crusty air and intertwined, to birth a delicate, ethereal mist of possibility.

> *God's gentle breath stirs creation to life, ventilates its soul, inspires it to be.*
>> *Deep. Steady. Connected*
> *Mouth-to-Mouth,*
>> *Out. then. In.*
> *Life-kissed.*

I stood at the doors of the undiscovered country.

It might take my breath away. And give it back.

> *Inhale. Exhale.*
>> *Breathe. Out, then In.*

My breathing slowed.

> *In. then. Out.*
> *(Out. then. In.)*
> *Spectral, soulful silence.*
> *Rolled, crushed wild basil.*
> *Argumentative reed frogs.*
> *Earthy, musky elephant dung.*
> *Melodic moans of mopane leaves.*
> *Hyena sniggers.*
> *A coucal's viscid gargles.*
> *An aroma of water.*

A heart open to the sunlight.

> *Fractal patterns converged and diverged in a tapestry of shifting,*
> *fractured images of light.*
> *Raindrop freshness.*
> *Embroidered harmony,*
> *Nature's genius.*

A holy, eucharistic moment.

> *Grace-filled, God-kissed.*
> *Blessed and shared, one heart to another.*
> *Mouth. to. Mouth.*
> *Smoke, honeyed and balsamic.*

Thin trails wafted to the heavens.
  'Campfires. Cooking fires, maybe?'
  'How far away, do you think?'

'Hard to say from here. Two clicks, maybe? We should get to some higher ground.'

'A protected village?'

I shrugged my shoulders. 'Only one way to find out.'

'We might get lucky.'

'Or not. It's unlucky to comment on your good luck, little brother. The rub of the green has favoured us, but for how much longer? I shouldn't tempt the serpents of fate any more than we have already.'

'So you keep saying. We're still here, aren't we?'

'Be careful Blaise, of hubris. Those serpents are likely to take a particular interest in us.'

'*Yada-yada-yada*. Time to disappear before they arrive on the scene to bushwhack our endeavours, then,' said Blaise with a wink.

I refrained from nibbling on his baited hook. 'Backpack check first.'

Family photo. *Check*. Journal and *No Longer at Ease*. Wrapped in plastic. *Check*. Three full water bottles. *Check*.

'Still hanging onto Achebe, I see.'

'I'm not done with him,' I said, packing it away.

'Don't clutch it too tightly, otherwise you won't be able to let go.'

With adroit fingers, Blaise removed the magazine from the 9-mm mamba in his hands.

Because of the United Nations arms embargo, Rhodesian engineers, through force of necessity, had designed and developed many of their own weapons for the bush war, including a local variation of the 9-mm, named for the deadliest snake in Africa, the black mamba.

Blaise cocked the weapon, moved its slide up and down a few times, checked its various steel parts and restored it to a state of readiness before returning it to the shoulder holster he had purloined from the dead guerrilla the day before.

The bloodied wound in that guerrilla's chest sailed into my mind, testament to the mamba's capabilities.

I strapped on the backpack while Blaise covered the evidence of our brief night-time sojourn as best as he could.

'Well done, Blazer-man. I couldn't have done better myself.'

He smiled. 'Aye-aye, Akela. I think I'm ready for that scout badge.'

'With a little more effort, you'll make a fine ranger apprentice.'

'I think I'll leave the rangering to you, Mr Crockett.'

'Hawkeye would be more appropriate.'

'*Hawkeye?* I would have thought Allan Quatermain. Who's this, ah, Hawkeye? Another of those nefarious characters from your stock of books?'

'I see you found me out. Hawkeye appears in Cooper's *The Last of the Mohicans.* He's one of those hybrid characters with European ancestry but naturalised with his Mohican family, Chingachgook and son, Uncas. He learnt the ways of the wild from his adopted family, and his name was legion in America's frontier wars back in the eighteenth century.'

'Why *The Last of the Mohicans?*'

'Long story cut short. Perhaps you should read the book? To pique your interest, it has all the ingredients of a good read: love, conflict, hate, war, set on a shifting frontier in a world of transition. Not unlike our own troubled times. Chingachgook becomes the last of his tribe, the Mohicans. I wouldn't want to spoil the details for you.'

'Sounds more like our story if you ask me, *The Last of the Rhodesians,*' said Blaise.

'That's a little premature, if not dark, don't you think?' I responded.

'More than that. Black, I would say.'

'An attempt at family black comedy without even trying, hey? Grandad used to say it ran in the Black family, that we were all tarred by the dark theatrical arts. I never understood him until now.'

'Wow, Baron, you're so *windgat*. Not sure what you're getting at.'

'Brother, reading. *R-E-A-D-I-N-G*, is the spice of life,' I said. 'Cooper's novel is one of my all-time faves. You should try it sometime when you're not so busy chatting up those convent girls or reading those international rugger magazines.'

'Reading is all fine and dandy,' Blaise said, 'but there's more to life than reading about it. How about you try living a bit? *L-I-V-I-N-G*.'

'From the little you've told me, anyway, I reckon Hawkeye sounds more like me than he does you. Or was Hawkeye a reader?'

'Well, Master Blaise, if that's the case, I'll call you Nat Bumppo from now on.'

'Nat Bumppo? Who in the hell is that?'

'Hawkeye's given name. Nathaniel Bumppo.'

'Funny, Baron. I'll stick to my given name, thank you very much. You can keep Mr Cooper and his character's name.'

'I think I might just do that.'

The words were hardly out of my mouth when it occurred to me Cooper described Hawkeye as pure-bred, 'a man without a cross'. Given my existential confusion, that did not apply to me at all.

We broke cover as the sun emerged from its slumbers. A gentle wind offered a temporary respite against the growing warmth of morning.

We cannot know the path of the wind, but we can claim kinship with other seekers and co-creators who, like fragile reeds, have submitted to its uncertainty and probing.

... where are you taking us...

A bilious undertone in my gut. The mopane worm 'feast' from the night before had unsurprisingly not quelled the spasms.

I thought of rock fig trees and their juicy, edible fruit. They had to be hiding in the labyrinth. My mouth watered. Memories of the 3W Weeks-Without-Walls *bundu*-bash backwashed in my mind.

Indigenous communities regarded the wild fig as sacred. In days of yore, the fig attracted voluntary human sacrifice during periods of calamity and hardship.

Apart from using fig trees as a source of bush tucker, local communities used their bark, fruit and leaves to combat mosquitoes, treat sores, eyes and teeth.

Given that malarial mosquitoes would be upon us in this damp sauna, such knowledge would prove useful.

It was the campfire smoke that gave me cause for the greatest optimism. It might just be our ticket home, the godsend we'd been looking for.

My spirit lifted at the prospect.

... ride...

... there's danger on the edge of town...

The sun sniped at the clouds, searching for any weakness. Apart from the occasional breach, the clouds held firm in their defence.

We rested in a nave of shady acacia trees that bowed over us.

The earth waited, breath inhaled, silent, hopeful but brooding, in anticipation of the at-once destructive and creative power of water's elemental life force, African style.

In that interregnum before exhalation, I felt my mind tugging me to that littoral space.

I did not resist.

Africa was the land of so many unfathomable incongruities and paradoxes. It was my spiritual home. This was where I felt I belonged. I was born here and regarded myself as African.

I wasn't a 'settler' – despite views to the contrary – and objected to the nametag. The blood of my colonial forebears lay co-mingled with those Xhosa, Zulu and Matabele warriors they fought against; blood seeped into the earth over generations in the Frontier Wars, at Isandlwana, uMgungundlovu, Rorke's Drift, Ulundi, the First Chimurenga, and along the Shangaan River, and now in the Second Chimurenga, the Rhodesian Bush War.

Yet the pillars of my understanding had shifted because of an in-the-wilderness confrontation with Thumbeza.

I had always assumed my birthright alone entitled me to claim my African place. Thumbeza had given me pause to reconsider the certainty of that view, compelling me to reconstruct my frames of reference.

My birthright did not entitle me to anything other than the unconditional respect and dignity all human beings warranted.

'The earth is a beehive, and we share one entrance.'

It was this shared humanity that tied me to others.

'Umuntu ngumuntu ngabantu.'

'A person is a person through other people.'

How could I claim any rights if I did not first claim the moral responsibility to ensure others enjoyed the same human rights of respect, dignity and compassion I enjoyed?

When I look back to this time, I see a self-absorbed, conflicted teenager, on the cusp of adulthood, shadowboxing himself, unable to discern fully the questions or answers, struggling to commit to the challenge of transformation.

I had launched my surf ski from a tranquil beach, intent on a prede-termined course, only to find I was an inexperienced paddler on an unsea-worthy vessel, adrift beyond the intertidal spaces, on a dangerous riptide in an uncharted bay.

To think, reflect, and act anew was a daunting prospect. To cling to customary and rigid formulae, practices and ideas, anxious about losing power and position, ignored the very fluid, variable and contradictory nature of the universe itself.

The younger me understood only that he had embarked on an elemental journey of sorts, defined by trial and detour, confusion, angst and pain, hounded by heaven and by monsters within and without.

It called for perseverance. Courage. Hope. Faith. Imagination.

Unlearning.

The later me came to realise the tides I sailed only had meaning if, time and again, in trust and faith, I checked my compass, recalculated my bearings, upgraded and maintained my equipment, and kept myself mentally and physically fit to survive its circuitous whims and wiles.

Beyond the littoral zone, I was in the paradoxical twilight.

No guarantees.

To find myself, I had to lose myself.

It warranted paddling beyond the shark-nets of old certainties, prompted by a willingness to lose sight of the safety of the beach and its reassuring shore-break to brave not only my own fears but also the unpredictability of that black ocean.

... of everything that stands...

IN THE BLOOD

THE COVER OF CLOUDS dissipated.

In the hushed African dawn, Blaise and I headed towards the trickles of smoke we could just make out in the distance.

We passed slithers of crocs, many somnambulant in the sparkling water pools, others lying inert on the sands next to them. Reptilian gladiators, they lay with mouths agape, armour-plated scutes bristling, the sun caressing their tough dragon spines.

Aware of their unpredictable nature, we kept our distance.

Bobbing pink-ringed eyes, cork-like ears and twitching nostrils sprinkled the many water cubbyholes, refuge to pods of almost fully submerged hippos. They eyed us, ears flicking, snorting water plumes heavenward. On cue, one emitted a maelstrom of deep-throated grunts and bellows akin to blasts from a tuba.

We crested a small *kopje*.

Nothing could have prepared us for the vista of silk clouds and earth that lay below. It was all that you'd expect from a picture postcard of an African flood plain, only more ruggedly beautiful.

Herds of elephant harrumphed their presence, perambulating down to the waters. Black rhino ambled in the tall grass. For the troops of swaggering baboons, it was playtime. A tower of piebald giraffes gambolled, harems of zebra wheeled and whinnied in elation, all abetted by a crush of ferocious-looking African buffalo, squads of smoky-blue, black-brindled wildebeest and sweeps of multi-coloured antelope – the full gamut – that roamed as far as the eye could see.

The massed choir was also in full voice, harmonious in its own way, by its own cryptic standards.

My soul soared at the spectacle. No escape – Africa was in the blood. *My blood.*

Once in the blood, always so.

Blaise and I kept up a steady pace. On occasion, we applied anti-tracking tactics to red-herring any pursuers. If they were on our tail, we did not detect any evidence.

We pushed on, keeping the puffs of smoke up ahead in our line of vision. They were further than we expected; we'd travelled for some time, and their spirals still wafted some way off.

... ride the highway... baby... yeah...

Distracted by our pursuit of the smokestacks, we were unprepared for an outburst of haunting *hoop-hoops* somewhere up ahead.

Startled, we sank into the tall grass. The whooping persisted.

Blaise parted the grass and pointed.

A lone bird squatted – half-folded, black-and-white striped wings outstretched, and tail low against the ground – absorbing the sun's rays. Lost in blissful preening, it primped its feather-crowned head.

Burdened by confused thoughts, ensnared in the labyrinth of my mind, how could I untangle my self-conscious knots to dwell in the moment unencumbered, like the bird before me?

Unaware, the bird engrossed itself in simple actions. Each delicate stroke of its beak through soft plumage spoke of contentment. Its actions appeared to be instinctual, guided by an innate wisdom humans had long forgotten.

How could I shed the cloak of self-awareness and tap into this source of tranquillity?

Phantoms of past and future distracted me from holy moments such as these.

The bird does not agonise over who and what it is. It does not fret over yesterday's flying or tomorrow's hunt.

It revels in being.

It lives in the now.

To live like that bird...

... to embrace the rawness of my emotions and thoughts without reservation, savour the sun's warmth, feel the caress of the wind, relish life's natural pleasures, and discard the masks I hide behind, are joys devoutly to be desired.

A spark ignited within me.

The bird transcended the mind-made manacles I had fashioned for myself. Its graceful, unchoreographed movements embodied an unburdened spirit.

Could I ever taste such freedom?

The path to such liberation may lie in rediscovering my spiritual self, to understand my weaknesses and strengths as wellsprings of happiness and sorrow pumping through my veins.

Blaise placed a hand on my shoulder. 'Did you hear what I said?'

'No, sorry. Beguiled by the bird.'

'Go figure. That's *Ngamfi*. African hoopoe,' he said. 'Herald of friends and much-needed visitors.' Before I could interject, he added, 'I too know something about local bird life.'

I wanted to offer a sarcastic rebuttal, but I bit my tongue.

We skirted the long-billed hoopoe and trekked onwards.

... calling us?...

Blaise grabbed me by the shoulder and thrust me onto the ground, falling on top of me. A venomous rebuke bubbled to my lips. He inclined his head towards an acacia thicket that nestled in a lacuna close ahead, to our left.

Everything had gone quiet. Blaise cupped hand to ear and pointed. 'You hear that?' he mouthed.

I shook my head.

'*There!*'

'You're having a laugh. Shadow-jumping, again.'

A faint plaintive whimper bumbled in the breeze.

'Human?'

'Can't be sure, but I think so.' Blaise flashed me a smug smile.

Before I could bite back, a cacophony of raspy hisses reverberated in the tall grass.

'Shit. What was that?'

Blaise frowned. 'I don't know, but it doesn't sound good.'

The whimper became a scream that shattered the morning. The anguished quality of it slammed into my ears like slivers of glass.

Above, a lone carrion bird wheeled in narrowing circles.

In that fractured lull, I was up and running towards the ring of acacia trees, a yelling Blaise on my heels.

... where are you taking us...?

QUO VADIS?

'WHOA. EASY, KWAGGA!' BLAISE pleaded from behind me.

'There's no time, Blazer.'

I stumbled into the shallow *donga,* scaled the far side and scrambled through the acacia trees to an amphitheatre at their heart and stopped, breathing hard, pulse racing.

Backs to the emerging sun, two formidable black-and-brown-winged birds sunbathed on a fallen blackened tree, its burnt arms spiking the sky. Pale grey, white-ruffed necks hinged on silky heads stared downwards at something beyond.

Izingwony zenkozi.

Blaise came to within a pace of me then slowed and inched his way forward to take up a position at my left shoulder.

The birds swivelled in unison to observe us. I held their gaze.

Birds of the king. Purifiers of the land.

Creatures of ambiguous omen.

Snuffling and squeaking, they adjusted their footholds.

No animal acts against its instincts.

Another penetrating cry from behind the lightning-struck trunk intruded to break the trance.

'Now what?'

'I think we should attack. Put the wind up them.'

'Baron? You lost your marbles?'

'I never was partial to playing with marbles. Vultures are carrion eaters. They won't feast on anything alive.'

'We don't know who's beyond that tree or the nature of their injuries.' Blaise looked away. 'This is a terrible idea.'

'We have to do something. And quick. Someone's in distress on the other side of that trunk,' I said, grabbing at Blaise's arm. 'Vultures are pack-hunters. Scavengers. And they miss nothing. The rest will be here soon enough. You saw the wheeling flight pattern. That was an invitation.'

'So, your bird-brained solution is *attack*?'

'You have any other ideas?'

'Apart from running in the opposite direction, no, can't say I do.'

'That's not a moral choice, is it? Find a weapon. Not the pistol. We don't want gunshot to attract attention from you-know-who.'

'With vultures gathering overhead, it might be too late already,' Blaise said with a shrug. 'But you've always had a soft spot for the underdog. It's what I love about you. Let's get to it, then,' he said, stretching for one of many branches littering the surrounding space.

I bent at the knees and picked up a rock the size of a grapefruit. It was smooth to the touch. I tested it, tossing it up in the air.

I sighed. *Déjà vu.*

Human choices recur in endless cycles, to weave eternal tapestries, transcending the confines of time, entwining generations past, present and future, here and everywhere.

'Ready? On the count of two.'

'*Two?*'

'Why not?'

From the other side of the fire-damaged tree, the sobs grew louder, insistent, and the birds shifted their concentration to its origin.

The vulture does not ask permission to feed.

'Two!' I yelled and rushed forward.

Taken by surprise, Blaise lurched a pace behind me. 'Holy crap, Baron. You could have warned me.'

'I did, Blazer. Why change a winning formula?'

Within three paces, Blaise was beside me as we advanced on our feathered foes. He had the branch raised above his head in both hands, poised for a downward stroke. In my fist by my side, I clutched the rock.

In a flurry of chitters and barks, both birds retreated in different directions.

'Blazer, take the buzzard on the left.'

'Gotcha.'

I hoisted the rock in line with my right ear and narrowed my gaze to align with the blood-orange chest of the vulture on the right. I unleashed the projectile with as much force as I could muster. It flew free from my hand, rotating and spinning in a downward arc towards its target. It looked to be on course for a direct strike, but it dipped and struck the earth a metre to the bird's front.

The stone ricocheted and struck the vulture with a glancing blow. In a burst of feathers, it rasped with hooked beak open and angry staring eyes and, with thrashing wings, sought the windless air. For a moment it teetered, found traction, then glided heavenward on a thermal.

I directed my attention back to the scene of battle.

Blaise had dispatched his adversary to the skies and was crouched over a human form in the shadow of the fallen tree.

I stooped over him.

A first glance prompted a deep inhalation of breath. Blaise gave me one of his *yeah-1-know* looks and redirected his attention to the figure on the ground. She lay muddied, bloodied, and half-trapped under the limbs of the toppled tree.

It unnerved me to read her face. Her features exuded a fiery serenity, but her eyes radiated a penetrating, hostile warmth and a wisdom that contradicted her youthfulness.

Blaise reached out to reassure her, but she knocked away his hand, and continued to stare at us, her expression steadfast and unafraid.

He tried again. She ignored him.

'Can she move, wriggle free?'

'If she could, she'd already have moved, so that's not good, Baron. It means the heavy branches have trapped her legs. They could also have crushed them under the weight.'

'She would be in pain if that were the case. I don't wish to frighten or antagonise her, so you should have a crack at telling her we're here to help. You speak Shona –'

'Better. I know. I'll try, but she strikes me as someone who doesn't scare.'

Blaise spoke, his dulcet tones faltering beneath her solemn gaze. After a lengthy, bumbling monologue, the animus drained from her face. She rubbed her brow and replied in her native tongue.

'Such a charmer. A gentleman to the last.'

'You're just jealous. Hurry, Bar, but mind your manners.'

'All over it. And while I'm doing that,' I said, handing Blaise one of our water bottles, 'offer her a drink.'

Blaise unscrewed the cap and offered her the bottle. Her humour resurfaced, and she pushed herself up and drank. He gestured for her to rinse head and face.

Mission accomplished, she gave back the bottle and reclined, supported by her elbows, to study his face.

Blaise dropped the bottle, followed by the cap. He scrabbled around, found it, let it slip again, picked it up, struggled to screw it back.

She chuckled.

In this time, I had cleared much of the foliage, removing smaller branches, and probed at the surrounding space near her lower limbs.

Careful to sign my intentions, I ran my fingertips across her legs, at which she remained composed, not uttering a sound.

'Blazer, if I can leverage this large branch here,' I said, 'you'll be able to slide her out.'

'Sounds like a plan.'

'You should tell her then.'

He tried, but he couldn't find the right words.

'You have a problem?'

'Yes. No. I'm struggling to find the right words. Not sure why?'

'You're not losing your touch, are you?'

His second try, while improved, remained below par. 'Damn, I'm finding her intensity disconcerting. She's put me off my game.'

'I know what you mean.'

'Third time lucky.' Blaise inhaled, fluffed his lines, bumbled an explanation.

The woman smiled and nodded.

'Success. I think I've made myself clearer.'

'If you say so, but it has less to do with your linguistic skills and more with her intuition.'

'*Ja*, whatever. Get a wriggle on, will you?'

'Give me a sec,' I said, crouched into a scrum-set position. 'You set?'

'When you are.'

'On the count of *three...*'

'You sure? Your track record's dodgy.'

'No shortcuts, I promise.'

I placed my shoulder below the knotted tree limb, took a firm grip, and bent my legs.

'Ready? One... two... and *three.*'

I flexed muscle, growled, straightened my knees. The branch nudged forward. 'Blazer, now's your time.'

Blaise grabbed her by the armpits and dragged her out. 'Clear,' he said.

I disengaged, and the tree thudded back into its place.

'What do we do now, Bar?'

'Ask her to lie still. We need to check for injury before we consider our next move,' I said. 'Check if she's okay with me doing this.'

She looked doubtful, but Blaise's silver-smooth tongue must have won her over, because she laughed and nodded.

'I see the blarney's returned.'

'Just as well I kissed the Stone. It worried me I'd lost the gift.' Blaise winked. 'A temporary blip. All good now.'

'We all kissed the Blarney Stone, mate. Didn't work for me.'

'You have to believe in its power, Baron, for it to work. Faith first. The rest, a poor second.'

'Touché, Blazer. I've no come-back to that. You may be right.'

'Would you repeat that for the record?' asked Blaise, a gleam in his eye.

'Don't push it,' I said, rubbing my chin, trying not to smile.

... everything that stands...

I knelt and examined the girl's lower body, starting with her feet, working upwards towards her pelvis. I searched for swelling, severe bruising over bone, any deformity.

Nothing.

She watched with a beguiling energy as I worked. I pinched her soles, and they reflexed. She did not quail when I applied finger pressure on her legs.

Encouraging signs.

'Does she have any sharp pins-and-needles pain anywhere?'

'I'll ask, but she might not understand me.'

'I suspect she understands more than she's showing.'

After a quick-fire exchange, Blaise said, 'She's stiff and sore.'

'That's not surprising. Apart from bruising, superficial scratches and minor cuts, I can't see any signs of serious injury. The acid test will be when she stands.'

'What do you mean?'

'If she can bear weight, she should be okay. Let's get her upright.'

We heaved her to her feet, Blaise gripping her left hand, me her right.

She took a few tentative footsteps.

Blaise and I let go.

She stretched, concentrated on bending her knees, then moved with increasing confidence.

'Time for the back-story. Will you do the honours? And try not to tie your tongue in knots.'

Blaise obliged. 'Baron,' he said, pointing at me. He prodded himself in the chest. 'Blaise.'

The two of them conferred once more.

'She says ours are unusual names.'

'Not wrong on that score.'

Directing a finger at each of us, with laughter echoing in her voice, she said, 'Bar-on. Blaise.' She patted her hand on her throat. 'Aizivaishe. *Aizi*.'

Aizi's age was difficult to establish. Initially I mistook her for a young teenager, but this assumption crumbled beneath the weight of her self-possessed gaze. Hers was an elusive and mystical presence. Much like the playful dance of light and shadow on rippling water, time seemed to swirl around her, defying any linear understanding. She evaded my linguistic attempts to do her aura justice.

I decided she was closer to our age, although she could have been much older.

'How did our mystery girl end up out here?'

'I was just about to ask.'

After an animated dialogue, Blaise offered his report.

'Aizi says she was out in a thunderstorm. The one that flogged us yesterday. She took shelter in this clump of trees. This tree *here*,' Blaise said, prodding it, 'was hit by lightning and fell, pinning her. She couldn't move and once the storm cleared, the vultures appeared. That's when we arrived. Why she was here at the old hanging tree, where she's from, or was going, I can't fathom. God knows, she might be on the run. I lost chunks of her story in translation. My gut tells me she lives nearby. Her home could be the source of those smoke signals we've been tracking.'

'It's unusual for a woman to be alone in the bush.'

'Let's not presume to understand any of this, more so of an older culture, more interconnected than ours.'

Silence descended. Blaise unsettled it.

'*Quo vadis*, Brother? Where to now? How do we cope with this complication?'

'Sometimes life throws a curved ball which is an opportunity in disguise.'

'That might be true, but given our precarious position, do you think she's safer with or without us?'

'It's a choice of two devils. We shouldn't leave Aizi to fend for herself, but it's her call if she wants to come with us. We can't force her. Nor should we hang about any longer. Will she lead us to the source of those smoke trails?'

'I'll find out.'

Before Blaise could utter a word, with eyes wide, Aizi pointed to the southern horizon at our backs, retreating as she did so.

With growing alarm, I traced the vector from her extended finger.

'What?'

From the foliage, a barrage of squawking, fluttering birds scattered to the air.

'Shit. *Move!*'

We ran, Aizi in the van, Blaise behind, me in the rear.

... where are you taking us? ...

MANNA FROM HEAVEN

Translucent mists of sweet-salty sweat.
  Heavy-soft breaths, a thrumming melody in the ears.
    Dogged. Irregular. Wavering.
Lungs aerated, smouldering.
  Labyrinths in my mind.
    Leaden-light feet.

WE FLED OUR PURSUERS, foot following foot, through the apricot arches of dawn, scrambling along phantomed footpaths, rushing to a sanctity elsewhere.

Prey and predator, shackled by chains of destiny.
  Persistent, tentative steps pounded, many after three,
  swelling and sagging, unharried, hounding.
    They beat a stifled, crimson-throbbing dread in my
    maculate heart.

Would they cease?

... the end, my friend...

Earth's muskiness humidified the air in shades of vermilion.
Rumblings of subtropical rain ripened, moistened soil,
sediment, stone.
Plant essences, bacteria and ozone, fused sweet potato and mari-
gold, co-mingled to secrete an organic,
soul-snagging, sensuous scent of water:
a novel yet familiar perfume.

Aizi slowed, held up her hand. We halted, breathing hard.

The shadowy woodlands angled downwards to compressed tree thickets, congested fluvial terraces, and the abundant Mana Pools floodplain.

The mountains in the distance advanced in shades of sandstone.

Implacable and unencumbered, the Zambezi slouched into view through a thin veil of vegetation.

All things living rise, intertwine at their source and fall, to return to their starting point to rise and fall again.

'This way.'

Aizi bounded away, a graceful gazelle, nimble feet dancing over the uneven terrain, her breathing fixed in the unfaltering rhythm of a long-distance athlete.

We struggled to keep pace.

'She's relentless. A force of nature,' Blaise puffed in admiration. 'And here's me thinking we needed to fend for her. She's doing the fending.'

'Her energy puts us rugger-buggers to shame.'

Aizi steered us towards the river on a swerving, gut-twisted route through aromatic African grasses, until a conclave of trees swallowed us into its shadow.

With a deft gesture of her right hand, she cautioned. We sank into the undergrowth.

The sweat clung to my eyebrows, dribbled to my cheeks and chin. I mopped it with my forearm. The mopane flies swarmed at the corner of my eyes, their murmuring loud in my ears. Blaise wore a half-smile on his face, but the quickness in his breath belied his calm exterior.

Aizi showed no signs of fatigue or distress; rhythm of mind, body, and soul fused in harmony: she was in the Void.

Her fingers flicked right.

We followed.

... a face from the ancient gallery...

Knee-high piles of yellow dung, embedded oval pad marks, a trail of broken branches and flattened vegetation betrayed the elephant long before we saw it.

'*Iko*. It is there. *Pedyo kwazvo*. Very close.' She pointed to a screen of savannah grass and tree-shadows.

Stillness.

Ruffle. Stir. Swish.

A rumour, a suggestion, a nuance of movement.

Ear. Trunk. Tusk. Limb. Bulbous body.

Half-parts merged to expose, in an *a-ha* moment, a rush of elephant.

A lone bull with discoloured tusks, a cluster of white oxpecker tick-birds hitch-hiking on its back, ambled past our position. I could trace the wrinkled arcs of its prehistoric grey skin folds.

It paused.

Had it sensed us?

Tension coarsened my breathing, and my gut fisted.

With flip-flopping ears, the bull uncoiled its trunk to pluck at and munch on the sheaths of head-high silver-coated grass-stalks surrounding it.

Another wait.

The elephant meandered away from our position to the trees.

Aizi signalled, and pivoted to her right. We moved sideways, followed her lead and picked up the pace.

... some stranger's hand...

She dropped to her haunches beneath the grass-line, beckoning for us to do the same.

'Is it safe to rest? Have we shaken them?'

'It's difficult to hide from someone who knows where to look,' Aizi said in English. 'And who does not give up.'

'I *knew* it. Aizi?'

She smiled but offered no answer.

No one spoke further. We crouched, ears and eyes straining.

Nothing.

'Where are they?'

'Close.'

Aizi started forward, darted glances left then right, searching for something.

'Don't move.' She melted into the shadowy matrices of abrasive elephant grass ringed by cadaverous tree trunks.

'I hope she knows what she's doing. I've lost my bearings.'

'Aizi's no slouch, that's for sure. I'm glad she's on our team.'

'We're on her team, if you hadn't noticed.'

'I can't help feeling like a startled *duiker* waiting for the leopard to pounce.'

'That resonates with me.'

'Where did Aizi go?'

At my invocation, she materialised from the bush.

'Holy sherbet.' I said, heart racing. 'How is it you keep sneaking up on us?'

'Here,' she smiled, 'take and eat.' She held out a handful of plump, oval-shaped, puce-coloured fruit. '*Mazhanje.*'

'Wild figs. They've been in my thoughts.'

The fig-skins were thin and tender to the touch. When I squeezed, they burst open to show crunchy seeds lining a fleshy rose-tinted inside wall.

'Can't remember when I last ate,' Blaise said, shovelling figs into his mouth.

'In our defence, something might have distracted us.'

'Never has food tasted so sweet and satisfying. I didn't realise they could be so luscious. Honeyed ambrosia.'

'Juicy and jammy. Manna from heaven. Just what we needed.'

Aizi shimmied up the closest acacia tree and squatted high on a crutch of branches hidden by tight foliage. She scanned the skyline, then pointed in the direction from where we'd come.

She raised her fisted hands. She opened them, flicked up her fingers.

'*Nine.*'

'Nine *what?*'

Aizi pointed her left forefinger and middle finger at her own eyes, straightened her arm to point southwards.

I waved. 'Almost a kilometre to the south.'

Another clenched fist, followed by five extended fingers on her left hand.

'*Five.*'

She repeated the action.

'*Plus* five.'

And again.

'Fifteen. *Shit.*'

Aizi slithered down to us. 'Come. We must hurry.'

We didn't need prompting.

... ride the snake...

We scrambled ever downwards, disappearing into a gully latticed by petrified trunks wrapped in foliage.

Damper. Darker. Musty. Mildewed. Decaying wood, rotting leaves.

The river's dissonance filled our senses.

'Stay alert. I don't think they can catch us, but keep an eye –'

The shrouded vegetation to my right unfurled.

A figure rushed forward with weapon raised. It flashed downwards. I ducked, stumbled, sprawled, a ripple of pain across my shoulder blades.

Before I could regain my feet, Blaise had drawn the mamba, thrust its muzzle into the figure's gut, and squeezed the trigger. Its report resounded near my head. The 9-mil round unzipped the man's abdomen. He screamed, bounced backwards into the undergrowth. The *panga* spiralled from his hand and clattered to the ground.

Fear gagged in the back of my throat. Rancid sweat wafted to my nose.

Blaise yanked me to my feet. 'You okay?'

The gun's echo pulsed in my ears.

'*Panga* caught me a glancing blow,' was all I could manage.

'You'll live, you big lug,' Blaise grunted. 'The backpack absorbed the blow. Lucky you. Lucky me.'

The ringing in my head subsided.

'Lucky us. I bear a charmed life, remember?' I said, dusting myself off.

'Dust and ashes, so don't get cocky.'

'No need to remind me. Morbid thoughts of death have preoccupied me enough.'

'Meditations on mortality keep us alive,' he grinned.

'Or bode our demise. I hope we haven't betrayed our position.'

'Too late to worry about that.'

Aizi had backtracked, and now appeared between the two of us. How she had managed such total surprise exceeded the limits of my imagination. In a single glance, she summed up our predicament.

'Aizi –'

'Wait here.'

She melted into the bush.

... limitless and free...

I snatched up the broad-bladed *panga* and ran my finger over its sharpened edge.

... on thy blade... gouts of blood...

I weighed and balanced the blade in my palm.

... hear not my steps, which way they walk...

'*Baron.*'

Blaise's sibilant murmur snapped me back, and I joined him behind the filter of vegetation. He stood looking at the spread-eagled body on the ground. A blood-spattered face, contorted in bewilderment, rasping for breath, stared in response.

For a moment, his eyes rested on Blaise's, and then shifted to mine. If eyes are portals to the soul, then this man's portals were frosted.

He lifted his right arm and pointed a finger towards the *panga* in my hand. The rattle in his breathing intensified.

'Lung-shot. He won't survive. We should end his misery,' said Blaise. 'It's the merciful thing.'

A bloodied face and a bloodier rock from the past rose unbidden in my mind. A shadow over my heart, I tried to speak but no words came. Bitterness filled my mouth. I lifted the *panga* above my head with the edge pointing downwards.

'I don't think I can do this.'

'This isn't the moment for hesitation, Baron,' said Blaise. He extended his hand. 'Here. I'll do it.'

I moved the weapon out of his reach. 'No. I must do this.'

'Do it then, brother. Time's not on our side.'

... into this house we're born...

I knelt next to the dying man. He cast me a penetrating gaze, difficult to discern. *Ambivalence? Resignation, maybe?*

I grabbed his hand and squeezed. His fingers responded, but his hold weakened.

My eyes watered.

I extracted my hand from his, clutched the *panga*'s handle with both of mine and positioned it above his heart, prepared for the *coup de grâce*.

The weapon quivered.

I forced my eyes to shut.

The moment fragmented.

I imagined the blade's downward thrust.

Reluctant at first, it resisted, but it bit into flesh, shattered ribs and heart, and exited into the earth.

My eyes sprang open.

I reversed my grip on the *panga* and wrapped the man's hands around its handle. I rose to see a pair of sightless eyes fixed on a spectral silence. On bended knee, I pressed them shut with my fingers.

'Rest now, *Mufambi*.'

'Should we take the blade? It could come in handy.'

'No. Nobody should dispossess a warrior of his weapon. He still has some way to travel.'

... into this world we're thrown...

'Where did he spring from, anyway?'

'I'd say he's the one on point, or the flank of the sweep formation, this bull's right horn,' said Blaise. 'It means they're closer than we thought. Now they know where to look...'

'They keep coming, don't they? What do they hope to gain? I can't make sense of it.'

'Who knows? Now's no time *to reason why...*'

'It's *the do and die* bit that's worrying me.'

'Not worth the worry. Dying's the rule, not the exception, despite our insistence otherwise. No escaping it,' said Blaise.

'Still, Death has his own surprises.'

'We're in a fight with it 'til the end.'

... the end...

A soft whistle.

A musical, lilting voice, a whisper from the wilds.

'Bar-on. Blaise. Come.'

'Time to blow this popsicle stand.'

We chased Aizi's shadow into the murky recesses of African bush.

... killer on the road...
... brain squirmin' like a toad...

We had stopped to regroup and to listen for sounds of pursuit, complicated by the swelling surge of the river.

Aizi scanned the bush.

'Over there!'

She pointed, crossed the space in two bounds, stooped, and removed a camouflaging of branches to uncover a canoe. It bobbed in the shallows, anchored by strips of animal hide secured at both ends around one of the many overhanging trunks.

This was no ordinary vessel: it was a *mokoro*. Hollowed-out from a single narrow tree trunk, it resembled a giant shelled pea pod. It featured a left-sided lateral support float – an ebony outrigger – fastened to the primary hull, bowline-knotted with strips of tanned nubuck hippo hide at two points, one forward, the other aft.

'She's not expecting us to punt down the Zambezi, is she?'

'Beautiful,' said Blaise, with widened eyes. From inside the *mokoro*, he picked up a sturdy piece of planed wood, smooth to the touch. It was a longer, thinner hardwood variation of a knobkerrie, the traditional cultural weapon favoured by African warriors.

'*Isilingo*,' Aizi grinned, miming the act of punting.

'A quant pole. I always wanted a second chance to punt on the Cam,' Blaise said, pursing his lips, flipping the ornate quarterstaff in windmill arcs back and forth. 'I'm a natural.'

'Anyone who saw Mum and you paddling first time round near the Clare College Bridge would disagree. As I recall, you almost catapulted us into the water, much to the amusement of the university wags lining the bridge railing.'

'Part of the show, dear brother. At least I had a go. Weren't you cowering in the boat's bow with your hoodie pulled down tight to hide your face?'

'Anything else in there? A paddle would be nice,' I said, ignoring his sarcasm. 'That pole isn't for the faint-hearted, or the unskilful.'

Aizi rummaged around in the canoe's stern and emerged with two short-handled assegai-bladed paddles. She handed them to Blaise.

'Catch.' He tossed one over to me. 'What craftsmanship,' he said, inspecting it.

Made of mahogany, each polished blade bore an intricate coiling snake-torso with dragonhead etched onto both sides.

'Unusual image. I'm sure I've seen this somewhere.'

'You have. It's Nyaminyami, the Zambezi snake spirit. Mom has a pendant with matching earrings. It was a birthday present from her brother Tom.'

'Yes. Now I remember. What's so special about Nyaminyami, oh Maestro?'

'He's the River Spirit. His Christian equivalent would be St Christopher. Protector of the indigenous people who inhabited the Zambezi basin for centuries, he acts as gatekeeper to the underworld.'

'Wonderful. I hope he prevents the uninitiated from entering that darklands.'

'As do I. For Odysseus' dilemma awaits us.'

'Here we go again. What makes him so special?'

'His choice between two evils is the stuff of myth: Charybdis or Scylla? Whirlpool or rocks? The whims of a wild, wanton river or the rancour of an aggressive cadre?'

'We might be stuck on the devil's horns, damned either way, but I think we've already made our choice,' said Blaise.

'The whirlpool and not the rocks?'

'We know what the terrs will do. With the river, we might have a chance.'

'For the record, Odysseus chose the rocks.'

'Shit. Let's hope we're not shooting the rapids on the Styx, then.'

'That depends.'

'On what?'

'The colour of your thoughts.'

... take a chance...

'It's time.'

Aizi's agile fingers untied the straps holding the boat in place. The *mokoro* wobbled, stabilised and floated free. 'Hurry. Our hunters are close.'

She must have sensed the trepidation in my face, because she gestured upwards. My eyes followed to where a peculiar bird, striped white and black, clutched a branch above us. With a puzzled look, it stared past us. Its oversized downward-curving beak looked to the sky.

'*Umkolwana.*'

I shook my head. '*Umkolwana*? The hornbill?'

'Yep, yellow-billed hornbill,' Blaise said. 'The *umkolwana.*'

Aizi's eyes sparkled. '*Umkolwana.* Little believer. *Umkolwana* always looks up. Her beak never droops earthwards. Her look says to have faith, even in times of uncertainty. In the end, all will be well.'

I smiled.

... not to the swift or strong... but to those who endure until the end...

The hornbill tarried for a moment, batted its lengthy eyelashes at me, uttered a piercing cry and, amidst a cacophony of whistles, launched itself into the air.

It plunged earthwards.

My heart fluttered.

At the pivotal point in its descent, *umkolwana* flourished her powerful wings, floated, and soared upwards.

No bird rises too high if it uses its own wings.

I will stay the course...

... unto the end.

Aizi firmed her grip on the *mokoro*'s gunwale. We clambered aboard, Blaise in the bow, me kneeling in the stern. The canoe protested, but the lateral support held its nerve.

Aizi guided the boat into the deeper shallows and let it go. Released from its shackles, the boat's momentum caused it to stray. Blaise and I manoeuvred the *mokoro* with our paddles, aligning it for a smooth exit between two sandbanks. To bolster its balance, Aizi waded deeper to seize the stern.

'Take my hand.' I stretched out towards her.

Aizi did not move.

'Quick, Aizi, before the current takes us.'

'I'm not going with you.'

'What do you mean, you're not coming with us?'

Protected by shoals and vegetation, pacified by Aizi's steely hold, the *mokoro* remained becalmed.

'Your path is not my path. My journey is not your journey. You have to find your own way, write your own story, as do I.'

I stared at her in disbelief. 'No. You need to come with us. God knows what will happen if you stay. You're safer with us in the boat.'

The *mokoro* tarried, expectant.

She smiled, shook her head.

'For a brief time, we have travelled the same path together, you and I. We have connected our stories; we are stronger for it, grateful we helped each other in a time of need.'

I opened my mouth to speak, but I could not.

'You are ready. It is time to blaze your own path. Craft your own tale or be enslaved by mine. We must part, to fulfil our own destinies.'

'I'm not sure I can do this by myself,' I said, holding out the paddle.

'You are never alone. How will you ever know if you don't leave the safety of the shore?'

I stared at her, uncertain, confused.

'The river hides the treasure you seek.'

The boat stirred, poised, open to the subtle signals of a surging, thundering current beyond the sandbars.

Is everybody in?
The ceremony's about to begin...

'Trust in the Spirit of the River. Have faith in your instincts. It is not as hard as you think.' I made to disembark, but Blaise intervened.

'No, Baron, she's spot on. Listen with your heart. Forget the heroics. You know she has a better chance without us.'

The river's strength pulled at the canoe, yet it still held back.

'It's a paradise lost.'

'And regained.'

... it hurts to set you free...

My shoulders slumped. I reached out my right hand. She responded, her fingers touching mine.

'Aizi, I –'

Tall grass on the far bank of the river morphed into a mishmash of combat fatigues and an eruption of shouts and bellows. The intrusion threw us off balance. The *mokoro* lurched, bucked and pitched.

Our hands separated.

Aizi was the first to regain her composure, applying weight to the gunwale to prevent the boat from keeling. Blaise and I followed her lead, and the canoe steadied.

Aizi's fingers tightened over mine.

Lingered.

Our eyes met, and terror grabbed at my throat. In that moment, I sensed what she intended.

'Aizi, please –'

Her expression softened, hardened, and reverted to that fierce tranquillity of our first encounter.

'*Hamba!* Travel well.'

'No, Aizi, don't –'

She strengthened her hold on the stern; bent her elbows. Her focus narrowed. With a loud cry, she shoved the boat towards the gap between the sandbanks. The *mokoro* bobbled and drifted sideways, rudderless.

Aizi slipped beneath the water.

I searched its ruffled surface for any sign.

The canoe trembled, wavered, swivelled.

'Shit. *Baron!*'

Blaise's shout snapped me back to the drama unfolding around us. '*Paddle.*'

Flicks and flitters in the air.

Tracer. Muzzle flashes.

I tried to glimpse Aizi, but in the pulsing moment, I could not. I dug in the oar, ducked beneath the *mokoro*'s shell, and lifted my head to paddle again.

Our oars found traction, rotated, edged forward.

Thuds. Rips. Thumps. Splintering wood.

The current strengthened, swirled, and sucked the canoe into its eddy, propelling it into and through the sand-banked channel to the churn of the Zambezi beyond.

... riders on the storm...

I scoured the vegetation, hoping to spy her.

A hint of movement on the embankment caught my eye.

Was it Aizi? Or the sun's reflections playing tricks on a mind open to suggestion?

I have never been sure.

... an island in your arms... a country in your eyes...

It is one of those many strange ironies that we live our lives forward, and only understand them backward, if at all.

I have often revisited my brush with Aizi. How one so centred came to us in a moment of need remains an enigma.

Who can understand the depths of the cosmos? Penetrate its mysteries? Aizi. Aizivaishe. 'Only God knows.'

From the many possible answers, I find solace in a single notion: the universe's heart conspired to beat with mine, synchronising my nature with something bigger, to recognise someone else in need.

In optimistic moments, I imagine it was Aizi's raised, fisted hand I spied on that overgrown sandbank beneath the trees so long ago.

I always regret that I did not acknowledge her act of humanity. The capricious current thrust the *mokoro* past the sandbank into its frothing bowels as Blaise and I struggled to keep it from capsizing. By the time we had regained control, Aizi had disappeared from view.

Despite our emotion-charged separation, Aizi remains with me, always.

... unto the end... my beautiful friend...

FISHERS

THE ZAMBEZI UNRAVELLED, SWOLLEN and untamed, an enraged *rinkhals*. Reptilian spittle and spray diminished sight; its rasps rattled the ears.

... sweat oozed from its shiny skin... a beast caged...

Our copper-skinned *mokoro* hurtled, swayed, lurched and pitched headlong among rocks, blurred past semi-submerged trees and sand-bars, dragged by a venomous undertow. Vortices of silvery-capped waves whirled us to face every direction in a vertiginous, turbulent torrent of terror.

'Right!' I yelled, thrashing the turgid white-water with an impotent paddle.

Constricted by the river's snake-like torso, our life-raft pivoted left, accomplishing an undignified pirouette.

Allegro.

Powerless to complete effective sweep strokes, we performed a series of ungraceful arabesques *en pointe*.

The rapids railed and rallied, rearing many heads, and spat us beyond its cataracts. We reeled, then righted into the calm below rushing falls.

And drifted.

Sideways.

The Zambezi, source and mirror of life and death, regained its composure and wrapped its coils around islands, sandbanks and our *mokoro*, looping and curling out onto the Mana Pools floodplain.

A river is an interwoven fishnet of eternity, too complex to untangle.

Golden clouds. Mauve sky. Blueberry-misted mountains.
The light-headedness subsided.
Head between my knees, I rested on my paddle.
'Wild,' I panted.
Gulping for air, Blaise lay over on his back. 'No desire to repeat that.'
'We might have to. No way of knowing what's ahead. Our pursuers are also aware in which direction the river's pushed us. We have to keep moving.'
'And Aizi?'
'I saw her in the water. At least, I thought I did. I hope to God she escaped.'
'She's better equipped than we are.'

... you won't know a thing 'til you get inside...

Desolate figures afloat on a silent water-wasteland, we canoed a sedate stretch of the river that radiated into calmer, narrower channels. We slipped through the waters, the dip and thrust of our paddle strokes lapping a soporific rhythm, interrupting the stillness of the bush.

To confront the Zambezi's floodplain-wilds from a canoe carries a mystery of its own. On foot, the overwhelming sensation is nasal. On water, the dominant impression is aural.

A muffled medley of sound pulsed across and amplified the flood-plain's waterways, signalling a mystical connectedness hidden in all things living.

An encyclopaedic knowledge of wildlife is one thing; direct experience of it another.

We shared the river with the full gamut of African bird life.

Garrulous ivory-crowned shrikes, trembling pied wagtails and red-beaked skimmers, mandibles trailing the water, flitted around our boat, uniting in an unsettled choral blessing.

Above, a brown and white snake eagle levitated on a thermal against an orange slackening sun. It serenaded us with a guttural *hok-hok-hok*.

Skittish carmine bee-eaters hawked and swarmed in expanding patterns, swooping in front of our bow; vivid aquamarine and lilac rollers spiralled in our wake like trapeze acrobats, their discordant *rak-rak* cries spiking the solitude; and an enthusiastic white egret with cantaloupe-tinted beak high-stepped along the peripheral muck to snaffle an unsuspecting catfish.

'*Blaise.*'

I leaned forward and tapped him on the shoulder.

'To your right. You see it?'

'Hard not to.' He nodded. '*Hungwe*. The eagle with many wings. *Ukosi*. Child of the Light God.'

From her acacia eyrie, Hungwe swooped to the river on midnight sable wings, gliding with grace and guile. As she skimmed the water, her wingspan arched, her legs stretched and clawed talons extended to snatch a rainbowed tigerfish.

'I never thought I'd get to see that,' said Blaise.

Snow-headed Hungwe, prey enclasped, rose with barely a beat of her powerful wings. She circled, returned to her throne. A gyrating fish imprisoned beneath her, she surveyed her watery realm. Satisfied, she ripped at her catch with tremulous twitches of her hooked beak.

To see an African fish eagle is to glimpse the divine...

Hungwe raised her head.

Her fiery eyes scrutinised our progress. In that idle moment, she fluted a single deep-throated, penetrating summons that swirled like an unflustered ghost across the waste.

... to hear her voice evinces the music of the spheres...

... darkly through a looking glass...
... a strange creature

In amongst the vast wetland richness, my attention settled on a solitary rainbow bird perched on a clump of forlorn adrenaline grass. Upright, tail downward, head bobbing to all points of the compass, he exuded an odd numinous beauty.

> *Strange, shadowy pilgrim:*
> *sacred, mythical inhlanzi;*
> *cloaked in luminous mist,*
> *setting-sun wounded breast.*
> *Hot-spurred, grail-blessed firebrand:*
> *nkosi yamanzi, water lion.*

His eyes pierced mine.

'What is it you seek? What ails you?'

He reminded me of gentler, halcyon childhood days when a similar malachite kingfisher visited our garden wash-line each year, a hopeful prelude to a joyful spring.

Blessing and blight of fish,
   mweya wemvura.
Soother and shaker of water,
   scout and sentinel.
Sky speckled, spine-feathered,
   Noah's first post-deluge bird.
Spirit-messenger between those living and dead,
   Alcyone-and-Cetyx, king among fishers.

'The answer to how I should live.'

Wise translucent eyes commanded a rufous face, framed by fluffed metallic blue-black crest feathers.

Thoughts rippled through my head.

'What is important is not the answer. This you should not speak.'

Short, rounded wings whirred in a blur.

The kingfisher dropped and fizzed low over nervous water and swept upwards. Suspended on high, the fisher king spear-dived to resurface with a shimmering yellow-bellied fish in his beak.

He rebounded and darted to his place of rest.

'Search within. The hunt unfolds first in the seeker's heart.'

The rainbow bird brandished his catch and shook it with vigour. He adjusted his foothold, tossed his meal in the air, gulped and ingested.

'The questions you swallow empower you.'

'Hey, Percival, off on another mind-quest?'

'More like a soul-quest, Sir G.'

'Distracted again.'

'By that kingfisher yonder. You see him?'

'Yeah.'

'Reminds me of our childhood. Things were simpler then.'

'Okay, Grandad, easy on the good-old-days nostalgia. You'll have me crying in my beer in a minute.'

The king-of-fishers tarried and, wings ablaze, melted into the scattered sun.

... waiting for...
you to hear my song...

⬬

Harsh daylight churned to butter and bathed the land in warmth.

In the languid mid-morning moments that followed, we watched bewitched as large herbivores and predators descended from the *fynbos* and wooded savannah, to feed on sweet-sour grasses and protein-rich acacia pods, and to take to the waters.

A family of elephants showered and sloshed in the shallows; a pair of buffalo mooched on the shoreline, impassive and mellow; and spiral-horned waterbuck appraised us with muffled amusement as we snaked by. And wherever the eye roamed, the ubiquitous croc and prevalent hippo slouched and slumped. Red and yellow ox-peckers peppered their sluggish hosts in an act of symbiosis.

Blaise broke the somnolence. 'Those crocs give me the hee-bees. How many?'

'At least a hundred. They're everywhere.'

On cue, one... two... three... four launched into the river, swift and silky, and disappeared beneath its surface without so much as a wrinkle.

Gone fishing.

Pairs of prehistoric eyes resurfaced on the waterline to our right. With an instinctive, primitive recoil, I pulled my hands inside the canoe, forgetting to paddle.

The space between heartbeats lengthened.

'Keep paddling, Bar,' said Blaise. 'Gentle movements. Arms in the boat as best you can.'

'If one gets too close?'

'Whack it with the pointy end of your oar.'

'What if we capsize?'

'Don't splash about like a *mampara*; it will attract their attention. Swim to the bank, or roll in a ball and let the current guide you to shore.'

'That's reassuring. Glad the current's agenda is the same as mine. What could be easier?'

Just below my line of sight, sharp and canny eyes sussed us out.

They dropped into the shadowy depths, somewhere beneath our tiny hull, to do whatever it was predators did.

'Ah, Bar, untamed Africa,' said Blaise. 'What's life without some feral titillation?'

'More than an adrenaline rush, Kemosabe. We're the enemy here. This is not our stadium. Our opponents play by hometown rules. And there's no referee.'

'In creation's grand scheme, humans are deadlier than any other predatory species, Baron. Don't get ahead of yourself.'

... ride the highway...

Red-muddied mounds of rounded flesh flopped on the far bank, hippo torsos half-in and half-out of the water.

Imvubu.

Hippos and more hippos.

Oh, ode to joy.

A highway of hippo happiness.

'Up ahead,' said Blaise. '*Imvubu*. Midstream.'

'I see them.'

Snorting vapour sprinkled the air.

'We'd best skirt them. They're territorial and if they have calves, well...'

We altered course, aiming to pass to their right, but the tide was persuasive. The space between us closed faster than expected.

They loomed large and languid off our starboard bow: pods and clusters of lazing hippo – too many to count – wallowed up to their nostrils, ears flicking and baleful eyes fixed on us as we paddled nearby.

The current quickened, tugging us towards them, and we fought it to keep our distance.

We had interrupted siesta-time, and the hippos were not shy to voice their annoyance at our impolite, awkward intrusion. Spinning hippo tails agitated the water, punctuated by a rising cacophony of insults and bah-humbugs.

A croak and a grunt...

One cow opened its immense maw to menace with its impressive lower incisors and, full-volume, gave a kettle-drum flourish. Magnified by the water, the fat lady's operatic interlude inspired the hairs on my arms to stand to attention.

One by one, hippos eased beneath the river's surface.

Irrational fear clutched at my heart. Were they submerged on the muddy riverbed, content to wait for us to pass, or were they skulking towards us underwater?

'Smack the water with the flat of your paddle.'

I obliged.

'And if it doesn't work?'

'Rap the blade on the canoe.'

'And that will scare them?'

'Just encourage them to keep their distance,' Blaise grunted. 'We can't outmanoeuvre them. They're submariners who bounce along the riverbed and remain submerged for long periods.'

'I prefer the old rod and reel fishing trips with Dad on Kariba Dam.'

'Paddle, Bar. Focus. Even strokes. The current's picking up.'

'Let's hope so. I'm done with big game fishing.'

A swollen-bellied bull on four undersized stumpy legs loitered on the riverbank, smirking at us. He sashayed forward a few paces and bellowed.

We whacked our paddles on the water's surface and he retreated.

We resumed paddling.

Emboldened, he swaggered towards us. We banged the paddles on the boat's gunwale. He backed off with a twinkle-toed shuffle, African style... front-to-back, side-to-side... back and forth...

'I'm worried he'll triple-jump off that bank. Then we'll be in a 3-tonne world of amphibian armour-plated pain.'

We slapped the paddles on the side of the *mokoro*.

'And if he does?'

The bull opened its monstrous mouth and bristled his molars.

'Paddle for all we're worth, and pray.'

His incisors were colossal.

With each paddle-slap, the strength in my arms diminished.

MUH-Muh-muh, the hippo bull muttered.

'Why don't I just swim over there and give him a kiss?' I scowled. 'Get it over with?'

'Out of your head, now, Baron. Paddle, *dammit!*'

More pop-ups. *Muhs*. Frothing bubbles.

Everywhere we turned, blunt, bobbing, growling snouts. Cows and calves sank and resurfaced all around. They resembled aquatic astronauts, water-moonwalking.

Flat-paddle smacks.

Hungry Hippos.

'Keep going, Bar.'

The current surged and thundered. We gained momentum and rocked with it, hippos hip-hopping in our wake.

A massive bull head surfaced behind us. We must have cannoned over him.

Was he guffawing, yawning, or just exercising his jaw ability?

In a frump of foam, he slipped into the river's depths.

Shit.

Behind us, a shadowy submarine silhouette bounded by waves of displaced water shot towards the *mokoro*.

It sprang, sank, shifted, swelled.

... a strange creature groaning...

A hippo's head ruptured the water close by. It bouldered forward with jaws agape, like a bottlenose dolphin sweeping through the surf. He lunged, and his mouth slammed shut on the boat's stern near where I cowered.

Subjected to the mastication of nature's perfect mulching machine, the *mokoro*'s rear dipped below the waterline amidst a spray of wood chips.

I tumbled backwards, engulfed in a lungful of hot sulphurous hippo-breath.

Snagged by jaws of life and death, I had an inkling of the dangers faced by ox-peckers and plovers that brave hippo and croc teeth.

The world reveals itself to those who venture up close.

Hefty herbivores rocking your boat can be educational.

Take the laws of Archimedes and Newton, for instance.

What goes down...

As the stern tilted downwards, the bow jerked heavenwards.

If a boat's weight is lighter than the water displaced by a behemoth of nature applying downward pressure, the height to which the object flies is disproportionate to the initial hippo-force applied.

The vigorous thrust of the burly hippo's jaws blasted the bow – and Blaise – into the air.

Every hippo-cratic action has an unequal, unfavourable and irrational human reaction.

A discharged projectile, Blaise spiralled upwards.

For an instant, he hovered; then, unable to avoid gravitation's caress, his buttocks smashed into the *mokoro*'s bottom as the hull splash-landed into the river's seething spate.

Conclusion: If we are to live meaningful lives, we must embrace and transcend life's ups and downs, its contradictions and paradoxes. QED.

The current crashed and crumbled, mugged our *mokoro* and manhandled it downstream, leaving a disappointed and prickly river-horse trailing. He grew smaller until he became an insignificant dark charcoal smudge on the floodplain canvas.

Apart from a missing chunk in the stern, we remained afloat, adrenalised, and alive.

We had little time to congratulate each other on our escape, to regroup, or to assess the full extent of the hippo-inflicted damage.

'Crap. V-shaped eddies.'

Whitewater.

Jets of pounding, fermented water ruffled and roiled.

'Lock and load, Bar.'

'You've got to be kidding me. Plucked from the hippo-drome to confront Yambeji's wrath.'

... let the serpent king sing...

The current's snarls intensified, then catapulted our canoe to where we had no wish to go but were helpless to prevent, in a blur of river detritus, protruding tree trunks, sandbanks and rocks.

Violent, unrelenting rapids and vortices side- and back-washed us on neverending hazardous water chutes.

Submerged debris latched onto the *mokoro*'s outrigger and swung us side-on. The float slipped from its rigid restraints and shattered into kindling. Exposed to the swirling current's unrestrained ferocity, the compromised *mokoro* copped a broadside, and flung us *bollemakiesie*.

My back slammed the water's surface, and the rapids whipped me away headfirst. I treaded water, tumbled and turned, but the river's heaving fluctuations sucked at my arms and legs. To keep my head and shoulders above water, I writhed and wrestled against the torrent, but a greater power held me fast. Pinioned by the undertow, decorum gone, I thrashed out in panic for much-needed oxygen.

Words bubbled to my surface.

Trust the river's spirit, Baron... Don't resist... Have courage to let go... To gain your life, you must be prepared to lose it. The adversary without cannot harm you if you quell the enemy within.

I abandoned my fate to the soul of the river.

I ricocheted off an underlying rock and smacked into another. Intense pain and a blinding flash behind my eyes ended in brain fog.

... where there's never any pain...

FORESHADOWED

... back in my brain...

'BARON. HEY, *BARON*!'

Stinging across my face. I opened my eyes to Blaise's hand, patting my cheeks. His action elicited a series of uncontrollable coughs.

Head half-in, half-out of the water, I floated on my back. A haloed Blaise stared at me from above.

'Tell me I'm in heaven.'

'Afraid not. Still in a vale of tears. Thought I'd lost you.'

I raised my head to take in my surroundings. 'No such luck. I remember being pummelled to pulp by boulders.'

'It's called *Slambezi* for a reason,' Blaise grinned. 'I fished you out on the far side of the rapids. You're one lucky soul.'

'I thought you hated fishing.'

'I guess. I could never understand what Dad and you saw in it.' He took a firm hold on the chest-strap of my backpack. 'It puzzled me the two of you could sit for hours together in sublime solitude.'

'You were always welcome.'

'I know. And I tried. After an hour, I'd lost the plot. And the bait and tackle.'

'I enjoyed my own company. It was a chance to process my thoughts. I guess Dad found those times out in the boat relaxing and prayerful, too.'

'Let's get you to safer waters.'

Blaise heaved me past a sandbar towards the relative calm of one of the many placid tributaries that pulsed parallel to the river's main current.

'You can stand.' He wrenched me upright. It took me a moment to find my footing.

'Odysseus had it wrong, Baron.'

'He did? How's that?'

'Scylla and Charybdis, remember? Sometimes your bookish waffle sticks. Odysseus opted for a lesser of evils. But he missed a third way, beyond rocks or whirling places: a steadfast course between extremes. The so-called *golden mean*. It worked for us.'

'Am I still in a brain fuzz or did I hear you right? And it nearly didn't work.'

'Right action comes at a cost,' said Blaise. 'Talking of cost, how's your body holding up?'

'Sore. Grazed. Battered. Grateful I'm alive. You now appear to have survived unscathed.'

'True. Apart from a few bumps and scratches, I am fortunate. I rolled up, avoided the rocks and whirlpools, and the river gods shunted me to its banks. It makes for a pleasant change,' said Blaise. 'By the way you're holding your wrist and that grimace on your face, I suspect you weren't as lucky.'

'Sharp pain in my left hand.' I held it up for inspection. The joint of my middle finger stuck out to one side.

'Swollen around the joint. A dislocation, methinks.'

'I can't move it. Hurts like hell. I must have jammed it or hyper-extended it,' I said. 'You must help me pop it back.'

'Won't that cause more damage?'

'It could. But what's the alternative?'

Blaise's eyebrows furrowed. 'How do we best do that?'

'I'll talk you through it. Push the finger forward, then pull it outward to loosen it up, get the bones back in place. Simple.'

'Easy for you to say,' said Blaise, running his fingers across his mouth. 'Let's get on with it before I lose my nerve.'

'Easier for you than me.' I gripped my left wrist with my right hand. 'On *three*. Ready?'

'Go for it. Surprise me.'

'*Three*.' Blaise pushed and pulled on cue. Needle-sharp pain exploded up my arm, burst in my brain. The finger shifted, then clicked into place.

'Feck, that was *eina*.'

'I felt nothing, Bar. What's your problem?'

'You,' I said, grinning.

'We need to splint it.'

'Tear two strips from my rugger jersey and strap it.'

'Our jerseys resemble windsocks after so many Heath Robinson interventions.' Blaise smiled, shook his head, nibbled at the seam and then ripped off narrow pieces from the left cuff.

'What's so funny?'

'This constant ebb and flow. How the tide has turned, again.' Blaise fashioned a makeshift splint with two strips torn from my jumper's sleeve. 'I wonder if it has a life lesson to teach.'

'Probably. Every experience does.'

'I wait with bated breath.'

He strapped the joints of my middle and ring fingers together, tying each off. 'The expectation is killing me.'

'We might not control life's currents, but we can prepare by training to ride them.'

'Forearmed is forewarned?'

'Something like that. Premeditate worst-case scenarios.'

'Couldn't we drown in a morass of negativity?'

'Not if we realise nothing happens to the wise against their expectations.'

Blaise's tongue protruded as he worked. 'Easier said than done. Now, this repair job *is* in our control.' He exhaled a final satisfied grunt.

'How's that feel?'

'Not half bad. We'll make a paramedic and philosopher of you yet,' I said, clenching and unclenching my left hand.

'How's that wonky ankle?'

'Good,' I said, rotating it. 'Strapping's still tight and in place.'

'Every silver lining has a dark cloud, I reckon,' Blaise said, smiling.

'Little brother, dark clouds are a sign of rain. Life. Benediction. *Grace.*'

'Touché.'

'What happened to the boat?'

'Noticed pieces of it on my way to find you.'

'So we're down-river without a paddle, or a boat. Any ideas?'

'Keep to the original plan. Reach those smoke trails. They can't be that far away. By my estimate, they'd be somewhere south-west of our present position. It shouldn't take long to rediscover them.'

'Agreed. And our pursuers?'

'Hard to say. They'll understand where the river pushed us. What they won't know is where we exited. Unless they come across our piece-meal boat. The current has shifted even that.'

'Stalemate again.'

'We need an exit spot and a safe place to regroup.'

... thru' each slow century of her moving...

My brother slogged and sloughed, wading through the chest-high sludge towards the dark, woody southern riverbank.

In places, we used the gentling leakage of murky water to nudge us on that route, always alert to the potential dangers lurking in the river.

'That's a suitable spot.'

Blaise pointed to a shaded, craggy cul-de-sac beneath overhanging clumps of weeping lovegrass.

'Works for me.'

We laboured towards it, using alternate leg thrusts and breaststroke arms. My breaths shortened, and every muscle ached and quivered as a prelude to cramp and fatigue. In that way, it reminded me of the rugby pre-season hours Blaise and I dedicated to speed and strength endurance training.

Close to our intended destination, Blaise pulled up, and I rear-ended him.

'Something's not right. You sense it?'

To still your inner self in such a hostile environment, to control your breathing on the cusp of exhaustion, was difficult.

'What am I meant to be sensing?'

'Difficult to express in words. *Unease*. It'll come to you if you concentrate. Shush now and listen.'

... for a fistful of silence...

'Can't you hear them? Yells. Shouts.'

'I'm picking up nothing, except for the river's hiss and fizz.'

Not for the first time, nausea and numbness overcame me. I chastised myself for succumbing to its wiles, and overpowered it with an act of the will.

'In that case, Blazer, caution trumps valour. Hurry now.'

Side by side, Blaise and I upped our pace. Arms heaved and hauled, and legs pumped and ploughed, piercing a resistant mud shield. We thrust ourselves forward, coasted into the eroded high-rise riverbank that reared above us, pressed ourselves against it, and sank beneath the water, up to our noses.

Mired in a putrid swampy muck, we waited.

... red are the hands of luxuriant cold stinging blood...

'Twitching at shadows again, hey, Blazer?'

'Maybe. I could have sworn I heard voices.'

'We've delayed long enough. Can't hang about here. It's too exposed. We need to dry –'

'Quiet.' Blaise grabbed my shoulder and shoved me back into the water.

Frost crackled through my veins. A currach of voices, subdued and indistinct, drifted with the light wind. Its chitchat grew louder, breezed towards us, and hove to.

In my head, space slowed and suspended its animation.

The jabber came about, hit the port side tack, and receded.

... climbing valleys into the shade...

Not until time emerged from its self-induced coma did Blaise and I move.

We exchanged glances, nodded. 'Safe as it'll ever be. You happy to lead?'

'Yep.'

'And your damaged finger?'

'Your shoulder's more of a worry.'

Blaise grinned. 'After you, then.'

I scanned the river's steep bank above me, searched for handholds and foot placements, mapped out a course to the top in my head, and climbed.

It was a painstaking, roundabout ascent.

Edge. Grab. Straight arms. Test. Pull. Hips side-on. Step. Eyes-on. Rest. Repeat.

With each step and grab, my confidence grew. I reached the halfway point, five-or-so metres above Blaise, and from my precarious lookout, caught the view, and my breath.

... shadows of trees witnessing the wild breeze...

A rigged windsail trapped a gust of voices and diverted it towards me.

The headwind of words intensified.

Dropped, becalmed.

I flattened myself to the river wall, every muscle taut and tingling, a sharp pain in my left hand, readied to drop into the water. Beneath me, Blaise's eyes caught mine. He shook his head. *Hang on*, he mouthed.

The sounds above wandered, wavered, whirlwinded.

A breathy bellow stilled their storm.

I tried not to look, but I couldn't help myself.

... night arrives with her purple legion...

Through a gap in the thick overhanging lovegrass in mopane shadows, I glimpsed the back of a head donned with a purplish military-style beret.

'Comrades.' A confident, authoritative voice grumbled in Shona. I recognised it from a time before. Quick-fire, terse, targeted words aimed and discharged. I could only pick up on the odd phrase: *boat destroyed... our net... caught nothing... no sign...*

The beret-bearing head whipped around to stare out over the river.

I lurched, teetered, lost balance, and my body surfed the bank's muddy surface. I reached out and grabbed at exposed tree-roots; they arrested my fall.

I prayed beret-man did not look downward.

In deep thought, he stood akimbo, gazing into the distance. He stepped closer to the lip of the riverbank, head tilting in my direction.

A yell made him pivot. He yapped a response, followed by a consternation of orders. They triggered a series of shouts and a flurry of movement.

The commotion faded.

After an over-indulgent wait, I scaled the bank and hauled myself up and over its lip. Wheezing, muscles limp, I lay, chin to chest, scanning the terrain.

I waved to Blaise and beckoned for him to ascend, which he accomplished with agility, relish and gusto. He reached me in a single tail-wag.

'You okay?'

'Apart from skinned hands and a bruised ego, yes.'

He pulled me to my feet. 'Aren't you a leaping leguaan? You should have led.'

'Monitor in motion, that's me,' Blaise grinned. 'Fear fires my lizard brain, lateral movements push me forward.'

'A metaphor for life's complexity. A sideways ascent. Better than my direct free-fall.'

'You still made it to the top, didn't you?'

... the lizard king can do anything...

'Check this out.'

'What?'

'Footprints. This is where they congregated.'

'How many?'

'Hard to say. Maybe a dozen.'

'The same mob that's been on our trail?'

'Highly likely. Look at the criss-cross design. It's the same I saw when following the hyena. The leader's voice was also unmistakable.'

'Did you pick up on anything he said?'

'Phrases, here and there. On a fishing expedition, were the words he used. Double-backed to check if they'd netted us. Their only catch was our boat wreckage. Fishing might not be their strength. Good chance they think we're dead.'

'Fingers crossed. Let's keep it that way.'

Tracks scored the earth, traipsed off to the east, then disappeared into dense bush.

Wet and weary, Blaise and I searched for a refuge beyond the reach of a churlish afternoon sun. We chanced upon a brace of fruiting fig trees in whose shade we rested.

'Shouldn't take long for our clothes to dry,' I said.

We sat in our undies and carried out a provisions check.

'The mamba's okay. Just needs cleaning.' He made the weapon safe, dismantled it and cleaned its parts.

'How's your shoulder?'

'I'll survive,' he said. 'And that finger of yours?'

'Ditto.'

'The rucksack?'

I unpacked it. 'Three bottles of water, intact. Here!' I tossed one over to him.

'And your beloved books?'

'They're fine. Wrapped in a plastic waterproof folder.'

'You're too clever for your own good.'

'I'm just a quick learner. Been caught out before. Only an idiot makes the same mistake more than once.'

Blaise and I foraged for figs, returned to our haven in the shadows, and gorged ourselves on them.

'Fruit diet's giving me the squirts.'

'Better out than in.'

'What I'd give for mom's home-baked bread.'

'A *boerie* roll wouldn't go amiss either. With all the trimmings, and a dash of Mrs Balls.'

'Stop, Baron. My mouth's watering. Think of something else.'

'In breaking open these figs, I can't help but remember Aizi.'

'I was just thinking of her. Whenever I see a fig tree, or eat its fruit, she's present in my memory.'

'She was a real godsend, wasn't she?'

'If it hadn't been for her...' Blaise choked up.

'She points to a deeper truth.'

'Be still my aching heart. To what?'

'To a greater mystery that connects us all.'

The floodplain's malarial and parasitical acolytes had found our cosy hideout, and escalated their interest in our presence.

'Does that mystical union include mozzies and tsetse flies?' asked Blaise.

'It's a package deal. No guarantees. The trick is to treat each thing as a blessing, rather than a misfortune.'

Blaise regarded me, a baffled look on his face coaxing me to elaborate.

'A case in point.' I plucked a handful of budding fig leaves, scrunched them in my hand, and passed them to him. 'Try this. Apply the sap to your exposed skin,' I said, not confident the remedy would ease the sunburn or keep the persistent mozzies at bay. 'Not sure if it'll work, but it's worth a punt.'

Ouma, a well-versed herbalist, often supplied the family with her own repellent brew of citronella, wild rosemary, catnip, mint and garlic.

'Baron,' I recall her saying. 'Nature is the ultimate teacher. She is never mistaken. Right and wrong are human constructs. For her, obstacles and opportunities are the same. Are you alert to the lessons she has to teach?'

I never remember if Ouma ever included crushed fig leaves in her homemade concoction, but much to my relief, the application offered respite.

'Point made,' said Blaise. 'I concede.'

'Of course you do,' I grinned. 'Our stuff's dry enough to wear. Let's get it done.'

Who among you will run with the hunt?

'One more thing before we head off,' said Blaise. 'The smoke trails.'

He clambered up the largest fig tree, scanned west and south, swung back to the ground.

'Closer than we thought, Bar. That direction.' He pointed. *South.*

'After you.' I waved him ahead with a smile.

... touch the earth... chase the scattered sun...

Replenished and renewed, repackaged and redressed, Blaise in the lead, we worked our way to the smokestacks.

They merged above us. A distinct smell of burning charcoal and charred meat on the breeze made me hungrier in anticipation.

The terrain scarped upwards, and we followed the ochred erosion scars to their apex. I scooped up a handful of the red soil and lined my face, arms, and legs with my muddied fingers.

'The ochre makes you look primal.'

'You should try it. I promise you, it'll reduce the sunburn. Good camouflage too. The ultimate fashion accessory.'

'Okay, but note, I'm doing it for the sunburn.'

We reached the summit after a mad scramble and squatted below the skyline in savannah grass. Within a large village of thatched circular mud huts – *rondavels* – a rustic stockade for cattle, or *kraal*, enclosed by an oval palisade of thorn-bush branches, nestled in the valley below.

Around the many cooking fires near its central point, a communal ceremony was underway. Laughter, singing, and beating drums drifted up to our position.

The sun hesitated, poised at its predestined sanctuary. Uncertain of our next step, we waited, scoping the lie of the land. It looked safe, but still we dithered.

... nothing left to do but...

'No sign of security or barbed wire, so not a PV. What do you think?'

'Agreed. Looks peaceful, even ordinary. Although I'm not sure what that normal is anymore,' Blaise said. 'Perhaps that hoopoe's call foreshadowed an invitation?'

I'd forgotten that encounter; it seemed like an event from long ago, outside recent memory.

Still, we tarried.

There was no obvious impediment to our approaching the locals for help, other than some craven scruple or vague feeling of unease. I could not help but think of the ambiguity of my snake dream two nights before and its relevance to our current position.

'Well, Bushmaster, we can't lie here feeling sorry for ourselves. We've got to do something. I vote to go down there and seek some support.'

Aizi's words bubbled into my consciousness.

How will you ever know if you don't leave the safety of the shore?

'I'm in. Nothing ventured, nothing gained.'

... come again... to the land of the strong, and the wise...

As we scrambled to our feet in the clumps of tall grass, a voice growled from behind us.

'What the f–?'

I lost my footing, tripped over Blaise, fell on top of him.

A sudden chasm of queasiness twisted in the depths of my gut, and dizziness pounded in my head.

OMEN

I UTTERED ANOTHER EXPLETIVE.

And a few more.

On his back underneath me, Blaise stared in the direction of the voice in total bewilderment.

'Get off me!'

Disordered and half-intertwined, we must have looked like a failed circus act.

A gnarled, sun-dried face grinned at us from the long grass.

Speechless and breathless, Blaise and I scrambled to our feet.

'*Hau!*' he cackled. '*Kurava mbudzi nedzisipo kurava nedzava matowo.*'

I looked over at Blaise. I could see his mind trying to figure it out.

'He said *counting other people's goats is like counting dead ones.*'

'What's he on about?'

'I believe he's suggesting we should not rely on something of which we are uncertain,' Blaise said. 'So, we should...'

'Abandon our plan.'

'Custom and respect dictate we greet. *Mhoro, Sekuru,*' Blaise said. 'Greetings, Grandfather.'

'*Mhoro wangu,*' he said, eyeing us. 'Greetings to you.' After a brief pause, he added, '*Uri sei?*'

At first glance, the man who stood before us exuded confidence and charisma. A mantle of soft leopard skin covered his upper body. Draped around his left wrist were various colourful bracelets bearing animal shells, ivory, bones, teeth, beads, and stones.

For local communities, leopards had special significance. They were protectors against the machinations of demonic forces. To wear leopard skins marked royalty.

The leopard, *Ingwe*, was a noble beast.

The Shona people recognised the man as a *nyanga*.

Individuals from every background sought advice from *nyangas*. They provided medical and spiritual guidance, and had extraordinary powers to tell fortunes, give advice, bless, heal, or even kill. *Nyangas* possessed a wealth of accumulated knowledge, passed on over the decades, from well before the onset of the colonial era. During the current *chimurenga*, politicians and guerrilla leaders had consulted them.

'*Tinotenda zvisinei*,' I said. 'We are thankful regardless.'

I worked to determine his totem from the clues in his attire, considered the usual suspects: *hungwe*, the fish eagle, *nzou* the elephant, *umvubu* the hippo. Given the number of croc teeth in his wristbands, and its distinctive outline carved into the head of one of his knobkerries, his clan's totem was, I decided, *ngwenya*.

It was odd he was out here by himself. The *nyanga* held pride of place in communal hierarchies.

'*Ndinotenda zvangu*,' he said. 'I am grateful.'

Shona culture has always valued civility and grace, tradition and expectation, dictating that individuals acknowledge the wellbeing of others to show they value the natural interconnectedness among people.

'Hey, Blaise.'

'Got it. I'll try to find out what he's doing out here.' He cleared his throat. 'We are well if you are also well,' Blaise faltered, in broken Shona.

The man looked in his mid-fifties, as suggested by his lined face and beads of grey at his temples. He was tall and sinewy, signalling that he didn't shy away from hard work and physical exertion. He had a simple, dignified look. His dark brown eyes sparkled, hinting at an alertness and powerful life force.

In his left hand he carried two polished *imbuia* knobkerries, the standard fighting sticks preferred by African tribesmen. Tucked into the leopard skin folds at his waist was an ornate ivory-handled dagger.

He and Blaise conferred, combining crude, improvised signs and a smattering of Shona. I picked up on the occasional word or phrase, but that was about all.

'He says his name is *Akashinga*, which translates as *brave one*. He once was the *nyanga* to the people in that village, but not anymore,' Blaise said.

'Guerrillas came and press-ganged the young men to train across the border,' he added. 'Two of them were his sister's sons and they died at the hands of the security forces. When guerrillas returned to recruit more young men, Akashinga objected, killing one recruiter after an argument got out of hand.'

Blaise paused.

'You'd understand he had to leave in a hurry. Now he's *kudzingwa. Banished, outcast*, I believe it means. He's been solo since. He says he followed us from the fig tree.'

'That's scary, seeing we had no inkling we were being surveilled. Ask if our plan to seek help in the village is in our best interests.'

'He already implied that it wasn't. But I'll ask him, just to confirm if we understood.'

Blaise and Akashinga chatted once more. After an animated exchange, Blaise reported back.

'He insists we should stay away. The villagers are divided over the war, split between those opposed to various cadres and militias and those against the Rhodesian military. There's much fear, and many are terrified of reprisals or retribution. They're the meat in the sandwich. A guerrilla cadre is there at the moment. They're looking for *vakomana vaviri vachena* – two white boys.'

Throughout Blaise's feedback, Akashinga studied us. It was unnerving.

'Just as well we didn't follow our initial plan. While there are many devils, angels likewise come in all colours and sizes,' I said, recalling our time with Aizi, and the snake's words in my dream. 'Do you think he'd be willing to assist us? Given his experiences, he might be a useful ally.'

'I'll ask.'

'If he could guide us to a safer settlement or a military base – the SAS or the Scouts? Do you recall what they were called in Shona?' I said.

'The Scouts, you mean? *Skuz'apo*. The pickpockets who bump you and mutter an apology as they take your wallet.'

The Selous Scouts were Rhodesia's feared and respected elite unit, committed to the clandestine elimination of terrorists both within and without the country. Finding them would be difficult if they chose to stay hidden.

Blaise and Akashinga spoke at length, as before.

'He says he can help us to the other side of this escarpment, to the east. We'll have to ford the river at various points, though.'

The snake vision from the night before popped into my head. Could he be the ancestral messenger in my dream? The snake morphed into Aizi.

'I believe we should trust him.'

'What do we have to lose?'

What did we stand to gain?

We needed savvy to survive, and the nyanga had it in great big spade-fuls. We had to tip the scales back in our favour. It was worth the risk.

'Apart from our lives, not much,' I said.

'My gut says *yes*. His story rings true. We need to ride this bus. Remember the bird of good omen?'

'I concur. Nor should we forget Aizi. I've also had some ochre-induced visions myself of late, consistent with that view.'

Blaise looked at me in confusion, shaking his head. '*What?* Don't tell me the red ochre causes hallucinations.'

'Prescient dreams, so the Shona believe. But you'll not let that worry you, will you?'

'Should I?'

'Nah.' I thought it best not to mention the ochre's use as a death mask. Instead, I said, 'You continue to astound me.'

'We're even, I reckon.'

Akashinga gestured for us to follow, setting off at a loping run. I fell in behind him, with Blaise to the rear. We picked up the pace.

To the east.

C'mon baby ... take a chance with us ...

Akashinga set a fast tempo. We avoided the *kraal* by a wide margin and made progress towards the low-lying plains to the east. We traversed at a swift pace, without a sound, keeping in the shadows, confident in Akashinga's hands-on awareness and knowledge of the bush.

Aka, as we called him much to his satisfaction, guided us in the subtleties and nuances of bushcraft, from navigational path-finding and foraging to water-sourcing and effective camouflaging; through counter-tracking and treating ailments and injuries to dealing with animals and insects.

He could solve any problem. In a single afternoon we learnt more from him than we'd ever discovered in our entire lives from everyone else put together.

I am humbled and embarrassed when I consider how, through western eyes, I might have dismissed Aka as inferior as recently as the week before.

It was I who was the student, he the mentor.

He was a hard taskmaster, driving us to up our efforts, but he was likewise thoughtful and patient.

'One who has set traps in burnt grass,' he'd say, 'no longer fears his apron getting dirty.'

He was well-versed in the accumulated ancient tribal mores and astute Shona insights into life. Often, they were riddles and paradoxes that needed to be unravelled to be grasped.

I only wished I could have remembered everything he said.

As a tracker, Aka was unsurpassed. He had a knack for observing and reading the clues, tracks and signs left by animals. He understood the landscape, the animal life and the ecological systems and patterns that made up his environment.

'You need a bigger head than belly. If you have a bigger belly, you become like a child,' he'd declare. 'Skill to find food is more important than mere appetite to enjoy it.'

He discerned multiple clues of the spoor: from prints, scat, feathers, kills, scratching and marking posts, drag marks, sounds, scents, to animal behaviour and habitat cues.

As the sun began its farewell ritual, we jogged onto the floodplain and closer to the river's arteries and its motionless water-basins, home to the most dangerous wildlife in the world.

Aka navigated a prudent path through these pools, threading the needle, so to speak. We gave the deeper, larger ones a wider berth, and forded many a river channel without incident. Although the water was at low ebb, we maintained a constant lookout for crocs and hippos.

While my efforts at appeasing my brother's infected wounds had borne success, Aka had supplemented my concoction with blends of his own herbal ingredients to speed up healing, so much so that within a short time, the infection was eradicated and Blaise, for all appearances, was back to his best. He accomplished similar success with my bruised ankle and dislocated finger.

That afternoon with Aka sped by. So engrossed in our learning, we paid little attention to the heat or time passing. Nor had we considered those in pursuit, which proved to be one of our poorer decisions.

By the time we had forded the river, the trembling sun, a sallow shadow of its daytime self, had sunk to a low beyond the amethyst hills, gathering his tattered *kaross* around himself, a fugitive from the oncoming posse of night, the ashen moon, and her pale-faced, frosty riders.

Who was I fooling?

The language of the western mind dissembles the simple complexity of African wisdom and folklore: Zuva, the sun, rises and sets without its histories or memories. And so with Mwedzi the moon, and Nyeredzi the stars. The sky wears the colours of the spirit, dyed by the quality of the human thoughts projected onto it.

We bunkered down for the night in one of the many impenetrable bush thickets.

Aka had chosen wisely. We were lodged in a nondescript compressed spinney of trees, saplings, shrubs and briars of undergrowth, dominated by acacia.

As we settled in, Aka disappeared into the fading dusk. A short while later, he reappeared with a large, skewered, gleaming and gyrating fish. It was a catfish or, as we knew it, *barbel*. He scaled, skinned and deboned it with dexterous skill, using his razor-sharp ornamental knife. He cut the fish into strips and then doled them out from the knife-tip.

'Not sure if uncooked fish is any better than squirming mopane worm,' I said to no one in particular.

'*Dya, mukomana,*' Aka said, smiling. 'Eat, young man.' He badgered me, gesturing with his hands for me to place the fish strip in my mouth and chew.

I hesitated.

He just sat watching and waiting, a mischievous glint in his eyes. '*Kuramba nyama yechidembo hunge uine yetsuro.*'

I looked over to Blaise.

'To refuse the meat of a skunk is to settle for hare.'

'What does that even mean?'

'It means, Bwana Baron, to decline a gift implies you have no use for it. Accept the gift, no matter how humble, to survive. Sometimes you have to eat humble pie, brother. Or sashimi.'

The experience of consuming mopane worms remained fresh in my mind.

'Come on, Baron,' Blaise said. 'Resist letting your imagined fear cloud the real joys of consuming raw fish. The last thing you want is to refuse Aka's hospitality. You don't want to offend him or hurt his feelings, do you?' He snickered and popped another piece of fish into his mouth. Blaise didn't have any qualms; he must have had guts of steel.

It couldn't be that horrible, surely?

I recalled how he loved to chew on ants and bugs.

'Just imagine you're eating *sashimi.*'

'Like your mopane biltong.'

I placed a long thin strip of fish between my teeth, chewing and grinning at Aka. I ripped at it with my teeth, force-swallowing with sips of water. At least it tasted better than my other personal 'favourite', refined beach-sand, also known as coarse and fibrous muesli. A tad more satisfactory than mopane bugs as well.

'*Waita zvakanaka*.' Aka smiled back at me. 'You have done well.' He lanced another piece of fish and flung it in my direction. '*Kudya kune nzira yekutenda*,' he said. 'Eating is a way of believing, of showing gratitude.'

A long, dark night of the soul awaited.

By the time we'd eaten, the sun had made its escape, replaced by his fickle sister, the sultry moon, under a star-spangled sky. The unvarying nocturne resumed, replacing the daytime shift.

In the light of that temperamental, silvery moon, I opened my journal. I wrote the date.

FRIDAY, 08 SEPTEMBER 1978.

I drew a blank.

I didn't know where to begin. *Unlike me*. I always had words to share. Thoughts tumbled into the *tabula rasa* of my mind.

Write something, *dammit*.

> *Is enlightenment not the hunt itself?*
> *Am I not paladin, penitent, priest, and pilgrim?*
> *Knight, fisher and grail? Is not each of these within me?*
> *At their best, they are a trinity of opposites. At their out-of-sync worst, they lay waste to a state of grace, and wait for the one question to restore them:*
> *What grail do I – should I – serve?*
> *Aizi. 'Only God knows.'*
> *Only the divine may know, but what I understand is this: human existence is a mystery to be savoured. And lived.*

No matter what, I should pursue a path worthy of my greatest efforts. I must venture into the uncharted waters to uncover an eternity of stars.

Is this the treasure – a pearl of great price – I found on the river?

My thoughts stirred, swirled, shifted to Aka. Once more I committed them to paper.

Aka is part of this mystery, this undiscovered treasure, this enigmatic grail.

But can my western gaze grasp at his depths?

How can my voice intertwine with other vibrant voices like his, or Aizi's, or Thumbeza's?

Is it possible to think and write from a post-cultural perspective?

I sighed, closed my journal, placed it back in its plastic sleeve, and into the backpack.

I glanced over to where Aka and Blaise lay. They nestled in the protective crook of two horizontal tree trunks that formed a natural bower. From appearances, both rested in the arms of Morpheus. It was time to join them.

But the sleep I craved was reticent, so I dozed, haunted and chilled by trans-spring gusts of skeletal, bloodied and disfigured faces.

... lost in a wilderness....

FOOL'S PARADOX

IN THAT DROWSY IN-BETWEEN state amid wakefulness and deep sleep, my eyes sagged, and my mind began its midlands meander.

... break on through to the other side...

For in that sleep of death, what dreams may come...

So it was...
    ... my spine tingled, conveying impulses to my entire body.
    I sensed its presence first.

Prowling, stalking.
    Throaty, haunting, resonant coughs.
    Circling.

Every exhalation produced a puff of hot, moist steam.
    A faint yeasty scent invaded my nasal passages, followed by a potent acerbic whiff of cat, not unlike the home-brewed fermented African beer, *umquombothi*.

Bright, burning, shining eyes.
    Silky-smooth pelage.

It crashed into my space and consciousness.

Fingerprinted patterns, shades of
    blackened rosettes on a golden palette.

It took me a while to grasp what it was. Then, with horror, it dawned
upon me. *Ingwe.*

Fearful Asymmetry.

> *Ingwe: profane visionary,*
> > *guardian of (un)earthly spirits,*
> > *adversary and ally of sovereigns;*
> > > *meek-and-muscled moxie.*
>
> *Arboreal nomad and sentinel,*
> > *silent hunter, shrouded in shadows,*
> > *quivering static-kinetic force;*
> > > *(un)restrained ferocity.*
>
> *Ingwe: tormentor and mentor,*
> > *captive boundlessness,*
> > *untamed yet docile;*
> > > *unified disunion.*
>
> *Liminal and (non)linear warrior*
> > *apex predator, at-risk prey,*
> > *mosaic of truthful secrets;*
> > > *(un)bridled power.*
>
> *Ingwe, mystical knight (errant),*
> > *caring yet crafty,*
> > *secular, spiritual, sacred, sublime;*
> > > *paladin, prophet, pilgrim, (priest?),*
> > > *with me once more.*

She rested her powerful forepaws on my chest, and I struggled to breathe. Her intense circular amber eyes absorbed me. I could look nowhere else. She offered a measured, understated growl that roused the darkness.

'Greetings, Baron, and welcome to the African night. My home, and the playground of your species.'

'Who are you?'

'Does that question need an answer? There are at least thirteen different ways of perceiving me.'

'Thirteen perspectives on shades of black?'

'Understand, Baron Black, I am present in all that you are, all that you know. *I am what I am.*'

'What are you asking of me?'

'Wrong question, Baron. Rather, what are you seeking from me? It is you who has summoned me.'

'I'm not sure what you mean by that.'

'Come on, Baron, you're not stupid. The slippery serpent and the stealthy leopard ought not to be awakened from their slumbers, nor invited into your home. But here I am, at your doors. Work it out.'

I thought for a moment.

Think or speak of the devil, and you stand on its curling white-tipped tail.

'Yes, guilty as charged.'

I'd been prodding the beast's belly with a long stick. The welcome mat lay at the doors. What did I yearn to know?

'I hope for an answer to the questions our brightest minds have grappled with over the centuries. I long to understand.'

'Come on then, spit it out.'

'What deity dares to seize such primal energy to form a creature so fearful and beautiful? To harness this vitality and ferocity, he must be even more savage and powerful than his creation, surely?'

'You're not asking the right question, Baron. Try again.'

'Perhaps the creator struggled to compress the potency of such a heart, almost losing control of the process.'

'That's not a question, is it?'

'Let me have another stab at it. I'm in awe of the one who hammered something like you into shape, but horrified this divinity would dare to grasp your tail and trammel such expansive energy. What the hell was he doing? What was he thinking?'

'Better, Baron. Once more.'

'Did the creator rejoice when he saw what he had made?'

'You know, those more eloquent and poetic than you have asked that very question.'

'True, but why are you avoiding it?'

The beast's chest rumbled.

'It is you who are skirting the issues, Baron. Let me help you,' she snarled. 'The creator fashioned a duality of opposites in all things mortal: virtues of grace that ease suffering through love, and egoistic traits that inflict misery through cruelty and arrogance. The former promotes human joy, while the latter undermines and destroys it.'

'I'm presuming that you're speaking metaphorically?'

'I won't dignify that with a response.'

'The lamb and you in harmony, together? The contrary states of peace and war, life and death, or self-sacrifice and tyranny, innocence and experience, good and evil in every human soul? All those interwoven dualities?'

'Now you're thinking more clearly.'

'I'm bewildered he could even consider creating such conflicting extremes in each of us.'

'Baron, you need not be. Both ends of the spectrum are part of the package. Without contraries, there is no progression. And I don't have to only signify destruction and evil. My savage prowess may likewise

symbolise an unconquerable spirit in all those who rebel against hypocrisy, injustice and oppression.'

'Your untamed energy might also embody the ugly natural desires
and instincts of the created world.'

'No guarantees, then. That's the risk. Creation is free to follow its
impulses. It can mean losing control.'

'I've experienced that loss recently myself, and it worries me. But
why take the chance? Should we be able to change our spots?'

'Why not? Why create something that has no choice? Where's the
joy in that?'

'It's the extremes in the opposites that appal me.'

'Baron, would you concede then that we have both extreme repul-
sive, and attractive qualities? Our burning presence in the darkness
causes human despair, as well as hope?'

'It could also be a matter of perspective. Perhaps the real question
is this: with what strength could this creator mould and control the
dynamic energies of creation and destruction in you? *In me?* What
prompted him to undertake a deed so formidable, so dreadful, so
painful and yet so beautiful in its consequences?'

'Much better, Baron. The pivotal question is yet to be asked.'

What was that supposed to mean?

'Trust your instincts, Baron.'

It dawned on me what that question might be. 'Could the creator
who framed the universe contain, within his very nature, both you and
the lamb?'

'Yes, Baron, at last. No longer becalmed. Now you're navigating with
a wet sail.'

'While speaking of the Almighty's nature, I find the opening scene
between the creator and his adversary in the *Book of Job* disturbing. The
creator doesn't emerge from that too well, does he?'

'You've missed the important bit in that book, Baron.'

'Have I? Taken as a whole, I regard Job as a kindred spirit. I find his story nothing short of inspirational. Now, let's just say God's performance is underwhelming in this narrative.'

'Now that you mention it, you're much like Job: defiant and knuckle-headed.'

'Hilarious. But in Job, I detect traces of existential heroism and endurance. He's bloodied, unbroken, honest, intelligent, uncompromising. And impatient. Job demands some integrity from his creator when he asks why he should trust him when he plays power games to amuse himself.'

'As far as I remember, the creator challenges Job from the midst of a whirlwind, Baron, asking him whether he can imagine or understand the creator's mind, and if he can supersede him in anything. He wouldn't be much of a creator otherwise, would he?'

'Spoken like a real comforter! Is that meant to placate me, or answer my questions?'

'It should, Baron. And yes, it offers an answer. As I remember it, God asks Job to consider two creatures, the behemoth and leviathan. If we are fearful of them, how could we ever challenge the deity who gave them life?'

'I suppose you're up there with the behemoth and leviathan?'

'It's not my place to say. I could counter by arguing that you're up there too. The point is this: you – or anyone – cannot subject the painful experiences of human existence to a meaningful analysis. The creator's workings are beyond our ability to fathom. We cannot see the bigger picture of the creator's purpose. We must learn to trust, no matter the circumstances.'

'Well, that's a cop out. When you consider how our creator treated Job, yours is a less-than-empathic reply.'

'You misunderstand, Baron. In the end, God intervenes to restore Job's health, wealth, and family to verify *His* faithfulness, compassion, and justice. While Job's righteousness and integrity are vindicated, so too, is God's supremacy.'

'Cold comfort for Job, who lost everything, including his children. If God treats his faithful with such disdain, what hope for the rest of us?'

'It's just a narrative, Baron. The Job-poet gives us a framework for contemplating the complexities of suffering and the human response to it. It's meant to prompt us to reflect on faith and resilience, and offers insights into the human condition and the search for meaning. It challenges simplistic notions of cause and effect, highlighting the complexity of moral and divine order. Its enduring relevance lies in its capacity to stimulate introspection and foster empathy.'

'That's a mouthful. While I understand the Job-text asks profound theological and existential questions in a textualising way, embracing the transformative power of metaphor and symbol, to evoke a sense of wonder, mystery, and open-ended inquiry, it also provokes anger.'

'What then, are you trying to ask, Baron?'

I expanded. 'Theodicy. The co-existence of God and the reality of suffering and evil. How does anyone argue with an omnipotent, invisible, and unsympathetic creator? He can't have it every way. He shouldn't be adversary, judge, and executioner at the same time. I cannot measure it. Almost all the explanations I've read have been unconvincing. It looks as if this conundrum is the best argument *against* God. Job grasped the paradoxes of it. What do you say to that?'

'Why seek to know what is beyond human understanding?'

'Who can ever say what is possible or not? That I can think, and feel, should be enough to justify my questioning. My doubt. My belief. *Nothing human is alien to me.* Is that inappropriate?'

'Ah, Baron, should there be definitive explanations? Perhaps there are none. Each soul must figure out its own meaning by living the questions before growing the answers.'

'I agree definitions are problematic. Some answer – however tentative – would be helpful. The creator's evasiveness is too convenient.'

Ingwe gave an annoyed, discordant growl. She adjusted her position on my chest. The weight of inevitability pushed down on me.

'Perhaps you're complicating things, Baron. Let's simplify the matter.'

'Can we do justice to a complex issue by simplifying it? The danger is that we might trivialise it.'

'Good point, Baron, but sometimes a reductionist approach can be useful. I think what you're proposing is this: the creator permits evil, or colludes with it. Am I right?'

'It's you who's said it. How do you reply to that allegation?'

'I'm not a mind-reader, Baron.'

'Why is God silent? I'm tired of talking to the big nothing. Why will He not front up?'

'The creator has his own agenda. You're also indulging in some stereotyping, Baron. You realise this, don't you? God has no gender or race, nor does he subscribe to a particular religion.'

'I don't know how to frame my ideas outside the limits of my language and my context ...'

'You're made in the divine image, aren't you?'

'What does that even mean? Isn't it the other way round? Don't we make *Him–Her–It* in our own image and likeness?'

'An interesting notion, Baron. I'm only trying to help to clarify the issues.'

'*Ja*, in the shadelands, the one-eyed creator rules...'

'That's pretty cynical, Baron. You should retract.'

'I'll rephrase. In the shadelands, the one-eyed creator doesn't rule. Perhaps he's no-eyed. *Better?*'

'Baron, you're in the jaws now, aren't you?'

'I'm beyond that, in the digestive tract.'

'You have a flair for the dramatic.'

'So I'm often told. But I'm no actor. Rather, I'm a product of a concocted experiment, akin to Frankenstein's creature,' I insisted.

'No, Baron, a postmodern Prometheus.'

'I'm beyond the irony, scepticism and incoherence of postmodernism. I'm looking for a critical style that's post-tragic, post-linear and post-rational. I'm more akin to a post-postmodern Job, or Odysseus.'

'That's a little dark, even for you, Baron Black. All this *post-post* wordiness can be confusing. I believe the term you're looking for is *meta-modern*.'

'*Meta*? That's above and beyond me. Why not toss in *trans-modern* or *hyper-modern*? They're more relatable.'

'That's the whole point, Baron. It has always been between, above and beyond.' Ingwe gave a half-laugh growl. 'You love the labelling, too, don't you? If we're going to use labels, the Promethean idea is a good fit for you. Perhaps disguised as a hybrid of Faust and Karamazov.'

'Are you trying to give me some sense of tragic nobility? Do you believe I should be bound to a rock for ravens to peck at my liver for eternity? Because I aspire to be more? Why not toss Aeneas, Oedipus and Lear into the mix, while you're about it?'

'Icarus, too.'

'Look what happened to him. If I question the creator's motives and demand he justify himself, will the same happen to me? Did I request that God create me? It's the creator who's the monster.'

'Now, now, Baron. Don't get so worked up. Do you imagine our creator is intimately attentive to me, or you? Doesn't he perhaps allow us just to be?' Ingwe asked.

... or not to be... yeah, that is the question...

'Not the free will stuff again. I'm done with that.'

'Isn't that the key, Baron?'

'No, I'm more interested in why the creator has withdrawn from taking responsibility for the defects in his design – suffering caused by evil. Why is he so quiet? Should we see this silence as hubristic or an admission of guilt? Is he in exile? On vacation? Or does he have other things on his mind? Perhaps evil is a by-product of his despotic needs, or of who he is. Maybe he feels he's failed,' I lamented. 'Or is it apathy? Maybe he doesn't exist, and we're living in a fool's paradox.'

'Baron, don't let your emotions get the better of you now.'

'He's a super-seagull,' I continued. 'Shits, messes and leaves, expecting us to clean up on his act. Is that fair?' After a moment, I added, 'Have I missed something?'

'Ah, Baron, there's no fair here. The creator picks on his friends and is more albatross than seagull.'

'I'm not sure if I'll ever be part of that august friendship circle. And we all know what happened to the albatross, don't we? People have worn its decaying carcass around their necks with pride rather than remorse ever since. That psychological weight is sapping my energy.'

'Not the whole God-is-dead thing again, Baron?'

'The God-is-dying and has-been-dying idea has been around for at least a century. Our need and desire for God is undergoing a radical shift in consciousness. And that's not a bad thing, despite the move to the secular.'

'You're not one of those last men, are you, Baron?'

'I see more potential in becoming a hybrid of the existential Christian and *Uber-mensch*, to be honest.'

'Another of those paradoxical fusions. You, my friend, have the makings of greatness. But tell me, Baron, can we ever – or even dare to – read the mind of the creator? Can we impute the creator's designs or his thinking?'

'I'm not sure I want to even try. Anyway, it's difficult enough to fathom *my* mind...'

'What should we infer from your questioning, then?' the creature asked.

'Perhaps it means the matter is in our hands. The search is everything. Every individual, if he tries hard enough, can redeem himself, humanity, and even the creator,' I said. *'The fault lies not in our stars, but in ourselves.'*

'Back to the free will thing, Baron. No getting away from it.'

'Do you mean that as a universal truth or a particular truth?' I asked.

'Baron, do you mean a particular universal truth, or is that a universal particular truth? After all, the most personal is also the most universal.'

'Stop smuggling my mind. Don't universals and particulars inform one another? Is evil within and beyond, immanent and transcendent?'

'I can't give a definitive answer.'

'By the same logic, would this not also apply to the good?'

'Makes sense.'

'Can we be certain?'

'I cannot speak for the creator. It's not my place to answer that.'

'This discussion is going nowhere, other than in vicious circles, akin to waiting for god-ot.'

Ingwe grunted. She shifted her position again, causing me to wheeze.

'You need to stop deferring to the creator all the time,' I quipped. 'It's doing you an injustice.'

Her golden eyes bore into me. 'No, it's not. Come on. Persevere. Join the God-dots.'

'What dots? Whose dots? You're deluding yourself.'

'Baron, careful now. Let's abandon the traditional view of the creator. Apply some reverse theology. Maybe He – or She – is not what we think. Perhaps our creator is not intimately involved in the minute detail of our lives, as you suggested. If that's so, what's left?'

'We dare not leave it all up to the creator, anyway. Isn't he-she waiting for us to do something? Isn't that why we're here?'

'Are you saying God is a *verb*? That the creator of all intervenes in creation only through the actions of all things living?'

'Yes. That's the point. God doesn't play dice with the universe,' I said. 'Why would she-he defy the natural law which he-she has created? Natural law is just another human construct. Scientific advancement and ethical complexification suggest the universe is more and more inscrutable,' I added. 'Our understanding of its skewed, absurd and chaotic nature is arcane, or sphinxlike, for want of better words. A mystery. Can we ever know the ways of nature? And by implication, the creator?'

'Creation has always been what it is, dynamic, evolving, as it should, along with our awareness of it. Where does that leave us?'

'Up the river covered in elephant dung.'

'Come on, Baron, you can do much better than that.'

'Okay. I have two options: I can choose either to follow my creative, or de-creative, urges. *Desire or grace.* Both are always present. The problem is that I'm finding they're intertwined. Maybe it's not *either... or*, but *both... and*. Or both of these concepts together. Maybe the de-creative and creative urge leads to something beyond the sum of their parts.'

'So, it transcends the creator? The resolution lies outside opposites, past good and evil? Beyond the entrenched positions? In No-One's Land? Not one or the other? Rather, in Dionysus and Apollo, together, melding in another kind of space?'

'It's a relative Garden of Eden. In the end, each of us must decide for ourselves,' I argued. 'The outcome will be our responsibility. Not the creator's.'

'Sounds creatively existential. Based on what values, Baron? What criteria? Whose standards?'

'Should there be any objective principles? Are there such things? If there were, should I not have some say in determining what those benchmarks should be?'

'Baron, it worries me you're so full of other people's wise axioms and dictums. It has the danger of becoming platitudinous.'

'Platitudinous? That's rich coming from you. How else can we progress? There's nothing either good or bad, but thinking makes it so...'

'There you go again. If it depends on thinking, then think for yourself. Trust your intuition. After all, untamed leopards are wiser than trained ponies. If you respect truth, you shouldn't subject it to too much analysis.'

'I'm an untrained pony, unsure if I could recognise truth, even if I sat on it.'

'That's where an honest search for truth in its many guises begins, Baron.'

'Where I stand depends on where I sit?'

'Stop chucking out clichés. Move beyond axiom and riddle. This line of enquiry will get you nowhere.'

'Perspective is everything. Reality is a hypothesis.'

'Cliché-touché. Spoken like a true relativist. Remember, there are more things in heaven and earth, Baron, than are dreamt of in your theology. Your standpoint shouldn't depend on your conditioning. Where you sit shouldn't depend on where you stand. If you are a thinking being, as you've argued, are you not able to unlock those mind-forged manacles that fetter you?'

For once, I had no comeback, apart from, 'Now look who's throwing out the clichés.'

'I see why your family calls you a disestablishmentarian,' she continued. 'You're pretty obstinate.'

'Do you blame me? It's in my nature to interrogate the pillars of human knowledge, those assumptions we take as gospel.'

'I grant you have a point. But, tell me, if we're all thinking differently, using our own personal frames of reference, how can there ever be any consensus on anything?'

I searched for words to frame a response.

'I'm tempted to say your question is subjectivity dressed in the borrowed robes of objectivity. Do you not see all points of view, all truths, need to address the pivotal question: according to what standard or measure?'

Ingwe chuckled. 'Ah, measure for measure. A solid rebuttal, Baron. At heart, you're a genuine scholar and sophist. From your perspective, there's no normal or abnormal, no right and wrong, just competing, swirling systems and provisional worldviews that give meaning to the life of each individual.'

'Yes. Consensus comes from the system the majority supports.'

'Then our evils, such as colonialism, genocide, slavery, sexism, racism, are okay if we all agree on it? Can you not see, relativism is contradictory at its very core?'

'Has absolutism been any better?'

'Point made. I respect the way you think,' Ingwe admitted. 'Perhaps the solution lies between and beyond the dichotomies, Baron. The relative and the absolute are not so opposed, after all. They might be enmeshed.'

'Yes, I alluded to that earlier.'

'So you did.'

'I'm trying to conceptualise it, and it's proving difficult.'

'That's the actual nature of this beast. Think of it this way, then. This might help: nothing is wholly bad or good. There's a continuum. A tension. Evil can have bewildering irrationality and good capacious resilience. They need each other.'

'What are you really saying?'

'Me and the lamb lying side-by-side. It's about balance. Or, even more radically, we mirror each other all the time.'

'Are you suggesting the dual impulses of the human heart are yoked? Yin and Yang. Passion and order. A disunion and union between Goldmund and Narcissus. An alchemist's red-hot crucible, a marriage of heaven and hell.'

'Atta-boy, Baron, you're on fire. We need to balance form and substance, élan and control. Where does this lead us?'

'Perhaps this persistent and ongoing conciliation of opposites is the key essential for human growth. It's requisite in the individual's quest for authenticity, self-knowledge and spiritual fulfilment.'

'You're flirting with an answer, Baron. You alluded to the crucible in the search for meaning.'

'Back to the simultaneous union and disunion of contraries. I can't seem to move beyond this idea.'

'Bear with me. Let's walk back the argument. Would you accept our sacred stories, myths, our art, music and literature, like the Job-story, while not historical fact, address spiritual truths that speak to the heart and feed the soul?'

'I'd concede that powerful artworks evoke and provoke both an emotional and intellectual response to challenge our sensibilities, and give us ways to imagine the metaphysical.'

'Would you agree their real power rests in the way they hold together all the intangibles and paradoxes the rational mind cannot process by itself?'

'They provide wisdom and insight into those questions that have perplexed humanity for centuries.'

'It must follow that such myths transport us into a deeper sense of time.'

'By *deeper* time, you mean?'

'All time, past, present and future, across all cultures and nationalities. This deeper time transfigures, even transubstantiates our consciousness.'

'That sounds trans-discombobulated, if you ask me.'

'Not a simple concept to grasp, I admit, but stay with it. Deeper time yields a perspective beyond the tyranny of the now. It joins us to the shared experience of humanity and reminds us we belong to a profound cosmic mystery greater than our little selves.'

'Makes sense so far. Less trans-discombobulated.'

'The first step to appreciating life's mystery is to recognise its contradictory nature. It is monstrous and beautiful all the time. We cannot bend the natural realm to our will or make it a rational abstraction. If we think we can create the cosmos in our own image, excluding pain, suffering and sorrow, redacting time, decay and death, then we are beating the cowhide drum for madmen to dance, and we become as foolish as they are, unfit for any form of enlightenment.'

'Poetically put. Most reflective people would have little trouble acknowledging this. What's your point?'

'Here it is. It would be useful to imagine a space where such deeper time conversations can occur, as a trans-rational space.'

'Please elaborate.'

'The western mind has preferenced a rational zeitgeist over the millennia and has explained human experience in terms of dichotomies. It has lost touch with the richness in its soul outside of such polarities. A way exists to restore balance.'

'That's in the trans-rational? Much like transcultural and transnational? A kind of trans-knowledge?'

'Yes, spot on, Baron. The trans-rational is that third way, beyond and between the rational and irrational. Some speak of it as the littoral zone or liminal space. But it's more than that. It's premised on paradox. It allows us to consider those complex experiences that often defy the rational, such as love, death, evil, suffering, God, and eternity, in a non-judgemental, non-sectarian, non-dualistic and unconstricted manner.'

'If I understand you correctly, within a trans-rational framework, we can probe those deeper wellsprings of soul, heart, mind, culture, and nationhood in an open-ended, imaginative, and honest space?'

'Yes, Baron. It's a shift from an egocentric to soulcentric worldview. We'd be unimpeded by ideology, rigid formulae and narrow definitions of culture and religion to explore life itself. Isn't that an exciting prospect?'

'While it sounds too good... and scary... to be true, it's still a framework.'

'We have to start somewhere beyond current paradigms. They've failed.'

'From ground zero?'

'No, Baron. But we should get out of our own way. Let go of our comfortable certainties. Destabilise our resistance to imagining something better; consider how to become better at being human, as individuals and as a civilisation. What we need is another renaissance, beginning with how we perceive, understand and sustain the world.'

'That's a big call. And nigh impossible to achieve.'

Ingwe emitted a growl.

'Our civilisation is approaching an inflection point, Baron.'

'The self-destruct point of no return, you mean? The so-called *pickle*?'

'If we are to imagine a new taste-fusion beyond its acerbity, we must first savour that pickle's every nuanced morsel, separate and identify each ingredient, to fathom how we are complicit in its creation. Have you chomped on it yet? Felt what its taste might mean for you?'

'I'm rather partial to pickles, but I understand what you're getting at.'

Ingwe growled. 'Do you?'

'Yes. To move forward, each of us must consider how we have personally flavoured the pickle, added to the existential predicament we find ourselves in.'

'To improve our chances of surviving and thriving, it helps to know what we are doing and why we do it. To rethink our world, Baron, we must understand our existing systems, our patterns of thought, our theologies, and virtues.'

'And the trans-rational impulse is the answer?'

'It could be, Baron, if we explore the undiscovered, spiritual country of our minds, and engage more creatively and proactively to nurture this trans-consciousness.'

'Most people would reject notions of trans-rationality, toss it in the too-hard basket. Nationalisms, group identities, and religious traditions offer more certainty, control and safety.'

'No one said it would be easy, but it would be worthwhile. People will surprise you if you give them a chance. There's no stopping an idea whose time is due. Now's that moment. Your invitation to deeper inner time awaits, Baron, to discover more about your own immaculate conception, and help others uncover theirs. Are you up to it?'

'That's an interesting way of putting it.'

'Each of us has a unique spiritual blueprint. Your life is a journey back to its source. From head to heart. The creator comes to you disguised as your life, Baron.'

'If so, how, where, do you propose I start?'

'You're the hero of your own narrative, Baron. Only you can write it, craft your destiny. Get started. Just begin, with grace and daring, in your small sphere of influence. This will bring you closer to the treasure you seek.'

'Whatever happens, I know I must hold on to something of profound virtue. On my thirteenth birthday, my father gave me a bronze medallion, which sad to say, I've lost. I don't think I ever valued it enough. *Until now.* Inscribed on it was Cicero's adage, *Summum Bonum.* 'The greatest good.' That's not a bad place to start.'

'There's a corollary to add, Baron. One last step.'

'I read it somewhere – I wish I could remember the text. The words have stuck with me.'

'Are you going to put us both out of this misery?'

'All things are atoned for, all things are redeemed by compassion and love.'

With a throaty purr, the muscled feline disengaged itself from me and vanished into the black recesses of the bush.

... break on through...

In me, Ingwe sniffs the lamb.

But when my lamb-scent dissipates, I realise with all the certainty of the Southern Cross pointing the way in the heavens, Ingwe will return.

She always does.

She has raided my fortress often, circling, challenging, probing for any weaknesses in my defences.

She has penetrated beyond the drawbridge and portcullis to claw at my inner citadel.

She is relentless.

She has the endowed and hereditary patience of her species.

Silent and serene, she waits for the darkest of nights,

for the witching hour.

When the sun's abed, the moon and stars are in anxious hiding, when my defences are lowered and I drowse, often smug in my certainty, most vulnerable to ambush,

she strikes.

In the ensuing chaos and carnage of her nocturnal assault, she withdraws to her tree-lair to contemplate her next strategic attack.

And I,

scarred, wary, and no longer at lamblike-ease,

I prepare as best as I can, for

her inevitable return.

LEVIATHAN

... lost in a roam'n wilderness...

AN INSISTENT WHISPER JARRED me from my slumber.

'Hey, *Baron.*'

It took me a short while to get my bearings. Blaise loomed large above me, almost mouth-to-mouth.

'Quiet now. We've got company.'

It remained dark, with hints of the pre-dawn sky. Absolute blackness had dispersed, replaced by a relative, eddying ash-grey mist, which had descended undercover of that darkness. The trees, portentous and eerie silhouettes, stood hushed and idle.

The two of us crawled over to where Aka lay, staring to the south.

'What's up?'

Blaise put his forefinger to his lips, cupped his ear. Senses sharpened, we scanned the terrain.

Stony silence.

Tension in our muscles eased, and we slipped into relax-mode. Aka cautioned us, motioned with his hand, and we remained where we were, senses tingling, primed and alert.

In the scrubland of my mind, I imagined dull footfalls padding the ground, delicate fingers ruffling the serenity of tree-foliage, gentle dulcet tones whispering from afar.

In the mist close beyond our position, a mild cadence rose and fell. It filled the space, stretched towards and around us.

Prickles on the spine.
Leopard? Lion?

We sat tight, unmoving, impassive.

From amongst molasses-blackened trees, several human shapes materialised in the misty haze a short distance to our front, narrowing into full focus.

Rice-flecked camouflaged jackets. AKs slung over shoulders.

Six? Seven?

They pushed forward in single file.

On their current trajectory, they would blunder into our position.

They had not yet uncovered our tracks, or they might have deployed by advancing to contact, in a sweep formation, ready for trouble. It was hard to tell if they had stationed any point guards to offer protection against an outflanking manoeuvre. We'd not seen any evidence of foraging scouts to the front, either.

Reports on the training and skill of the guerrilla cadres circulating in city circles were mixed. Like many things in this war, clouded by weapons of mass persuasion and propaganda, it was difficult to determine their accuracy.

The figures ambled towards us.

Was this the same cadre pursuing us? The numbers did not add up. Where were the rest of them?

If they drew close, we would have to defend ourselves.

Blaise had drawn the mamba, expecting confrontation, and Aka grasped his knife and knobkerries. Without a word, he passed one to me. I nodded my thanks, grasped it. It rested, a snug fit in my palm.

With a few gestures, Aka signalled a makeshift battle-plan. Blaise and I followed his hands and acknowledged understanding.

We kept count as they shuffled closer.

Seven.

They clumped together, not evenly spaced: a trio bunched in the front, two further back, and two lagging.

... the snake... he's long...

We held our position.

The cadre ambled to within a few metres.

Stopped.

Hesitant, they awaited instructions.

The front three huddled, muttered amongst themselves, pointed and argued in subdued tones. One of them, wearing a burgundy beret, turned to his comrades behind and signalled for them to hurry. His over-energetic arm movements suggested agitation.

Was he the same man from atop the riverbank?

The three conferred again. The man in the beret persisted with his gesticulations.

Were they lost?

We hung in the air like dragonflies, suspended in that crucial moment before decisions or actions of pith and consequence.

After much finger-pointing and head-shaking, the cadre headed left into the latticed mist, in the same formation. Their footfalls receded into the gloom.

Tension eased. Pulses slowed. Breathing settled.

The easing was short-lived. More jabbering floated in the ghostly stillness.

Bliksem! Just as well we'd waited.

More bodies crystallised from the mist, from the same direction as those before them, in a similar formation.

I counted them off as they drifted closer.

One... two... plus two... and another... one more. Six, and the earlier seven.

Unlucky thirteen. The numbers corresponded.

The same cadre chasing us.

We could do nothing but wait.

If they maintained their current route, we would avoid each other. One by one, they drew abreast, passed into the mist beyond us. Again, I counted them.

Six... five... four...

So focused on counting, I shifted my aching feet, my thigh knocking the knobkerrie from my hand.

It thudded to the ground.

It wasn't more than a flutter, but in my ears, it was a raucous charging hippo. One guerrilla must have sensed something amiss because his head jerked in surprise in our direction.

He swore under his breath.

Before he could dispel a warning or unsling his rifle, Blaise discharged his firearm into the formation. The mamba shattered the silence, a series of resounding thunderclaps.

Aka had, in that instant, rushed from the bush thicket and smashed his knobkerrie into the rear-marker's skull, and as he fell with an ululating cry, Aka thrust a shining dagger into the man's neck. He extracted the bloodied blade; it emerged with a slurp.

'I have eaten!'

The man died before he slumped to the ground.

Yelling, I burst from the bush, swung the knobkerrie at guerrilla number five's head. I missed. The club swished in the air.

My opponent had stepped back, avoiding my lunge. If it had connected, it might have decapitated him, such was the force I threw behind what was a square cut rather than an aggressive downward *coup de grâce*. I over-balanced, staggered, sprawled, and tumbled headfirst into the ground.

Winded, dagger pain in my left ankle, and stinging grass burns on cheek and palms, I rolled over.

In a single graceful movement, the terr unslung his AK, pirouetted, raised and pointed it at me. From behind, two loud cracks in quick succession erupted in my ears and the man crashed on my ribcage, a look of total disbelief stamped on his face. He gurgled, blood spurting from his mouth as he fell. It froze, paralysed, in a half-open, silent scream.

Staring into those lifeless, protuberant eyes within an inch of mine, the only thought I had was, *God, he... she was so young.*

In abject horror, I remained transfixed by the smooth and rich brown mysteries of her face and the unsettling realisation of what had just happened. They thrust at me, a thousand swords of disbelief and dis-ease, disintegrating my already unravelling sensibility.

I pushed her limp body from mine, careful not to show any disrespect. Dazed, with thrumming ears, I studied the woman's face.

Her regal, dignified features reminded me of the young woman my parents had employed to act as nanny when Blaise and I were much younger.

Her name was Fadziso, 'one who brings happiness', but we called her 'Faddy'. We had considered her part of our family. She was 'the girl' who did our bidding. It mattered not that she was a young adult, an employee, worthy of our greatest respect.

So many years later, to my shame, I have no recollection of her full indigenous name, the richness of her story, or what became of her.

So little I knew. Less had I understood.

There were others. Their pick-locked faces rolled in sequence through me, soft as thunder. Lena. Valerie. Janet. Rose. Linda. Clementine.

Each trapped in the shadowy coils of a guilty heart.

Echoes reverberated over the *veld* as Blaise, advancing, swivelled and shot at the front two terrs, who scampered off into the mist in total disorder.

Aka loped to my side. 'A baby snake is a snake; it is never too small. When it is in the house, you do not worry about its length, its age or its sex.'

He scurried off again.

I wasn't sure if his simple, unambiguous wisdom was ever going to placate me. A poisonous snake may be lethal, even from birth, but we were all bloody snakes. We'd scotched this one, pissed it off.

Aka leapt from body to body, eviscerating them. To the western mind, disembowelment looked brutal and unfeeling, but he was paying them a warrior's respect by aiding their spirits to the ancestral realm beyond.

'You gonna be all right?' Blaise grabbed the front of my jumper, dragged me to my knees.

'Head's spinning a bit. Struggling to breathe. Think I've cracked a rib. Some ankle pain. Sorry about that slip-up.'

'Forget it. Shit happens. Now, get up.'

He hauled me to my feet.

Aka came over to us, a smile chiselled on his face. 'He who ate *sadza* dry now dips it into relish; he who dipped it into relish now eats *sadza* dry,' he philosophised while wiping the blood from his dagger on the grass.

When would the blind and fickle Lady Fortuna break the spokes and fellies of that revolving wheel and pronounce our turn for a double dose of tribulation?

Blaise checked the mamba's clip of ammo. 'We need to haul ass before they regroup and return. Only three bullets left. The sun will burn off this moisture. The odds are again spinning in their favour.'

'*Famba!* Move. Or die,' said Aka. 'Those at peace are dead; as for us who live, a spear to our rear prods us. Follow me.'

With a wave, he strode back towards the river. I shook my head. He was full of poetical and paradoxical words of wisdom, even in moments of crisis.

What did he mean? Don't try to live forever? Beware the Spear of Destiny? Shadows and dust?

Whatever he intended, we were in borrowed heaven.

Through the mist, the light softened to a royal blue.

Time waited not; we had to squeeze from its marrow every morsel of life.

I snatched up our rucksack and took tentative steps. The pain in my ankle and chest were acute, but I fell in behind Aka, Blaise bringing up the rear.

Shift happens too.

We ran at the double. *South.*

The sun had yet to appear, but his dressing-room door stood ajar. He'd received his entrance cue.

In the misty, semi half-light, Aka held up his hand. We slowed to a walk. With no word spoken, he gestured for us to conceal ourselves. We went to ground in a shallow *donga* in the brush.

Not a moment too soon.

We heard our adversaries emerge from the savannah grass. They almost fell in on top of our location.

The cadre had regrouped, turned at an acute angle to its retreating trajectory, and in a clever counter-ambush manoeuvre, headed back towards our position at a tangent.

Our pursuers passed nearby then stopped. A voice called in Shona, 'Any sign of them?'

'Spread out. They can't be too far away.'

The mist swirled, scurried and shrank. First light was upon us all. In moments, it would expose our position. Heads down, weapons at the ready, bodies tense, we dared not move.

The voices passed. Silence wrapped its arms around us once more.

... driver...

We fell in behind Aka as before, worked our way back onto a course towards the south at right angles to our hunters.

... where are you taking us?

The sultry, coquettish mist lifted, and the sun, now tired of its flirtatious dalliance, searched for amusement elsewhere.

The three of us reached the river in rapid time. It was as we'd left it the day before. At a depleted level, we could cross waist-high at its deepest point. We splashed in, wading with thrusting arms and legs.

We scrambled onto the far bank and hurried in the wash of Aka's footsteps. He took us on a murderous, weaving run through a maze of alluring pools. What lay beneath their dark and tantalising surface, we could only imagine. There was no time to care.

Behind, we heard shouts, yells and sporadic bursts of automatic gunfire. Tracers whined and whizzed above, but we were beyond effective range.

Realising we'd given them the slip, our hunters had once again doubled back.

... the lake... the ancient lake, baby...

Aka had used an alternative route.

We reached a narrow finger of pulpy land, three to four metres wide and twenty long, between two glassy pools. Aka slowed and motioned for us to be silent, to step where he stepped.

Thus, we began our hellish trip along a slim promontory between two lifeless and ominous watering holes.

If you're going through hell...

We scanned the uninviting water to the left and right as we advanced, but we could detect nothing.

Gunfire had ceased; the guerrillas were obscured by one of the many dead, eroded earth scars that disfigured the landscape.

We inched forward, stepping without panicking.

Looks can be deceiving.

My chest fluttered and my palms grew moist. I concentrated on my breathing.

Deep, even, slow. A step at a time.
  Be in the moment.

When we had reached the centre of that marshy neck of land, Aka shot up his hand. We halted in our tracks, caught in an unprotected position. My heart quivered in my gut. Every fibre wanted to burst free, but

I had wedged myself amidships between Aka and Blaise. I crouched, rigid, waiting for his next instruction.

We were at our most vulnerable. It was a kill zone. The water and its surrounds remained still.

... there's danger on the edge...

Aka waved us forward, and we resumed our ponderous trek. We'd reached the bluff opposite when the waters to our left shifted, as if someone had inhaled and exhaled without pausing.

The water's surface lifted, disturbed and displaced in a surge of bubbles and ripples.

Aka saw it a fraction before I did. 'Move!' he shouted. *'Famba!'*

A rush, a thrash of foam and wake, erupted to our rear. We scrambled, piled up the far incline, and collapsed in a heap at the top.

An enormous underwater silhouette of a Nile crocodile, nearly five metres from snout to tail tip, lazed away, zigzagging without a sound to vanish into the sky-blue depths beneath a shimmering surface.

'Crap, that was too close for comfort.'

Blaise emitted a nervous laugh. 'No kidding.'

The mist was a wispy shadow of its former self as we found ourselves on an embankment above the pools. To our right, a smudge of dense low-lying vegetation jagged the sky, and as we moved behind Aka, he instructed us to conceal ourselves.

What Aka had planned, I did not know, and by the confused look on Blaise's face, neither did he.

I inclined my head in Aka's direction, as I caught Blaise's eye.

'Hey, Aka,' said Blaise, 'what are you up to?'

Aka looked from Blaise to me in mild amusement. 'The quiet pool is the one in which the crocodile lives,' he said. 'Do not underestimate your enemy. It is the thing you despise that kills you.'

What was he on about?

He melted into the bush.

The penny dropped. Aka was preparing a warm and unexpected reception for our soon-to-be-arriving guests. I laughed out loud.

'What's so funny?'

'Nothing.'

'C'mon, Baron...'

'Revenge is a dish best served cold.'

'What?'

'Do you remember our rugby mantra before playing?'

'We had many,' Blaise said. 'Which one?'

'Warm from the neck down. Calm intensity.'

'So?'

'We must achieve victory first between the ears. With the head, then with the heart. First, *nous*. Then *gees*.'

'You've lost me.'

'Don't disturb the enemy while it's making a mistake.'

'Stop the riddles, Baron. You're doing my head in.'

'It's not that hard, Blazer. Simple strategy. We've adopted it ourselves. Use the opposition's anger and over-confidence to your own advantage. The wily Aka is going to conjure a crocodile.'

'That I have to see.'

'Watch and learn from the bush master.'

... weird scenes...

We did not have to wait long.

Our cadre of friends limped into view, nine in all, two in the van, two in the rear, the rest in the middle, in a ragged skirmish-line across space the width of a rugby field. At its centre, the man in the merlot beret marshalled his militia around him.

He was the head of the serpent.

To pass between the owl-eye pools, the cadre slowed, ambled to a halt. Confined space dictated they'd have to take the gap in a single file.

I recalled how vulnerable and anxious I had felt on that restricted, exposed headland. For an ambush, it was a perfect spot.

Beret-man barked a few commands, and his men sprang to life. They advanced in traditional column, loose and in well-spaced groups of two, stepping in unison, the expanding and contracting bellows of a concertina, negotiating the narrow strip of land between the two symmetrical, reflective pools.

... ride the snake...

For Blaise and me, the unravelling scene triggered memories of childhood front-row seats at a Saturday afternoon matinee. The only item we needed to add was popcorn.

The skeletal mist had lifted and was replaced by a sweaty, heat-induced sauna.

A wary alpha group, the tip of the spear, scanned the waterway on either side for hostiles. Beret-man cajoled them, brandishing a mahogany cane; its crested ferrule gleamed in the morning sunlight.

As the vanguard reached the mid-point, Aka arose from the scrub. He did nothing but stand, staring at his foes, from a small mound on higher ground, thirty metres to our left and in front of the guerrilla cadre.

In disbelief, Blaise and I stared at him.

He raised his knobkerries above his head and knocked them together. They click-clacked an eerie, unearthly rhythm, beating a cadence that rose to fill the entire wetland amphitheatre.

Surprised by the echoing groan and rattle of wood on wood, and staring into the morning sun, the guerrillas struggled to pinpoint the source of the disturbance.

The two men of alpha group shouted, pointed and brought their firearms to bear on Aka.

His voice resonated above the thumps of the knobkerries, across the space to the water holes.

'*Mweya Mukuru!*' he commanded. 'Oh, Great Spirit! Hear me.' He repeated his exhortation. '*Ngwenya*! Great Swallower.'

The guerrillas' AKs spewed in Aka's direction, bullets despoiling the brush and thudding into the ground where he had stood. He had side-stepped and melted into the undergrowth. The men below us rushed forward, looking up, searching for any sign of their quarry, oblivious to the danger lurking in the waterholes.

As before, on the surface, the pools remained tranquil, passive, sparkling.

... the killer awoke...

The attack was inevitable, but even I was unprepared for the ferocity of its violence.

An amphibious assassin from the shallows ambushed the two men. It exploded from the water, propelled by its back legs and long, brawny tail, its mouth clamping shut around the front man's head. He gave a hoarse scream, but it ceased as the force of the powerful jaws crushed his skull. Falling back into the shallows in a ferment of fizzling bubbles, the crocodile dragged the man with it and disappeared beneath the pool's surface.

Bursts of feeble, spasmodic automatic rifle fire sputtered and rattled from further afield, but the attack was so swift and decisive, it was over in a thrust of a croc-tail.

The water settled.

Given its tranquil idyll, I couldn't imagine how such aggression and hostility were possible.

Convulsive movements bubbled in the opposing waterhole. A second guerrilla wallowed on his back. The croc's power had blown him sideways, and he had toppled into its shallows.

He bore a look of dazed confusion, and then of growing fear, as the reality of his predicament dawned on him. He struggled to regather his feet, but could not gain any traction. Heavy webbing and rifle retarded his efforts to stand and extricate himself from the soapy water.

As he thrashed around in the bog of mud, another gladiatorial giant, bigger than the first, swept towards him. Its rear legs churned the water, and its burly tail, at least half of its total length, swished back and forth in graceful s-shaped movements. Within three tail thrusts, it was upon him.

The man must have sensed the approaching monster because, in a panic, he redoubled his efforts. His arms and legs flailed, but he could not escape the quagmire he'd created for himself.

The mega-reptile slammed into him with the speed of a bullet train and snapped its massive jaws around his right arm and shoulder.

I shuddered at the impact; I could not look away.

The man arched his spine and head backwards and mouthed a short, gut-wrenching shriek, the timbre of which chilled the bones.

The croc hauled him into the depths and dismembered him in a frenetic ballet of rotations, ripping and tearing flesh and bone. It disappeared beneath the indifferent waters, dragging the tattered remnants to the depths.

The rest of the guerrilla cadre had retreated in a disorderly fashion, well beyond the narrow headland, and had regrouped under beret-man's baton.

Aka materialised next to us.

How he achieved such surprise, only Africa comprehends. He pointed to the west, and off he galloped, with us chasing his shadow.

C'mon baby, take a chance with us...

PASSING ELEPHANTS

AKA LED US ON a similar route to the one Blaise and I had traversed before our encounter with Aizi. The escarpments, *kopjes*, and panoramic vistas of wildlife bore a familiar look.

A jornada continua.

The journey unravels and entwines, a bewitching interplay of infinite possibilities. It weaves and reweaves, a sacred pattern of becoming.

So do our narratives flow, currents in the vast ocean of collective (un)consciousness.

They converge and diverge, always in search of (un)familiar shores.

... nothing to do, but run, run, run with the hunt...

The sun was high in the sky, in its usual spot, doing what it normally did.

Beneath it, we toiled, determined to leverage time and widen the gap between our pursuers and ourselves. The trailing cadre would have regrouped and renewed the chase. We were under no illusion; they had shown they would not bend the knee.

Despite the machinations of an unrelenting sun, we kept at it, conscious of the outcome should our chasers catch up to us.

Run for your life.

I was tired of it, but until we found help, or it found us, we didn't have many options. Our bodies had taken a pounding, but on we soldiered.

Aka's loping strides dropped to a shuffle; behind him, Blaise ambled, cradling his injured arm and shoulder, while I limped in the rear.

The ache in my chest had intensified; each time I sucked in air or moved my upper body, stabs of pain shot through my ribcage. To add insult, my left ankle was tender, an aggravated courtesy thanks to an old rugby injury.

Aka called a halt, and Blaise and I threw ourselves on the ground in the shade of an acacia thicket. We quaffed most of the water in our possession. As we were in a wet zone, replenishing our supply was no longer an overriding concern.

'Blazer-man, how're those wounds feeling?'

'Sore, but okay. Your work, and Aka's, has done the trick. Just need a breather.'

'We should check anyway.'

'I don't think it's urgent. All's good.'

I moved towards him but corrected myself, stopped in my tracks.

Blaise could resolve matters for himself. It was about time I recognised that. I needed to treat him like the equal he was.

'All right then, you make the call. If you're happy, so am I.'

Blaise gave a knowing, secretive smile, and an imperceptible nod, as if he had sensed a shift in consciousness. All I could do was reciprocate.

... my only friend...

'Bar, Aka's struggling. Something's not right.'

Aka sat crouched over, propped up against a tree trunk. He grimaced and clutched at his abdomen. Blood seeped through a makeshift bandage from a wound near his hip.

He and Blaise conferred.

'Looks as if a stray bullet struck him at the water hole. I thought his action foolhardy.'

'I'll take a look.'

'I don't think he'll let you.'

He shook his head when I crouched before him. '*Utsva hworurimi hahuna marapiro*,' he said. 'A burn on the tongue cannot be treated.'

While I understood what he meant, I persisted. '*Ndapota*. Please, Aka. *Ini ndininzwisisa*. I understand. *Rega nditarise*. Let me look.'

After a gentle exchange, Aka yielded. I removed the stopgap dressing around Aka's lower torso.

An AK-round had punctured his abdomen near the left hipbone, its destructive force weaving a mangled tapestry. Aka's once smooth belly was all jagged edges, exposed tissue, and torn skin at the point of entry, much like a fractured looking glass.

Blood and visceral fluid intermingled and seeped from the wound, its crimson hue clashing with the pallor of Aka's skin. It oozed, misaligned with his rebellious pulse. Where looped internal organs once nestled within the abdomen's sanctuary, now they lay bare, their intricate design defiled and disfigured. Worse, I could not find an exit wound.

My heart clenched. Aka had one of the worst possible injuries. Untreated or treated, the outcome was inevitable: a slow and painful death.

... the end, my friend... the end...

Despite valiant attempts to conceal visible signs of pain, Aka's face strained and furrowed, contorted by spasms of agony. Each laboured breath, every shift of his damaged body, testified to his struggle, his tenacity, and indomitable spirit.

Eyes that were once vibrant now mirrored a mixture of distress and doggedness. Aka's flicker of determination burned bright. He remained poised and unbowed, masking his suffering behind a stoic façade. The clench of his jaw and the unyielding grip of his trembling hands were acts of a warrior's fortitude and defiance in the face of a relentless assault on his body, and his soul.

That he had hiked with such a wound resisted belief.

'What do you think, Bar?'

'It's bad. It's a mess in there. He's suffered severe abdominal trauma, and his organs have perforated.'

'So where does that leave us?'

'Right at the top of shit street. He's lost a lot of blood. Leakage of body fluids into the abdominal cavity also means serious infection is inevitable.'

'Just give me the bottom line, Baron.'

'He needs emergency care. Otherwise, he'll die.'

The bullet needed to come out. Either way, sepsis was unavoidable. But of this I said nothing.

'Not sure what I can do. What we can do.'

'Could you remove the bullet using Aka's dagger?'

'This is not the movies, Blaise. That's more dangerous. How do we sterilise it? It's not just a flesh wound, like yours. And that was bad enough. An AK-round has punctured his organs.'

'We could make a fire and heat the blade.'

'That will be a homing beacon for our cadre friends.'

'We can't let him just die,' said Blaise. 'We have to do something.'

'I understand your frustration. I feel the same way. But think. We have limited choices.'

'Any other ideas?'

'Apart from cleaning the wound, strapping it as best as we can, and trying to get him to some help, no.'

'It's Aka's decision, isn't it?'

'You're right,' I said. 'We should ask what he would he like us to do to help him. I think I already know what he wants.'

Blaise nodded.

He and Aka spoke at length.

'So?'

Looking thoughtful for a moment, Blaise said, 'You heard what he said earlier. For him, there's no solution. He stands by that. Strap him up and let's get going. He'll also be true to his promise to get us out of here.'

I admired my brother for his *gees* and grit. But I was in awe of Aka's raw courage.

At Aka's instruction, and with Blaise's help, I cleaned the wound as best as I could, then applied a herbal poultice from a bagged collection of goodies he carried in the folds of his leopard skins, and strapped a pressure bandage in place.

'Not much more I can do.'

... look into your eyes...

Aka's eyes, eloquent in their silence, offered a thank-you that reverberated in my core. Unspoken gratitude shimmered between us, a sacred bond beyond words. I smiled, eyes watering.

... again...

'*Ndatenda.* Thank you. *Ndatenda hama dzangu.* Thank you, my brothers,' he said, eyes shining.

'No, thank *you*, Brother,' I said. 'Rest now.'

He closed his eyes and drifted into a fitful sleep.

I checked his vital signs. His pulse, elevated and errant, persisted. Shallow, restrained, and measured, his breaths belied an underlying toughness. His moist and clammy skin and hot forehead signalled growing fever and potential sepsis.

Déjà vu.

But in these circumstances, the outcome would be different. Aka had a mortal, life-threatening wound, and neither Blaise nor I could do anything to heal it.

... desperately in need...

'B, I've been thinking. We should wait for it to cool down before heading off. If we leave now, we won't get too far in the afternoon heat. We'd get further in the cool. It'll also help Aka. Give him rest time. We'd be taking a chance, but hell, we've taken so many of those, what's one more?'

'Why not? Now's not the time to be cautious. *Faint heart...*'

'*... never won fair maid.* Yeah, I know.'

... waiting... waiting...

The damage of a single bullet never fails to blur the boundaries of my perception.

Such destructive force can become more, if we allow it.

A simple account of violence and suffering has the potential to be a greater meta-narrative of meaning.

Aka's trial by combat inspires me to wrestle the vibrant paradoxes intrinsic to my journey. His steadfast spirit shatters my binary notions of suffering and transcendence, individual and shared experience, conversion and stagnation, culture and race.

His struggle is mine, and not mine.

Minha luta continua.

It is also more.

A luta continua.

It is beyond both and more...

Over the years, Aka's simple philosophy has challenged me to enter the paradoxical labyrinth where irony and sincerity fuse, and wounds are gateways to ever-shifting landscapes of meaning. He stirs me to seek truth, to question the constructs that shape my worldview, to transform those ideas I must, and to act on them *summum bonum.*

... waiting... waiting...

The sun dipped towards the horizon.

Under an expansive canopy of cloudless, pink-fuchsia sunset sky, we moved out.

Aka led us, although the verve and spring in his step were missing. A true warrior, he put a brave face on his discomfort and pain. Instead of skirting the plains of wildlife, as Blaise and I had done earlier on our outward trip, Aka led us downhill through a landscape of miombo woodland, past thorny acacia, dotted *kopjes* and greening savannah grass, to the glossy water lagoons, to the heart of the lowlands.

On the wide floodplain, from a safe distance we saw in the many waterholes rafts of crocodile, bloats of hippos and vast numbers of carmine bee-eaters, burrowing nests into the sandy riverbanks.

The big five were prominent. Herds of perambulating elephant; *inyathi*, the life-giving buffalo; *ingwe*, the lone tree-lazing, tongue-lolling leopard; a lounging, indolent and fatigued pride of lion; a pair of wandering and grumpy *umkombe*, black rhino.

The plains also teemed with black-and-white sable antelope; spiral-horned *kudu*; sunlit-skinned, dewlapped eland; a sun-dance of *tsepe*, the holiest of antelope, the gold-and-white springbok; smelly, disagreeable brown-eyed waterbuck; grazing herds of children-of-the-moon zebras and stiff-necked, far-sighted, skewbald giraffes.

Above, two banded *inyoka* eagles flew in lazy circles; a couple of gliding yellow-billed kites drifted on the air currents, and the continent's kings of carrion, the vultures, pursued their business with noisy efficiency.

A lone bateleur eagle roosted with locked claws in the low foliage of a winter-thorn branch.

It scrutinised our every move.

Words from my transcendental birdsong at the airport bubbled to my mind's surface: *'Dare you push against the doors?'*

... on the edge...

Often, we stopped for Aka to rest. As the sepsis took hold and his condition deteriorated, he struggled to keep moving.

After a laborious trek through the grassland, we reached the shade of a single white-thorn tree. A throng of elephant calves and cows shambled and browsed nearby. In the acacia treeline, they snapped, shook and hammered for tasty morsels. The herd ambled and foraged, enjoying the late afternoon light.

Apart from an encounter with the single bull on our river jaunt, I had never seen a group of elephants close-up. I'd read all about such encounters in books, but the experience in real life was different. To stand in the shadows of an acacia, uncertain of the intentions of the largest land animal on the planet, stirred the blood, uplifted the soul.

As they meandered past us, one of them detached from the herd and strolled over in our direction.

She drew closer.

Should I run or hide? Blaise and I looked at each other.

'*Usafambe,*' Aka said. 'Don't move.'

We trembled as the matriarch of the herd trundled towards us. The withaak beneath which we stood, however, kept its peace, silent and vigilant.

The old lady, her ears flopping in the light evening breeze, was at least four metres in height with a weight to match. She sported a set of large stained tusks, and her probing trunk swayed lazily towards the ground.

I searched for tell-tale signs of agitated behaviour – aggressive ear waving, trunk raising, coiling and slapping, and angry shakes of the head. A discontented elephant is one of the most dangerous and unpredictable animals of all.

'Stay still,' Aka said under his breath.

She displayed none of these mannerisms as she moseyed on over to say *g'day*.

Have you ever wondered why individuals, when confronted by untenable, life-threatening predicaments, can't extricate themselves by fleeing?

At that moment, as the elephant wandered over to us, I think I knew why. It's not a problem with the head, or desire, or intention. It's more a question of the legs. Limp, they refused to move, even though I wanted them to.

As the elephant towered above us, I closed my eyes, anticipated the worst.

I re-opened them to see the wise Old One – *Wakare* – advance to within a few metres of us and halt. In confidence, Aka had stepped forward and held up his right hand in a royal salute.

'*Hau! Nzou. Mukuru*,' Aka cooed. 'O Elephant! O great, godly One.' He maintained his position and posture. '*Ambuya!* Grandmother, Blessed One.'

For a moment, *Ambuya* paused, then stepped to within a stride of him, staring down with bright, old eyes. She blew a hushed sound I have never forgotten, much like a novice playing a *vuvuzela* for the first time.

I had the sense she and Aka were old friends.

She stretched out her thick *boomslang*-nose, like a stethoscope, and examined him. She patted and probed, first on the top of his head, then his face and shoulders, working her way downwards, massaging with her proboscis, until she reached the abdominal area, his pierced stomach. Her trunk tarried.

Dumbfounded, Blaise and I could only stand rooted to the spot.

All the while, Aka remained still with his arm extended upwards, patting the bridge of Ambuya's lengthy nose. After her brief inspection of his abdomen, the elephant raised her trunk and stroked his upraised hand, offering some understanding and consolation by returning his greeting.

She cleared her nasal passages, trumpeted a tranquil farewell, wheeled on the solid pillars that were her legs and slouched off, commodious hindquarters swinging, to rejoin her family as it promenaded past us.

None of us budged. We watched... and watched, as the elephants rambled off into the amphitheatre of tall savannah.

... weird scenes inside...

Blaise and I remained transfixed.

Aka disturbed our preoccupation. 'Those that have grazed at the same anthill have become friends,' he said.

I looked at Blaise, wondering what Aka meant. After a few moments, Blaise said, 'I think he means those who have shared a common experience now share a bond.' He paused. 'Almost brothers of the blood. Such experiences, once shared, unite people forever.'

My brother's insights continued to floor me.

'What's he really saying? I get the sense he's telling us something more.'

'Not sure if I follow.'

'He's saying goodbye.'

Aka stood watching us as our exchange unravelled.

'That's a little premature. And anyway, we've got to get him some help.'

I shook my head. 'Blaise, it's too late. He's beyond that.'

'No, Baron, we're still in with a chance of saving him.'

'Blaise...'

He turned his back and stomped off.

'*Blaise!* Look at me.'

He swung round and eyeballed me. His eyes were moist and red. He wiped them with what remained of his tattered shirt-sleeve. 'I... we... *surely...* we can save him?'

'Don't you see, Blaise? We don't need to save him.'

'How can you be so certain?'

'In his own eyes, he has redeemed himself, to become a warrior once again. He has reclaimed his story, his song, and his dignity, and can now face his shades, his ancestors, with pride and respect.'

Aka intervened.

'It's a deliberate choice to die from the wounds of tattoo marks,' he said. 'My life is my responsibility,' he added. 'I don't blame others for the consequences of my choices. This is the simple wisdom of the elders.

Ndatenda, hama. Thank you, brother,' he said. He turned to Blaise and repeated his thanks. 'You have restored my life to me.'

Blaise was poised to say something, but I cut him off. 'You must let this go. If you respect Aka at all, you'll let this rest.'

Blaise shut his mouth, bit his lip, and remained silent.

Aka smiled at each of us and said, 'I salute you, my brothers. Remember, some problems have no solutions. Sometimes we must accept the things over which we have no control. We must live our lives, responding to the circumstances, opportunities and challenges unfolding before us.'

He looked into my eyes and said, 'We miss the passing elephants if we fail to look for them. Travel well.'

'*Hamba.* Travel well too, *Baba*,' I said.

Niebuhr's prayer popped into my head.

God, grant me the Serenity to accept the things I cannot change; Courage to change the things I can and Wisdom to know the difference.

Serenity, that elusive quality of inner quietness, is the term I would use to describe Aka.

Tranquil intensity.

He turned to Blaise, spoke briefly. Blaise nodded, and then he too smiled.

'We will meet again.' He held his hand high in a last farewell.

We responded in kind.

... it hurts to set you free...

With heavy hearts, we watched Aka disappear into the sunset.

'What did Aka say to you as he was leaving?'

'The last part of the plan for our pursuers.'

'Come on, then. Pray, spill.'

He did. It was crazy, but it just might work.

We waited for a while, giving Aka time to put some distance between us, and then we put the plan into action.

Beyond our position, a few hundred metres to the south, herds of antelope grazed in the afternoon half-light. We skirted them, moved west, then south.

Blaise grunted with satisfaction. 'This should do it.'

He pulled out the mamba and checked the clip. 'Three bullets left.' Flipping the safety catch, Blaise cocked the weapon and fired it twice into the air. Its discharge reverberated across the *veld*.

The results were spectacular: the various herds charged off in all directions, to the southeast. The stampede would cover our tracks and confuse our foe, delaying them, giving us a chance.

So we believed.

And Aka? He was the decoy.

We settled into a loping run in the opposite direction, to the southwest.

... ride, baby... ride...

BLACK-BLEACHED

THE UNRULY SUN HAD run off, replaced by the pouting moon.

... day destroys the night... night divides the day...

Polarities. Binaries.

Innocence and Experience.

Apollo and Venus. Black and White. Good and Evil. Heaven and Hell. The Feminine and Masculine.

Light and Dark.

Dawns and Dusks. Sun and Moon. Risings and Settings.

Beginnings and Endings.

Order and Passion. Comings and Goings. Births and Deaths.

I was over it all. I'd had enough.

The earth spun and revolved. As did the moon. The sun did neither, taking no interest in interplanetary pageantry. No more, no less.

Who cared? Another day and night. Another luni-solar moment.

Did it matter?

We lay camouflaged in yet another of the many bush thorn thickets. Given our injuries, we had covered the ground at a fair pace while the sun and moon played childish games about whose turn it was to bully lesser mortals.

Blaise snapped me out of my ruminations. 'Baron, I've been thinking.'

It was on the tip of my tongue to be a smart arse by saying, *I'm not sure whether you do that very often*, but I desisted. Instead, I said, 'Come on, then.'

'We spent time the other night seeking to understand the nature of suffering and evil. We kind of got carried away,' Blaise said. 'I just wanted to add a final two cents' worth.'

'I'm sure your thoughts are worth much more than *that*,' I said.

'Maybe. But this is where the rubber hits the road. I've had an aha-moment since meeting Aka. In the light of all that's happened to him, and us, to an extent, he's shown an incredible serenity to deal with it.'

'It's funny that you should use that word. It's a word I too would've used to describe Aka. *Serenity*. And stoical forbearance.'

'Yeah, that's random.'

'Random's not the word. Rather, *interconnected*. Sometimes disconnected ideas and experiences align. You know, earlier this year, long before we embarked on this journey, our R.E. Teacher, Mr A, had pointed me to Frankl's *Man's Search for Meaning*. Heard of it?'

'You are such a book nerd. I've heard of it, but can't say I've read it.'

'Frankl survived the Nazi death camps and reflected on that experience in this amazing text,' I said. 'He lost everything and everyone close to him, but he maintained an immense capacity for life.'

'A bit like Job. Now that would be an interesting read.'

'It was. *Is*. Two things stand out to me.'

'I'm listening.'

'First, he said the only thing we can control in traumatic situations is our response to them. Confronted with a reality we cannot change, we are challenged to change ourselves.'

'That sounds like uncommon sense. And the second thing?'

'It relates to spirit and belief. Words to the effect that if we believe in something beyond us, we can endure and survive any form of suffering or circumstance.'

Blaise thought for a moment. 'I believe I owe you an apology for my earlier cynicism about books and their relevance.'

'Apology accepted,' I said, grinning. 'What else is on your mind?'

'As you present them, Frankl's thoughts appear very apt for our current situation. I've been trying to verbalise something similar. His views appear to be a lot like Aka's, emphasising freedom, shifting responsibility onto individuals for their actions. Forget the metaphysics and pie-in-the-sky stuff.'

'Aka and Frankl together? That's an interesting notion.'

'It sounds bizarre, but it's not really. Just engaging with Aka, his worldview has an uncomplicated, down-to-earth wisdom. *Taking responsibility,*' Blaise said. 'Taking control of what you can control. To use a rugby term, playing what's in front of you. Not to place the blame anywhere else if things go haywire. Forget about the existential questions. Forget about definitions. They don't help.'

Blaise inhaled and continued. 'Does it matter if the heart is in a state of civil war? Or where God fits? All those other questions, too. How do they help us?'

'A new way of seeing, a new way of being?'

'Yes, Bar. We need to embrace the paradoxes of life, with a dose of good humour, humaneness, courage and gratefulness. To become better versions of ourselves.'

'No certainties, then. Goodness is its own reward; evil is a natural and necessary part of the package. But we need to add three key ingredients to the recipe.'

'Yeah, and what are those?'

'The theological virtues.'

'You mean faith, hope and –'

'Love.'

'And what of this love?'

'That's a loaded question, Blaise. Love is a double-edged sword. To connect our hearts to the source of all life, the Eternal Heart, love crowns and crucifies.'

'Sorry I asked...'

'Yeah, that's a tale for another sequel, another time, another book.'

'Amen to that.'

... the end of everything that stands... the end...

The light was all but gone.

Blaise had passed out and there I sat, compelled to write in my journal after slim offerings the night before.

My mind was a twirl of jumbled thoughts.

Just write. It's not an exam.

SATURDAY 09 SEPTEMBER 1978

Is my Black(white)washed mind any clearer after all that's happened?

I'm a prince of my darkness. My inky night of the soul continues.

God's question to the prophet Jeremiah is stuck in my head, looping over and over: 'The heart is devious and perverse above all else. Who can understand it?'

I recognise the writer of the text, in imputing this question to the creator, wants his readership to ponder this very question.

Nothing is more dangerous than narcissistic self-deception. It's the sworn enemy of our ability to learn and grow. It is impossible for me to learn what I believe I already know. How can I become a better version of myself if I already think this is what I am? How do I unshackle ego's manacles?

Questions.

I underlined the word.

> *It's our questions about who we are as humans and what life means that frustrate us.*
>
> *Perhaps we need to flip our thinking.*
>
> *Life asks questions of us. How we live our lives is an answer to those questions. If we choose not to ignore the questions, our attitudes and values can give meaning, even to our deviousness and darkness.*
>
> *We must take ownership of our lives, even in the face of what may be unchangeable.*

Niebuhr's prayer sprung into my head again, this time with a unique spin. I recorded the words.

> *Lord, grant us the serenity to navigate the complexities of our world with curiosity and compassion; the courage to challenge those worldviews and assumptions that dehumanise and marginalise; and the wisdom, grace and faith to transform as we seek truth, justice, and inter-connection in all that we do.*
>
> *Suffering, death and evil may be unchangeable, but they do not rob life of its meaning.*
>
> *When we are not able to shape our lives, our situation can only be endured. It is the quality of how we confront these moments that determines our humanity.*

My discussion with Blaise about Aka, and Frankl's text, barged into my head like a rhino.

I put pen to paper once again.

> *Hamlet asked, 'What is this quintessence of dust?'*

In answer, Frankl observes the essential spark within us is spiritual. The answer rests 'at the still point of the turning world.'

To search for, to recognise this point-of-no-turning, is our life's journey.

Death, suffering and evil have no authority there, and far from stealing life from us, they challenge us to explore, in humility and grace, the undiscovered country of our spiritual selves and to live in the potential holiness of each moment.

I sighed, shut my journal.

I had travelled far, but I wondered if I was any closer to more coherent answers. With more answers came jumbled thoughts and more questions.

The darkness, a tempting aphrodisiac, snuggled up to me, nuzzling my earlobes. The moon had taken the night off and was also abed, her heavenly candles snuffed out.

Paint it Black.

A weighty summons settled upon me. I was over-tired, yet I could not sleep.

... I look inside myself and see my heart is Black...

Darkness is a strange companion.

It can beguile, befriend and bewitch as quickly as it can befoul, benight and bedevil.

... It's not easy when your whole world is Black...

The dark possesses a certain mystique, acting on its own seductive whims and caprices, by its own set of unpredictable non-rules.

It can present as an impenetrable, suffocating and claustrophobic weight or as oozing, tacky oil, smothering and overwhelming. An odourless vapour, it can also stifle and suffocate the sensibilities.

The darkness is a very disturbing and persistent suitor indeed.

In an exhausted and enervated state, I surrendered to the wiles of its darkest wooing, drifting into a restless slumber, invoking *Inyathi*.

... weird scenes inside...

An unearthly rustle and crackle in the brush to our left slapped me out of drowsiness.

My pulse quickened.

I did not know what stumbled in the never-never, but given the intensity of the noise, it must have been large.

Between Blaise and me, no words were necessary: our shared look was an instinctive and subtle enough hint to remain calm, to ready ourselves, despite the adrenaline rush.

A dark silhouette transposed behind the tall grass.

In the deathly shadows, I fumbled around me, seeking for a weapon of sorts. My hand closed on one of the many rocks littering the ground. Blaise had drawn the mamba and pointed it in the direction of the disturbance in the bush.

Life continues, oscillating between echoes ancient and patterns nascent.

Inyathi.

He ambled into view, headed in our direction.

My fingers tightened on the projectile.

Our eyes met. Inyathi held my gaze, noted my presence with what seemed to be a perceptible nod, and resumed grazing in the *fynbos* close by.

Blaise had sensed the moment's strangeness and had not reacted, lowering his weapon.

Last light suspended its struggle against the encroaching night. On cue, the large creature shifted direction, meandered closer to where we sat, munching as he moved.

His demeanour showed no obvious hostile intent, but given my previous experience of the power and ferocity of Inyathi, and his unpredictable, unforgiving nature, the squeeze on the object in my hand intensified, to the point my fingers numbed from the pain.

As I anticipated the worst, and made to lift my arm to defend myself, with a satisfied grunt, Inyathi plopped down between Blaise and me, within spitting distance of each of us. Curling onto his side, he propped his head on his front legs and tucked in his hindquarters toward his belly, still chewing.

Each time Blaise or I tried to move, he grunted, so we remained where we were.

When I relate this story to those who would listen, I am greeted with smiles, sarcastic commentary, nods of the disbelieving kind, and knowing, conspiratorial winks reserved for bar room bull-shit artist gatherings.

'How did you get away from the buffalo, hey?' they'd ask. 'Did you give it a kiss and frighten it away?'

'No,' I'd say, 'the buffalo spent the night protecting my brother and me. We could hear the grumbling lions and the smirking hyenas circling throughout the night. Yet old Inyathi remained on guard at his post.'

'And I suppose you shared a slap-up breakfast in the morning,' someone said, winking.

'You think I was dreaming? You don't believe me,' I'd say. They would reply, trying not to laugh, 'But we do,' adding, 'So, what happened the next morning, in the light of day?'

'Nothing strange or startling,' I would respond. 'The night had been restless and chilly, but the scarred old bull rose before the sun's first light, glanced at us as if to bid farewell, and shambled off into the scrub.'

Even now, many years later, I still wonder if I'd dreamt it all. The experience's eerie, otherworldly quality haunts me still, and I have thought of the old bull often.

Apart from Blaise, I could never talk about its trancelike oddness and charm to anyone who would listen without winking.

Still, I record the story as I re-remember it, and the rest is outside my Black-bleached philosophy. Only Africa, and the dark undiscovered country of my soul, in their intimate, contradictory and interwoven wisdom, might hazard an understanding.

... the end of night(s)...

BEYOND THE DOORS

THE REFRACTING SALMON-PINK SUNLIGHT STRETCHED OUT her elegant fingers, offering a relaxing massage after the black of the night. Scented, spicy air and the sirenic harmonies of the bush softened the dawn with a sympathetic encore.

On second thoughts, in the current context and from a trans-cultural, trans-linguistic perspective, *flame-lily-fingered dawn* might be more appropriate and authentic as a description.

I shook Blaise's foot. His eyes trembled open.

'Come on, *Bru*. We must keep moving. We're almost there. I can feel it.'

'The buffalo gone?'

'Yep. Before first light,' I said.

'Even you have to admit that was weird,' Blaise said.

'Too true,' I said, pulling him to his feet.

... get here and we'll do the rest...

I strapped on my backpack, straightened and turned around. Before me stood a tall, square-set man dressed in a green and rice-flecked camouflage jacket. He sported navy-blue reflective aviator sunglasses, and a faded cerise beret pulled down at a rakish angle. Tucked under his left armpit, he gripped a polished cane.

355

Behind him lounged a small troop of his military cadre, in various flavours of rice-flecks and sage-green leopard spots.

The serpents were all gathered in one place for an (un)holy last supper.

'So you thought you could give us the slip?'
I recognised his gruff voice. Then came the full realisation.

The purple beret at the river. At the crocodile pools. Beret-man in the swirling dawn mist. In conversation with Thumbeza. At the Hunyani crash-site.

'You may have won a few minor skirmishes along the way, but you will lose.' He whipped out his cane from beneath his armpit with his right hand and pointed it at us. 'A *luta continua,* but our victory is assured. And it is close at hand. Soon we will reclaim the ancestral land you settlers stole from us. The time of reckoning is not far off.'

Blaise and I did nothing but stare at him. I would not dignify his words with a response.

'Ah yes, that traitorous *nyanga* who tried to help you. We've known about his sympathies for a while. He won't be bothering us again.'

He held up a pair of bloodied, tattered ears and drew the fingers of his right hand across his throat, making a strange sibilant sound between gritted teeth.

'He is now crocodile meat himself,' he said, giving a little laugh. 'Strange thing, though. It was as if he wanted us to find him. He led us on a merry dance until that moment.'

His callous words confirmed who and what he was, and our associated kinship.

The *mysterium iniquitatis.* We were old sparring partners.

'A pity for you,' he said. 'You almost made it. What you seek is just beyond the next ridge. However, here you are. The predator has caught up to its elusive prey.'

He appeared to be enjoying himself.

He took his time drawing his sidearm, no doubt to heighten the theatrics and to impress his assembled protégés. Smiles all round, they focused on the unfolding drama.

'So, my friends, I'm a kind man. I'll give you a moment to say your farewells.'

He wiped his brow with a black cravat he removed from around his neck.

Blaise and I exchanged glances. Words were unnecessary.

My brother took a step forward, and with his back to our adversary, hugged me. His grip was firm, charged with calm intensity. With his right hand he thrust the handgun into my waistband.

His whisper wounded our silence. 'One bullet, in the chamber. Safety's off. Do your best.' He winked and smiled, a transcendent glint in his eyes. 'We never got to finish that *indaba*, Baron. Perhaps another time, another place. Forgive me.'

... fuck you... mother...

I knew what he was going to do. But before I could intervene, Blaise turned and launched himself at the guerrilla leader.

In the brief fracturing of the divisions of time, my brother's injured shoulder smashed into the man's midriff, and his grasp locked onto the guerrilla's gun hand.

I drew the mamba, dropped to one knee. It trembled in my palm, its heaviness a blessing and burden.

My aim vacillated between the two wrestling figures.

I struggled to separate foe from friend, moment from mind, fiction from fact, memory from mis-memory.

The pair thumped into dust and shadow. They rolled head-over-heels in a life-and-death embrace.

My grip steadied.

With Dad's mantra, 'aim narrow, miss narrow', looping in my head, my focus tightened.

Breath suppressed, I squeezed the trigger.

Two shots in quick succession echoed across the veld, scattering birds and wildlife in all directions.

... everything that stands...

When the world stopped spinning, Blaise's face-down body lay still.

The mamba slipped from my hands.

Disoriented, beret-man sat on his backside beside Blaise. He struggled to his feet, dusted himself off, readjusted his beret.

'A fitting end for a brave cub,' he scoffed. Across the void that divided us, he glared at me with cold eyes. 'And you, huh? Would you also like to dance, *white boy*?'

I remained kneeling, glancing from my fallen brother to the weapon hiding in the frail grass.

Beret-man stooped to retrieve his sunglasses, cane and pistol, all of which Blaise had dislodged in their scuffle. His comrades, weapons shouldered, grinned with mocking bravado.

My gaze fixed on Blaise's motionless body.

A flurry of unspoken thoughts and misunderstood emotions coursed through me.

The abandoned mamba pressed down upon me, its weight expanding to fill the present yet absent space connecting us.

... the end of nights we tried to die...

With a single blood-curdling scream, giving vent to my bloodlust and all the bottled-up frustration and anger that had been brewing within me since Blaise and I had been thrust into this fateful journey, I fixated on his beret and charged at him, intent on ripping out his throat.

... c'mon, f-uck, yeah... kill, f-uck, kill...

I stormed forward in a red fog. Beret-man secured his weapon. He raised his arm and aimed the pistol at my chest as I bore down on him.

A sjambok crack, a muzzle flash.

I did not stop or flinch. No matter what, I was going to smash him to a bloody pulp... *rip out his intestines... I knew how it was done...*

Before I could reach him, the man had dropped to the ground. Confused, I slowed, the adrenaline and anger still throbbing in my head.

Military figures emerged from the shadows.

The gathered cadre stood no more; their bodies littered the ground.

I stopped and leaned over, straining to breathe, pain in my ribcage. After a pause, I straightened up and moved over to the man I had desired to kill, who had just attempted to kill me.

He lay, sans sunglasses, convulsing, staring upwards, gasping and gurgling for breath, a look of disbelief etched on his face. His discoloured camouflage jacket seeped blood outwards from the chest.

I squatted down beside him and watched as his life ebbed away. I could not bring myself to feel anything.

... of-everything-that-stands...

My eyes drifted beyond to where Blaise lay unmoving a short way off.

I made to stand, but as I did so, an arm yanked me downwards. Taken by surprise, I resisted by jerking backwards, but flailing *tokoloshe*-hands pawed, snatched, gripped and wrenched at me. They repositioned and grabbed once again, left hand clutching behind my neck and right hand gripping my left upper arm.

... arms that chain us... eyes that lied...

Left with no choice, I stared into the man's blood-spattered face. He tried to speak but managed only an emphatic burble and gargle of blood. He shook me, but the shallow panting and sputtering from almost closed lips masked his words.

... your eyes...

We held each other's gaze.

In that fragmented moment, I saw what I could only construe as an inscrutable disconnect, an incomprehension, a hatred in the intensity and glare of his staring eyes, and an involuntary recoil at my own glazed indifference to it.

... can you picture what will be...?

The world telescoped outwards, to that temporary, trans-space, beyond our anger and alienation, our difference, our strangeness, our otherness, to somewhere more profound, deeper beyond deep.

For I not only saw.

I discerned.

I felt.

Connected. Grokked. With his humanity. With his spirit. His energy and fire. His core.

This welding awoke in me emotions I had never experienced, and for which I had no words.

... stranger's hand...

I squeezed his hand, but could not say with any certainty if he responded. His irregular breaths faded and ceased.

His hold on me weakened, luminous eyes glassing to an unfocusing darkness.

... the end of everything...

I struggled to my feet.

After a few steps, unsolicited, I bent over at the hips and retched till there was nothing left to share.

Overhead, the familiar *dak-dak-dak-dak-dak* of the Rhodesian Fire Force vibrated in my ears. The air cavalry had arrived.

Red smoke canisters phished and clouded. A pair of choppers hung in the air like long-legged dragonflies, and as they dipped toward the ground, belched their innards. Dust and debris blew in rotating funnel-shaped wind vortices.

The SAS had breezed in to secure the area.

I wiped my mouth on my jumper's tatty sleeve and cast a glance over at Blaise.

Could it be?

I detected a slight movement in his arms and legs.

I hobbled over.

Rolling my brother onto his back, I cradled his head in the crook of my arm.

He looked up at me and gave me his trademark impish grin. 'Hah! I always knew that you had that fire in you...' he wheezed. 'Sorry... sorry for being so reckless...'

Crimson blood petals frothed at the side of his mouth.

I tried to speak.

'I thought I had him covered. It was a monster tackle, hey?' He coughed.

I wanted to tell him so many things, but could not. I wasn't sure how.

'Tell Mum and Dad I love them... I regret... I wish I could have been more like you... the fortunate son...'

His voice faltered.

I leaned closer and managed, 'No, Blaise, I'm sorry. It's me who wanted to be more like you.'

I will always be glad I spoke those words. It was the only direct affirmation I ever gave him. But it was heartfelt.

Blaise half-smiled and beckoned me to come closer. I placed my ear close to his lips and took his hands in my free right hand and squeezed. He did likewise, but his strength weakened.

'*Remember...* brother...' He whispered into my ear.

I nodded.

Then his head slumped backwards.

... you'll never follow me...

Medics swarmed around us. One of them looked over at me and shook his head.

Scouts spread out in a defensive perimeter.

Two shimmering Alouettes surveyed the terrain from above, like bateleur eagles sunning themselves.

... so limitless and free...

Blaise lay with a half-smile on his face, but his once green-eyed intensity was no more. I closed his eyelids, kissed his check, sat beside him, holding his hand.

... I'll never look into your eyes again...

And I wept.

For losing my brother and closest friend.

For all that he was, and for all he could have been.

Gone too soon.

For the loss of those on the *Hunyani*.

Men, women and children, with their own interconnected lives, their interwoven hopes and dreams.

Gone too soon.

People who had enjoyed the warmth of a shared sun, looked up in awe to a communal moon, and the tapestry of stars.

Gone too soon.

I wept for the *nyanga*, the brave and wise Akashinga.

For his wisdom and humaneness. For his selfless and courageous act, which had given Blaise and me a chance at life.

Gone too soon.

I wept for those men and women who had died at our hands.

Inspired to fight, to struggle for their rights, for a better world, a better life, fired by aspirations similar to my own.

Also gone too soon.

And I wept for myself.

For seeing my mirror image, my double, as I was:

a mongrel, conflicted and contradictory, a man with a cross.

... of everything that stands...

I had believed the simple wisdom of 'unnatural deeds do breed unnatural troubles'. In having disturbed those dark and subversive serpents that entwine the soul, I was no longer certain. Perhaps it was better to flip that simple wisdom: natural troubles do prompt unnatural deeds.

Our condition may have been troubled to start with. As a species, we couldn't help ourselves.

I wanted God in the dock to answer the allegations brought against him.

What kind of creator would be bold enough to forge such a synthesis of contradictions, and would he take responsibility for the boldness of that decision?

But the Lord of the Absurd is elusive.

A divine Jekyll and Hyde.

In amongst this spinning twizzle of thoughts, I had one consolation.

Despite the machinations of the creator, or because of them, it may be possible to live beyond, beyond a spiritual wilderness. But first, we must confront and recognise our darkness, and then make a conscious decision to be warriors of, and for, grace and light.

It was part of the existential conundrum.

To act or not to act. To overcome evil results in the very evil you seek to destroy tainting you. But act you must, with relative freedom, faith and fortitude, with good intentions, and a spirit of humaneness, in each moment.

... came to a door...

As these thoughts cascaded in my conscious mind, not unlike the Zambezi waters crashing over Mosi-oa-Tunya, several questions drifted unscripted into my thoughts.

The mist cloud lifted and, as I pushed against them, the doors creaked open.

... looked inside ...

Was there a way to balance the many binaries, the irresolvable tensions within the creator and his creation and how they mirrored each other?

I yearned for a non-dualistic, non-linear way of thinking and being.

Was there a face of the creator I had yet to consider?

Our creator may have seemed absent, silent and disinterested in the tragedies that beset human existence *because it was we who had created a divine other*, confining him to the limitations of our own human image and likeness.

My image of God creates me.
    God is the ultimate paradox.

Close and between. Without and within. Both, and All, and...
    God is the unfathomable, the strange and radical other, beyond-beyond the limits of human expression and understanding: the nameless, unsayable, and ineffable, deep within the human heart.

No one can fathom God from beginning to end.

In and through all things, God is closer to us than ourselves, in the past, in the here and now, in the time yet to be.
    We are calligraphic inscriptions on the divine palm.
    God has woven eternity in our hearts, stitched the essence of unsighted horizons into the fabric of our souls.
    If God is different, who amongst us can ever know the divine mind?
    Job asks God: *Why do you allow good people to suffer?*
    The Job-poet responds: *You were not present from the beginning. How could you know? Your thoughts are not my thoughts, your ways, not my ways.*
    Some things are inexplicable, only partially discerned and understood. They can, however, reveal the problem we are to ourselves, opening new opportunities for learning and loving.
    God may be present in our suffering, may even want to explain its purpose, but will we ever have the capacity to understand?

Aizi.

Only God knows.

The path open to us is to live the best we can in the tension of the mystery.

It hadn't helped that we had moved out of God's earshot. *Had we not ignored the invitation to relationship within a cosmic Christhood?*

... the falcon cannot hear the falconer...

Could it be, by stretching the imagination, the creator suffers in exile with creation because he loves it so much?

We are just incapable of perceiving this face because our narcissistic drumming deafens us.

In gifting us a creation, through whatever lens we opted to view it, the creator had opened himself to one clear and dangerous vulnerability: *a love without conditions.*

If you could choose love, then you could also choose its opposite.

Did evil exist so love remained a possibility?

Even in the darkest of hearts, freedom to choose, or reject, remained.

Was our creator grieving, watering the heavens with tears? Had he been suffering with us at the loss of every life on the *Hunyani,* and every death and tear shed before and since?

Was it possible our creator knew human grief and pain? Did he walk in that suffering with us, even though we may not have felt he did?

Could I have misunderstood?

Was this the reason I was a man with a cross?

Had the creator crafted an admixture of contraries, where suffering and pain were realities, for this very reason? Was this his way of accepting responsibility for such a paradoxical creation?

He may have been responsible for allowing a world to evolve where the effects of moral and physical evil created injustice and suffering. But was he liable for the human refusal to make the hard choices that would transform the world, even though he was often accused of that very thing?

There was also a difference between a creator allowing for the possibility of suffering and evil, and a creator perpetrating it.

The world was not thus. Thus had we, ourselves, made it.

Blake and Huxley's doors, that had stood ajar for a moment, shut. The mist descended once again, to shroud my mind once more.

Errant pilgrims, prophets and paladins who return through the doors are never the same as those who depart.

They are unsure, yet wiser. Restless, and happier. Less trusting, but compassionate. Not submissive, yet humbler. Serene rather than satisfied. Less rational, but better able to contemplate and express the incarnational mystery, and how it unites the paradoxes embroidered into the very fabric of the universe.

I sat for what seemed a very long time, confused in thought, grief, and shame.

... it hurts to set you free...

I heard a cough behind me. I scrambled up and turned in its direction. Before me stood one of the military scouts. He'd been waiting, out of respect, not wanting to interrupt my farewell.

'McKenzie. SAS. We've been on their tail for two days and caught up with you here. A moment too late for your friend, I'm afraid. I'm sorry.'

I nodded, wiped my eyes.

'You gonna be okay?'

'Thanks. Yeah... No... I'm okay, I think.' After a moment, I said, 'And he was not just my friend; he was my younger brother. He saved my life.'

And my soul.

The casevac was professional, well-rehearsed, efficient, an assassin's knife thrust.

In and out.

... the blue bus is calling us...

The Alouettes floated downwards and bee-like, sucked in their precious cargo.

Driver, where are you taking us?

For a drumbeat they hovered, before their rotors' song rose into the bloodstained sun.

IN THE CITADEL

THE THUNDEROUS ECHO OF jet engines snaps me back to the present moment.

A rainbowed South African Airways Airbus rises in the sky on its chosen trajectory, a majestic eagle at the start of its next long-haul journey. Its silver wings glow red in the pinkish half-light of sunset. It grows smaller and smaller.

When I look back towards the memorial, my wife and second eldest daughter are standing on either side of me.

Words seem unnecessary.

From my right, my wife hands me a bouquet of flame lilies laced with sprigs of rosemary. I hand it to my daughter.

With furrowed brows, she looks at me. 'Are you sure?' she whispers. I nod.

She moves to the memorial, bows and places the flame lilies on the steps at the middle of the monument, at the spine of its open book.

She returns to take up her position beside me.

I invoke the novena prayer of John Bradburne. The three of us pray it together.

God's love within you is your native land.

So search none other, never more depart.

For you are homeless save God keeps your heart.

We observe a moment's silence.

I make a mental note to fulfil a bucket-list promise to undertake a pilgrimage to Mutemwa in Zimbabwe to climb Chigona Mountain, to walk the Way of the Cross, to visit John B's shrine.

In the stillness, I open my old, shabby, blood-splotched and dog-eared journal to the last entry.

I need not read it. I know the content by heart.

MONDAY, SEPTEMBER 11, 1978

So, here I am... alive, and he's dead.

I was meant to save him. I tried to save him.

In the end, he saved me.

The irony is not lost on me. He died so I could live.

To the full.

This was a life – like so many others – snuffed out by a conflict without victors.

How many more lives will we sacrifice before we come to our senses?

What is the cost of a single life? Can one life make a difference?

I have no adequate answers. For losing my brother and the manner of that loss, I feel resentment, bitterness and revulsion at my complicity and irrational bloodlust.

I know every new birth must have its blood. But this birth, this death, has been – is – difficult.

I also know this dry winter season will come to pass.

For it was Blaise's last words – the whispers of a dying brother – that resound in my head and heart and give me some hope and comfort in my desolation.

'Remember... brother... hunyani. Baron... hunyani is our bond.

The hottest fire forges the strongest metal. Be that molten metal of reconciliation. Of grace.

Don't be bitter.

We must forgive before we can overcome any cruel injustices committed against us. Forgiveness is the only road to peace.

Begin by forgiving yourself.

I love you. I forgive you. You should – must – forgive yourself.

Promise me you'll forgive. Promise you will pursue peace.

Someone has to help transform the clenched fists into handshakes, the spears into ploughs. Let it begin with you.'

Vale, Brother.

This is not the end. I can picture what can be. We no longer need to be desperate strangers in a desperate land, and I will look into your eyes again.

No, my beautiful friend, this is not the end.

Not yet.

For I am determined to keep your flame alive, committed to honouring your red-metal spirit by beating on against the human current of natural and unnatural troubles, to echo your whisper like thunder from the ochred hilltops.

I turn to my wife.

'Anne, have I kept the *hunyani* flame alive, as I promised?' I ask. 'Have I made a difference? Have I honoured my brother's memory, and those who died? Please tell me my life has not been a waste. That he – they – did not die in vain.'

Her sky-blue eyes sparkle. 'You cannot undo what was done, nor should you atone for decisions that were not yours. It's not an all-or-nothing matter, or a binary distinction between useful and wasteful.'

'I understand I didn't create the problem. I get that it's beyond a black-and-white issue,' I say. 'Of all people, you would know I'm a relativist at heart. Life exists in the shades-of-grey sea, beyond the tides. However, the question remains, what contribution have I made in the name of grace and peace? Have I lived against the grain of popular culture?'

'Against the grain? Your mother called you a disestablishmentarian. What do you think?' She laughs. 'As for the rest, I can only see the issues in real, practical terms.' She gestures with her arm.

'Look to our family. You must see their optimism. *Their hope.* Your daughters are people of integrity,' she says. 'They are making positive and courageous contributions in their careers, in their communities and in a country desperate for moral leadership. Your sons are living meaningful and just lives. Then, our beautiful grandchildren. They are our legacy: the blazing torch we hand to the next generation. You shouldn't forget what we have achieved, however small, in the other public areas of our lives as well.'

'But is that enough? It seems insignificant when you look at the global context.'

My daughter interjects. 'It's easy to be overwhelmed by the troubles of the world. Remember, Dad, we are shaping a future that is not our own. We don't know what will become of the seeds we plant. We must plant them, nonetheless. Always in good faith, according to our talents and resources in our small spheres of influence. We can do no more. Take some comfort in that.'

'Aren't we called to do, to be more?' I persist. 'I feel as if I have failed in my struggle for peace and justice. For Eldorado.'

'You and Eldorado. Like that fresco of the Man from La Mancha mocking me in the sitting room. How like you. Well, it gives me the itch,' Anne says. 'I'm tempted to toss it in the trash. Off tilting at wind-mills to achieve the impossible dream.'

Suppressing a smile is hard. 'But I'm trying to be true to myself.'

'Here's something to think about. In trying to be true to yourself, can you say you're not confusing loyalty with integrity? You must deal with the here and now, by bringing that truth to the present moment. The past is written, the future unscripted. Your pursuit of Eldorado is noble and idealistic, but impractical. We live in the real world,' Anne says. 'Yes, each of us can always do more. And be more. But you cannot take responsibility for something that you did not cause.'

'You don't understand. *Eldorado* is an idea that whispers to me from the mists of uncertainty beyond entrenchments. It's this fragile vision of a better world that sustains me. I have to believe it's out there somewhere.'

'While you're searching for this elusive Eldorado, you still have to be present in the now,' my daughter remarks. 'Inside out, not outside *in*. That's the key. If I can help one life, I save the world. You taught me that. That's a good place to start,' she says. 'Don't forget: you are not alone. Many believe in the Eldorado you speak of. Isn't that enough? You have helped to shape so many lives. So many Eldorados. Take some satisfaction in that too.'

I'm about to argue the toss further, but Anne takes my arm and says, 'Makes sense to me. Don't over-analyse things. You always thought too deeply about everything. Your life's not over, either. Not yet, anyway. The best is yet to come. There's no reason you shouldn't believe that.'

With a sigh, I close my frayed, blood-fingered journal, my permanent companion down the years and, taking a knee, place it on the step beside the bouquet of flame lilies and rosemary.

It has reached a resting place. It has found a home.

My throat swells.

Can a stone memorial temper grief or bind up wounds of loss, guilt and anger, lift the weight of memory, or erase the shame of witness and participation?

Wreaths, names, inscriptions on monument walls may offer consolation, but are they enough? Can they restore the promise and potential of those no longer with us?

Can I, and my grail, ever atone, bring healing and reconciliation?

I remain kneeling, staring at the flame lily bouquet and the grubby, tatty journal beside it. The rosemary's minty-pine scent fills my senses. I am held captive by its fragrance, unable to move. A myriad of thoughts and emotions snake through my tortured mind.

... of everything that stands...

Amidst the static, a mishmash of blood-splattered faces and disparate, incongruent, interconnected voices from my constricted past vie for attention. Like the entwining coils of an African python, their visages and auguries squeeze my chest, clamp my heart, suffocate my brain.

'Remember, brother, search within. Hunyani is our bond... Milo... my young friend, is that Africa in you? Which grail do you serve? The foolish build dams... we are all prisoners. Be careful, white boy, not to make those different from you in your image and likeness. We miss the elephants, our worldviews conditioned by our language. We are all serpents, predator and prey... Lungisani. The river hides the treasure you seek. We live our lives, responding to circumstances and challenges. The wise build bridges... how will you ever know if you do not leave the shore? The hunt unfolds in the seeker's heart. Time to create your own path, or be enslaved by another's. It's grit. Remember.'

Part of me longs to loosen the tourniquets, to let the blood flow, to feel again what I have stemmed for so long. Another part knows that to do so is to risk the agony of wounds reopening, to expose the bleeding and pain I have worked so hard to staunch.

Over time, they say, memories soften, pain wanes, and joy waxes.

In my experience, the opposite has been true.

I recall the discoloured, blurred family photograph that accompanied me on my journey into the Rhodesian wild so many years ago. Like that fading photo, happy memories distort and disembody. Hurtful memories, though, invoke and illuminate, sparked by everyday moments: a plane's engines surging overhead, chargrilled meat sizzling on red-hot coals, the whiff of petrol fumes, a red and white footy jumper.

Such moments awaken in me a flood of images, sounds and smells accompanied by stabs of fear, guilt and grief re-remembered, despite my attempts to quash or dispel them.

The leather-bound journal lies open at the foot of the memorial, its pages lapping in the soothing breeze. Without it, I'm out of my depth, treading water in a truncated and dissident riptide of memories.

The journal has been with me for so long, it defines who I am.

'Dad?' A hand rests on my shoulder.

I recognise the voice, but it takes me a moment to work out from where it came. The rest of the family, who had been waiting a short distance away, has now gathered around me. I pick out his lanky frame, woolly ginger *kuif* and cheeky smile.

'I thought leaving the journal here would be cathartic. I believed that by letting it go, I could erase my guilt and anger, and gain some kind of closure.'

His lengthy, muscled frame leans down, and his large hands gather up the journal. 'Maybe the journey doesn't end here,' he says, holding it towards me. 'Maybe it never ends. Who can say where anything begins or ends? This could just be another pit-stop.'

I stare at his outstretched hand offering the journal. 'What do you mean?'

'There's another way.'

'I still don't quite follow.'

'You need this journal. To record its story. *Blaise's* story. *Your* story. The *Hunyani's* story. It needs to be told,' he says. '*You* need to tell it. It's time. Lest we forget. You owe it to the family to tell it. You've always harped on about finding the right material to write your novel. Well, *write* it. You have all the ingredients in this journal. You have the nous. The lived experience. What's stopping you? If anyone's going to tell it, why not you? Time to apply that *hunyani* resolve for real. After all, it's part of our history, and it's also part of a much greater narrative,' he says. 'It's in writing this story that I believe you will face up to your past and tame those serpents that still haunt you.'

'I'm not sure I can ever tame those serpents, nor do I know if I can do justice to this story in a balanced, dependable way.'

'Sounds like impostor syndrome to me,' he grins.

'After all these years, I am still haunted by so many anguished faces. How can I – *how should I* – reconcile the dissenting voices that are part of it? My memories are too clouded and jaundiced. And my views, partisan.'

'Does that trivialise your journey and the memory of it, making it unworthy of the telling?' my eldest daughter challenges me, smiling. 'Is there such a thing as a reliable record of the past? A dodgy filter's wedged between the reality of the past and how we remember it. That past is disremembered or reremembered in a forever changing narrative. It's all a perceiving, and a renegotiated one at that.'

'Spoken like a dedicated literature and philosophy teacher.'

'Dad, the past is never dead,' my son says. 'It's not even past. It also messes with the present. You might as well bring your version of it into the light.' Before I can interject, he adds, 'Yes, there's a danger you might sacrifice aspects of the story at the expense of others, misremember things, and even misrepresent those culturally different from you. But what else do we have, if not our memories? I read that somewhere, but can't remember where,' he smiles.

I'm at a loss for words. My children have become the parent of this man, their father.

The tightness in my chest subsides.

Resurrection, beyond-beyond the turbulent paradoxes of the experience itself, may be possible, in an organic, evolutionary, mystical and incarnational sense.

Such an understanding might bring healing if we allow it.

Blaise is not lost. He will never be unremembered, disremembered or misremembered.

Neither is he alone.

We still remember him, and all those who perished on the Hunyani and Umniati.

I cannot bring any of them back from the dead. Nor can I remove the weight of memory.

But I can ease its burden.

I can give their lives meaning.

I can resurrect their humanity; restore it to the tabernacle of memory. Transfigure it with words.

With all their eruptions, erasures and exclusions, memories can be reconceptualised and relanguaged. Words can seep into memory's uncharted, ill-defined cracks and percolate a deeper meaning to the surface.

By de-silencing the past and making sense of what Blaise and I lived through, I can give my brother's life sacramental meaning.

And my own.

'So, are you up for the challenge? Dare you write it?' pipes the voice of the youngest and most ebullient of my children. 'I can help. I have so many ideas I can't get them down quickly enough.'

More giggles.

I look around at each member of the family, shaking my head and smiling. I reach out and take the journal from my son.

'It's so much nicer when you smile,' Anne says. 'You should do it more often. We're all tired of the grumpy old bum.'

'Who're you calling *old*, huh?'

A chorus of assenting chuckles ensues. My eldest son offers his hand. I grab it, and he pulls me to my feet.

'Group hug!' Amidst the shrieks of delight, everyone crowds in, including a barking Scout, our labrador and fifth child.

'About the mythical *City of Gold*,' I say. '*Egoli. Eldorado. Avalon. Arcadia.* Whatever you like to call it.'

A collective groan disrupts my train of thought.

'We're so over that,' the youngest says, rolling his eyes.

Nods and grins all round.

'You're right, but hear me out. I promise, this will be my last word on it.'

'Well?' Anne raises her eyebrows.

'It's dawning on me. I've had it wrong all along.'

'You're in danger of becoming wise, Dad,' my youngest says, a broad grin etched on his face.

'Eldorado is not out there somewhere, beyond the mountains of the moon. It's not a place. It's amongst us. Right *here*.' I incline my head to the huddle's centre.

'In *here*.' I gesture to my chest.

'And *here*, between the ears.' I point at my temple. 'Its potential is within each of us, in the citadel of our very being. Together, every day, we collaborate in its creation. We bring it with us wherever we are and share it with whomever we encounter. We build and live it in the holiness of each moment. In this moment. It's all we have, and it's all we need.' I look each family member in the eye. 'Sorry it's taken me such a long time to fathom it.'

The sun has all but disappeared. The departing Airbus has reached the point of no return, a dust-speck in what remains of the dusk on the distant horizon.

As it slips out of sight, it occurs to me that each of my memories of the *Hunyani* experience is, like that diminishing airbus, a minuscule but persistent particle of a bigger story.

To draw from and shape the varied and shifting particles of that narrative, sensitive to how they might prompt me to weave a coherent, imaginative and post-conventional account that resonates with the past and my memory of it, offers another challenge, another beginning, another opportunity for grace.

Such an undertaking can only ever be equivocal. At the onset of an African night, the skeins of our memories, with their many charms and consolations, feats and failures, stases and shifts, divergences and dalliances, erasures and embellishments, misappropriations and misperceptions, amidst the many competing and spiralling voices, are all we have. We owe it to ourselves, and the generations that follow, to record them with candour and justice, no matter how dislocated we feel they may be.

The cost of not doing so would be so much higher.

Together, as family, we turn to face the memorial and stand silent and reflective. I step forward, put three fingers to my lips, reach out and allow them to brush across Blaise's name, chiselled into the black-flecked marble.

Words from a song favoured by my father stray into my mind.

To everything there is a season...

... turn...

As we turn and take our leave, a sharp gust of wind inundates us with jacaranda flower-kisses.

... a time for every purpose under heaven...
... turn...

With the three boys fossicking and tumbling amongst the descending blossoms on the scented carpet beneath the trees – Scout in playful tow – Anne and I cannot help but laugh as we drift, hand-in-hand, in the company of children and grandchildren, towards the twilit horizon sprinkled with floating pinhole stars above the memorial grove of honeyed jacarandas.

... my story is like the wind...

The Byrds' folk-rock homage to *Ecclesiastes* mutates into Johnny Clegg's soulful, trans-cultural life-anthem.

... a highway of stars across the heavens...
... a hope and dream at the edge of the sky...

One of my many struggles may be at an end, but another is about to begin.

I'm searching for the spirit of the Great Heart...
(Guga mzimba, sala ntliziyo)
to stand me by...
that beats my name inside...
under African sky...

Minha busca continua.

AFTERWORD

HISTORICAL CONTEXT

The Rhodesian Bush War, alternatively known as the *Second Chimurenga* or the *Zimbabwe War of Liberation* (1964-1979), pitted Ian Smith's white-led Rhodesian Government against two national liberation movements: Joshua Nkomo's Zimbabwe African People's Union (ZAPU), and Robert Mugabe's Zimbabwe African National Union (ZANU).

These movements fought the war to remove colonial dominance, dismantle white minority rule, and address land dispossession. The white community viewed the conflict as a fight for survival to protect the 'Rhodesian Way of Life' in what they considered the 'Breadbasket of Africa'. The brutality and chaos of the liberation struggles in Kenya, Ethiopia, and the former Belgian Congo to the north, Angola to the west, and Mozambique to the east were also compelling incentives to resist the winds of *Uhuru* blowing through Africa.

Any analysis of the civil conflict in Rhodesia must also consider the significant role played by the Cold War. Throughout the 1960s and 1970s, the Soviet Union and the People's Republic of China (PRC) trained and funded the many African armies of liberation to pursue their national interests, expanding their global influence to gain access to more and better natural resources. These superpowers often competed and hence, the militia of the two liberation movements, ZANLA (the military wing of ZANU) backed by the PRC and North Korea, and ZIPRA (the military wing of ZAPU) supported by the Soviet Union and East Germany, engaged in separate guerrilla wars against Ian Smith's Rhodesian Security Forces. ZANLA fighters were primarily Shona, whereas ZAPU fighters were mainly Ndebele.

The protracted hostilities, incurring well over twenty thousand casualties, many of which were civilian, eventually led to the end of white minority rule, introducing universal suffrage, and the establishment of the Republic of Zimbabwe in 1980, with Robert Mugabe at the helm.

THE HUNYANI TRAGEDY

On 3 September 1978, at a critical juncture in the war, members of ZIPRA downed Air Rhodesia Flight RH825, using a Soviet-made SAM-7 (*Strela*-2) heat-seeking missile. The civilian aircraft, a Vickers Viscount named the *Hunyani*, was en route from the resort town of Kariba to the capital Salisbury. The missile struck the *Hunyani's* starboard wing, forcing the pilots to execute an emergency landing. Of the 52 passengers and four crew, 38 perished in the crash.

Shortly afterwards, a cadre of ZIPRA insurgents approached the wreckage, rounded up the survivors and killed them. Three passengers survived by taking refuge in the surrounding bush, while a further five escaped as they had gone in search of water before the guerrillas arrived.

Nkomo took responsibility for the attack, claiming he had received intelligence showing the *Hunyani* was a legitimate military target. He denied issuing orders for the killing of survivors.

METAMODERN IMPULSE

The *Hunyani* atrocity, documented across a range of sources, has inspired this narrative. While I have changed some elements to align with the narrative's artistic vision, they remain faithful to the memory of the actual incident. As the text is a work of fiction with its own metamodern, theopoetic and creative concerns, readers should embrace, enjoy and critique it within this framework.

Wittgenstein's assertion that 'the limits of my language mean the limits of my world', has spurred me to push against linguistic boundaries to grapple with the organic and complex relationship between culture and human thought.

The intentional inclusion of multiple languages in this narrative points to this intricate and interconnected dynamic and plays a pivotal role in tracking the protagonist's journey from modern through postmodern to metamodern realms. While some might perceive this approach as exotic or culturally disrespectful, the interweaving of these languages seeks to capture the multi-dimensional nature of the human experience and promote cross-cultural understanding, sensitivity, and empathy. My aim, guided by a post-rational spirit, is, and has always been, to imagine, enchant and explore uncharted literary territories.

Underpinning the cascade of multilingual terms lies a rigorous process of research and linguistic exploration. These terms draw in the main from Afrikaans, Latin, Shona, Ndebele, Zulu, French, and Portuguese. To enrich the text and mitigate any risk of misappropriation or misrepresentation, I have taken great care to ensure translations and meanings transcend cultures and languages with authenticity and nuance. Any translation errors, although unintended, fall ultimately on my shoulders.

ACKNOWLEDGEMENTS

To raise a child, African wisdom contends, takes a village. Similarly, it takes a team to complete a writing project. While I penned the initial draft of this novel in 12 weeks, the subsequent stages of reframing, drafting and editing extended over a far longer span.

It is with appreciation I acknowledge those who have played crucial roles in this endeavour.

I want to extend a special thanks to Jon den Hartigh, who provided invaluable support with his evocative front and back cover design concepts, and unwavering encouragement during the early and often arduous dry white season of re-writing and re-drafting. Nick Evans provided valuable insights on the *oeuvre* of Antonin Artaud, while Stephen Chatelier offered an astute postcolonial critique. Heartfelt thanks to Gavin Fuller, for our shared conversations on the works of Hesse, Shakespeare, Aurelius and Seneca, with red wine thrown in for good measure.

To those who generously offered their time to proofread, beta-read, sub-edit, and advise, providing helpful input, I also record my thanks. Specifically, I want to acknowledge Stephen Calvert for his constructive feedback and editing suggestions.

I am also indebted to the teams at Greenhill Publishing and Bookmark Edits for facilitating this project in its final iteration.

Last, I reserve a special tribute to two members of *Holts Inc.*, who prompted the telling of this tale in its current form. To Anne J, for sharing her recollections of life in Rhodesia during the Bush War, which were adapted and retold by Sean B, in his sweeping reimagining of those memories. Full credit to them both. Without their inspiration, this story might have remained hidden in the recesses of a preoccupied mind.

Having served in the SADF in the late Seventies, I have very intimate ties to many of those who endured, fought, and perished in the

Rhodesian and the South African Bush Wars. Through this narrative, I hope to contribute to the collective memory of those troubling and turbulent times, honouring especially those who lost their lives aboard the *Hunyani* and, five months later, on the *Umniati*.

This text stands as a testament to them all.

Gone too soon, but never forgotten.

A jornada continua.

Jeremy Holt
September 2023

GLOSSARY

CHAPTER BY CHAPTER

TITLE PAGES

Everything that Stands Words from *The Doors'* song, *The End* (1971).

Kahlil Gibran (1883-1931) Lebanese American writer and artist, best remembered for his mystical and inspirational work *The Prophet* (1923).

Ecclesiastes Old Testament wisdom text (author unknown) dating from the 3rd Century BCE, reflecting on the meaning and purpose of life, the vanity of human endeavour, the role of God, and the value of wisdom.

Anthony de Mello (1931-1987) Indian Jesuit priest, psychotherapist, spiritual teacher, writer and public speaker, best known for his texts *The Song of the Bird* (1982) and *Awareness* (1990).

The Tyger Published as part of the *Songs of Experience* (1794), Blake's poem explores the nature of God and creation through a series of rhetorical questions.

Ben Okri (b.1959) Nigerian-born British poet and novelist in the postmodern and postcolonial traditions, best known for his text *The Famished Road* (1991).

A LUMINOUS DARK

Scatterling One who has no fixed residence, a vagabond, vagrant.

FORGET-ME-NOT

Voortrekkerhoogte Precinct of SADF military bases on the southern outskirts of Pretoria during the apartheid years.

1-MIL Premier military hospital, located in Voortrekkerhoogte.

Ratel Named for the honey badger, a South African light armoured military vehicle providing firepower and strategic mobility for mechanised infantry.

Apartheid System of institutionalised racial segregation that existed in South Africa (1948-1994).

Ian Smith Prime Minister of white-led minority government in Rhodesia (1965-1979).

Robert Mugabe Revolutionary and politician, leader of ZANU-PF (1980-2017), 1st PM (1980-87) and then 1st president (1987-2017) of Zimbabwe.

ZANU-PF Acronym for *Zimbabwe African National Union-Patriotic Front*.

Abel Muzorewa Methodist Bishop and politician, 1st and only PM of Rhodesia-Zimbabwe (1979-1980).

Lancaster House Agreement Signed in Lancaster House, London (21 Dec 1979), this effectively terminated armed conflict in Zimbabwe and paved the way for democratic elections in April 1980.

UDI *Unilateral Declaration of Independence*, a statement adopted by the Cabinet of Rhodesia (on 11 Nov 1965), announcing that Southern Rhodesia, a British territory, regarded itself as Rhodesia, an independent sovereign state.

Limpopo River Africa's second largest river, called *Espiritu Santo* (*Holy Spirit*) by the Portuguese explorer Vasco da Gama, flowing 1700 km through South Africa, Zimbabwe, Botswana and Mozambique to the Indian Ocean.

South-West *South-West-Africa*, now independent Namibia.

Rundu Namibian city on the Kavango River, bordering Angola.

Kavango River Runs 1600 km south-east from central Angola to northern Botswana.

Operation Askari Military operation (Dec 1983-Jan 1984) in Angola, undertaken by the SADF during the South African Border War (1966-90).

Rhodesian Bush War Second *Chimurenga* or Zimbabwe War of Independence (1964-1979).

Viscount Memorial Located in the Voortrekker Monument Heritage Site (erected in 2012) to honour the victims of the Rhodesian Bush War Viscount tragedies.

A vida continua Portuguese phrase, meaning *Life continues.*

Sic transit gloria mundi Latin phrase, meaning *Thus do the joys of this world pass us by.*

Requiescat in pace Latin for *Rest in peace.*

Voortrekker Monument Designed by South African architect Gerard Moerdijk (1890-1958), a granite structure and the spiritual home of the Afrikaner, built to commemorate the 100th anniversary of the voortrekkers' journey to escape British colonial rule (1836-1936).

Thaba Tshwane Replacement name for *Voortrekkerhoogte* (1998), motivated by the post-apartheid desire to be more inclusive and representative of local culture and history.

Adamastor Mythological character, created by the Portuguese poet Luís de Camões (1524-1580) in his epic poem *Lusiads* (Book V, 1572), to personify the Cape of Storms:

... Grotesque and enormous stature
With heavy jowls, and an unkempt beard
Scowling from shrunken, hollow eyes
Its complexion earthy and pale,
Its hair grizzled and matted with clay,
Its mouth coal black, teeth yellow with decay.

SAM-7 Also known as the *Strela-2* (Russian for *arrow*), Soviet-designed, shoulder-launched, surface-to-air missile developed in 1959, and first deployed in 1968.

Hunyani AR Vickers Viscount, named for the Hunyani River, shot down by guerrillas (Sept 1978).

Umniati AR Vickers Viscount, named for the Umniati River, shot down by guerrillas (Feb 1979).

Vickers Viscount British designed medium-range turboprop passenger airliner, used by Air Rhodesia between 1967 and 1980.

THE-YOU-KNOW-WHAT

Ja South African colloquialism for *yes.*

Ag Afrikaans interjection expressing frustration or resignation, similar to *oh* or *ugh* in English.

Salisbury Now Harare, capital of Zimbabwe.

Fothergill Island Named for game-ranger Robert Fothergill, a small island located in Lake Kariba, part of Matusadona National Park.

Matusadona Declared a national park in 1975, known for its diverse fauna and flora, including the Big Five.

St George's Jesuit College, founded in Bulawayo (1896), relocated to Salisbury in 1927.

David Livingstone Scottish physician, missionary and explorer to Africa from 1841 to 1873.

Queen Victoria Monarch of the British Empire, on which *the sun never set* (1837-1901).

Zambezi (River) Named by the Tonga people, *Zambeze (River of God)* is the fourth longest river in Africa (3540 km), rising in Zambia and flowing through Angola, Namibia, Botswana, Zimbabwe and Mozambique to the Indian Ocean.

Seongo Indigenous Tonga name for the Victoria Falls, meaning *Place of the Rainbow.*

Mosi-oa-Tunya Indigenous Tonga and Lozi name for the Victoria Falls, meaning *The Smoke or Cloud that Thunders.*

Niagara (Falls) A group of three waterfalls on the Niagara River, marking the border between Canada and the USA.

Iguazu (Falls) A series of cataracts on the Iguazu River, which forms the border between Argentina and Brazil.

Nyaminyami Zambezi River God or Snake Spirit, depicted with snake-body and fish-head; protector and sustainer of local communities, his image often worn to ward off evil spirits.

I wait upon thy leisure... Exchange between the brothers using lines from Shakespeare's *Macbeth* (1603).

Touché *French fencing term, meaning touched, or point scored, and in argument, acknowledging a good or clever point made.*

Eeyore Friend of Christopher Robin, the pessimistic, gloomy old grey donkey who appears in Alan Milne's *Winnie-the-Pooh* (1926).

Mozambique Country situated on the southeastern coast of Africa, bordered by Tanzania, Malawi, Zambia, Zimbabwe, South Africa and Eswatini (formerly Swaziland); achieved independence from Portugal in June 1975.

Chimurenga Shona word referring to the revolutionary wars-insurrections in Zimbabwe, embodying the spirit of resistance, and the struggle for self-determination.

Salisbury Woolworths' store bombing (06 August 1977) 11 civilians were killed and 76 injured in an attack carried out by members of Nkomo's ZANLA.

St Paul's Musami murders (06 February 1977) Guerrillas killed three Jesuits and four Dominican nuns at the Catholic Mission in the Murewa district.

Elim Mission massacre (23 June 1978) Guerrillas attacked the Pentecostal mission and killed 12 British missionaries and their children.

Beit Bridge Spanning the Limpopo River, BB connects Zimbabwe and South Africa, and is named for Albert Beit, a British South African financier who funded its construction (1929).

12.7-mm Browning American-made mounted machine gun, capable of firing up to 600 rounds per minute, used by the Rhodesian military.

Donga Zulu word for *ravine* or *gully*, eroded by water.

Kopje (*koppie*) Dutch, South African and Afrikaans term for *small hill* or *hillock*.

Deo gratias Latin phrase for *Thanks be to God* or *God be praised.*

The Wombles Created by children's author Elisabeth Beresford (1968), pointy-nosed, furry creatures living beneath Wimbledon Common who aim to help the environment by collecting and recycling rubbish in creative ways.

Terr Derogatory contraction of *terrorist,* as opposed to guerilla or freedom fighter.

Uhuru Swahili word meaning *freedom*, popularised in African states who fought for independence from colonial powers.

Krugerrand South African gold coin, 1st minted in 1967, to promote SA's gold industry, bearing the image of Paul Kruger, former ZAR president, and a pronking Springbok on the reverse.

Gawain In Arthurian legend, archetypal grail knight who symbolises honour, integrity, loyalty and prowess in combat, his name derived from the Welsh meaning *white hawk [of the battle].*

Percival Archetypal grail knight who represents the quest for spiritual enlightenment, and whose name derives from the French, *to pierce the vale.*

Ouma Afrikaans for *grandma.*

Boet-Bru Afrikaans and South African colloquialisms for *brother.*

Padkos Afrikaans for *food for the road.*

ALWAYS ENDING

Gareth Edwards-Barry John Legendary rugby half-back duo for Wales and the British Lions in the late 1960s and early 1970s.

Creedence Clearwater Revival Or *CCR*, an American rock band active in the late 1960s and early 1970s, known for their distinctive swamp rock sound.

Simon and Garfunkel American folk-rock duo, Paul Simon and Art Garfunkel became famous in the 1960s for songs such as *The Sounds of Silence* and *Bridge over Troubled Water.*

The Rolling Stones Enduring English rock band (formed in 1962), whose music spans six decades, and whose legacy transcends music and culture.

Pink Floyd English rock band (formed in 1965), best known for their album *Dark Side of the Moon* (1973), which explores aspects of human life such as conflict, greed, time, decay and death.

The Doors American rock band (formed in 1965), known for their psychedelic blues sound, as well as their poetic, provocative and disestablishmentarian lyrics, drawn from a range of literary, philosophical and religious sources.

The Fall of Icarus (c.1555) Attributed to Flemish Renaissance painter Peter Brueghel the Elder, a painting depicting a scene from Greek myth, showing Icarus' fall from grace and the indifference of the onlookers.

Jim Morrison Lead singer and songwriter of *The Doors* (died at age 27 in 1971), considered the most iconic and influential figure in rock history.

William Blake (1757-1827) English poet, painter and printmaker, known for his innovative and visionary works, specifically *The Songs of Innocence and Experience.*

Huxley (Aldous) English writer and philosopher, best known for his dystopian novel *Brave New World* (1932), and *The Doors of Perception* (1954), a record of his experimentation with psychedelic drugs.

Brak Afrikaans for *mongrel* or *crossbreed.*

Junior Springbok Brand of leather rugby ball.

Waterford Oldest city in Ireland (founded by the Vikings in the 9th Century) famous for, *inter alia*, its crystal industry which dates to 1783.

Malacca cane Durable, flexible walking stick made from rattan palm, originally from Malacca, in Malaysia.

Miraculous Medal Devotional medal also known as the *Medal of Our Lady of Graces* or the *Medal of the Immaculate Conception*, originating from French nun Catherine Labouré (1830), following her encounters with apparitions of the Blessed Virgin Mary.

Gees Afrikaans for *spirit*, or *zest for life.*

SENTINELS

Rhodesian SAS Special forces unit of the Rhodesian Army during the Bush War (1961-1980), specialising in parachute operations, raids, and small unit tactics.

Paton (Alan) South African writer and anti-apartheid activist (1903-1988), best known for his first novel, *Cry the Beloved Country* (1948).

Achebe (Chinua) Nigerian novelist (1930-2013), best known for his novel *Things Fall Apart* (1958) which explores the impact of colonialism on local indigenous communities.

No Longer at Ease Achebe's sequel (1960) to *Things Fall Apart.*

Karanga Major subgroup of the Shona people, tracking back to before the medieval City of Stone, the Great City of Zimbabwe.

Bateleur Eagle associated with the Zimbabwe Bird, derived from the French, meaning *acrobat* or *tumbler,* and called *Shiri ya Mwari*, meaning *The Bird of God.*

Zimbabwe Bird National emblem and bird of Zimbabwe, associated with the bateleur.

Sit Nomine Digna Latin phrase meaning *May she be worthy of the name*, the motto on the Rhodesian Coat-of-Arms.

Existentially creative Term coined by Ben Okri (in 2021), referring to a new mode of writing to address the extreme truths of our times, and to inspire people to do something about it.

Kusimba Shona for *strength, courage, bravery, resilience.*

Mooi Afrikaans for *beautiful* or *lovely.*

Meisies Afrikaans for *girls.*

Mysterious Island Jules Verne's novel (1875) that tracks the survival of individuals on an uninhabited island, ironic counterpoint to Golding's *Lord of the Flies* (1954).

Heart of Darkness Controversial novella by Joseph Conrad (1899), which examines the horrors of western colonialism.

The River Between Novel by Ngugi wa Thiong'o (1965), Kenyan author and activist, known also for his text *Decolonizing the Mind* (1986), which placed linguistic imperialism at the heart of literary discourse.

AR Flight RH825 Air Rhodesia flight from Kariba to Salisbury (03 September 1978), shot down by guerrillas at the height of the Bush War.

The Jungle Book Collection of stories by English author Rudyard Kipling (1894-5) centred on Mowgli the man-cub, and a host of animal characters.

Kintsugi A term meaning *golden repair*, referring to the traditional Japanese art form of repairing broken pottery, built on the idea of celebrating the beauty of imperfection.

Minha busca continua Portuguese phrase, meaning *My search continues.*

IN THE SHADOWS

Magee War poet and Spitfire fighter pilot, John Magee's 1941 sonnet *High Flight* was written three weeks before his death (aged 19) in a flying collision.
Calliope In Greek mythology, the chief of all muses, presiding over eloquence and epic poetry.
Pliny (the Elder) In his *Historia Naturalis*, Pliny (23-79) notes 'Africa always brings [us] something new', a reference to Africa as the source of all things hybridised.

BEYOND... BEYOND

Whamira (Hills) Rugged granite-capped Zimbabwean mountain range.
Skinder Afrikaans for *gossip.*
Sjambok Afrikaans and Dutch for *large whip*, made from leather.
A luta continua Portuguese phrase, meaning *The struggle continues.*
Hamba Zulu for *get going* or *get out of here.*
The 7th Voyage of Sinbad American fantasy film (1958) directed by Nathan Juran, where Sinbad must undertake a quest to an island of monsters to prevent war by rescuing an abducted princess.
Parabats South African military term, a contraction of *parachute battalion*, specialised airborne infantry.
Braaied Afrikaans word for *barbecued.*

INTO THE BELLY

AK-47 Famous assault rifle developed in the Soviet Union by Mikhail Kalashnikov (1947); known for its simplicity, reliability and durability, it became a symbol for resistance, revolution and independence, but also synonymous with terrorism and violence.
Mhoroi Shona for *hello.*
Buia lapa Shona for *come here.*
Gajima Zulu exhortation to *run* or *move.*
Panga Broad bladed African machete.
Cessna Lynx Light attack aircraft used by the RhAF to conduct air assaults, reconnaissance and close air support against guerrilla forces.
Coucal Species of cuckoo found in southern Africa.
Benediction Term derived from the Latin, meaning *blessing.*

CLASH OF KUDUS

Unjani igama lakho? S Ndebele for *What is your name?*
Ungubani wena? S Ndebele for *Who are you?*
Ufuna njani? Ndebele for *What do you want?*
Angizwsisi S Ndebele for *I don't know-understand.*
Uyabhubhisa S Ndebele for *You are careless-negligent.*
Kudu African antelope, the male has long spiral horns that can grow to 2m.
Ubuntu Nguni term for *humaneness*, premised on the idea we are humans only through other humans: *Because we are, I am.*
Minha luta continua Portuguese phrase, meaning *My struggle continues.*
Kuhle ukukubona S Ndebele for *It's good to meet-see you.*
Indaba Zulu term, meaning *gathering,* where parties come together to discuss and negotiate important matters; it has gained broader significance to convey the idea of inclusive and constructive dialogue.
Sala kuhle-Khamba kuhle S Ndebele term of farewell, *Stay well-Travel well.*
Sala kahle-Hamba kahle Zulu term of farewell, *Stay well-Travel well.*
Lungisani Name of Zulu origin, meaning *One who mends.*
Thembelani Name of Ndebele origin, meaning *One who has faith-trust.*

TALISMAN

Tekkies Or *tackies*, South African colloquialism for *running shoes* or *trainers.*
Bosque-Boscages Derived from the Spanish term for *woodlands.*
Inyathi Zulu word for *African buffalo.*
Imbola Zulu and Ndebele term for *red clay* or *ochre*, a naturally occurring reddish-brown pigment used for a range of practical and spiritual purposes.
Memento mori Latin and Stoic phrase, meaning *Remember you must die*, a prompt for the inevitability of death, and an exhortation to live each moment to the full.
Inyoka Zulu and Ndebele for *snake*; in this context, a puff adder.
Puff adder Member of the viper family, responsible for the most snakebite fatalities in Africa.
Phoenix... Nyangani These mythological names are linked to snakes, which have influenced art, literature, culture, music, medicine and beliefs across cultures and civilisations, and are associated with many meanings and attributes, such as fertility, rebirth, healing, wisdom, chaos, and evil.
Axis mundi Latin for *still point of the turning world,* symbolising the order and harmony of the cosmos, the quest for God, and the search for spiritual enlightenment.
Ophiomorphic As opposed to anthropomorphic, derived from the Greek, meaning *snakelike in form.*

BEHEMOTH

Umlungu Zulu for *white person* of European descent, derived from *ubulungu*, meaning *white foam of the sea.*

Musasa Zambezi teak tree, with wide canopy.

Umsenge Ndebele and Zulu term for the *nurturing tree*, the baobab.

Thembesi Or *impisi*, Zulu for cleanser and purifier, the *hyena.*

Umfaan Derived from Zulu, meaning *young boy.*

Bwana Swahili word for *sir* or *master.*

LABYRINTH

Groot Trek Northward migration of Dutch-speaking settlers who travelled by ox-wagon trains from the Cape Colony into the interior of South Africa from 1836 onwards, seeking to escape British colonial rule.

Commedia dell'arte *16th century Italian theatre form, characterised by improvised dialogue, masks, and colourful stock characters.*

En garde! ... Touché! *Sequence of French fencing terms.*

Biltong Dutch and Afrikaans word for cured or dried meat meaning *strip of beef,* akin to *jerky.*

Stoep Afrikaans for *verandah.*

Dr Barnard South African cardiac surgeon who performed the world's first heart transplant at Groote Schuur Hospital in Cape Town (1967).

Bundu South African and Zimbabwean slang for *large uninhabited wilderness.*

Obi-Wan, Yoda and Master Luke Characters from the *Star Wars* saga.

RLI, SAS, Selous Scouts Rhodesian military units: Light Infantry, Special Air Services, and Black Ops.

Springboks and All Blacks National rugby teams of South Africa and New Zealand.

Galileo Famous Italian scientist (1564-1642), supporter of Copernican theory, who made significant contributions to astronomy, physics, mathematics, and philosophy.

Southern Cross Constellation of stars in the southern sky in the shape of a cross, used for navigation, in astronomy, culture, religion, and art.

Nkosi Nguni word for *king* or *lord*, used to address a superior.

Gwelo Former name of Gweru, a city in central Zimbabwe (dating from 1894), derived from the Ndebele word *ikwelo*, meaning *steep place.*

Bulawayo From the Ndebele word *bulala*, meaning *to kill*, second largest city in Zimbabwe, founded by Matabele King Lobengula in the 1870s, and acquired by the British in 1893.

Gulliver Main character of Jonathan Swift's text *Gulliver's Travels* (1726), a satire of human nature and the *travel tales'* genre.

Sherlock Holmes and Dr Watson Famous detective duo created by Scottish surgeon and author Sir Arthur Conan Doyle (1859-1930).

Doctor Doolittle Children's literature character who could speak to animals, and who appears in *The Story of Doctor Doolittle* (1920) and *The Voyages of Doctor Doolittle* (1922), created by American writer and civil engineer Hugh Lofting (1886-1947).

Archimedes (287-212BCE) Leading scientist and mathematician of classical antiquity, hailing from Syracuse, Sicily.

Euclid (300-260BCE) Greek mathematician dubbed the *father of geometry*, best known for his treatise *The Elements*.

Uriah Heep Fictional villain in Dickens' *David Copperfield* (1850), a byword for one falsely humble.

Jis Short for *Jislaaik*, South African colloquialism, derived from Afrikaans, expressing a range of emotions from astonishment and approval to dismay and regret.

Caprivi A narrow strip of land that extends from the NE corner of Namibia to the Zambezi River, named for German Chancellor Leo von Caprivi (1890); with the added *captain*, a sarcastic term for those who think themselves skilled in combat and bushcraft.

Henry Rider Haggard (1856-1925) English writer of exotic adventure fiction, best known for *King Solomon's Mines* (1885), *She* (1886) and *Allan Quatermain* (1887); creator of characters such as Umbopa, Twala, Gagool and, of course, the great frontiersman, explorer and hunter, Allan Quatermain.

She-who-must-be-obeyed Or Ayesha, a fictional character in Rider Haggard's *She*; a supernatural, powerful white queen of a vanished African city who has lived for millennia.

Flesh being proud... *From Shakespeare's The Rape of Lucrece.*

Be courageous... *From Deuteronomy 31:6.*

Jammer Afrikaans for *sorry.*

Skeef Afrikaans for *skew.*

Ibhubesi Zulu for *judge* or *ruler*, referring to the lion, the king of beasts.

Umganu Zulu word for the *Marula* tree.

Kwadira Zulu term for the grey lourie, the *go-away bird*, that makes sharp sounds to warn people of imminent danger.

BUTCHER BIRDS

Karongwe Shona for *cockerel*, signifying the Flame Lily, *Gloriosa Superba*, the national flower of Rhodesia; *Amakukhulume* in Ndebele, and *Ihlamvu* in Zulu.

Sisyphus Famous figure from Grek mythology, condemned for eternity by the gods to roll a boulder uphill only to see it roll back down; a symbol of human resilience and defiance in the face of existential futility and absurdity.

Carpe diem From the Roman poet Horace, a Latin phrase meaning *pluck-seize the day*, urging one to make the most of the moment.

Mosu Setswana for *umbrella thorn-acacia* tree.

Sangoma Zulu term for one who practises *ngoma*, a philosophy based on a belief in ancestral spirits and traditional African medicine.

Nyanga Or *n'anga*, a Shona term for a traditional healer.

Paradoxigma Neologism joining the words *paradox* and *enigma*.

Ingonghulu Zulu and isiXhosa word for the bateleur eagle, the Alpha-and-Omega bird, holiest of all birds.

Gabriel de Jongh Dutch-born South African landscape artist (1913-2004).

Withaak African umbrella thorn tree with wide-spreading branches at the top which provide good shade.

Memorare From the Latin, meaning *Remember*, Catholic prayer seeking the intercession of the Virgin Mary, originating from the 12th century but popularised by Fr Claude Bernard in the 17th.

I lift up my eyes... From *Psalm 121.*

Morpheus In Greek mythology, a god of sleep and dreams.

Finisterre (Africanus) From the Latin *finis terrae*, meaning *the end of the earth*, or known world, a reference to Cape Finisterre in Galicia Spain, marking the unofficial endpoint of the Camino de Santiago; in this text it refers to an African endpoint, a *Field of Stars.*

When I am weak... From *2 Corinthians 12:10.*

Veld(t) From the Dutch and Afrikaans meaning *open country*, Old English *feld*, meaning *field.*

Butcherbirds Thorn-birds or hangman birds, the African shrike impales its prey on sharp objects.

Gwabi Zambian place name, associated with the Zambezi, signifying *creative, compassionate, generous* and *loyal.*

BLUNDERLAND

Impundulu In Zulu folklore, the lightning bird or *thekwane*, that summons lightning and thunder with its wings and talons.
St Anthony of Padua (1195-1231) Franciscan friar, Doctor of the Church, patron saint of the poor, lost and stolen articles.
Novena Derived from the Latin *novem*, meaning *nine*, a Catholic form of worship consisting of special prayers on nine successive days for a specific intention.
umNcaka Zulu for the *Red Ivory* tree, the giver of fire-energy, producing tasty and medicinal fruit, believed to symbolise survival, and inspire spiritual and emotional strength.
Skrik Afrikaans for *scare* or *frighten*.
Slaan my dood Afrikaans expression for *Knock me down, dead.*
Laurence Olivier Acclaimed English director and actor (1907-1989), best known for his Shakespearean performances.
Tabula rasa Latin for *blank slate* or *scraped tablet*, referring to the idea popularised by John Locke, that the human mind is blank before experience shapes knowledge.
We might not make our sun stand still... *Lines from Andrew Marvell's metaphysical carpe diem poem, To His Coy Mistress (1681).*
Né *Afrikaans interrogative particle, meaning Isn't that so? or Not so?*
Manne Colloquial Afrikaans term of affection, meaning *men, mates, fellas* or *guys.*
Dankie, Meneer Afrikaans for *Thank you, Sir.*

BLOOD TRAIL

Hades In Greek mythology, the underworld, named for its king, where souls go after death; divided into Tartarus (for the wicked), Elysium (for the righteous) and Asphodel (for the mediocre majority).
Hadrian's Wall Defensive fortification of walls, ditches and forts (118 km), constructed by the Romans at the command of Emperor Hadrian in the 2nd Century CE, to mark the northern boundary of Britannia.
Mana Pools UNESCO heritage site of 219600 ha, wildlife conservation and national park in northern Zimbabwe (derived from the Shona word *mana*, meaning *four*).
Joggie Jansen South African rugby centre who destroyed the All Blacks with his ferocious tacking in the 1970 Test series.
Mamba Native to Africa, genus of snake (includes black, green and Jameson mamba) that is fast moving, agile, and possessed of a powerful neurotoxic venom fatal to humans; the nickname for the Rhodesian 9-mm semi-automatic handgun.
Madame Fortuna Roman goddess of luck, chance and fate, often depicted as a wheel, a cornucopia, or a rudder.

PLEXUS

Miombo Swahili for a genus of woodland trees across south-central Africa.

Plexus Medical term, derived from the Latin meaning *braid*, or *network*; metaphorically, describes complex, intricate interrelated systems.

Petrichor Refers to the smell of rain on dry soil or rocks, from the Greek meaning *blood of the gods.*

Red Adair Famous American oil well firefighter (1915-2004).

Red Baron Nickname for famous World War 1 fighter pilot, Baron Manfred von Richthofen, who died in combat aged 25 (1918).

Deville Wood, the Somme, Ypres Major battles of World War 1.

Baasboy Afrikaans compound word for *boss-boy*, derogatory term for one who collaborates with the authorities.

Imvubu Zulu word for *hippopotamus.*

Enterprise In the original series of *Star Trek*, penned by Gene Roddenberry (in 1966), Captain Kirk's starship.

Che Guevara (1928-1967) Controversial Argentinian Marxist revolutionary.

Muti Derived from the Zulu, Xhosa and Ndebele word *umuthi*, meaning *tree*, it refers to African traditional medicine.

Mashonja Shona word for *mopane worms.*

Lekker South African colloquial term, derived from the Afrikaans word for *nice, fantastic, superb.*

Hors d'oeuvres Derived from the French, meaning *outside the main course.*

Hors de combat French term, meaning *out of combat* (due to injury or damage).

Alea iacta est *Latin term for the die is cast, the decision is made, there's no turning back.*

Ave Caesar, morituri te salutant *Latin phrase, supposedly used by gladiators, meaning Hail Caesar, those about to die salute you.*

Shongololo *Derived from the Zulu and Xhosa word ishongololo, meaning to roll up, referring to the millipede.*

SEEK-AND-HIDE

Antonin Artaud (1896-1948) French surrealist writer, who developed the concept of the *Theatre of Cruelty*, best known for his texts *Jet of Blood* (1925), and *The Theatre and its Double* (1938).

Dark satanic mills Words from Blake's poem *Jerusalem* (1808).

Carwyn James (1929-1983) Welsh rugby player, visionary coach, philosopher, and decent human being.

UP-RIVER

Mysterium iniquitatis Latin phrase, meaning *the mystery of evil.*

Stygian From Greek mythology, relating to the river Styx, the boundary between the living and dead, meaning *dark, gloomy* and *forbidding.*

Mysterium bonum Latin phrase for the *mystery of the good.*

Ad infinitum Latin for *to infinity* or *repeating without end.*

Kak Afrikaans slang, meaning *crap* or *nonsense.*

Second order idea Refers to *an idea about an idea*, and the process of reflecting on the validity of one's own thoughts, beliefs and assumptions.

MORE THAN LITTORAL

Windgat Afrikaans colloquial, derogatory term for a *windbag.*

Spiritus mundi Latin term meaning *inter alia, world spirit*, the collective unconsciousness, the spirit that gives breath to creation, source of universal memory, or the muse of poetic inspiration.

Genius loci Latin term referring to the protective spirit or deity inhabiting a particular place, and its distinctive atmosphere or ambience.

Litany Bird Name for the nocturnal Nightjar, so-called for its prayerful and repetitious song.

Brother Sun and Sister Moon Zeffirelli's filmic homage to St Frances and St Clare (1972), and tribute to nature and our interconnected relationship with it.

Eucharistic Derived from the Greek, meaning *thanksgiving*, the term refers to a sacramental moment of grace, gratitude, interconnection, celebration, compassion, and reconciliation.

Hubris Greek word referring to excessive pride or arrogance that leads to a downfall.

Last of the Mohicans James Fenimore Cooper's novel (1826), documenting an American frontier in transition.

Last of the Rhodesians Appropriated from the subtitle of Karl Greenway's chronicle, *The Gokwe Kid.*

Isandlwana, Rorke's Drift, Ulundi, uMgungundlovu Sites of battle during the Anglo-Zulu War of 1879.

First Chimurenga Revolutionary struggle or Second Matabele War (1896-97), fought by Matabele and Shona people against British colonial rule.

Shangaan River Reference to skirmishes of the First Matabele War (1893-4), a localised conflict between King Lobengula's Matabele and the British South Africa Company, over land ownership.

Umuntu ngumuntu ngabantu *Zulu phrase, meaning A person is a person through other people.*

Littoral English word referring to the intertidal zone on the shore of sea or lake; metaphor relating to liminality, or the third space.

Ngamfi Zulu for *African Hoopoe.*

QUO VADIS?

Kwagga Subspecies of zebra, now extinct.

Izingwony zenkozi Zulu for *Birds of the King*, or vultures.

Aizivaishe-Aizi Shona male and female name, meaning *God knows.*

Quo Vadis? Latin for *Where to now?*

MANNA FROM HEAVEN

Iko Demonstrative Shona pronoun, indicating place, [it is] *there.*

Pedyo kwazvo Shona for *very close*, or *right nearby.*

Duiker From Afrikaans, meaning *diver*, a small, skittish antelope found in sub-Saharan Africa.

Mazhanje Shona for *black plum*, wild fig tree fruit, also meaning *envy, jealousy.*

Manna from heaven In the Book of Exodus, God provides the Israelites with this bread-like substance (derived from the Hebrew *man*, meaning *what is it?*) during their journey through the wilderness; an expression used to describe an unexpected, miraculous gift.

Coup-de-grace French for *stroke of grace*, referring to the death or mercy blow.

Mufambi Shona for *traveller* or *wanderer.*

Mokoro Tswana for type of canoe.

Gudo-Isilingo Shona-Zulu term for *long oar.*

Umkolwana Zulu for *believer*, referring to the red-billed hornbill.

FISHERS

Rinkhals From Afrikaans meaning *ring-throat*, referring to the ring-necked spitting cobra.

Allegro Italian ballet term for *brisk, sprightly, cheerful.*

En pointe French ballet term for *on the tip* (of the toes).

Hungwe-Ukosi Zulu for the *godly, multiple-winged* African fish eagle.

Through a looking glass darkly Allusion to *1 Corinthians 13: 12.*

Inhlanzi Zulu word for *kingfisher.*

Nkosi yamanzi Zulu for *king of the water.*

Mweya wemvura Shona for *soul of the water.*

Alcyone and Cetyx Characters from Greek myth, turned into *Halcyon* kingfishers by the gods in an act of compassion.

Fisher King In Arthurian legend, the maimed king, protector and embodiment of the lands, whose injury renders him impotent and his kingdom barren; he spends his time fishing, awaiting the hero-knight (Percival) who has the nous to heal him.

Holy Grail From the Latin *gradale*, meaning *dish* or *platter,* (or old French *sang-real*, meaning *royal blood*), sacred object or relic believed to be the cup Jesus used at the Last Supper, and that may have caught his blood during the Crucifixion; it has come to symbolise the quest for spiritual enlightenment, meaning and truth, faith and redemption, a source of inspiration, renewal and power, the union of opposites (male-female, king-land, knight-maiden), and hidden or lost truth.

Fynbos Afrikaans for *fine bush*, referring to a wide range of vegetation.

Mampara From Tswana, meaning *idiot* or *imbecile.*

Kemosabe Supposedly meaning *faithful friend* or *trusty scout*, used by Tonto, Native American companion to the Lone Ranger; characters appearing in the American western series *The Lone Ranger* (1949-1957), created by George Trendle and Fran Striker.

Yambeji Spelling variation and personification of the spirit guardian of the Zambezi, Nyaminyami.

Bollemakiesie Afrikaans for *head-over-heels.*

FORESHADOWED

Between Scylla and Charybdis Two mythical sea-monsters from Greek mythology appearing in Homer's *Odyssey*; an expression which has come to mean, *between a rock and a hard place*, or *to face a choice between two equally bad options.*

Eina Afrikaans word, meaning *ouch.*

Currach Irish boat with a wooden frame covered by animal skin or canvas.

Boerie-roll From Afrikaans *boerewors*, or *farmer's sausage*, braaied and served on a bread roll, with chutney and onion.

Mrs Balls Popular South African brand of chutney.

Rondavel From the Dutch, meaning *round hut*, with conical roof, widespread amongst African indigenous communities.

Kraal Afrikaans word, derived from the Portuguese *curral*, Spanish *corral*, meaning *pen* or *enclosure* for animals.

OMEN

Kurava mbudzi nedzisipo kurava nedzava matowa Shona expression, meaning *Counting other people's goats means counting dead ones.*

Mhoro, Sekuru Shona for *Greetings, Grandfather-Elder.*

Mhoro wangu Shona for *Hello, my friend.*

Uri sei? Shona for *How are you?*

Ingwe Shona and Zulu term for *leopard.*

Tinotenda zvisinei Shona for *We are thankful regardless.*

Nzou Shona for *elephant.*

Ngwenya Shona and Zulu for *crocodile.*

Ndinotenda zvangu Shona for *I give thanks for that.*

Kudzingwa Shona for *banished, outcast.*

Akashinga Shona male name, meaning *Brave one.*

Imbuia Hard durable wood, native to Brazil.

Knobkerries Standard wooden fighting sticks of African tribesmen.

Vakomana vaviri vachana Shona phrase for *two white boys.*

Skuz'apo Shona term for the Selous Scouts.

Zuva, Mwedzi and Nyeredzi Shona for *sun, moon*, and *stars.*

Barbel Afrikaans for *catfish.*

Dya, mukomana Shona for *Eat, young man.*

Kuramba nyama yechidemb hunge uine yetsuro Shona expression, meaning *Rejecting the meat of a skunk is to settle for rabbit.*

Sashimi Japanese dish of thinly sliced raw fish or meat served with soy and wasabi.

Waita zvakanaka Shona for *You have done well-the right thing.*

Kudya kune nzira yekutenda Shona for *Eating is a way of believing, of showing gratitude.*

FOOL'S PARADOX

Umquombothi Nguni traditional beer made from maize, sorghum malt, yeast and water.

Job Old Testament existential hero and rebel, who loses everything but retains his dignity.

Odysseus Legendary Greek hero of the Trojan War, and King of Ithaca who appears in Homer's epic poems *The Iliad* and *The Odyssey* (8th Century BCE).

Metamodernism Cultural and artistic movement that seeks to marry and balance elements of the modern and postmodern.

Faust Famously explored in Goethe's 2-part play *Faust* (1808-1832), legendary German character who makes a pact with the devil in exchange for knowledge, pleasure, and power.

Karamazov Refers to the family central to Dostoevsky's *The Brothers Karamazov* (1880), a novel that explores issues of faith, family, morality, and the nature of evil, through the interactions of the three brothers.

Prometheus In Greek myth, a Titan who defied the gods by stealing fire and gifting it to humanity to advance civlisation; his story is seen as a symbol of human striving and rebellion.

Aeneas In Roman mythology and literature, legendary Trojan hero and founder of Rome, his journey recorded by Virgil in *The Aeneid* (29-23BCE).

Oedipus Tragic figure in Greek mythology, who unknowingly fulfils the prophecy that he would kill his father and marry his mother, the basis of Sophocles' play *Oedipus Rex* (429BCE).

Lear Titular character of Shakespeare's play *King Lear* (1608), which explores ideas of power, betrayal, family, and madness.

The fault lies not in our stars... *Lines from Shakespeare's Julius Caesar (1599).*

Uber-mensch From the German meaning *superman*, Nietzsche's concept in *Thus Spake Zarathustra* (1883-85) of the individual who transcends contextual conventions.

Goldmund and Narcissus Characters in Herman Hesse's novel *Narcissus and Goldmund* (1930), where their differing paths and choices are contrasted.

Summum Bonum Cicero's life maxim, *the highest* or *ultimate good*, tied to questions of what constitutes a virtuous and fulfilling life.

LEVIATHAN

Bliksem Afrikaans word, derived from the Dutch, meaning *lightning*, used to express shock, anger, or as a vulgar expletive to threaten violence.

Fadziso Shona girl's name, meaning *One who brings happiness.*

Sadza Shona word for *cooked porridge,* consisting of water and stiff maize meal.

Famba Shona word for *move.*

Nous From the Greek, meaning *mind*, a philosophical term referring to intellect, and reason.

Mweya mukuru Shona for *Great Spirit-Soul-Breath-Wise one*

PASSING ELEPHANTS

A jornada continua Portuguese phrase, meaning *The journey continues.*

Utsva hworurimi hahuna marapiro Shona expression, meaning *A burn on the tongue cannot be treated.*

Ndapote Shona for *please.*

Ini ndinonzwisisa Shona for *I understand.*

Rega nditarise Shona for *Let me take a look.*

Ndatenda hama dzangu Shona for *I thank you, my brothers.*

Déjà vu French term for *already seen*, referring to the eerie sensation that one has experienced the current situation before.

Umkombe Zulu for *black rhino.*

Insepe Shona for *the rays of the sun*, the springbok.

Usafambe Shona for *Don't move-walk.*

Yekare Shona for *Ancient One.*

Ambuya Shona for *Grandmother.*

Vuvuzela Zulu compound word of *vuvu* (*vuvu*-sound) and *zela* (*protest*), referring to 2-ft long horn which produces a loud buzzing *vuvu*-noise.

Boomslang Afrikaans for *tree-snake.*

Ndatenda, hama Shona for *Thank you, brother.*

Baba Shona-Zulu word for *father.*

Niebuhr American theologian and ethicist (1892-1972), credited with crafting the *Serenity Prayer* which first appeared in 1943, although authorship is contested.

BLACK-BLEACHED

Frankl (Viktor) Austrian neurologist, psychiatrist and Holocaust survivor, best known for his text *Man's Search for Meaning* (1946, 1959).

Jeremiah Old Testament figure, referred to as the *Prophet of Doom.*

BEYOND THE DOORS

Tokoloshe Mythical, mischievous and malevolent Zulu and Xhosa creature, with supernatural powers, depicted as small and hairy with long, strong arms.

Grok(ked) Term from Robert Heinlein's *Stranger in a Strange Land* (1961), meaning *to understand something deeply and intuitively,* to the point of becoming one with it.

Alouette Derived from the French, meaning *skylark*, French-Canadian military re-con helicopter.

Jekyll and Hyde Taken from Robert Stevenson's novella *Strange Case of Dr Jekyll and Mr Hyde* (1886), the phrase has come to symbolise the dual nature in a person.

Casevac Military acronym that stands for *casualty evacuation.*

IN THE CITADEL

John Bradburne (1921-1979) British poet, artist, lay member of St Francis, who lived and worked in the Mutemwa leper mission (Zimbabwe); a man of strong faith and service, murdered by guerrillas during the *Chimurenga*, his cause for canonization as saint is underway within the Catholic Church.

The Man from La Muncha Spanish author Miguel de Cervantes' protagonist Don Quixote in the novel of the same name (1605), which explores the boundary between imagination and reality.

Kuif Afrikaans for (hair) *fringe.*

Eldorado The mythical City of Gold, the title of Edgar Allan Poe's last published poem (1849), emblematic of the search for meaning and fulfilment, the futility of unrealised dreams, and the inevitability of death.

Egoli... Arcadia Mythical cities akin to the City of Gold, Shangri-La, or *heaven-on-earth.*

The Byrds American band (formed in 1964) known for their innovative fusion of folk, rock and psychedelic music, most notably the iconic *Turn! Turn Turn!* (1965), based on *Ecclesiastes* (3:1-8).

Johnny Clegg (1953-2019) South African musician, singer, and anti-apartheid activist, known for his fusion of Western pop and traditional Zulu music; his song *Great Heart* (1987) is an anthem of unity and hope.

Guga mzimba, sala ntliziyo Zulu expression, meaning *Body grow old, heart stays young.*

LAST WRITES

Finis coronat opus Attributed to the Roman poet Ovid, from his text *Metamorphoses* (8CE), Latin for *The end crowns the work.*

KEY SOURCES

I am indebted to the wisdom and existential inspiration of the following creators who helped me pierce the veil of my certainties:

Chinua Achebe, *Things Fall Apart; No Longer at Ease*
Dante Alighieri, *The Divine Comedy*
Kenneth Appiah, *In My Father's House: Africa in the Philosophy of Culture*
Thomas Aquinas, *Summa Theologica*
Aristotle, *Nicomachean Ethics; Poetics; Metaphysics*
Karen Armstrong, *The History of God; The Battle for God; The Case for God; 12 Steps to a Compassionate Life; Sacred Nature*
Bill Ashcroft, Gareth Griffiths & Helen Tiffin, *The Empire Writes Back: Theory and Practice in Postcolonial Literatures*
Margaret Atwood, *Negotiating with the Dead: A Writer on Writing; In Other Worlds: SF and the Human Imagination; Burning Questions*
Augustine of Hippo, *Confessions; The City of God*
Marcus Aurelius, *Meditations*
Mikhail Bakhtin, *The Dialogic Imagination*
Robert Cardinal Barron, *Vibrant Paradoxes; Towards a Postliberal Catholicism; The Priority of Christ*
Roland Barthes, *'The Death of the Author'*
Jean Baudrillard, *The Transparency of Evil*
Zygmunt Bauman, *Liquid Modernity*
Peter Baxter, *Bush War Rhodesia 1966-1980; Rhodesia: A Complete History 1890-1980*
Mark Behr, *The Smell of Apples*
Homi Bhabha, *The Location of Culture*
The Bible, *The Book of Job; Ecclesiastes; Wisdom; Psalms; Isaiah; Jeremiah; Four Gospels; Letters of Paul; Book of Revelation*
Steve Biko, *I Write What I Like*
William Blake, *'The Tyger'; 'The Lamb'; 'London'; 'The Sick Rose'; 'The Marriage of Heaven and Hell'; 'Jerusalem'; Illustrations to the Book of Job*
Herman Charles Bosman, *Collected Stories*

Pieter Breughel, *Landscape with the Fall of Icarus*
Thomas Bulfinch, *The Age of Fable*
The Byrds, *'Turn! Turn! Turn!'*
Joseph Campbell, *The Power of Myth; The Hero with a Thousand Faces*
John Caputo, *What Would Jesus Deconstruct?*
Nick Cave, *Introduction to The Gospel of Mark*
Gilbert Keith Chesterton, *Introduction to Job*
Duncan Clarke, *The Last Rhodesians: A Society Adrift*
Johnny Clegg, *'Great Heart'*
Paulo Coelho, *The Alchemist*
John Maxwell Coetzee, *The Life and Times of Michael K; Waiting for the Barbarians; Disgrace;*
    Stranger Shores
David Coltart, *The Struggle Continues: 50 Years of Tyranny in Zimbabwe*
Confucius, *Analects*
Joseph Conrad, *Heart of Darkness*
James Fenimore Cooper, *The Last of the Mohicans*
Francis Ford Coppola (dir.), *Apocalypse Now*
Creedence Clearwater Revival, *'Fortunate Son'*
Tsitsi Dangarembga, *Nervous Conditions*
Mark Danielewski, *House of Leaves*
Louis de Bernières, *Introduction to The Book of Job*
Alain de Botton, *The Consolations of Philosophy*
Teilhard de Chardin, *Science and Christ*
Henri de Lubac, *Paradoxes*
Anthony de Mello, *The Song of the Bird; Awareness*
Louis de Wohl, *The Quiet Light; The Restless Flame*
Neil Diamond, *'Done Too Soon'*
The Doors, *'The End'; 'Celebration of the Lizard King'; 'Riders on the Storm'*
Fyodor Dostoyevsky, *The Brothers Karamazov*
Fr John Dove SJ, *Strange Vagabond of God*
Alexandra Dumitrescu, *'What is Metamodernism and Why Bother?'*
Umberto Eco, *The Name of the Rose; Foucault's Pendulum*
Thomas Stearns Eliot, *'The Hollow Men'; 'Journey of the Magi'; 'Preludes'; 'The Wasteland'*
Epictetus, *Enchiridion*
Tony Eprile, *The Persistence of Memory*
Emilio Estevez (dir.), *The Way*
Fr Sean Fagan, *Does Morality Change?*
Frantz Fanon, *Black Skin, White Masks*
William Faulkner, *Requiem for a Nun; The Sound and the Fury*
Pink Floyd, *'Us and Them'*
Michel Foucault, *'What is an Author?'; 'Self Writing'*
Viktor Frankl, *Man's Search for Meaning*
James G Frazer, *The Golden Bough*
Hans Freiheit, *The Listening Society*
Athol Fugard, *Master Harold... and the Boys; A Lesson from Aloes*
Jostein Gaarder, *Sophie's World*
Neil Gaiman, *American Gods*
Kahlil Gibran, *The Prophet*
Terry Gilliam (dir.), *The Fisher King*
Peter Godwin, *Mukiwa – A White Boy in Africa*
William Golding, *The Lord of the Flies*

Nadine Gordimer, *July's People; Burgher's Daughter*
Stathis Gourgouris, *Perils of the One; Does Literature Think?*
Ciro Guerra (dir.), *The Embrace of the Serpent*
Pierre Hadot, *Philosophy as a Way of Life*
Henry Rider Haggard, *She; King Solomon's Mines; Alan Quatermain*
Dag Hammarskjold, *Markings*
Bessie Head, *When Rain Clouds Gather; A Question of Power*
Herman Hesse, *Narcissus and Goldmund*
Linda Hogan, *Confronting the Truth: Conscience in the Catholic Tradition*
Ryan Holiday, *Ego is the Enemy; Stillness is the Key*
Homer, *The Odyssey; The Iliad*
Gerard Hughes, *God of Surprises*
Basil Cardinal Hume, *Basil in Blunderland*
Linda Hutcheon, *Narcissistic Narrative: The Metafictional Paradox*
Aldous Huxley, *The Doors of Perception*
Kazuo Ishiguro, *The Buried Giant; Never Let Me Go*
John of the Cross, *The Dark Night of the Soul*
Paul Johnson, *Quest for God*
James Joyce, *Ulysses; Finnegan's Wake*
Carl Jung, *Answer to Job*
Richard Kearney, *Anatheism: Returning to God After God*
Richard Kearney & Jens Zimmermann, *Toward a Metamodern Theology: The Emergence of an Otherness Paradigm*
Catherine Keenan, 'History's Uncivil Wars' (*Spectrum, The Sydney Morning Herald*)
Matthew Kelly, *Perfectly Yourself; Holy Moments*
Bernadette King, *Guide to Snake Dream Symbols & Meanings*
Stephen King, *On Writing: A Memoir of the Craft*
Peter Kreeft, *Between Heaven and Hell; Doors in the Walls of the World: Signs of Transcendence in the Human Story*
Antjie Krog, *Country of My Skull*
Hans Küng, *On Being a Christian*
Alex La Guma, *The Stone Country*
Anne Lamott, *Bird by Bird*
Benjamin Larson, 'Participation and Evil' (*Currents in Theology*)
Ursula le Guin, *Steering the Craft: A Twenty-First-Century Guide to Sailing the Sea of Story*
Fr Richard Leonard SJ, 'Where the Hell is God?'
Doris Lessing, *The Grass is Singing; Africa Laughing: Four Visits to Zimbabwe*
Neil Levy, *Moral Relativism*
Clive Staples Lewis, *God in the Dock; Mere Christianity; The Problem of Pain*
Jean-Francois Lyotard, *The Postmodern Condition*
John Magee, 'High Flight'
John Manoussakis, *God after Metaphysics: A theological aesthetic*
Yann Martel, *Life of Pi*
Cormac McCarthy, *The Road*
Iain McGilchrist, *The Master and his Emissary; The Matter with Things*
Zakes Mda, *The Heart of Redness*
Chris Mears, *Goodbye Rhodesia*
Thomas Merton, *Seven Storey Mountain*
Lance Morrow, 'An Essay on Evil' (*Time Magazine*)
Credo Mutwa, *Wildlife Campus: African Folklore*
Susan Neiman, *Evil in Modern Thought*

Cardinal John Henry Newman, *'The Mission of My Life'*
Friedrich Nietzsche, *Beyond Good and Evil; Twilight of the Idols; Thus Spake Zarathustra*
Albert Nolan, *Jesus Before Christianity*
Michael Novak, *No-one Sees God*
Martha Nussbaum, *Upheavals of Thought*
David Oderberg, *'Why I am a Relativist'*
John O'Donohue, *Anam Cara*
Diarmuid O'Murchu, *Quantum Theology*
Ben Okri, *Tales of Freedom*
Blaise Pascal, *Pensées*
Alan Paton, *Cry the Beloved Country*
Scott Peck, *Children of the Lie: Hope for Healing Human Evil; The Road Less Travelled*
Josef Pieper, *The Four Cardinal Virtues*
Luigi Pirandello, *Six Characters in Search of an Author*
Plato, *The Republic; Symposium; Phaedo; Meno; Phaedrus; Apology*
Edgar Allan Poe, *'Eldorado'*
Steven Pressfield, *The War of Art*
Ian Pringle, *Green Leader: Operation Gatling, the Rhodesian Military's Response to the Viscount Tragedy; Murder in the Zambezi: The Story of the Air Rhodesia Viscounts*
Thomas Pynchon, *The Crying of Lot 49*
Karl Rahner, *Spirit in the World; Hearers of the Word*
Richard Rohr, *Falling Upward; The Universal Christ; Yes, And...; Job and the Mystery of Suffering; Quest for the Grail: Soul Work and the Sacred Journey; The Wild Man and the Wise Man; The Wisdom Pattern*
Rolling Stones, *'Paint it Black'*
Jonathan Rowson, *'Metamodernism and the Perception of Context: The Cultural Between, the Political After and the Mystic Beyond'; 'Perspectiva in 10 Premises'*
Robert Ruark, *Uhuru*
Salmon Rushdie, *Midnight's Children*
George Rutler, *Beyond Modernity: Reflections of a Post-Modern Catholic*
William Safire, *The First Dissident: The Book of Job in Today's Politics*
Edward Said, *Orientalism*
Seneca, *Letters from a Stoic*
Sipho Sepamla, *Ride on the Whirlwind*
Mongane Serote, *To Every Birth its Blood; Sounds of a Cowhide Drum*
William Shakespeare, *Hamlet; Julius Caesar; King Lear; Macbeth; Othello; The Tempest*
Mary Shelley, *Frankenstein*
Wilbur Smith, *When the Lion Feeds; A Falcon Flies*
Gayatri Spivak, *'Can the Subaltern Speak?'*
Wallace Stevens, *'Thirteen Ways of Looking at a Blackbird'*
Oliver Stone (dir.), *The Doors*
Brian Swimme, *The Universe is a Green Dragon*
Richard Tarnas, *Passion of the Western Mind; Cosmos and Psyche*
Charles Taylor, *A Secular Age*
Henry Treece, *'Conquerors'*
Desmond Tutu, *God is not a Christian*
Lao Tzu, *Tao Te Ching*
Robin van den Akker, Alison Gibbons, & Timotheus Vermeulen, *Metamodernism: Historicity, Affect, and Depth after Postmodernism*
Robin van den Akker & Timotheus Vermeulen, *'Notes on Metamodernism 2.0'*
Christopher Volger, *The Writer's Journey: Mythic Structure for Writers*

David Wallace, This is Water; Infinite Jest
Ngũgĩ wa Thiong'o, Decolonising the Mind; A Grain of Wheat; Petals of Blood; The River Between
Gunther Weber, I Believe, I Doubt
Morris West, The Clowns of God; The Last Confession
Elie Wiesel, Night
Hannes Wessels, A Handful of Hard Men: The SAS and the Battle for Rhodesia
William Butler Yeats, 'The Second Coming'; 'Long Legged Fly'
Richard Young, White Mythologies: Writing History and the West; Postcolonialism: An Historical Introduction; Colonial Desire: Hybridity in Theory, Culture and Race

Finis coronat opus

Milton Keynes UK
Ingram Content Group UK Ltd.
UKHW040833071024
449371UK00007B/776